Praise for Wendy Holden's bestselling novels SIMPLY DIVINE, PASTURES NOUVEAUX, FAME FATALE, AZUR LIKE IT and THE WIVES OF BATH:

'A frothy, naughty, Evelyn-Waugh-on-speed take on literary and media life, pulled off with great aplomb by a writer firing on all cylinders. A real hoot' *Daily Mail*

'So funny and readable you worry about the calorie content' *The Sunday Times*

'Devilishly witty' *Elle*

'The perfect antidote to the blues' *The Times*

'Sparkling' *You* magazine

'Holden writes with delicious verve and energy. Lie back and enjoy it' *Mail on Sunday*

'Savagely amusing; the satire is deadly, the plot addictive and the pace exhilarating' *Metro*

'Restores the pun to literary respectability, an amazing feat' *Esquire*

'Fiendishly witty' *Marie Claire*

'Witty, frothy and dancing with excess . . . an irrepressibly joyous novel' *Good Housekeeping*

Also by Wendy Holden from Headline Review

Simply Divine
Bad Heir Day
Fame Fatale
Azur Like It
The Wives of Bath
The School For Husbands

WENDY HOLDEN

FAME FATALE

headline
review

First published in 2002
by HEADLINE BOOK PUBLISHING

First published in paperback in 2002
by HEADLINE BOOK PUBLISHING

This edition published in paperback in 2006
by HEADLINE REVIEW
An imprint of Headline Book Publishing

A HEADLINE REVIEW paperback

4

ISBN 978 0 7553 2976 2

Typeset in Garamond by Avon Dataset Ltd, Bidford-on-Avon, Warks

Printed and bound in Great Britain by Clays Ltd, St Ives plc

HEADLINE BOOK PUBLISHING
A division of Hodder Headline
338 Euston Road
London NW1 3BH

www.reviewbooks.co.uk
www.hodderheadline.com

For Emma and Matthew

Thanks to my wonderful editors, Jane Morpeth and Flora Rees, for everything, and my fantastic agent Jonathan Lloyd, without whom nothing. Also to my friend Mark Goodwin, for lending me his pen-name and, as always, to my husband for lending me his endless help and support!

CHAPTER ONE

Grace stood on the edge of the party, clutching a glass of warm white wine and peering round hard for Henry. Concentrating on the search was difficult; everywhere she looked she saw someone distractingly famous.

A mere paperback's toss away, Nick Hornby was deep in conversation with Helen Fielding, while, just behind them, V.S. Naipaul and Joanna Trollope were laughing uproariously at something Robbie Williams had just said . . . *Robbie Williams*? Grace did a double-take. But yes, there was no mistaking that elastic, humorous face. Of course, Grace remembered, he'd been asked to be a Booker judge this year.

The St Merrion Festival, long renowned for the number of celebrities it attracted, had clearly excelled itself this time round. Anyone doubting that books were the new rock and roll, Grace thought, only had to be here, at the festival's cocktail reception, to see how much more like a film première it looked than anything to do with the traditionally fusty world of writing. Hair shone, teeth gleamed, laughter tinkled. Everyone looked tanned, sleek, wealthy and confident; everyone, moreover, seemed to have film deals.

'So Warner Bros have just *optioned* your book, then?' a blonde in diamanté mules to Grace's left was asking a brunette in a leather jacket.

The brunette gave a self-satisfied nod.

'What a shame. Disney have *bought* mine outright,' simpered the blonde, tossing a cloud of split ends. 'Much more money that way, of course.'

Jenny Bristols and Sassy Jenks, Grace registered. Two of the best-selling young female writers in the country and bitter rivals in the same publishing house.

'You shtill on your own?'

Grace's toes curled at the voice she had hoped not to hear again that evening. Looking down, she saw the short, florid, former solicitor known to millions of readers as Lucinda McCann. The discovery that the 'Queen of Romance' was actually a man and, judging by his wandering hands, a straight one at that, had been disconcerting.

'Like all the greats, I write about love,' he had explained to Grace earlier. 'Tolstoy wrote about love. Shakespeare wrote about love. So tell me. What's the difference? What else is *Lord and Master* about than love? *Say Yes, My Darling* – it's all about love. So why are *my* books not classics? I'll tell you why,' Lucinda raged, as Grace realised the question was rhetorical. He threw an arm out to the glittering crowd around them, his colour heightening with anger. 'Because of the snobbery of the literary establishment, that's why.'

'Is that what it is?' Grace had murmured, longing for Henry's untidy head to make an appearance and rescue her. It was ridiculous he was not here yet, not least because, as an author whose own mother would describe as obscure, it was a miracle he had been invited to the St Merrion in the first place.

'But I'll show them,' Lucinda had seethed. 'The book I'm working on at the moment,' he confided in garlic-laced gasps, staring into Grace's cleavage with excited eyes, 'has got Booker written all over it. It's going to be about sexual awakening written from the point of view of a fourteen-year-old girl.'

In the end, an invented visit to the loo had been Grace's only escape. But now here Lucinda was again, hot little eyes fastened once again on her breasts, sandy toupée noticeably askew, clearly several over the eight.

'Shame,' he said. 'Nishe girl like you, all by yourshelf at a party.'

Grace considered another loo dash, but decided in the end that it was safer to stay put. Mainly because it maximised the chances of Henry finding her, but partly because in her eagerness to escape from Lucinda last time she had trodden on Louis de Bernières.

'My author should be here any minute,' she said firmly.

But Lucinda, suddenly, wasn't listening. His eyes, narrow

with loathing, were focused on someone in the crowd. 'There'sh that bashtard Mark Lawson. He ripped *Lord and Mashter* to shredsh on *Front Row* the other week. I'm just going over to give him a piesh of my mind.'

'Good idea,' said Grace, taking a grateful sip of her wine.

Snatches of literary gossip drifted over.

'... so she came to the end of her author talk and the chairman said, "Well, now, do the audience have any questions they'd like to ask Miss Atkinson?" and someone put their hand up and said, "Yes, I want to know where Kate bought those shoes ..." '

'... so there I was saying goodbye to Gore – Vidal, you know – and when I turned round, Melvyn Bragg had stolen my taxi ...'

'... yes, apparently she bookmarks all her rivals on Amazon to see how they're doing. And writes all her own Amazon reviews, so no wonder they've all got five stars ...'

'I suppose you've heard I've been nominated for the Lemon,' Sassy was saying loudly to Jenny. Grace raised her eyebrows in surprise. If this was a competition, that was definitely fifteen love to Jenks. The Lemon, after all, was no empty boast. Aiming to recognise what it saw as 'challenging modern fiction', it was one of the most prestigious of the literary prizes. More so even than the Booker, in some eyes.

In reply, Jenny shot smoke out of her nostrils. It rolled like a thundercloud straight into her rival's face. 'Well *done*, darling,' she trilled. 'And marvellous you can be bothered, really. Quite frankly, the prize money wouldn't keep me in fags.'

Fifteen all for such bravado on the Bristols part, Grace thought. Everyone in the book world knew how carpet-bitingly incandescent Jenny had been when *Shooting Up*, Sassy Jenks's first novel, had not only been snapped up for a record sum by the publishing house Ptarmigan, but had garnered the blanket acclaim of the book world into the bargain. A book world which, so far, had failed to recognise the genius of Jenny Bristols. And in particular, her new novel, *Airhead.*

So universal had been the *Shooting Up* reviews that Grace could remember them; they were, in any case, much the same. 'Funky, urban and literary' (*Guardian*); 'Urban, literary and funky' (*Independent*); 'Literary, funky and urban' (*The Times*). The remaining reviews had been variations on the theme of 'the humour, power and unflinching realism with which Jenks portrays life as a teenager on a South London sink estate'.

The reason Grace could remember this so clearly was because many of the authors she looked after herself, in the publicity department of Hatto & Hatto, had constantly drawn Jenks's success to her attention, the implication being that they deserved similar acclaim and it was her fault they hadn't got it. Henry Moon, for all his lack of punctuality, had been practically the only Hatto writer not convinced that Grace's incompetence alone stood between him and worldwide domination.

'In any case,' Bristols drawled, '*Airhead*'s won more than its fair share of prizes. The Dyno-Rod Book of the Year, for instance. The Tipp-Ex Editor of the Year Award. And we're just waiting to hear whether it's won the Spud-U-Like PR Campaign as well . . .'

Thirty fifteen, Grace thought.

'Yes, I heard things were complicated by the entries being an even lower standard than usual,' interjected Jenks with a sweet smile.

Thirty all.

'. . . not to mention *Airhead*'s notching up almost half a million in paperback sales,' retaliated Jenny, tossing back her strawlike frizz. So much money, Grace thought. And yet apparently so little conditioner.

An angry red spot, she noticed, had appeared on each of Sassy's high cheekbones. Bristols had slammed in an ace there. Just as well known as the fact Jenks's literary acclaim annoyed Bristols was the fact Jenny Bristols's huge sales figures irritated Jenks. Forty thirty.

'And I hear congratulations are due on your Bad Sex Award nomination,' Sassy purred, barely missing a beat. 'They say *Braindead*'s almost certain to win.'

Deuce, Grace thought. *Braindead*, Jenny's last novel, had sold phenomenally well. Grace had seen its retina-frying pink cover so often on Underground posters that the book's cover line, 'A barnstorming bestseller set in the sex-'n'-scalpels world of neurosurgery', had almost become etched on her brain. This was, however, the first she had heard of the book's being a contender for the most notorious literary award of all, the prize no author wanted to win and every author dreaded being nominated for, the annual prize given by the *Literary Review* for that year's worst sex scene in a novel.

Handed over each year at a famously lavish party, this most infamous of literary gongs invariably attracted much humorous newspaper comment. Yet, given that publicity and prizes were all authors seemed to want, their wish to avoid the Bad Sex one at all costs always struck Grace as odd.

Irritation momentarily creased the Bristols brow. She paused for a second before once again firing both nostrils straight into Jenks' face. 'Yes, *marvellous*, isn't it?' she beamed, showing all her teeth. 'The Bad Sex Award is such a *fantastic* honour. I'm so excited, especially as there's a rumour Mick Jagger's presenting the award again this year and I'll get to meet him.'

Advantage Bristols, thought Grace, hiding a smile in her wine which was getting nearer and nearer the bottom of the glass. She looked for a waiter, and saw that she was not the only one. Beth Allardice, literary editor of the powerful mid-market tabloid *The Globe*, was staring hopefully around with an empty glass in her hand.

'Beth!' Grace suddenly heard Sassy yell. 'It's been *ages*.'

Back to deuce, Grace decided, watching confusion ripple the Allardice features as both Sassy and Jenny, elbows out, plunged towards her at speed.

'We've met of course,' Jenny urged, flashing all her teeth once more. 'Jenny Bristols. *Airhead*.'

Advantage Bristols again, Grace thought. Jenny was certainly quickest off the mark.

'And Bad Sex Award nominee,' added Sassy sweetly.

Back to deuce. Grace looked at Jenny. Yet there was something odd about the Bristols expression. She had not risen to the Bad Sex bait before; why, wondered Grace, was she doing so now? Jenny's eyes were bulging and her lips were drawn back in what could equally have been a rictus grin or an expression of agony. Her arms were rigid, the hands tensed and clenched like claws.

Her gaze dropping further, Grace saw that, just above floor level, the Jenks stiletto, a thin, sharp shaft of what looked like steel, was currently plunged straight into the Bristols big toe. As she watched, the stiletto twisted. Game to Jenks, thought Grace as Jenny gave Sassy a mighty shove and stumbled off into the crowd, face twisted with pain and loathing. Set and match, she added, as satisfaction spread like butter across Sassy's haughty face.

There was a sudden movement beside her. 'Hi, Grace.'

'Henry! Where the hell have you been?'

His thick, dark hair was, as usual, standing out in all directions. The bags below his eyes swelled tired and purple. Heavy brows the thickness of a finger pressed down from above. The overall effect was that Henry Moon's organs of sight were almost entirely hidden. More so when he curved his mouth in a smile as big as a slice of watermelon.

'You look rough,' Grace said, trying to sound stern. Henry in theory was easy to be angry with; as always, it was almost impossible in the flesh. Or what flesh there was – Henry's skin stretched taut across the frame of his tall, broad-shouldered body like the canvas on a kite. She had always found it impossible to imagine him alone with a rucksack, exploring the Himalayas for a lost and legendary tribe who ritually sat around with pebbles in their mouths, yet he had, and *Sucking Stones* was the result. 'Dreams, drama and dysentery; the pursuit of a personal challenge by the last of the gentlemen explorers', as Grace had put it on the press release. She had been reluctant about the dysentery, but Henry had insisted. 'Makes it sound less serious,' he said.

'But it *is* serious,' Grace had replied. 'You're a serious explorer.'

'No I'm not. Well – I'm an *explorer*. But I'm not serious.'

And about book promotion, Grace knew, he was particularly not serious. There was nothing she could do to make Henry regard the business of touting his tome as anything but a hoot at best, mild humiliation at worst. Even when the St Merrion Literary Festival, to whose organisers she had written in the confident expectation that absolutely nothing would come of it, had replied expressing its interest in having Henry come and talk about *Sucking Stones*, he had seemed oblivious to the great honour that was being done him. So oblivious, in fact, that in the hours just passed before he finally made his appearance, she had become increasingly certain he had forgotten about the festival completely.

'Where have you *been*?' she demanded again, noticing, as Henry grabbed a glass of wine from a passing tray, that he looked not so much tired as shattered. 'Burning the midnight oil?' He had, she knew, been having difficulty starting his next book, yet refused to admit he had writer's block. Henry hated to whinge about anything.

'Midnight oil of a sort,' Henry confessed, the wine restoring faint colour to his cheeks. 'I had a curry in Brick Lane at half past one this morning. Washed down with tequila slammers,' he added ruefully. 'Didn't wake up till eleven, so I had to get the train after the one you said to catch. But I'm here now.' He shot her a winning grin.

'So we'd better get going,' Grace retaliated. 'I need to get you round as many newspaper and radio people as possible – the party's nearly over. Come on.' She seized Henry by the arm. 'That's the editor of *Woman's Hour* over there, and in that corner are the editors of the *Sunday Times* Style section.'

Henry suppressed a groan. As he stumbled after her, he accidentally trod on the foot of someone deep in conversation with Melvyn Bragg.

'Ouch,' yelped Louis de Bernières.

Following the party, Grace directed Henry into the village of St Merrion to check in at the only bed and breakfast with vacancies at the time the green light came from the Festival.

'Past the church and down the lane to the right. You can't miss it. It's called Ivanhoe.'

'Very literary, I'm sure.' Henry grinned, brows lifting to reveal eyes of red-rimmed hazel.

'I'll wait for you here in the writers' marquee,' Grace told him.

The fact that the Festival boasted an official writers' area had been a surprise to Grace, more accustomed to the grotty corner of the bar that, at most literary events of her experience, passed for a writers' common room. The facilities offered by the St Merrion to its participants – a large and splendid tent strung with fairy lights and piled with rugs, cushions and long divans – were a revelation. It was towards this tent that Grace hurried, determined, now her charge had finally arrived, to soak up some literary atmosphere at last. Not to mention the free wine and sandwiches with which The Yurt, as it was known, was allegedly plentifully supplied.

Grace's entry to The Yurt was blocked by someone she did not recognise – a tall, silver-haired man, clearly a writer, who was having his photograph taken. He had a tanned, slender Spanish elegance about him; no doubt, Grace thought, some magically realistic laureate from the land of García Márquez. She hesitated before him; he inclined his head but did not move. Seeing his slightly questioning smile, Grace realised that he was expecting her to produce a book for him to sign. When she confessed that, actually, she was only trying to gain access to The Yurt, he stepped aside and in she went, feeling embarrassed already.

With luck, there would be someone in here she recognised. As long as it wasn't Lucinda McCann; but he mercifully seemed conspicuous by his absence. Very much present, on the other hand, was a group of large, black-clad and bra-less women with frazzled grey hair and bare legs tucked up under their generous bottoms. They glared at Grace suspiciously. One of them wore a T-shirt bearing the slogan 'Men Should Come With Instructions'.

Scurrying past, Grace was gratified to spot Jane Lewis, author of *Fromage*, chatting to Mike Bloke, wild-haired, bespectacled star of the Lit Lad firmament. 'Yes, it was wonderful when Brad agreed to star in the film of *Fromage*,' Jane was reminiscing, a beatific beam on her face, while Mike looked tense. Grace smiled to herself. This was more like it.

She walked over to the refreshment table, revelling in the strange feel of carpets spread over grass. She poured a glass of white wine and helped herself gratefully to a couple of prawn sandwiches. They were curling at the edges but welcome nonetheless. Mounted above the table was the writers' notice board. Munching, Grace inspected it.

The board was peppered with missives to someone called Lucy Love. Grace furrowed her brow before remembering that, of course, it must be *that* Lucy Love, the attractive, Titian-haired wife of multi-millionaire rock star Mike Love, whose recently published novel had generated much interest. An interest, Grace recalled, directed mostly at the Titian-haired attractiveness, not to mention the multi-millions, but there was no doubt Lucy was a decorative addition to the literary scene.

As Grace gazed at the festival programme, also pinned to the board, a warm glow overcame her that had nothing to do with the wine. There, listed among the events of tomorrow, such as V.S. Naipaul previewing his latest novel, Gore Vidal's insider's view of American politics, and a 'Meet the Author' with Margaret Atwood and Doris Lessing on science fiction, was – roll of drums, fanfare of trumpets – 'Henry Moon talks about his latest work, *Sucking Stones*'. Gazing at it, Grace could feel the tears pricking the back of her eyes. She had never managed to interest the mighty St Merrion in any Hatto author before. Getting Henry here had been an achievement. In more ways than one.

Just then, Henry himself appeared through The Yurt's elaborate wooden archway entrance. 'My God,' he said loudly, looking round in amazement at the intricately carved domes, the cushions and kilims. 'Takes me straight back to the Khyber Pass.'

The women in black glared and whispered furiously to each other. While Grace, straining her ears, could hear phrases like 'colonialist bastard', Henry made a beeline for the drink.

Suddenly, there was a ringing sound of laughter at the entrance, and in sashayed a beautiful young woman surrounded by at least ten men, their faces turned so eagerly towards her that some of them were walking backwards in front of her, like the Lord Chamberlain in front of the

Queen. The woman was shaking her long curtain of glossy red hair, undulating her compact, curvy body and showing small, perfect teeth as she laughed and clutched a folder to her small, perfect breasts. Lucy Love, Grace recognised, seeing, with a jolt of jealousy which surprised her, Henry lower his bottle of Becks from his mouth and stare at the new arrival in open admiration. Grace, suddenly keenly aware of her own lack of curves and excess of height, her practical blonde bob, her unremarkable grey eyes, unrelentingly nose-shaped nose and unastoundingly mouth-shaped mouth, felt a sudden sense of sisterhood with the bra-less coven in black who were staring at Lucy with unmitigated loathing.

'Lucy darling, you were *wonderful*,' breathed one of the throng, a pale young man with orange-framed glasses and a prominent Adam's apple.

'Yes, *brilliant*,' chorused the others fervently. Although Lucy accepted the praise heaped upon her with pretty smiles and high-pitched words of thanks, Grace detected a certain impatience on her part, a covert watching of the tent entrance.

After a few minutes, a man in chauffeur's uniform appeared and Lucy wiggled to the door, gasping, 'Must fly, darlings,' to her admirers. The farewell, Grace imagined, was literal; Lucy's husband famously had at least five houses as well as a passion for air travel.

'Where's she gone?' Henry asked, shuffling up.

'Off in one of her many helicopters to one of her many

homes, I should think,' Grace said, trying to steer her tones to the airily uninterested side of seething envy. With no great success, judging from the amused way in which Henry was regarding her from over the top of his bottle.

'Would you like to know who else is here?' Grace muttered, reddening. 'That's Jane Lewis over there. Author of *Fromage*.'

'Never heard of it,' Henry said cheerfully.

Grace stared at him. 'But Henry, it was the publishing sensation of last summer. All about this piece of over-ripe Camembert, and how it unlocked memories of the war for this old soldier . . . no?'

Henry, biting into a sandwich, shook his head.

'Made into a film with Brad Pitt?' Grace prodded, lowering her voice as Mike Bloke walked by. 'And that's Phil Plant over there,' she added.

'Who's he?'

'Stand-up comedian, wrote a book called *With A Ferret Down My Trousers*, about walking from Land's End to John O'Groats with, well, a ferret down his trousers. Sort of comic travel book. Sold like hot cakes.' Grace stopped, uncomfortably conscious that Henry's travel book had done less well. Significantly less well. Quite badly, in fact. She looked at him apprehensively.

Henry's attention, however, had moved on.

'Who's that woman?' he asked, as Jenny Bristols entered, shrieking excitedly at a weaselly looking man Grace recognised as being from one of the newspaper diaries.

'Absolutely *dreadful*, isn't it?' Jenny was yelping. 'Classic flash in the pan syndrome. Poor Sassy.'

'Just *awful*,' agreed the man, scribbling rapidly. 'So the rumour is that *Shooting Up* was written by someone else entirely?'

'Yes, but *I* didn't tell you that,' Jenny said, lowering her voice to a mere thunderclap as she swept past Grace and Henry. 'We agreed unattributed quotes, remember? I mean, *imagine*,' she added, collapsing on a divan in the corner. 'I'd *die* if my editor told me *my* second book was *so* bad, *such* utter rubbish, *such* crap, that it needed to be *completely rewritten*. Started absolutely from scratch. There's talk of returning half the advance and *everything*. Sassy's devastated,' Jenny added in a stage whisper, thrusting her breasts forward with her elbows.

'Putting a brave face on it though,' the diarist remarked, looking across to the entrance where a very-obviously merry Sassy, champagne bottle in hand and pair of boxer shorts on her head, had just arrived and was performing the cancan with Germaine Greer and a man in a bra.

'But she's crying inside,' Jenny said determinedly, looking down at her big toe and wincing.

'I need to get out of here,' Henry said suddenly to Grace. 'Fancy a walk? It's still light and we might catch a sunset.'

Taken aback, Grace nodded.

The farm on whose land the festival was being held occupied a lofty position atop a Cornish peninsula. They walked between the tents of the temporary festival village –

Henry stumbling here and there over the guy ropes. The warm evening air, scented with fresh-cut hay, spiced with the faint salt tang of the sea, swirled around them. As Grace and Henry turned out of the flag-fluttering festival entrance and into the lane, hedges superabundant with flowers flanked them; bluebell, garlic, foxglove, buttercup, cow parsley, valerian, gorse, campion, London Pride; all entangled so artistically it seemed, Grace thought, impossible that they had not been deliberately arranged by some fashionable florist. When, feeling rather ingenious, she mentioned this to Henry, he looked horrified. 'They look *much* better than that.'

Her similies thus checked, Grace decided not to mention how the sky, streaked in all the glowing colours of sunset, reminded her of cavorting deities on stately home ceilings. High up, clouds like slashed gold velvet revealed salmon-pink islets in seas of duck-egg blue. Below, the sinking sun glowed into the clouds like a flame held to mother-of-pearl. All that was missing were a few bearded muscular gods and luxuriantly plump goddesses clutching immodest scraps of cloth.

As they walked along, Grace pointed at the sheep gathering in the dusk around an electric pylon. 'Why do you think they're all sitting there?'

Henry shrugged. 'Dunno. Maybe they get a buzz out of it.'

Grace giggled. It was very pleasant, this, striding along next to Henry beneath the Olympian sky. Even if, she realised, tuning in guiltily a few moments later, she had not been listening to a word he was saying. Something about his travels, by the sound of it.

'. . . woke up one night in Kenya to the sound of water. I thought it was a rainstorm until I heard a growl and realised a *lion* was pissing on the side of my tent.' His eyes sparkled. 'Talk about lucky.'

'You'd never just want to go to the Caribbean?' asked Grace, to whom this sounded anything but lucky.

Henry groaned. 'The thought of lying in the sun on a beach all day makes me want to lose the will to live.'

'Does it?' Grace sighed wistfully. She had, in recent weeks, been fantasising about a stretch of golden sand by a turquoise sea. The kind of place where you stuck flags in the sand when you wanted another cocktail. Perhaps it was being with Sion that had done it, a man whose idea of a seaside holiday was the Socialist Workers' Party convention at Skegness . . . But I'm not thinking about that, Grace told herself sternly. Part of the reason she had come here was, after all, to stop obsessing about Sion.

'Absolutely,' Henry confirmed. 'But honestly, you'd love some of the places I've been to. Did you know there's a part of Eastern Europe where they still have bubonic plague?'

Grace shook her head vigorously.

'And North Korea is just wild. Like being in a different solar system. They've never heard of Princess Diana, even.'

He pulled on his cigarette. What Grace could see of his eyes looked far away. 'I've been chased down the Amazon by armed drug dealers. Been reduced to eating my own dog in the jungle. Dined on steamed silkworms with Chinese gangsters.'

Grace grimaced. 'Ugh. How could you?'

Henry flicked her a narrow-eyed glance. 'Like I said, it was with Chinese gangsters. You eat what you're given in those circumstances. And they're quite nice, really. Sort of subtle-tasting. Rather like . . .'

'Chicken?' guessed Grace. Anything odd-sounding, after all, usually did.

Henry nodded, beaming. 'You've had them then?'

'Of course. Hasn't everyone?'

He rolled his eyes, realising he was being teased. 'Travelling. There's nothing like it.'

'I loved *Sucking Stones*,' Grace leapt in eagerly. 'I thought it was wonderful.' Diplomatically, she did not add what a surprise this had been. Not naturally drawn to tales of Himalayan derring-do, Grace had approached the book with professional resignation and personal reluctance, but had been gradually drawn in by its drama, humour and general air of *joie de vivre*. So much so that she had twice missed her stop on the Tube while reading it. 'That bit where you come over the mountain ridge to find the whole tribe sitting there with huge stones in their mouths? *Amazing*.'

They had just come over the top of the hill themselves and were looking down the darkening finger of land pushing out into a sea of liquid gold. 'It's so beautiful,' Grace murmured.

Henry smiled at her. His eyes, she noticed, were rising

slightly out of their cushions of bag; slits of amber in the setting blaze of the sun. Turning to her, he raked a hand through hair that had clearly not seen a brush for some days. Less bed hair, Grace thought, than hair that had never made it up the stairs in the first place. 'It's good to be here,' he said. 'I'm having a great time.' His voice seemed oddly low and gruff; with extra meaning? Grace wondered. Or early stage emphysema?

'Good,' she replied, higher and more breathlessly than intended. 'The St Merrion Festival is very prestigious.'

'I'm not talking about the bloody festival,' Henry stared unrelentingly at her as she reddened. He took a long, contemplative draw on his cigarette. Silence fell.

Grace's heart was rushing about her ribcage like a dazzled rabbit. 'Shall we go back and have a drink?' she squealed.

CHAPTER TWO

Back in the festival bar – they had eschewed The Yurt on account of what Henry called 'those scary motherships' – they drank steadily and copiously. Grace felt excited, nervous, unsure what exactly Henry had meant out there on the promontory, and uncertain how or whether to make further enquiries. The way back had not offered much in the way of elucidation; furthermore, she had Sion to consider. Perhaps it was best to let providence – or the Pinot Grigio – take its course. She sipped warmish glass after warmish glass, increasing her intake steeply after the two packets of nuts eaten in lieu of supper. Her head was starting to spin. And she had long since stopped counting how much whisky Henry had drunk.

Henry's attention was no longer on her in any case. He

was watching an inebriated Mike Bloke make grinding gestures with his pelvis up against the main tent pole whilst grinning lasciviously at the waitresses. 'Lad novelists,' he chortled in a manner implying that he regarded the genre with little respect. 'Boy meets girl. Boy drinks too much beer . . .'

Grace blinked. The scenario sounded familiar. The beer, certainly. Had she and Sion not had a huge row only the week before about him coming in late and drunk long after she had gone to sleep?

'Boy comes home late . . .'

Of course, she understood that Sion's PhD thesis on *Why New Labour Are Bastards* required him to interview MPs on the extreme left wing of the party. What was less understandable was why these interviews invariably involved the consumption of large amounts of beer. Increasingly recently, Grace had retired to bed leaving the door of her flat unlocked because of Sion's late night protracted sessions of putting the world to rights. Or lefts. On one or two evenings he had not turned up at all.

'Girl finds out he has been sleeping with someone else . . .'

Grace had tried not to mind too much about the fact that, as chairman of the local Revolutionary Socialists, Sion spent Saturday mornings rattling buckets with impressionable women outside supermarkets. Nor about the eager female students on the course he taught on The Obstretics of Oppression: Blair and The Birth of the Nanny State at the University of Penge. Apparat-chicks, Grace had labelled them, trying to make a joke of it, trying not to worry exactly what Sion was teaching them about The Third Way. Many of the Apparat-chicks left messages on Grace's answerphone – Sion's own flat lacked one, its tenant considering them bourgeois affectations – in which they addressed her boyfriend in awestruck tones. She guessed many were in love and was not surprised; tall, red-haired, impassioned and trailing all the romance of his Celtic-sounding name, Sion presented a dashing figure, particularly on the frequent occasions he was late for his Penge-bound bus. Reliability, Grace reflected, was hardly his middle name. She had been rather surprised to find that Graham was.

Yet Grace was not *excessively* worried. She worried just as much as anyone in her position would. It was difficult not to suspect, especially after evening meetings from which he arrived back in the early hours of the morning, that Sion was sowing more than the seeds of revolution.

'Girl finds out . . .' chortled Henry.

Grace blinked. There was no hard evidence, certainly. Apart from that strange pair of knickers in his washing basket. Sion's garbled excuse that he had bought them for her at a Socialist Worker jumble sale and felt they needed a pre-presentation wash had been wildly unconvincing, even given his legendary parsimony. Actually, she had been pretty angry about the whole episode.

'Girl smashes up boy's CD collection . . .'

Unfortunately, that had not been an option. Sion was

too mean – or too anti-capitalist culture as he put it – to buy music of his own. And about hers he was merciless, denouncing her Vaughan Williams as bourgeois and her Billie Holidays and Nat King Coles as proof of a patronising and superior attitude towards ethnic minorities.

'Girl dumps boy . . . Want another drink?' Henry got uncertainly to his large feet.

Grace nodded. She certainly did. In more ways than one.

How different Sion had been in the early days of their relationship. Grace had been on the rebound, if such an energetic word could be applied to the end of the affair with Tom, a prematurely grey City banker who had swept her off her feet at a garden party – literally; she'd been too drunk to walk to the car. She had woken the next morning to find herself with a man with lots of money, little time and no interest in anything besides vintage cars and the accumulation of wealth, neither of which much enthused Grace. The fact that he was hopeless in bed and what political views he had were wildly at odds with her vague but liberal own were part of the reason the relationship was in difficulties even before the night Tom's 1965 E-type Jaguar was, much to his fury, clamped outside an expensive Park Lane restaurant.

His forcibly expressed view that the removal of an expensive vintage car outside Nobu symbolised the breakdown of the fabric of society had been the final straw. Grace had, in any case, realised that Tom's ultimate intention was to immure her in a slice of prime Putney real estate and impregnate her up to five times. He had even told her he considered her 'good breeding stock'.

And so it was that when, a week later, Sion appeared on her doorstep passionately urging her to back his Socialist Worker candidate in the local government elections, he had seemed to Grace a knight in shining armour. Well, not shining exactly – nothing about Sion, whose outward appearance leant towards a Jarvis Cocker-like unkempt greasiness saved only by his physical beauty, shone as such – but at least he was the exact opposite of Tom. Motivated, passionate and bursting with conviction. Moreover, like her, newly single: his last girlfriend, he told her, was extremely politically committed and had left the country to take up a missionary position. It had not taken too much prompting for Grace to do the same.

'Girl dumps boy,' Henry reprised, returning from the bar and slamming their drinks on the table. 'Girl's mother is delighted.'

Grace gasped. Far from being funny, this was uncanny. Her mother would certainly be delighted if she and Sion split. She was aware – via twice-weekly reminders by telephone – that Lady Armiger's intentions for her, now the approved-of Tom had left the scene, turned determinedly on one of the sons of the Foreign Office mandarins or foreign aristocrats that she, as wife of the British Consul in Venice, met in the course of professional duty. Not the least of my problems, Grace reflected, is having a mother not so much a social climber as a social astronaut. She sighed and took another slug of wine.

'Not the sort of thing you have problems with, I imagine.' Across the table, Henry was regarding her with a swaying head but an intense gaze. She started, realising she had lost the thread.

'What's that? What don't I have problems with?'

'Blokes. Got them queuing round the block, I imagine.'

Grace reddened. 'Hardly . . .' struggled out from between lips pressed tight with sudden emotion. It was the drink. Had to be.

Henry's face registered woozy surprise. 'Oh. Sorry. Didn't mean to upset you.'

' 'S'all right.'

'Bit of boyfriend trouble then?'

'Sort of.' Struggling to an upright position, Grace realised not all her limbs were obeying her commands. At least, not immediately. There was a brief, awkward silence. 'You need cheering up,' Henry announced. 'What's more,' he slurred, pointing to her empty glass, 'you need another drink.' He tottered off to the bar where, as she watched, he slid to the front of the crowd with astonishing ease.

'I've had an idea,' he declared, returning with a bottle of red wine. 'Let's play a drinking game. I know a great literary one. Perfect for here.' He nodded his head in the direction of the bar, by now almost full with shouting, smoking, staggering writers and their satellites. Over in the corner, she could vaguely make out a woman in tight white trousers dancing on the table. Whether the furniture or Jenny Bristols's seams were most in danger, Grace could not decide.

'What drinking game?' Grace was apprehensive. Tom had enjoyed drinking games, in particular one involving dashing wine into every third person's face after someone else had failed to answer a question correctly.

'It's called Worstsellers.'

'The opposite of bestsellers, you mean?' Through the thickness in her brain, Grace wondered if Henry was having a dig at Hatto & Hatto. Her authors' success in featuring in the all-important *Sunday Times* top ten bestsellers list was admittedly limited; put bluntly, utterly nonexistent. Grace had her doubts about the defence that Adam Knight, Hatto's Head of Fiction, invariably cited whenever the subject came up: 'Hatto & Hatto will defend to the end the right to publish books that no one reads.'

'That's right,' Henry chortled. 'You have to think of an unsuccessful version of a famous book. *Alice In Sunderland*, for example, instead of *Alice In Wonderland*.'

This rang a vague bell. 'Don't they play this on the radio? On *I'm Sorry I Haven't a Clue*?'

Henry nodded unsteadily. 'Except this is different. If you think of a Worstseller, I drain my glass, and vice versa. You start.'

Grace paused, her mind a swirling blank. Then, suddenly, amazingly, surfaced. '. . . *Zorba The Geek*.'

'Very good.' Henry drank his glass of wine and refilled hers. '*Lady Chatterley's Liver*.'

Grace giggled. '*The Hound of the Basket Meals*?' Her head was spinning faster.

'*Ron Juan.*'

'*A Room with a Trouser Press*,' snorted Grace, emptying her glass down her throat. It had been a long time since she had laughed so much.

'*Mansfield Car Park*,' yelled Henry, tipping off his chair into a crowd of chattering writers behind him.

'Mind my foot,' snapped Louis de Bernières.

'*The Merry Wives Of Widnes.*' Grace's eyes were streaming. The world was whirling, full of excitement and laughter.

'*The Portrait Of Muriel Gray.*'

'*Oliver Pissed*,' Grace shouted triumphantly, vaguely aware of an odd, sliding sensation. She realised that she too had fallen off her chair.

'We'd better get out of here,' Henry muttered, helping her to her feet.

They swayed out, Grace leaning on Henry's shoulder, to find the bright sky had faded to a dark-blue velvet cushion on which stars lay scattered like diamonds. They stopped and faced each other.

Grace was dimly aware of Henry's face approaching. As his lips touched hers, she took deep, slow breaths of his scent. Top notes of Colgate, a warm whiff of sweat and garlic, a faint tang of eau de Cologne. Plus base notes of distinct promise.

Henry was a committed kisser, hungry, greedy, even. The thought of Sion loomed briefly, then faded. Payback time for all his extracurricular activities, Grace thought, with a recklessness shot through with triumph.

Henry slowly detached his lips from hers. She felt him pull on her hand and lead her away among the tents, picking through the guy ropes with amazing dexterity given his alcohol intake. They reached the edge of the field, where a large tree bulking against the moonlight cast a deep black shadow. To Grace, gliding along, a glassy grin on her face, it seemed both natural and inevitable to follow. She felt no guilt, just eager anticipation.

Next morning, Grace stirred her spoon round her cereal bowl. The clank of metal on china was amplified by her hangover and the dank silence of the breakfast room. From the evidence of the abandoned tables around her, she was the last to surface – everyone else had eaten and gone, everyone else, that was, apart from the forbidding proprietress now approaching with Grace's cooked breakfast. Grace avoided Mrs Ivanhoe's eye; possibly she had heard their giggling, crashing return the night before. Definitely, Grace realised, as the plate met the table rather more emphatically than might have been expected.

Grace surveyed the cakey tops of the fried eggs, the shrunken bacon, the blackened mushrooms, the orange gunk bleeding from the fried tomato. As the savoury smell rose to her nostrils, her stomach rose to her throat.

She pressed the cool inside of her elbow against her boiling forehead. Why were breakfast rooms always so hot? Or was the source of the burning combined self-disgust and guilt?

Last night. Oh God. Why had she done it? It was so unprofessional, apart from anything else. She'd come here to work, to do a job, to help Henry through the perils of public performance. Not help him shag her senseless. Although she had not been senseless, she remembered, taking a deep breath. She had felt everything; that sunburst in her knees, soles and groin, those waves and shudders of pleasure. Henry, for all his apparent gangling ineptitude, was a surprisingly skilful lover, more so even than Sion and infinitely more so than Tom.

Sex with Tom was thankfully a fading memory, but Grace could still recall that feeling of crushing claustrophobia, pinned beneath the heavy duvet, his body scrambling painfully over her like a soldier on manoeuvres. Sion, by contrast, had taken her with a thrilling, rather brutal force, but always swiftly and always putting his own pleasure before hers. But Henry had been all solicitude, his knowing fingers lighting flames of delight all over her body, bringing her to a peak of gasping excitement before finally releasing himself.

But she should not have done it. She was still officially with Sion; she shouldn't have slept with a man she hardly knew. Not that slept was the word – Grace now recalled with hideous clarity her animal writhing, her moans, the way she had pushed herself against him as if unable to get enough of him inside her. Did he think she did this with all her authors? Apart from a handful of regrettable university encounters, Henry was the only one-night stand she had ever had. Did this make things better or worse?

Grace looked miserably down at her breakfast. Was there something mockingly, indecently suggestive about the lewd angle of the burst sausage protruding above the top of the tomato? The arrangement of the fried eggs? In tribute to its status as the least innuendo-loaded item on the plate, Grace gingerly pricked the top of her mushroom. Thin black grease ran out.

The only compensation was not having to face him physically. Perhaps Henry had eaten breakfast already; perhaps, Grace thought, flicking her eyes towards the ceiling and wincing at the pain this produced, he was up there now in his room, the same guilty thoughts clattering in the same painful dryness of his similarly dehydrated brain. He might well have a Significant Other as well. He hadn't mentioned a girlfriend, but she hadn't asked. Or did he have sex with relative strangers all the time? Given the places he had been, this was a thought too hideous to contemplate. Grace scooped the tomato onto her fork where it promptly disintegrated and dripped down between the tines. God. What a mess.

If only Ellie were here. Her friend and colleague in the Hatto press office, a self-styled expert on men, would certainly have views on the matter. The fact that her relationships rarely lasted beyond a month – making Grace's six with Sion look positively Darby and Joan – did not, in Ellie's view, in the least compromise her ability to pronounce on those of others. 'Those who can't, teach,' she would grin. What would Ellie say, Grace wondered. She had, after all, overstepped the author-publisher divide by several hundred miles. Getting paralytic and opening her legs to all comers was hardly the act of a consummate professional. 'Although a consummating one, certainly,' she could hear Ellie cackle.

As the breakfast-room door opened, Grace, fearing Mrs Ivanhoe again, dug her fork into the bacon and lifted it to her mouth with every appearance of enthusiasm. It remained suspended in mid-air, trembling, as she recognised in the doorway the tall, dark-haired form of Henry Moon. Her intestines surged in shock.

'Hi there,' he grinned.

'Hello,' she muttered, frowning with pain as he sat down opposite and shook a noisy cascade of Rice Krispies into a small, floral bowl.

'You look great,' he told her.

Disarmed and amazed, Grace could only stare at him. *Great?* The most fleeting of glimpses in the mirror – all she could bear – had told her that her eyes were piggy and bloodshot, her hair stuck out like straw and her face was streaked with mascara. She contemplated replying that she never came down to breakfast in anything other than full make-up. Last night's full make-up, in particular.

'How are you feeling?' Henry asked.

Grace opened her mouth. Now there was a question to which there were several answers. Terrible? Regretful? Wishing none of it had ever happened? But, as the door opened and Mrs Ivanhoe came in carrying Henry's cooked breakfast,

Grace cleared her throat and muttered, 'Fine, thanks,' in as dignified a tone as she could muster.

Henry's breakfast had clearly done its time keeping warm in the oven. Henry, however, stuck his fork into his aged, blackened sausage with every appearance of enjoyment. 'Delicious, thank you,' he called after Mrs Ivanhoe. She paused at the door, her cross, careworn face melting into something perilously close to a smile. 'You're welcome,' she replied, with a growl that was almost coquettish.

Henry dug into his breakfast. To Grace's relief but also to her confusion, he offered no further comment About Last Night. Yet he clearly wasn't pretending nothing had happened. There was an intimacy in the baggy-eyed glance which held her eyes for a second or two longer than was necessary. An added width to his monkey grin, even as he asked neutral and straightforward questions about the talk he was due to give at that morning's festival. Grace, striving to create a distance, answered in as clipped and formal a manner as her compromising appearance and obvious hangover would allow. Yes, the talk was at eleven o'clock, in the Spiegeltent. No, she hadn't the faintest idea what a Spiegel was.

'I'm just going up to sort myself out,' she said eventually, feeling, as Henry tore messily into a small plastic packet of brown sauce and squeezed it in a pool beside his eggs, that her bucking stomach would bear no more. Eating one Ivanhoe cooked breakfast had been unfortunate; to sit through another struck her as carelessness.

In her room, Grace attempted to brush her hair, clean her teeth and put on fresh make-up without calling on the mirror. Contemplating the wages of drink and lust was not an attractive prospect. And guilt was never a good look.

She lingered over her toilet as long as possible – at times literally, given that the fried eggs were attempting a last-minute bid for freedom – before descending the swirling Axminster staircase, whose alcoves bore bowls of potpourri and whose walls hung with gilt-framed school photographs of plump-faced Ivanhoe grandchildren.

Henry was waiting downstairs, flicking through the books section of the *Daily Mail.*

'Seen any reviews of *Sucking Stones*?' he asked, as they left Ivanhoe and struck out along the sunny lane towards the festival.

Grace shook her head too quickly, wincing as her swollen brain slammed against her cranium. 'But I haven't seen all the newspapers,' she hedged. It was true in a way. She hadn't seen the *Racing Post*, for example, for ages. Or *Pigeon Fancier's Weekly*. She had, however, been scouring the book review pages of almost all the others since *Sucking Stones*'s publication day, despite the knowledge that none of the literary editors she had approached had been remotely interested in it.

'Well don't bother,' Henry said easily. 'None of them has anything about *Sucking Stones.*'

'But the good thing about that,' Grace countered, seizing on the oldest publicity department excuse in the world, 'is that at least no one's been negative about it.'

Henry grinned. 'I suppose so. But actually, I wasn't talking about the newspaper reviews, or lack of them. I meant the Amazon ones.'

'Oh, right,' Grace said guardedly. The online bookshop's customer review pages were famous for not pulling their punches. They had certainly not done so with Henry. Oh God. She'd been hoping he wouldn't log on. Or know how to.

'Actually,' Henry admitted, 'I looked twice. The first time there was only one stinker. I was 300,012 in the sales charts then. But when I looked again later,' an expression of wonderment crossed his face, 'someone from Germany had left a two-word review which had had an incredible effect on the sales.'

'Great,' Grace said, relieved. 'What did they say?'

' "Very disappointing." So now I've dropped to about three million and three.'

'Ah.'

'My fault of course,' Henry grinned. 'Looking at Amazon reviews is a mug's game. For a start, if you discount all your bad ones, you can't take the good ones seriously either.'

'I suppose not.'

'Then there are the mad ones,' Henry continued. 'Those wordy ones written by people who'd like to be professional critics but aren't, and those weird ranty ones written by survivalists that say "This Writer Is The Antichrist". I suppose the only comfort,' he added, getting into his stride, 'is that no one is immune. Not even God. If you look at the King James Bible you'll find some loon has filled in the author's comment section, signing himself Jehovah aka The Lord etc., followed by something like "This nonstop rollicking look at humanity throughout the ages will ensure not a dry seat in the house. There are fires, floods, wars, tortures and puzzles. Something for everyone".'

Grace could not help smiling. Reluctant, however, to be lured back into friendly intercourse with Henry, let alone any other variety, she strode ahead, enforcing their distance both physically and psychologically. Henry, however, his much longer limbs shifting easily into gear to keep up, strolled alongside, chatting, forcing her to walk even faster. Thus, at near-marathon speed, through hedges uproarious with July, Grace and Henry reached the festival site.

Grace noticed that the air, wonderfully hay-scented yesterday, now had a sour tinge of manure. Yet – perhaps it was the vigorous exercise – she was definitely feeling better. The sun was shining, the sky was blue and, judging from the various other grey-faced people stumbling uncertainly about the site, she wasn't the only one to have done something she regretted the night before. Moreover, whatever personal misdeeds had been committed with the author, there was no doubt that Henry's approaching talk was a professional triumph. It was the first time any Hatto & Hatto writer had appeared at so prestigious a festival; still less, one so gratifyingly keen to have him. And she, Grace, had set the whole thing up. Penetrated this inner literary sanctum. Perhaps there were reasons to be cheerful, after all.

They arrived at the Spiegeltent twenty minutes before Henry was due on. This made the large, female crowd sitting inside, restive and expectant, all the more gratifying a sight. Among them, Grace was amazed to see, sat the black-clad coven from The Yurt.

'Stay here,' she said to Henry, not quite meeting his eyes. 'I'll just check the bookshop's stocked up for your signing session afterwards. Looks as if there'll be quite a demand.'

At first sight, the bookshop seemed innocent of a single copy of *Sucking Stones*. Obviously she was not looking properly. Grace went round again, noticing as she did so that the large sign by the doorway announcing 'On in the Spiegeltent' listed the 11 a.m. event to be not '*Sucking Stones*: Henry Moon, Last of the Gentlemen Explorers, Discusses His Adventures' but 'Talking 'Bout Our Genitalia: Marilou Honigsbaum, Feminist and Creator of *The Clitoris Chronicles*'.

Grace gasped and pointed at the notice. 'There's been a mistake,' she hissed urgently at the diffident young man stacking up copies of *Airhead* and *Shooting Up* in Manhattan-like piles. 'It's not, um,' she squinted disbelievingly at the sign again, '*The Clitoris Chronicles* on now. It's Henry Moon and *Sucking Stones*.'

'There's been a change of plan, apparently,' said the bookshop assistant.

'What?' Grace stared at him, incredulous.

'They've just changed it. About an hour ago.'

Grace's mind whirled and clicked through any number of sensational possibilities before settling, with great effort, on the calmest and most logical. Henry's talk had been moved for some reason. Shifted up the schedule a bit. It happened sometimes. Sometimes, Grace thought, gripped by a sudden excitement, because demand for a particular talk outstripped the original venue and the show had to be moved to another, bigger one. Yes. This was obviously what had happened.

'What are *The Clitoris Chronicles*, anyway?' she asked, conversationally, picking up the top volume from the pile. 'Over 400 Women Talking Frankly About Their Clitorises', announced the cover. The assistant reddened. 'I see,' said Grace.

'Very big in the States, apparently,' the assistant mumbled, his blush intensifying. Grinning, Grace placed the book back on the pile and returned to the Spiegeltent, looking both for Henry and an official to explain the changed plan. Neither seemed much in evidence. *The Clitoris Chronicles*, however, were about to start.

Grace elbowed her way through the crowd to where she had spotted a tall, frizzy-haired man in a creased white suit and a festival official badge. His arms were folded and a look of pleasurable anticipation suffused his face. He looked benignly at Grace as she pushed purposefully up to him.

'Why have you changed the time of Henry Moon's talk?' she hissed.

'Sssh,' snapped a woman with a fringed blonde bob in front of her.

To deafening applause, a dark-haired woman in jeans and a T-shirt announcing 'Clit Girl' in glittery lettering had appeared on the stage.

'GOOD MORNING, I'M MARILOU HONIGS-BAUM,' shouted the woman in a cawing New York accent. The crowd hooted appreciatively.

Grace prodded Creased Suit questioningly on the arm. 'Excuse me. Can you tell me why Henry Moon's talk has been moved?'

'WE'RE HERE TO REACH PEACE WITH OUR VAGINAS,' yelled the Clit Girl. 'TO ACHIEVE CLOSURE WITH OUR CLITORISES.' Whoops and yells greeted this.

'It's not been moved,' Creased Suit said absently, staring at this stage. 'It's been taken off the schedule altogether.'

'Taken *off*?' Grace felt her voice rise hysterically. The blonde woman turned angrily.

Creased Suit nodded.

'I WANT YOU TO ANSWER A QUESTION,' the Clit Girl was shouting to her audience. 'IF YOUR CLITORIS WORE A HAT, WHAT SORT OF HAT WOULD IT BE?'

'A French beret,' roared Blonde Bob.

'Why?' roared Grace at Creased Suit.

'Why *not*?' roared Blonde Bob, whirling round with an insane gleam in her eye. Grace backed away and trod on someone behind her.

'*Ow*!' snapped the voice she had now come to associate with the author of *Captain Corelli's Mandolin*.

'A wimple,' shouted someone else.

'A crash helmet,' yelled another, to general hilarity.

'Look. I need to talk to you,' Grace insisted to Creased Suit, pulling him to the side of the tent. His name, she saw from the badge, was Eustace. 'I don't understand what has happened,' she hissed. 'You were dying to have Henry Moon and *Sucking Stones* at the festival. In fact, I distinctly remember it being said that he would electrify the audience and you hadn't had anything so interesting for ages.'

'Ye-es,' Eustace admitted. 'But we hadn't quite realised then what the book was about. I mean, you know.' He shrugged helplessly.

'Not realised? But I sent you a press release about Henry,' Grace countered. ' "The Real Indiana Jones",' she quoted. ' "The Millennium Hemingway".'

'Mmm,' Eustace said. '*Explorers*. It's just that they're . . . ah, how can I put this?' He rubbed his chin. 'A bit five minutes ago, I suppose. A bit boring.'

'Boring? "The fascinating story of one man's journey to discover a lost tribe"?' Grace spat indignantly. 'Do you realise what Henry went through? How he—?'

'Yes, well,' Eustace interrupted. 'Um, I suppose we sort of focused on the title – you know how busy things get, no one has time to read a whole *release* – and, um, well, I suppose we sort of leapt to conclusions.' A note of embarrassment had crept into his voice.

'What conclusions? What on earth did you think *Sucking Stones* was about?'

'Um, well, I suppose we sort of assumed it would be about um, well, *groupies*.'

'*Groupies?*' Grace gasped. 'What, Plaster-Caster, I'm-with-the-band sort of groupies?'

Eustace's eyes were fixed firmly on his feet. 'Well, Rolling Stones groupies, to be precise. *Sucking Stones*, you know, well, it is quite a misleading title. We sort of thought . . . you know.'

Grace grappled simultaneously with her temper and the urge to batter Eustace to death with a tent peg.

'So why leave it so late?' she demanded. 'Why have you only cancelled it this morning?'

'We didn't realise until the author turned up.' Eustace turned strained features to hers. 'You see, we thought Henry Moon would be a woman.'

'A *woman*?'

'Henrietta, you know. An understandable mistake . . .' He grinned helplessly at her.

'C**t, c**t, c**t,' the women inside the Spiegeltent were shouting. Egged on by Marilou Honigsbaum, they were evidently well on the road to closure with their clitorises.

Grace, some way off anything similar with hers, stomped off to break the news to Henry. As she walked, the smell of manure in her nostrils grew stronger.

* * *

Grace could not look at Henry on the train home. She had long since stopped feeling embarrassed in every pore and nerve end; pores and nerve ends were no longer distinguished as such. Each had melded with the other, making her entire body a sheet of shame. Her burning face was turned determinedly to the window and the passing fields and cattle which seemed so placid and cool by comparison. If only I were a cow, thought Grace. If only I were anything but someone who works in book PR.

What had made everything worse was Henry's sanguine, horribly reasonable response to the catastrophe.

'But it makes perfect sense,' he insisted. 'Yes of course, *ideally* they could have read the book, but I can see how they thought a rock groupie would draw in the crowds. No one cares about explorers. I should write about something else, really. Maybe,' he added with a rueful twist of his large mouth, 'I should even start writing Lad novels. That's where the money is, after all.'

He had been almost unbearably jolly, cracking jokes for what seemed like hours to cheer her up. None of them did, of course. As the London-bound train had – after what seemed a wait of some weeks – finally dragged itself into St Merrion station, Henry had pushed down the tall metal handle of her upright suitcase to amusingly mimic a detonator. Some people on the platform had laughed, but their number did not include Grace. Henry's ridiculous good spirits sprang, she was certain, from the fact that he found her ridiculous. Of course he did. And who could blame him? After letting him screw her – in spite of the fact that she had a boyfriend – she had proceeded to screw up his event at a prestigious literary festival. She deserved to be laughed at. She was absurd. Worse, he was probably even sorry for her. The fact that Last Night had still not been mentioned struck Grace as increasingly sinister. Worse still, he seemed determined to assure her that the Festival cock-up – the other Festival cock-up, that was – was in no way her fault.

Tantrums Grace could have coped with. Vicious assaults on her professional incompetence would have been balm in comparison with his ghastly brand of amused resignation, his insistence that none of it mattered, that he hated reading to audiences anyway.

'Besides,' Henry added, as they emerged at Paddington, 'I only came down because of you. Last night . . .'

'What?' Grace rasped, panicking. The moment had come. Last Night was being mentioned. Oh God. 'Last night . . .?' she bleated.

'Was wonderful,' Henry said gently.

The purple zoomed up Grace's face like a high speed lift. She groped for a reply. 'But you never said anything,' was the best she could gasp at such notice. 'At breakfast . . .' she added, helplessly.

Henry grinned, the hazel flickers of his eyes gleaming in the station lights. 'I've never thought it particularly good form to bring up the night before over the breakfast table.'

'Oh.' Grace felt obscurely annoyed. How relevant was good form, given the circumstances?

'And anyway,' Henry added, 'it all sounds a bit complicated. You already being with someone, and all that . . .' His voice tailed off; Grace could not identify its tone. Regretful? Or relieved?

'Yes,' she said, sounding harsher than she meant to. 'It's complicated.'

She could hear what he was saying clearly enough. That she should shuffle off back to Sion with never a backward glance. That he was not interested, even if she was, which of course she wasn't. Why would he be interested? She was a disaster. In every possible sense of the word. No right-thinking man, and definitely not a man who, like Henry Moon, had experienced her sluttish incompetence at first hand and had more reason than most to be wary, would want to touch her with a bargepole.

'I'd like to see you again,' Henry murmured.

This not being in the expected script, Grace took a couple of seconds to register it. Then she rallied: of course, he had to say that. The last of the gentlemen explorers. Never forgetting the thank you with the wham, the bam and the ma'am. Of course he did not mean it. As if he *could*.

Grace looked down, sudden tears pricking the back of her eyes. 'It's complicated,' she repeated.

'Are you happy with him?' Henry asked her softly.

A clever question, deliberately put, she thought. However she answered, she would sound stupid. And he, irresistible.

She was happy with her boyfriend, yet she had slept with *him*; she was unhappy with her boyfriend, she had turned to him to forget. She shrugged. 'Yes. I'm happy.'

Henry nodded. 'Well, then, I'd better leave it.'

'Yes. You better had.'

Was it relief that now suffused his face with colour? He was knitting his broad brow, no doubt to conceal a smile. Good riddance, he must have been thinking.

'But if anything changes, will you let me know?'

Grace quickly converted her expression of amazement into a taut smile. That was all the reply she gave him as she turned and trudged, with her detonator suitcase, in the direction of the Underground.

CHAPTER THREE

'I know, I know,' Ellie cried, bursting into the office half an hour late. 'But I've got a good reason.' She waved her newspaper at Grace. 'According to *The Globe*'s health pages, I can't get out of bed on time because I'm immobilised in the absorption of everyone else's negative energies.'

Grace stared. 'What?' Ellie's excuses were always impressive, but this one beat the lot.

'They're running this series called "Chi Whizz: Know Your Motivations",' Ellie continued breathlessly. 'It's amazing. Has an explanation for *everything*. Apparently the reason I'm always so late is because I'm a people pleaser.'

Grace raised an eyebrow. Fond as she was of her assistant, there was no doubt that the person Ellie sought most often to please was herself.

'I take on all sorts of tasks I don't really have time to do,' Ellie continued.

Ye-es, Grace thought. Ellie's in-tray had residents more ancient than those of the average old people's home.

'I let things stack up.'

True, too. Via emphatic underwear, Ellie brought the impression of great buxomness to a rather flat chest. Via full Oscar ceremony make-up on all occasions, she made ordinary features go further. At all times her hair shimmered with expensive highlights and she wore heels of a height that made Grace wince.

'And the reason I'm such an awful driver is because my parents split up when I was five,' Ellie finished.

'I didn't know your parents got divorced when you were five,' Grace said, all sympathy.

Ellie looked uncomfortable. 'Well, they didn't, actually. But they could have done. There must be some reason why I can't pass my driving test. I've taken it fifteen times now.'

'Fifteen times!' Grace was astounded. 'Why don't you change your instructor?'

'I couldn't. We're mutually dependent now.' Ellie hung her denim jacket up on the battered stand by the door, walked to her desk, sat down and sighed. 'Christ, what a bummer of a weekend.'

You said it, Grace thought. She had changed her mind completely about asking her colleague's advice and was thankful that, so far, Ellie had not asked one question about the weekend at St Merrion. Thankful too that the next half-hour would be dedicated entirely to another of Ellie's colourful, largely luckless and invariably fascinating romantic adventures. Entirely preferable, Grace thought, to having to give an account of the Henry Moon disaster. Or disasters. 'So what happened?' she asked.

'After a lovely meal in an exclusive Thai restaurant,' Ellie began with the Pooteresque delivery she reserved for these stories, 'Chris, who up until that point had been a perfect gentleman, lined up all the food we hadn't eaten and flicked it across the restaurant. When a prawn wonton hit a waiter between the eyes, I got my coat.' She pulled a face. 'What is it with these blokes I get fixed up with? Take Jez, the one I saw on Friday. Gorgeous. Straight out of a style magazine to look at. Talk about naff, though. We'd just got our drinks, when he fished the ice cubes out of mine, threw them on the floor, jumped up and down on them and said "Now I've broken the ice . . ." ' Ellie shook her head in disgust and looked at Grace. 'Can you imagine a more pathetic sense of humour?'

'No,' Grace said, the Henry Moon detonator joke springing uncomfortably to mind. As well as the one about the sheep and the pylon.

'I don't know what it is about me,' Ellie sighed. 'I just attract freaks, that's all. Take Pete from last week. When he told me he'd planned a picnic, I was so touched. We drove for miles until we found the perfect spot.' Ellie paused, her brow wrinkling. 'The first warning bell should have sounded when he spread a pink-satin-edged blanket on the ground that still had his name tag on it from when he'd been camping as a Scout. But the final straw came when I thanked him for the wonderful feast. "Don't thank me," he said. "Thank Mummy. She made it." '

'You've had a lot of dates recently,' Grace remarked, grinning despite herself.

'Gotta make hay while the sun shines, babe. Which reminds me of Griff from a few weeks ago – remember him?'

'Oh yes,' Grace said, smiling. 'That gorgeous farmer who drove down from Hertfordshire in his Range Rover and asked you without a trace of irony if you'd been to a Harvester before.' She giggled.

'It's all right for you,' Ellie grumbled. 'You've got a bloke. Even if you could definitely do better.'

'Honestly, Ellie. You sound just like my mother.' Sensing the latest lecture on The Unsuitability Of Sion coming up, Grace tried to keep her tone light, even as dark guilt gathered in her heart at the memory of the weekend's events.

'Pretty girl like you should be having a good time,' Ellie remarked. 'Not hiding away at all those SWP solidarity events Sion's always making you go to.'

'A better time like you, you mean?' flashed back Grace.

'Those that can't . . .' Ellie grinned. 'Come on, Grace. Sion's hardly love's young dream, admit it. If I remember rightly your first date was a Christmas anti-capitalism disco in the Wanstead Flats Mechanics' Institute.'

'So what?' Grace was defensive. 'Sion did invite me to dinner afterwards.'

'To a *restaurant*?' Ellie looked amazed. 'Burger King, I suppose. Oh no, I forgot, he hates corporations. The Hare Krishna soup kitchen?'

'His flat, *actually*.'

'What did he cook for you? I'm assuming,' Ellie said airily, 'that he didn't get Gordon Ramsay in to cater the event.'

Grace hesitated. 'Not exactly.'

Ellie sighed impatiently. 'Come on. Amaze me. Tell me he's one of those cooks that can just open the fridge and conjure up something delicious from absolutely anything that's in it.'

Grace brightened. 'Well, he did make dinner out of what he could find in the fridge.'

'And what did he make?'

'Er, carrot omelette.'

'*What?*'

'Well it could have been worse,' Grace snapped. 'The other things in the fridge were sardines and cream.'

There was a pause while Ellie put her hands to her throat and mimed being sick. 'Grace, fond of you as I am, I'm with your mother on this one. Poor old Lady A. No wonder she worries about you. Be honest. You're only going out with him to piss her off.'

'Of course I'm not,' Grace protested, stung. 'Mum's a diplomat's wife. She doesn't get pissed off. She gets on the phone. And stays there.' She rolled her eyes. 'And *stays* there.'

Ellie looked unconvinced. 'So what's so irresistible about

him? Although I suppose,' she conceded, 'he's quite good-looking. In an unwashed sort of way.'

Grace bridled. As far as she was concerned, there was nothing quite about it. From the moment she had encountered Sion on the doorstep, she had fallen for him. He had a face like a Renaissance angel's, and a clean-cut body to match; even now, if he walked in the room, he could make her knees melt with a look. There was, aesthetically speaking, no comparison between him and Henry Moon. In terms of obviously appreciating her, however, the latter had won hands down. Hands everywhere, come to that. But that was irrelevant now. It had been a one-off. Never to be repeated. Or referred to. Or thought of. She fixed Ellie with a warning, steady gaze.

Ellie, however, had returned to contemplation of her own problems. 'And now,' she groaned, 'I'm back to the most exciting prospect of my working day being if Luigi at the sandwich bar puts an extra spoonful of tuna and sweetcorn mix in my poppyseed roll.'

'Oh, Ellie. It's not that bad.' Relieved to move on from the subject of Sion, and to have apparently skipped altogether that of Henry Moon, Grace looked almost fondly round the PR department of Hatto & Hatto. If, that is, such a grand term could be applied to the small, shabby room set aside for the purposes of book publicity. Grace had tried, but the A4 sheet of paper on which she had written 'Publicity Dept' had peeled away from its Blu-Tack many months ago and now hung, abashed and curling, from the back of the door.

Among the office's few nods to the twenty-first century was a hideous strip light crowded with the corpses of flies, a vast and ugly filing cabinet and two cramped desks on which squatted cumbersome and outdated computer screens.

But Grace did not mind this overmuch. She did not even mind the only 'facilities' being a small, chilly lavatory on the next half-landing. Wooden-staired, warreny and still sporting the elegant Georgian ceilings and fireplaces installed by the original owners, Hatto & Hatto's office represented, to Grace, the Platonic ideal of what a publishers should look like. Ellie, she knew, did not share this view. Nor, unlike Grace, did she consider, given the competition for jobs in publishing, that she was lucky to work here at all. Ellie had from the start been bent on higher things, of which her vertiginous heels were only one.

'Think of working at Hatto as a challenge,' Grace urged her colleague now.

'Well, it's certainly that,' Ellie acknowledged. 'Tackling the irreversible decline in most of our authors' careers is not for the faint-hearted.'

That Hatto & Hatto's stable of authors was not quite as well known to the outside world as it might be was indisputable. Not only were press, radio and television utterly uninterested; they seemed, despite Grace and Ellie's efforts, more uninterested all the time.

'But that's because Marian's just left,' Grace said bravely. 'Things will pick up when they get someone to replace her.'

Marian had been the cheery Head of Sales. Had been the cheery Head of Sales when she arrived, that was; more recent months had marked a rapid decline in Marian's readiness to trade a smile and a friendly word. According to Gladys the septuagenarian general secretary, in whom Marian had confided, this was due to her discovery that selling Hatto titles 'had been like pushing fog uphill'. Marian's additional discovery that her grand title of Head of Sales translated in reality to The Only Person In Sales had apparently also contributed to her disillusionment.

Yet Grace could not quite ignore that fact that, since Marian's departure, things had gone from bad to worse. Evidence that the company's output, always slow to reach the bookshops, wasn't reaching them at all now was piled up the stairs and round the edges of each room in the form of brown cardboard boxes stamped 'Books With Care'.

'And when they get someone to replace Adam as well,' Ellie said. Her low opinion of the Head of Fiction was, Grace had long ago guessed, informed by the fact that Ellie secretly had her sights set on an editorial job herself. The entire reason Ellie stayed at Hatto & Hatto at all, Grace suspected, was in the hope of penetrating the realm of Adam Knight. His realm was, however, a small one; having once presided over an office of no less than four editors, Adam was now Head of Fiction in the same way Marian had been Head of Sales. And the same way, Grace imagined, she herself would soon be Head of Publicity. If the department wasn't abolished in its entirety, that was.

'That's a bit harsh,' she murmured, although she wasn't sure that it was, really.

'Is it?' Ellie's eyes were burning between the layers of mascara. 'Have you read the manuscript of that book he's just bought? *The Curate's Ego*, or whatever it's called.'

'That one by Inigo Thongsbridge?'

Ellie nodded. 'Completely incomprehensible. According to the synopsis Adam sent out with it, it's a sort of satirical reworking of the Tibetan Book of the Dead based around the martyrdom of Saint Sebastian who is inhabiting the body of an artist in residence at Tate Modern. Adam thinks it's a work of genius.'

'Mmm.' Grace was unwilling to admit she hadn't even waded through the synopsis.

'Personally,' Ellie huffed, 'I think he's losing his marbles. And as for Thongsbridge . . .' She rolled her eyes in annoyance. 'These days Adam seems incapable of distinguishing between art and . . .' She paused. 'Fart.'

'Morning, Adam,' Grace called suddenly, spotting the editor's creased, stained, stone-coloured mac as it shambled past the door. A balding head with a few wild strands of hair pasted haphazardly across its spongy surface peered into the publicity room over a pair of wonky half-moon spectacles. Bundled under Adam's arm was a thick wedge of dog-eared paper bound with a rubber band.

'Well, at least he hasn't left that one on the bus,' Ellie observed as Adam shuffled off to his book-heaped cubby-hole at the end of the corridor. The Head of Fiction was notorious for abandoning original manuscripts on the Number 19.

Ellie sighed and began to shuffle the papers in her in-tray. 'How was *your* weekend, anyway?' she asked suddenly.

'Um, all right,' Grace hedged. She was tempted to lie, but couldn't summon up the necessary creativity. 'A bit of a mess, really,' she confessed eventually.

'Look,' Ellie said. 'I know it's none of my business, but I hope you don't mind me saying . . .'

Grace blushed violently. Had Ellie guessed? Or, even worse, *heard*? Had someone *said* something? It was far from impossible; the book industry was rife with gossip, even about those as lowly as she. She swallowed nervously, remembering the drinking game in the bar. It must have been abundantly obvious how drunk they were; what was more, practically the entire literary establishment had seen them. And very possibly, Grace supposed miserably, practically the entire literary establishment had not been quite as drunk as it had looked. 'What do you mean?' she demanded of Ellie, determined to tough it out.

'Well, it *is* a bit of a mess, isn't it? The whole thing, really. Disaster area, let's face it.'

Grace groaned inwardly. The game was obviously up. 'Well, I expect Henry and I will get over it,' she said, trying to sound breezy despite her painfully curled toes. 'After all, I don't suppose I'm the first publicity officer to get hammered at a literary festival and sleep with an author.'

Ellie's eyes were on stalks. '*What?*' She clapped a hand to her forehead. 'Christ, of course, the St Merrion Festival. You went there. I'd forgotten.'

'Isn't that what you meant?' Grace's hands felt suddenly clammy.

'You're all moony about Henry Moon,' teased Ellie delightedly. 'Who would have thought it! Well done, girl. Got lashed and got laid, in the best literary festival tradition.'

'I'm not moony. I'm *not.*' It was the only part Grace could rebut.

'But why not? He's quite good-looking, isn't he? For a complete flop, that is.'

'He's not a complete flop,' Grace said automatically, then wondered why she was bothering. What was Henry Moon to her, after all? Or she to Henry?

Ellie shrugged. 'Face the facts, babe. That's publishing. One day exploring's the new big thing. The next, it's the new raffia work.'

Ellie was very proud of the accuracy with which she was able to predict publishing trends. Only a few weeks before, she had foretold with great accuracy the extent to which a work called *A Humorous Look At Pain* would fail to justify Adam's confidence that the author, Tenebris Luks, was the next Martin Amis.

'But look at it this way,' Ellie added. 'Promoting Henry will be a hell of a lot more interesting if you happen to be bonking him as well.'

'*I'm not.*' Grace felt her face flood with shame. 'It was just – I don't know. A moment of madness.' She touched her forehead briefly. Probably about four bottles of madness as well. Two days later, the hangover had still not quite left her.

Ellie grinned. 'If I dropped an egg on your face now it would fry in seconds.'

'Piss off,' Grace snapped, feeling she had sufficient egg on there already.

'And Henry's *much* nicer than Sion,' Ellie added slyly. 'Do I take it from this little, um, *episode* that it's over between you two?'

'No,' blustered Grace, guilt and panic fighting for dominance within her. 'Not at all. In fact, Sion's taking me away to the country this weekend.'

Ellie's eyebrows shot up. '*Really?*'

Grace nodded emphatically. 'Yes, really.'

In truth, the proposed trip was as much of a surprise to her as it was to Ellie. Yet her urgings that for once they leave the Saturday morning bucket-rattling behind them and spend the weekend somewhere in the country seemed finally to have had an effect. Arriving back from the festival, feeling grubby inside and out, Grace had been confounded to find a message from Sion on the answerphone. Initially, because he had overcome his antipathy to speaking after the tone and subsequently at the recorded suggestion they leave London for a few days.

'I think,' Grace told Ellie, 'that he's realised we need to sort a few things out.'

'So where's he taking you?'

Grace shrugged. 'No idea. I haven't spoken to him yet.' Her hopes were already high nonetheless; fudge-tin cottages, their gardens crammed with hollyhocks, had already begun to line the scented lanes of her imagination. As had, admittedly even less realistically, country-house hotel terraces and the fringed curtains of four-poster beds. Perhaps, in such peaceful, perfect surroundings, they might really sort their problems out.

Ellie snorted. 'It'll be a Marxism for the Millennium conference in Basingstoke or something, you just wait.'

Grace scowled at her. She was determined to believe that things with Sion were about to improve, that the rot of his neglect was about to be stopped. 'So you see,' she pressed, 'things with Sion aren't really that much of a mess.' Ellie's remark about disaster areas had obviously referred to her relationship rather than the literary festival.

'Actually, I wasn't talking about things with Sion being a mess – although they obviously are. I was talking about your flat.'

'My flat? What's wrong with my flat?'

'It's a bomb site.'

'Well, at least I don't polish the pavement outside my house in case someone comes back for the night.'

'Neither do I,' snapped Ellie. 'Mrs Clarke does it for me.'

Grace felt cross. That her flat fell somewhat short of Ellie's *House & Garden* standard had been made perfectly clear the handful of times Ellie had visited it.

'Frankly, darling,' Ellie continued mercilessly, 'you're living like a slob. Don't you think you need a cleaner?'

'A slob? A *cleaner*?'

'Either that or I get the Social Services to put you in sheltered accommodation. Fortunately,' Ellie held up a hand, as Grace, red with indignation, looked set to interrupt, 'I've thought of the perfect solution. Mrs Clarke . . .'

'Mrs Clarke?' Grace asked in surprise. 'But you're always complaining about her. The things she breaks, the dust she misses.'

Ellie nodded. 'I know. But she's practically part of the family. She knew my sister was pregnant before my sister did, possibly because she spends so much time rummaging in drawers. But we're mutually dependent now. Like my driving instructor.'

'So what are you saying? That I should let Mrs Clarke rummage in my drawers as well?'

'Not her, silly. She has this friend, an East European woman called Maria. Incredibly hard-working, according to Mrs C.'

'Er . . .' hedged Grace.

'She's had *such* a tragic life,' Ellie said, widening her eyes persuasively. 'Apparently she had a successful business in Eastern Europe somewhere. But it went under because of the civil war.'

'Oh dear,' Grace was struck by compassion for anyone who had worse luck at work than herself. 'How awful.'

'More than awful. She lost her flat and everything. And

then, just as it seemed things couldn't get any worse, her husband died.'

'Oh the poor thing,' Grace murmured.

'So she came here, got a temporary visa and now she cleans for a living,' Ellie finished, her voice breaking dramatically.

Grace blinked hard. In the face of this poor woman's misfortunes, her own problems were fading to nothingness.

'But she's *desperately* in need of nice clients,' Ellie pressed, sensing her advantage. 'Got some woman who's absolutely vile to her at the moment, no matter how hard she tries. Pays her peanuts, shouts at her . . .' Grace's eyes, she saw with triumph, were glistening. 'Basically, she's cleaner heaven, even though her English is a bit iffy.'

Grace gave her a trembly smile.

'So what's the problem?' demanded Ellie, swooping for the kill. 'Don't you want to try and make this poor woman's life better?'

'Well, yes, but . . .'

'But what?' inquired Ellie crisply, waiting a few beats before assuming a contemptuous expression. 'Oh, don't tell me. Sion. You're worried he'll say cleaners are a bourgeois affectation perpetuating the existence of an, um, underclass.'

'Not at all,' Grace insisted, though she could not have put it better herself.

'When of course,' Ellie continued relentlessly, 'there's nothing *remotely* bourgeois or affected about the way he calls himself Sion when his real name is Simon.'

Grace scowled again at her colleague. *Why* could Ellie not let a week pass without bringing up the subject of Sion's name-change? Grace had regretted letting this slip in the wine bar almost more than any other act she had ever committed. Apart from the Henry Moon at St Merrion act, that was.

'That's settled then,' said Ellie decisively.

A cleaner probably wasn't such a bad idea, Grace thought, returning to her flat that night. Her gaze fell on the crumb-scattered carpet, the half-empty glasses of water crowded round the bottom of the sofa, a plate bearing a half-eaten, half-forgotten piece of toast sitting on top of the dusty television. She looked at the latter with interest. So that was where her breakfast had gone this morning. She'd looked everywhere, from the hair-balled, tissue-scattered underneath of the bed to the grey-scummed top of the bathroom cabinet, after which gruesome sight her appetite had disappeared entirely. Her eye caught the grey sheets on the long-unchanged bed (Tracey Emin had nothing on her), and the Olympic symbols of drinks rings covering every hard surface. It was impossible not to admit all this was less than ideal. Perhaps Ellie *had* put her well-manicured finger on something.

Somewhere under a pile of magazines on the floor, the telephone rang. Grace rummaged desperately to find it. Sion? Ringing about the weekend? And possibly even giving her some idea of when she could expect him tonight?

'Darling heart!'

'Mum!' Grace said, resignedly. 'How are you? How's Venice?'

'Wet as ever, darling. Are you still in touch with Ludo Cleft-Baring at all? Such a nice boy. Do you remember him? You used to go to lots of gymkhanas together.'

Grace gritted her teeth. 'No. Why?' Ludo, Grace remembered, was the only child more frightened of horses than she was. They had got on well enough, but once school and university had intervened, Grace had felt no urge to renew the acquaintance. In particular, not the type of acquaintance her mother clearly now had in mind.

'Lord Cleft-Baring's not very well. As his son, Ludo's definitely got *prospects* . . .'

'Mum, in case you've forgotten, I've got a boyfriend.'

'Yes, but . . .'

'But *what*?'

'Darling, Sion's so . . . chippy.'

'At least he believes in something besides Rule Britannia and the Royal Family,' retorted Grace. The one and only time her boyfriend and mother had met, Lady Armiger had been impressed at Sion's assertion that he had met a member of the Royal Family and had a photograph to prove it. Her approval had turned to horror when Sion dug out of his wallet an old newspaper cutting showing him throwing an egg at Princess Margaret who was making a visit to his university. The rest of the meeting with Lady Armiger had been awkward. It had also been unrepeated.

'Really, Grace. I do wish you'd get over this idea that everyone who has a title is ghastly,' her mother continued. 'Some of the nicest people I know have titles.'

'*Everyone* you know has a title.'

'Not necessarily, dear, I'm sure there's *someone* who doesn't. *Anyway*, my point is that *not* having one doesn't necessarily make someone a better person. Any more than eating with one's mouth open, slurping one's wine and not leaving a scrap of food on the plate for Mr Manners makes someone more charming.'

'I hope that's not a dig at Sion,' said Grace. She had never quite found the words – still less the courage – to explain to Lady Armiger that Sion's eating style was deliberately designed to confront and confound the accepted bourgeois orthodoxy on salt-passing, butter-knife management and the rest of it.

'Out again tonight, is he?' Lady Armiger inquired breezily, going, as usual, to the heart of the problem with all the subtlety of a cruise missile.

'He's gone to the launch of a book about how the multinational conglomeration of the corporate face of capitalism is damaging both culture and democracy,' Grace recited, wondering if she had got it quite right.

'I'm sorry I asked,' sniffed Lady Armiger. 'Still, at least he's not making you spend your evenings teaching drug addicts how to use the internet any more. And then letting them steal your computer.'

Grace gritted her teeth. After a stern lecture from Sion

on the subject of her bourgeois selfishness, she had felt much more ashamed of her assumption that the laptop was hers by right. Sion was unbending in his belief that all property was theft, and that the cinema, to which she occasionally suggested they go, was American cultural imperialism at its most brazen and seductive. And, post-cinema, pouring money into overpriced restaurants who callously exploited the Third World labour markets was yet more heinous. 'But I'm only suggesting Pizza Express,' Grace would bleat.

'Actually,' Grace said triumphantly, 'Sion's taking me for a weekend in the country. Just the two of us. Romantic, don't you think? Four poster beds, the lot,' she added, crossing her fingers and hoping it was true.

There was a brief, stunned silence from the Venice end. 'Well, all I can think is that it must be true what they say about SWP types.'

'What do they say?'

'That they only have one thing on their mind.'

'Class war, you mean?'

'No, darling. Sex.'

CHAPTER FOUR

'Call this a *table*?' spat Belinda. She stabbed a red-tipped finger into the thickly woven silk tie of the hapless maître d'. He looked helplessly at the piece of furniture in question. A circular surface, covered by a generous white cloth, silver cutlery set out with the mathematical exactitude of one of London's top restaurants . . . yes, it looked *exactly* like a table to him. He was happy to confirm it to this angry-looking woman with the black hair, emphatic make-up and extremely tight leather mini-skirt, who seemed for some reason to expect him to have heard of her.

'Well, it's not,' Belinda flung back. 'It's not a *table* at all. It's bloody Siberia.' She cast a quick, furious look round at the other diners. 'Actually, it's not even Siberia. It's the fucking Gulag.'

Belinda took the maxim that one should dress for the next job one wanted a stage further than normal. She believed one should *behave* like the next job one wanted as well. It was a cause of constant irritation that the job Belinda wanted – *believed*, indeed, she was born to do – was currently held by one Maureen 'Mo' Mills, *The Globe*'s star interviewer and chatelaine of a fortnightly four-page interview slot with a major celebrity. Almost more than she longed for wealth and fame, Belinda longed for that interview slot. Mostly because she believed, having got it, wealth and fame would naturally follow, either as a result of her brilliance in the job or through meeting and marrying a superstar. Either would do – Belinda wasn't fussy. Yet exactly how she was to get the job remained for the moment unclear. Mo Mills had been the paper's star interviewer since the early 1960s and showed no sign of flagging. She was, Belinda thought furiously, as immovable as the Rock of Gibraltar. And about the same size.

'But this is the second best table in the restaurant,' trembled the maître d'.

'Exactly,' roared Belinda. 'Do you know who I am? Belinda Black of *The Globe*, that's who. I want the *best*.'

'But Princess Diana used to sit here quite happily . . .'

'And look what bloody happened to her,' cut in Belinda. 'I rest my case.'

She was satisfied she had made enough of a fuss now. No one in the restaurant could possibly be unaware of who she was unless they were blind, deaf and dumb – poor excuse though *that* was. Belinda sat down with much loud scraping of her chair and began rummaging in her handbag.

She snapped open her compact and checked the reflected room for celebrities. None, really, apart from the Duchess of Kent in the corner and some camp designer with a Ronseal tan on Jeffrey Archer's old table. As usual, all the women in the restaurant were watching her in disgust, while the men slid looks of covert lust her way. Cheered, Belinda pushed her breasts out further. This tight suede top, deliberately two sizes too small, never failed to provoke the desired effect – i.e. one of desire. Belinda had at an early age mastered the tricks to make herself irresistible to men, which in her view boiled down to the Three Ls – Long Hair, Legs and Lots of Cleavage. Tossing her shining raven mane, sucking in her cheeks and swivelling her bottom to ruck the leather mini up still further, Belinda swung one long St Tropez-tanned leg over the other and wondered where the hell her lunch date was.

How *dare* society shoemaker 'Stinky' Cheshire, daughter of the Earl of Alderley, turn up *even later* to be interviewed than she herself had arrived to ask the questions? She had been twenty minutes behind schedule herself; but that was to be expected. Had Belinda Black of *The Globe* time to arrive punctually? Of course not. The fact that she had instructed the cab to circulate Piccadilly until the twenty minutes were up was neither here nor there. Shoemaker my arse, Belinda thought viciously, eyes trained for signs of Stinky on the restaurant's revolving black and silver door. But cobblers, certainly.

Handed a menu, she studied it scornfully, her mind far from the delicate world of marinated scallops and courgette-flower beignets. No doubt Stinky would have turned up on time for Mo Mills and her vastly superior – well, *bigger*, anyway, Belinda hastily corrected herself – interview slot. Would she ever get her hands on it? Mo Mills, after all, had the depressingly sound constitution of an exceptionally robust ox. The fact that, in over thirty years, she had famously Never Had A Day Ill, despite obvious weight problems and a face the colour of sweaty putty, was only one of the legends that surrounded her. Legends which, to Belinda's infinite boredom and irritation, all dated back to her sixties heyday. Who the hell, Belinda wondered, tearing murderously into a bread roll, cared about the sixties any more?

Who cared if, back *in* the sixties, Mo had swung with the Swinging Blue Jeans, hung with the Maharishi, shared a Dormobile with Bob Dylan, got Mick Jagger to reveal his recipe for Mussels Marinara and been the first to interview the Beatles after they'd had their hair cut in their signature style? The Moptop Interviews were, Belinda knew, widely regarded as a ground-breaking piece of celebrity journalism – but what ground did they *break*, exactly? Mo hadn't even found out what sort of shampoo the Fab Four used, for Christ's sake. Let alone made probing inquiries about conditioner.

'Aperitif, madam?' ventured a waiter.

'Glass of champagne,' Belinda snapped. The waiter glided

off, his face expressionless, but a muscle ticking vigorously in his cheek. Belinda watched. Despite La Garrigue's august reputation, it seemed there were certain of its staff who were just not used to dealing with stars. With people at the top of their profession. Or nearly.

Her boiling thoughts returned to contemplation of Mo Mills. That Mo held the title of Nicest Woman In Fleet Street struck Belinda as particularly pathetic. How hard *was* that, after all? Ditto, how interesting was it that her other plaudits included being One Of The Last Of The Great Characters, The Ultimate Professional and most famously, The Woman Who In Thirty Years Had Never Got A Fact Wrong? No wonder her interviews were so boring. For what could possibly be duller than the truth?

As for that line of description, under her byline photograph: 'The Woman Who Asks The Probing Questions,' Mo should be sued under the bloody Trade Descriptions Act. Take that Joseph Fiennes interview last week. Opening with the controversial humdinger, 'Joseph, you're the heart-throb of millions. How exactly does that make you feel?' it, in Belinda's opinion, had been a piece with all the sexual chemistry of a frozen fish finger. Not just a waste. A nuclear waste. The Woman Who Asks The Probing Questions. Ha! In her shoes – and not Mo's habitual bloody Birkenstocks at that – Belinda would have been probing in a different way altogether.

One small compensation was that Mo had not become rich on the back of her column. She had, in Belinda's scornful but largely relieved view, utterly failed to make hay while *The Globe* shone and snap up a rich and famous man from among the many with whom she had spent hours alone in hotel suites. Instead of flirting for Britain, she had actually wasted valuable time asking them *questions*. As if anyone *cared* what Bob Dylan really thought of Jacqueline Kennedy or what Paul McCartney really thought of John Lennon. Or, more recently what Bill Clinton really thought about George Bush and what Tony Blair's real views on Gordon Brown were. And the only concrete benefit Mo reaped from decades of getting intimate with the famous was an invitation each summer to Mick Jagger's box at Lord's. In Mo's position, Belinda would have been trying to get into a different sort of cricket box altogether.

But perhaps it wasn't so surprising; Mo was hardly well-equipped for flirting. To say she looked like the back end of a bus, Belinda thought smugly, catching and holding the eye of a flush-faced septuagenarian tackling his cheese course, was an insult to the backs of buses. Licking her lips suggestively, she grinned as the septuagenarian choked on his Stilton and had to be helped to the Gents.

But where the hell was Stinky bloody Cheshire? Belinda snatched the arriving champagne out of the hand of the waiter. Her teeth clanked angrily against the glass. Well, on Stinky's head be it. The longer she was in arriving, the nastier Belinda would be about her. Despite the fact the 'Tea Break' column hardly offered much room for personal opinion. Or offered anything else. The chance to meet megastars, least of all.

Tea Break, which had spent the previous twelve months in Belinda's reluctant charge, was *The Globe*'s weekly short question-and-answer-with-a-minor-celebrity item. It was found at the back of the paper, with the crossword and horoscope, rather than the front with the news like the Mo Mills Interview. To Belinda's chagrin, Tea Break was, and quite deliberately so, the polar opposite of the Mo Mills Interview. Where the Mo Mills Interview aimed high, Tea Break aimed low.

It wasn't just, Belinda thought, that Tea Break lacked prestige. Tea Break lacked interest as well – formulaic questions to formulaic sub-celebrities with bit parts on sitcoms, adverts and *The Bill*. Tea Break was, in short, a travesty of her talents; beneath her to an extent that would be laughable were it not so tragic. It was Tea Break, after all, that Belinda could thank for putting her on Christmas-card-receiving terms with the entire Who's That? of British television. Knowing what Ainsley Harriott's hamsters were called and being on a first-name footing with Antony Worrall Thompson, Fern Britton and the middle strata of the *Coronation Street* cast was also something she could lay fairly and squarely at Tea Break's door.

Tea Break haunted Belinda. She feared she would never escape it. She would wake, shuddering, from Tea Break nightmares in which she was locked in a Sun Hill police cell at the age of eighty, asking Charlie Dimmock what it would most surprise people to know about her. Belinda thought she hated Tea Break as much as it was possible to hate anything until the day she discovered it to be the part of the paper most popular with factory workers and manual labourers. After that, her loathing knew no bounds.

Belinda desperately wanted a break from Tea Break. Even more desperately, she wanted Mo Mills's job. But it would take a miracle to move Mo, and the precise nature of what that miracle might be occupied most of her waking thoughts.

Suddenly, a pink pashmina on legs came flying through the revolving doors. 'I'm so *sorry*!' exclaimed a toothsome blonde emanating a cloud of perfume so strong it caught the back of Belinda's throat. Not for nothing, it seemed, was this girl called Stinky Cheshire.

Belinda smiled nastily and mentally sharpened her claws. As she was not yet Chief Celebrity Interviewer, she would simply have to compensate herself by behaving as though she were. Or, to be precise, as she would *if* she were.

'Where have you been?' demanded Fran the Features Editor as Belinda arrived back in the office late that afternoon.

Belinda looked at her pityingly. Fran had obviously been down to the monastery barber again – who else, after all, could be responsible for that disastrous fringed hairstyle which only accentuated how exactly like a nose stuck on a ball her face looked? Lipstick the colour of poached salmon hardly helped. As for that scoop-necked top with what looked like cat bells round the collar, it should be a sacking offence. Merit a written warning, at the very least.

'Lunch,' Belinda snapped, as if that explained everything.

'Yes. I gathered that from the smell of alcohol. The only thing is, it's now half past four.'

'Keep your hair on,' Belinda told Fran, resisting the temptation to add, on second thoughts, that it might be better off. 'I've been doing a Tea Break with Stinky Cheshire. Who was late, by the way.'

Fran looked blank. 'Stinky who?'

'You know. That brain-dead socialite who goes water-skiing with Prince Andrew. Graciously agreed to a Tea Break in order to plug her fascinating new venture as a shoe designer.'

'Oh yes. What was she like?'

Belinda dragged out her Dictaphone and flicked the switch. 'Listen.'

A throaty female voice floated out of the microphone. 'Oh yah. It's been an amazing learning process. It takes nine months to have a child – and nine months to produce a pair of shoes!'

Belinda's own voice then cut in.

'Well, that's fascinating, Stinky. And is it true you recently arranged for your pet dogs to get married?'

'Oh yah. Absolutely. Those dogs really love each other.'

'Gwyneth Paltrow it wasn't,' Belinda observed acidly, switching off the Dictaphone. 'Chance would be a fine thing,' she muttered.

Fran stuck her chin into the air. 'Belinda, you know perfectly well that, while we all think you do a great job on Tea Break . . .'

Belinda looked at her boss narrowly, concealing her surprise. Hen's teeth were more common than praise from Fran.

'. . . and you definitely have a real knack for interviews . . .'

True, Belinda knew. Asking not-very-leading people not-much-more-leading questions and carefully editing the answers made all the difference between a good read and a mediocre one. Or, more accurately, between a mediocre read and a bad one. There was an art to Tea Breaks, albeit one she profoundly despised.

'. . . and we appreciate it, here on *The Globe* . . .'

Of course. The penny dropped. Is Fran's sudden recognition of my talents, Belinda cynically wondered, anything to do with the fact that *The Globe* has recently suffered a haemorrhage of features staff to the *Daily Mail*?

'. . . you're not quite ready to take on the bigger stuff yet.'

'So when,' Belinda inquired icily, '*will* I be ready?'

But she knew the answer. When Mo Mills dropped dead . . . . hang on, what had Fran just said?

'What did you just say?' she demanded.

'That I'm sure we could think about it if Mo ever went away,' Fran repeated crisply. 'There might be a window of opportunity.'

Belinda stared. *If Mo ever went away* . . . this was a first. Fran had never before admitted there was the faintest chance of her taking over the Mo Mills Interview. She was obviously under instruction to keep her staff happy. Or just keep her staff, full stop. Belinda's mind raced, before encountering an obstacle in the road.

'But Mo never goes away,' she protested. 'Never even takes a bloody day off.' Her voice was savage with disappointment. Window of opportunity – like hell. This was not, in actual fact, the tiniest opening of the door of potential. Not even a hairline crack in the cat flap of possibility.

Fran shrugged and turned away.

Belinda sulked over to her desk. The telephone rang. Belinda snatched it up. 'Yeah?'

'It's Amber. From Ace PR.'

These PR women, Belinda thought with professional weariness, were always called bloody Amber.

'I wondered,' Amber continued nervously, 'whether you'd made up your mind yet. You were thinking about putting some of the actors I represent in Tea Break.'

'Oh . . . yes.' Belinda brightened. There were worse ways to pass the time than PR-baiting. 'Congratulations,' she said.

'That's wonderful,' Amber breathed in relief.

'Congratulations, I mean, on having a stable of actors too dull even for Tea Break,' Belinda snarled. 'Quite a feat, that.'

'Wh-what?' There was a faint crash at Amber's end. Part of her brain falling off, Belinda imagined.

'But Jim Friedlander,' gasped Amber. 'He's huge . . .'

'He's a dwarf.'

'What do you mean?' Amber sounded horror-struck.

'I mean,' Belinda said, 'that Jim Friedlander barely tops five foot five.'

'He's very handsome,' Amber faltered defensively.

'He's also very short,' Belinda sneered.

'He's got a great sense of humour. He could give you lots of anecdotes.'

'Yes – if I got on my hands and knees to hear them,' Belinda cackled. 'Face it, babe. He's a midget.'

Oh, this was fun. This was power. This was infinitely more like it. And what harm was there in it? She had to spend her entire life with the humiliation of Tea Break, could she be blamed for humiliating someone else?

'But that's so unfair,' Amber protested feebly. 'To judge an actor on his height is so . . .'

'Heightist?'

'Jim's very talented,' Amber persisted bravely. 'His *Hamlet* was critically acclaimed. The *Guardian* loved it—'

'I bet it did. A dwarf version of *Hamlet* would be right up the *Guardian*'s street. But you're not talking liberal left-wing press here, sweetie. We're *The Globe*. We like our stars to look like stars. Which means tall.'

'But he's being considered for the next James Bond,' Amber said in a strangled voice.

'As what?' chortled Belinda. 'Mini-Me?' Christ on a bike, when would these bloody actors' PRs come up with a different line? If the number of putative James Bonds they claimed to represent was anywhere near accurate, the 007 casting directors must be at it 24/7. They must be overwhelmed with applicants. Just as she herself was overwhelmed with all the has-beens and never-would-bes desperate to be interviewed for Tea Break.

'Come on,' she urged the now-audibly-sniffing Amber. 'Who else have you got? Anyone famous, by any chance?'

Belinda knew perfectly well that megastars were about as likely to consent to Tea Break as the Queen was to do *Through The Keyhole*. But that need not stop her trying. 'Ace PR handles Mason Mackenna, doesn't it?' she asked suddenly.

'When she's in London, yes,' snuffled Amber.

'Ah. Well, now you're talking. Big Hollywood actress. Very glamorous. A no-holds-barred interview with her would be more than acceptable.'

'I think,' Amber said, gathering the shattered remains of her dignity about her, 'that she's unlikely to do a Tea Break. If Mason did anything on *The Globe* it would be the Mo Mills Interview.'

With a noise midway between a howl and a snarl, Belinda hurled the receiver back into its cradle. 'I'm going for a tea break – I mean a cup of tea,' she said, flouncing out of the office.

'But you're only just back from lunch,' muttered Fran.

* * *

Belinda stood in the tea queue. As she contemplated, revolted, the dirty earplugs abandoned in the cheeseplants by *The Globe*'s printers, her mobile rang. She checked the number.

'Che Guevara!' Belinda cooed delightedly into the instrument.

'Don't call me Che Guevara,' snapped the voice on the other end. 'He used to be a bank manager.'

'So when am I seeing you?' she purred.

'Dunno. I've got a meeting in, um, Westminster first. Problems arising from the government having abandoned their traditional left-wing principles . . .'

With an effort, Belinda hauled back her drifting attention. Although politicians weren't her usual beat for Tea Break, there was no doubt that 600 words worth of Cherie would electrify the slot and simultaneously her career. And Che, bless him, had promised to deliver. Their meeting had been fortuitous.

She had been, initially, extremely reluctant to attend the launch of *Das Capitalist*, a grindingly dull-sounding tome about the economic future of the planet. Her enthusiasm remained unkindled even after Fran had pointed out to her that the author was a friend of the paper's Deputy Editor, Warren Street, and it was her duty to go. 'But you know the only duty I care about is duty free,' Belinda had retorted. She realised, however, that she had no choice.

The reality had been worse than her wildest imagining.

In the fusty bookshop, listening to the author of *Das Capitalist* endlessly drone on, Belinda had sipped beer with a grimace, shifted from high heel to high heel and reflected that the only economic future she was interested in was her own.

'Yawnerama,' she grinned unsteadily at the person next to her. He was, she thought, handsome in a green-eyed, flat-featured, Christopher Walken sort of way, despite lank red hair and clothes that looked utterly unacquainted with a washing machine.

'What do you mean?' asked the ginger-haired man.

'Well, you can't possibly be *following* all this,' Belinda yawned.

'Let me ask *you* a question.' The green eyes glinted. 'Where do you stand on dialectical materialism?'

'Is that another word for bias cut?'

The man stared at her. 'Do you know *nothing* about left-wing politics?'

'Do you know who I am?' countered Belinda, indignantly. 'Belinda Black of *The Globe*, that's who.'

This had a gratifyingly spectacular effect. Minutes later, he had drawn her into a corner, was eagerly expounding on his PhD thesis and telling her it was about time she got some serious political stuff into the paper.

'You must be joking, Che, darling,' Belinda drawled. 'My section's idea of political debate is whether Cherie wears big pants or thongs.'

'I could find that out for you,' Che said quickly. 'I know

Cherie really, really well. And Tony. And Alastair. In return, I could do with a bit of exposure myself.'

'That,' Belinda purred, thrusting her breasts at him, 'could be arranged.'

Astride him later that night, Belinda tried to ignore the toast crumbs in his sheets. Let alone the general squalor of his flat – he didn't even have an answerphone, for Christ's sake. Still, she thought, grinding and clutching like an HGV, it would all be worth it for a Tea Break with Cherie. If that didn't make Kevin Grayson, the paper's Editor, realise she was promotion material, nothing would.

The tea queue moved suddenly forward. 'Got me my interview with Cherie yet, by the way?' Belinda hissed into the mobile – you never knew who was listening – whilst pretending to choose between Lemon Zester and Red Zinger. 'You said you were seeing her last night.'

'Yeah, well, something came up,' said the other end of the line quickly. 'But it'll be cool. Cherie'll do anything for me. Even if her husband's a smarmy git who's betrayed the working classes of this country. Could probably get you a Coffee Break with him, as well.'

'*Tea*, darling, tea,' Belinda corrected through gritted teeth, unwillingly reminded that Coffee Break had come out in reader surveys as being too aspirational a name for the slot.

'So I'll see you tonight.'

'What about tomorrow?' Belinda was unsure she could face the toast crumbs so soon.

'No can do. I'm – um – going to the country for the weekend.'

'How terribly middle-class.'

'So, do you want to meet tonight then, or what?' His voice was defensive.

Belinda sighed. 'I suppose so,' she said ungraciously. 'I'll see you at my club.'

'Nah. It's full of self-satisfied media wankers.'

'Of *course* it's full of self-satisfied media wankers. That's the whole point of it. Listen, big boy. No one ever changed the world by not going to Soho House.'

CHAPTER FIVE

'This boiled egg is delicious, Janet.' Grace smiled, breaking the silence that had reigned since they all sat down. Since she and Sion had arrived last night, in fact.

'I didn't realise,' Grace had whispered, as they took their bags up to the small, twin-bedded room allotted to them, 'that when you said we were going for a weekend in the country you meant we were going for a weekend with your parents.'

'What's wrong with my parents?' Sion snapped, his pale, delicate face red with indignation. 'Just because they're not diplomats and knights and whatever.'

'Nothing,' Grace said quickly, seeing that it would be both pointless and unpleasant to argue. If Sion's idea of a rural getaway was a twee semi outside Kettering called Janavid, so be it.

'*You* wanted a weekend away,' Sion snapped.

Grace rolled her eyes. Of course. It was all her fault. How could it not be?

'And they wanted to meet you,' Sion growled, as if why, exactly, was a mystery to him. 'And they've been nagging me for bloody ages to come up. Three birds with one stone, I thought.'

'Admirably economical,' Grace had remarked, remembering how Sion, suddenly unable to locate his wallet at St Pancras, had made her pay for the tickets.

Now, over the breakfast table Sion's mother nodded. 'Yes, my new egg-boiler's wonderful.'

'The one you showed me last night?' As Janet moved her chin up and down in eager affirmation, Grace was conscious of Sion, opposite, watching her suspiciously. 'The one that's shaped like a hen?' She was determined not to let slip the tiniest hint she found any of this bizarre. If Sion's parents were addicted to mail-order homeware catalogues, so be it. Among the items Grace had been invited to admire were bottle bibs to stop nasty sticky ring marks in the kitchen cupboard, a Heath Robinson machine to peel and core apples, and what looked like a large test tube with 'Olive Oil', 'Vinegar' and 'Mustard' marked on the side. 'Just add the ingredients and shake,' Janet had said, her voice wobbling with the vigour of her demonstration, 'and it makes perfect salad dressing every time.'

'You showed me the Wonder Cooker as well,' Grace smiled at Janet, ignoring Sion's scrutiny. 'The one with the lid that concentrates heat in the pan so it cooks from the bottom and the top simultaneously.'

'Sealing in the flavour and reducing the cooking time,' chimed in Janet enthusiastically.

'And don't forget the bacon crisper,' added David, Sion's father, looking up from the *Radio Times*. 'Amazing. Made of cast iron – it just presses the bacon against the pan to maximise the contact. Works a treat. I even wrote to the customer director of the catalogue to thank them. They printed my letter as well, Simon,' he added proudly, turning to his son. Who, Grace saw, flinched at the reference to his real name.

'Don't think I didn't notice you,' he snapped later as, Janet having disappeared into Janavid's garden wielding her secateurs and David having filled up his car-washing bucket, Sion and Grace took the bus into Kettering.

'Notice me doing what?' Grace asked innocently.

'Pretending to be interested. I saw you, when my mother read the bit out of the catalogue about the Dudley Duck Popper.'

'—"Making a large bowl of delicious fat-free popcorn for all the family to enjoy in front of *Stars In Their Eyes*"? But I wasn't pretending,' Grace protested. 'And, for what it's worth, I loved the milk frother.'

'And you were sniggering at that butter thing.'

'No I wasn't.' Grace had in fact been quick to recognise the value of the patent butter curler. To her mother's endless dismay, Gennaro, the chef at the Consulate, had never got the hang of them. Something requiring him to 'simply push down the base and up pops a dish of delightfully presented curls' would, Grace knew, save Lady Armiger considerable stress at the diplomatic dining table.

'And you obviously thought the chip-maker was crap.'

'That's just not true.' Although why Janet needed chips was anyone's guess, she thought ruefully. Her son had enough on his shoulder to supply the whole of Harry Ramsden's. 'Sion, why are you saying all these things? I really like your parents.'

'Yeah.' His tone was sneering. 'Don't you just. Love their house as well, don't you? Just like the one you grew up in, I'm sure.'

Grace sighed. 'I do like them,' she insisted. 'I just don't understand why *you're* so embarrassed about them.' Oh God. She hadn't quite meant it to come out that way. Still, the point of the weekend was to discuss difficult things.

'Embarrassed!' Sion's face went pink with fury. 'Why the hell would I be embarrassed about them?'

'I don't know. But I know you are.'

It had, after all, been he, not she, who had winced when Janet opened the *Radio Times* and began to mark with pink highlighter pen the programmes she intended to watch; David later did the same with blue. Sion had, in addition, looked furious at David's instructions to 'use the downstairs loo for solids during the night, Simon, as the upstairs one flushing wakes up Mum'.

'And why,' Grace asked, thinking she may as well be hung for a plain-speaking sheep as an upfront lamb, 'did you change your name from Simon to Sion anyway? Your poor mother gets in a terrible fluster about it. She doesn't know what to call you.'

Sion stomped off furiously down the pavement. Grace, ran after him, and tugging his sleeve, stopped him and turned him to face her.

'Sion, what's the matter?' she asked gently. 'The *real* matter, I mean.'

Something serious, she already knew. Because the main event of the weekend, the one even her mother had anticipated, had failed to materialise. There had been no sex. No banging of the airforce-blue Dralon bedhead against the artex walls in passion spiced by parental propinquity. Grace had gone to bed fairly aching with anticipation, and woken up in much the same condition. She had lain expectantly in the narrow single bed, alert to every movement of Sion's body swishing against the poly-cotton sheets several feet away. But the sudden whisper, the anticipated assault on the candlewick bedspread that would herald illicit, carpet-burned ecstasy, never came. Surely this, of all things, needed explaining? The dread possibility that Sion had found out about Henry Moon had been – with great relief – ruled out. Sion had no contacts with the book world apart from her. So what else could be the problem?

'Surely you're not still cross about that loo business?' Grace probed.

The week before, apparently unburdening himself of a long-held grudge, Sion had informed her that it was elitist of her to refer to the toilet as the lavatory. Instructed, in addition, that her revolutionary duty was to sit in a lounge, not a sitting room, and on a settee, not a sofa, Grace had been stepping on eggshells ever since. Battery eggshells at that; Sion considered anything free-range or organic part of a bourgeois-capitalist-conspiracy.

'Don't be so frivolous,' Sion snapped.

'Is it my job then?'

'What business is it of mine if you choose to spend your days pandering to a decadent and outmoded elite?' Sion snarled, his narrow eyes flashing.

'Working for a publisher, you mean?' Grace said in amazement. 'It's only a little business.'

'All capitalism, and in particular the multinational conglomeration of its corporate face, is damaging both culture and democracy.'

'I don't disagree with you, Sion,' said Grace, exasperated, 'but really, what's remotely capitalist about Hatto & Hatto? They don't even make a profit, as far as I know.'

'That's what they tell *you*. That's the boss class all over. Keep you in the dark and feed you shit.'

The idea of Adam Knight craftily salting away the profits made Grace want to laugh out loud. Adam's hands had started to shake so badly recently he could barely salt his lunch.

'Publish shit, as well,' snapped Sion.

Although this was one of the few points on which Ellie, Grace knew, would agree with Sion, she felt compelled to defend her employers. 'But Sion, you were very keen for Hatto & Hatto to publish your PhD thesis. You must have asked me a hundred times whether Adam had read *Why New Labour Are Bastards* yet.'

She stopped; Sion's temper was hardly likely to improve with the reminder that the publishing company had passed on the opportunity.

Yet she didn't feel this was the reason. Grace tried again. 'It's the cleaner, isn't it? You're cross because I've hired a cleaner.'

Sion, storming ahead over the rain-slicked pavements, turned and threw her a burning glare.

'But it'll be wonderful,' Grace urged cheerfully. 'I'm sure you'll love it.' Maria was due to start on Monday. There was no going back now.

'Love it?' Sion's face was twisted with irritation. 'That the existence of an underclass is being perpetuated by a bourgeois exploitative?' He spoke with no more emphasis than he had on anything else, however. Was there something she had missed? Had there been signs she had failed to pick up as determinedly as Sion consistently failed to pick up the 'Support the Striking (Fill In Here)' posters he had some time ago dumped in a box in her hallway?

'Is there someone else?' she croaked eventually. It seemed the only thing left.

Sion looked at her, the expression on his handsome face poised between exasperation and scorn. 'Oh *yeah*,' he sneered. 'Sure. Actually, I'm shagging an ambitious nymphomaniac hack with huge tits who wants me for my brilliant political connections.'

Grace's mood of sober concern evaporated. Her shoulders shook. 'Oh, Sion.' At least, despite everything, he could still make her laugh.

'What a shame you have to go early,' Janet said next day as David started the car outside Janavid.

'I'm awfully sorry,' Grace gabbled. 'But Sion insisted we can't stay for lunch. He's suddenly got something urgent to attend to. Something about Cherie – but I probably didn't hear properly. Anyway, I'm sure he'll tell you when he comes out.' She glanced, irritated, at the net-curtained window of the room where, for the past twenty minutes at least, Sion had been deep in conversation on his mobile – with whom she was not sure.

She had not dared go in – and was now uncomfortably aware she had forgotten to check the bottom of the bed for knickers.

'I was so looking forward to showing you my apple turnovers,' Janet sighed. 'That baker's prick is nothing short of a miracle.'

Grace strapped herself into the front seat of David's Proton.

Janet leant in through the open window and gave her a quick peck on the cheek. 'Well, hopefully we'll see you again soon,' she said brightly. 'You know,' her voice dropped to a whisper, 'you're the nicest girl Simon – I mean *Sion*,' she added uncomfortably as David, in the driving seat, raised his eyebrow, 'has ever had. By far the nicest. David and I are very much hoping . . .'

'Si*mon*!' David, unrepentant, called in the direction of Janavid. 'Where *is* the boy?' he muttered, irritated.

'Don't leave yet. I've got something for you.' Janet scuttled off. With pantomime timing, as soon as she had disappeared through the front door, Sion appeared out of the side one and got into the car.

As he slammed the car door, Janet rushed out again, bearing something on a tray. 'Here, take this.' She reached deftly through the window and plonked the brown plastic oblong into Grace's lap. 'I didn't want you to travel without a square meal inside you,' she added. 'I thought you could eat it on the way.'

Grace looked down in amazement at a plate of homemade fish and chips, complete with lemon wedges on the side.

'Oh, and there are these too.' Janet rummaged in her apron pocket and dropped onto the tray a handful of tiny packets of salt, vinegar and ketchup that Grace could tell had been collected from cafés, pubs and aeroplane meal boxes. She had already noted how the Janavid bathroom cabinets were well stocked with miniature bottles of shampoo, shower gel and moisturiser emblazoned with the logos of various hotels.

'And you'll need this,' Janet grinned, handing over a plastic knife and fork in a plastic bag stamped 'British Airways'.

'Thanks,' stammered Grace, thinking it certainly gave a whole new meaning to meals on wheels. 'You really shouldn't have gone to all this trouble. Honestly.'

'No trouble,' Janet beamed. 'I've got a tray just the same for Sion in the kitchen. Hang on, I'll just bring it out.'

'Don't bother,' said Sion brutally.

'No, don't,' David agreed, drumming his ginger suede-gloved hands impatiently on the steering wheel.

'Oh well, if you're sure,' Janet said, disappointed. 'Drive carefully,' she instructed her husband. 'I don't want to be cleaning chips out of the footwell when you get back.'

The following Monday evening, Grace paced about the flat nervously. Ten minutes to go before her first visit from Maria.

In anticipation, Grace had sought to impose some order on her home. Her home, however, had shrugged her efforts contemptuously off. Attempts to relieve the mirror of its layer of dust had only succeeded in the creation of great Van Gogh swirls of polish on the surface. The mysterious dark stains on the bottom of the kitchen sink showed as profoundly brown as ever, particularly in the pitiless glare of the overhead light. Looking at the bare bulb, Grace remembered she had taken the grease-and-fly-encrusted shade down to clean some weeks ago and, having failed to find anything to do this with, had forgotten to put it back. She had no idea where the shade was now.

Ellie was right. She *had* been living like a slob. Her

windows were, now she came to notice them, filthy to the point where it was hard to see out and she'd probably been risking tetanus every time she used any of the china, cutlery or glassware in the kitchen. Her feet sticking to the long-unwashed bathroom floor, Grace peered apprehensively into the gritty bottom of the bath. She had just noticed the spattered mirror and the lumps of toothpaste behind the taps when the door buzzer sounded.

Grace was seized with panic and guilt. She had no idea what someone whose life had gone wrong on the scale Maria's had might look like. She imagined eyes large with pain and worry, brow creased with misery, hands gnarled with a lifetime of bashing potatoes into submission in some grim concrete tower block. Perhaps, Grace thought, going to the door, I'll just show Maria to a chair and give her a cup of tea. After everything she's gone through, the last thing she'll want is to clean my flat as well.

Opening the door, Grace was confounded to see standing before her an attractive, denim-clad woman with blonde hair shot through with streaks of brilliant pink. A large bag was slung over her shoulder. Grace looked at the stranger inquiringly. Jehovah's Witness? MORI pollster? 'Can I help?'

The woman flashed a big, toothy smile.

'I ham Maria? I come to clean for you?' She smiled again. It was, Grace thought, amazed, like looking into the beam of a particularly bright lighthouse. Far from being a limping, downtrodden bulk, Maria was slim, lithe and radiated energy.

Embarrassed, Grace led the way to the kitchen. Maria looked calmly around, then rummaged in her large bag to produce several cloths and bottles covered in pictures of shining tiled floors. 'Bleach,' she grinned, waving a big plastic bottle in violent yellow. 'Ees good. Verray strong.' The thought of all that bleach swilling down her U-bend made Grace swallow. Salmon had only just come back to the Thames after all.

Maria's blouse, Grace noticed, was immaculately well-pressed. A wild longing suddenly struck her. The words were out before she could stop them.

'Um, Maria, I don't suppose you do ironing?'

The cleaner's blue eyes swelled with surprise. Wrong question, Grace thought. *Of course* she doesn't do ironing. Not all cleaners do.

'*Ir-roning?*'

'I'm *sorry*,' Grace cried. 'Silly of me to have asked.'

'Of course I do ir-roning. What else I here for?'

Grace beamed at her in wonder, thinking of the scrunched-up pile of shirts at the back of the cupboard. Maria had paid for herself already. She had tripled Grace's wardrobe in an instant.

Shown the bedroom, Maria cast a businesslike glance across the rumpled sheets which Grace, sniffing that morning, had decided would just about do for another week. 'Zay need changing.'

Suddenly, Maria snatched at something in a silver frame on the bedside table. The photograph, Grace realised, of

Sion throwing eggs at Princess Margaret. It had been her Christmas present from him.

'But what ees thees?' Maria was peering closely at the picture. 'Thees man here,' she said, stabbing a blue, sparkling fingernail on the image of Sion, 'he throw something? He ees not nice.'

'Um, actually, that's my boyfriend.'

Maria stared at Grace, then back to the photograph, in amazement.

'But Madam Grace,' she chided. 'Ees not good, thees man. I tell. I know these theengs.'

Indignation welled within Grace. She had enough of this from her mother and Ellie not to have to pay to hear it from the cleaner into the bargain. With an effort, she suppressed her irritation. Did she or did she not want ironed shirts?

'How do you know these theengs – I mean things?' she asked, not sure this was the proper subject to be discussing when they had met less than five minutes ago and were in a master-servant scenario to boot.

'My family,' Maria answered. 'My grandmother, she knew how make spell.'

Oh Christ. A mystic cleaner, no less. When all she wanted was a clean flat, with as little trouble as possible. Grace put her hands firmly, if regretfully, on her hips. Time to show who was boss. 'Erm, Maria . . .' It came out less authoritatively than she was hoping.

'Madam Grace,' cut in Maria, her eyes wide with excitement. On her slender, athletic hips, her hands were placed with equal firmness. 'I haf idea. One hof my customers verray nice man. He by heemself. He nice for you.'

Grace tried not to flinch at the thought of Maria's male clients who lived by themselves. Men with bulgy bellies and, no doubt, hairy backs who sat in front of daytime TV in grubby vests. Or else ass-kicking, sleazy City types whose cutting-edge bedside tables held a fine powdering of cocaine. Neither much appealed.

'No thanks, Maria. Now, look . . .'

'But why?' Maria insisted, eyes large and wounded. 'My customer, he verray kind man.' She pointed at the picture of Sion. '*He* not verray kind man.'

Grace felt her heart sinking. In amongst the heartrending details, Ellie had neglected to mention that Maria was stark raving bonkers. Just what had she let herself in for?

CHAPTER SIX

Belinda looked balefully at the actor sitting opposite. It was almost too much of an effort to switch on her Dictaphone and start the interview. But he was supposed to be an up-and-coming television star, and she needed *something* for Tea Break. And, unlike Jim Friedlander, this actor at least possessed the virtue of being above knee level. If only he wasn't so pathetically grateful at being interviewed. It was enough to make her want to puke.

Belinda finally mustered the energy to press the tape recorder button. 'So, Tony . . .'

'Toby,' said the young man apologetically.

Belinda rolled her eyes irritatedly. The most infuriating thing about these wannabes was their pernickety obsession with pathetic detail.

'It *sounds* a bit like Tony, though,' the actor added helpfully. 'I can understand why you confused it.'

Belinda, pointed the small black machine at him as if it were a gun. 'Tell me,' she demanded with weary resignation. 'How *are* the foothills of fame?'

The blond young man's eyes sparkled. 'Brilliant. I've always hoped television would give me something, but never something as big as this. In the last few weeks, I've done *Celebrity Weakest Link*, *Taste Today With Anthea Turner*, presented a youth award with Sebastian Coe and opened a BT Cellnet shop and a Somerfield. Amazing, isn't it?'

Belinda blinked, momentarily stunned by the exactness of this precis of Z-list hell.

'Tell me about your huge new part,' she commanded. 'Haven't seen the press release, I'm afraid.' Toby's PR had, in fact, sent her several copies by fax, email and post, none of which Belinda had quite managed to drag her eyes across. 'Involves Dawn, doesn't it? Personally, I've never been a big fan of fat girl comedy.'

'Oh, it's not a comedy. Not *quite*.' The young man's eyes were fairly straining with the fear of offending her. 'More of a drama, really. Quite violent, too. I get tied to a post by a gang of men . . .'

Belinda sat up slightly, rucking her skirt to expose yet more thigh. The action was more habit than serious intention to seduce; Toby was hardly her type. Too thin, too blond. And far too obscure.

But . . . being tied to a post by a gang of men definitely

sounded more interesting than she had expected. And a homosexual rape storyline was quite a departure for Dawn French. Hardly *The Vicar Of Dibley*.

'Sounds quite kinky,' Belinda observed. She narrowed her small, heavily made-up eyes. 'Any uniforms involved?'

'Oh yes. *Lots*,' beamed Toby.

'Animals?'

Toby looked doubtful. 'Well, there were a few freeze-dried rats.'

Vermin. Very post-watershed.

'When you throw them in the mud, they swell up and bob about,' Toby added. 'Looks very realistic. Horrible, really.'

Belinda nodded approvingly. 'And at what stage does Dawn come in?'

The actor looked confused. 'Sort of at the end.'

'And then the laughs really start, do they? Once she gets involved?'

'Erm, well, not laughs, exactly.' Toby looked troubled. 'Not as such.'

'What did you say this programme was called?' Belinda demanded, suddenly suspicious.

'*Shot At Dawn*,' said Toby politely. 'I play a First World War deserter who . . .'

It was with more than the usual feeling of tension that Belinda returned to *The Globe* office. *Sanity? What sanity?* inquired a screensaver in the advertising sales department as she walked through. As Belinda stalked past the fashion desk, the fluting tones of Ticky Sinclair, *The Glode's* Fashion Editor, could be heard in heated debate with Warren Street, its Deputy Editor.

'Look, I won't say this again,' Street barked in his nasal voice. 'The Editor wants a piece about how suits are back.'

'But we, you know, like, *can't.*' Ticky wafted her long hands about helplessly.

'I'll say it again. The Editor wants a piece saying suits are fashionable.'

'But they're not. Suits are . . .' Ticky rolled her eyes languidly, ' . . . so *over.*'

'That does not matter. What does is that the Editor's wife wants to carry on wearing hers.'

Ticky sighed and flicked blunt-cut brown hair back over skinny shoulders, one of which was fully exposed in a striped nylon slashed top.

'But suits are so ten minutes ago. So *wrong*. So not cool.'

Street's sharp eyes flashed fire in his thin, tanned face. 'If *The Globe* says they're –' he scowled at having to say the word – 'cool, they are.' His pager bleeped. Street pulled it distractedly out of his pocket. 'Look, I've got to go – got to finish The Funny Things Dogs Do spread. Just get on with it, will you?'

As Ticky glowered after Street, Belinda grinned to herself. Seeing someone else have a hard time always made her feel better.

She passed the subs' desk. 'But this section is a bit confusing,' Laura, the chief sub-editor was saying worriedly into her receiver, presumably to some contributor. 'For instance, are we sure here that it's the daughter speaking and not the dog? And when you say "pants" can we change it to "trousers"? "I took my pants off" doesn't sound very family newspaper . . .'

At the features desk, Fran was deep in conversation with the Health Editor, Aurelia 'Potty' Potter. Belinda's lip curled. Potty, she considered, was completely *noisettes*. Despite having a coveted company parking space, she insisted on turning up to work on an ancient bicycle covered in anti-world-trade-organisation slogans. She then followed her exertions with a shower using a concoction made of salt, sugar, honey and hemp oil which nonetheless sounded, Belinda thought, more edible than anything on *The Globe*'s cookery pages.

'*Chi-Whizz* explains all sorts of mysteries,' Potty was telling Fran. 'Tomorrow's piece is about how people who have an aversion to alcohol, for instance, may find it's because they were married to someone who had a drink problem in a former life.'

'Or in this life,' Belinda observed sweetly, smiling dazzlingly at Fran, whose face flushed with fury. Yet is it *my* fault, Belinda thought, that Fran had a terminally useless writer husband who spent his time sunk in a morass of self-pity and Tio Pepe? Even Fran refused to risk her reputation by commissioning him. Still, what else could one expect of someone called Inigo Thongsbridge?

Belinda finally arrived at her desk and stared unenthusiastically at the latest pile of press releases and invitations sent in daily by PRs hoping the actor/film/TV programme/book/brand of margarine they represented might prove suitable for a Tea Break. On top was a summons to the relaunch of a range of tofu and vegetarian terrines. And that, Belinda thought, ripping it in half, just about sums the whole damn thing up.

Swinging her bag contemptuously into the heap, Belinda scattered it to the four air-conditioned winds.

'Excuse me,' Margaret the features secretary said acidly. 'I've actually just spent ages sorting those out and piling them up.'

Belinda shot Margaret a look of dislike. Her loathing was, she knew, returned with interest. And expressed in other ways as well. Faxes addressed to Belinda frequently went missing, expense forms were invariably queried and anyone calling with complaints about pieces Belinda had written were encouraged by the features secretary to fax their concerns, not to Belinda or Fran, but directly to Kevin Grayson, the Editor.

Belinda plunged reluctantly into the press releases. It was like diving into a freezing, slimy pond, but with none of the glamour and interest that implied. Nonetheless, there had to be a Tea Break here somewhere.

'*In a new TV series,* Charlie's Garden Boot Camp, *Ms Dimmock leads a gang of real shoplifters on a project to build a provençal-style garden against the east wall of a young offenders' institution . . .*'

Belinda ground her teeth and bowled the first press release into the bin. She picked up the second.

'Star Ready Steady Garden. *Team leaders Davina McCall and Norman Wisdom are both given 30 minutes to transform a patch of rough ground outside Rotherham . . .*'

Slam dunk, thought Belinda, watching the paper curve through the air.

'Real Gardeners From Hell. *Leylandii wars in a small Derbyshire village turn very nasty indeed, while a West Yorkshire woman plants rockery dwarves in extremely acid soil . . .*'

Underneath the TV blurbs were press releases for forthcoming films. Belinda skimmed through them. Hollywood it wasn't. Mo Mills, of course, had got first dibs on the big stuff.

'The Brothers. *A boxing champion is abducted by Nazis and replaced by his evil sibling . . .*' Nope.

'Voodoo Song. *A classical composer visiting a friend's jungle plantation is attacked by a boa constrictor and nursed back to health by the chieftain's daughter who inspires him to write a jungle concerto . . .*' I don't think so.

'Kiss Off. *An unwitting beauty consultant is lined up to kill a presidential candidate with poisoned lipstick . . .*' *Kiss Off*, thought Belinda, could piss off.

'Circus. *In a neat reversal of the running-away-to-join-the-circus idea, an equestrian clown runs away to the city to become a stockbroker but ultimately returns to save the family act . . .'* Like hell.

'Howdy Doody. *A man moves into a haunted house where his ass is possessed by a demon called Captain Howdy . . .'* Hell's fucking bells, thought Belinda, lobbing Captain Howdy at the bin and starting on the book releases.

'With A Ferret Down My Trousers *by Phil Plant, Parrot Publishing, £5.99. In this follow-up to* Playing The Ethiopians At Bingo, *the celebrated stand-up comedian and holder of a first-class degree from Oxford describes his hilarious adventures walking from Land's End to John O'Groats in the company of a live mammal . . .'* Not on my page, he doesn't, Belinda thought, screwing both Plant and his mammal into the tightest of balls.

'*Shampoo and sex,*' read the next book release, printed in red on dazzling pink paper. '*As he ran his fingers through her hair, she yearned for the feel of his tong . . .'* Jesus. 'Airhead, *by Jenny Bristols. Ptarmigan, £5.99. In this laugh-out-loud follow-up to last year's barnstorming bestseller set in the sex-'n'-scalpels world of neurosurgery,* Braindead *author Bristols tackles the lust-'n'-lowlights world of hairdressing. In this bubbly tale of a love rhombus set in a Mayfair salon, Jess's cutting remarks are making frothy Rosie feel blue, while Matt bobs helplessly in the wake of Cairo, who consistently gives his advances the brush-off. Zak, meanwhile, combs his past for an answer, but will it lead to a tragic parting?*'

Attached to the page was a small, glossy postcard

depicting a neon-pink hairdryer set on a fizzing blue background. It was, Belinda realised, an invitation to the *Airhead* publication party. 'The Naked Launch', it announced, giving the address of a Soho pole-dancing club. Taped to the back was the dress code information, 'As Little As Possible', and a bright pink thong. Twirling the scrap of neon nylon round her forefinger, Belinda pitched it into the bin.

The next press release could not have been more different. No laminate, no colour and certainly no pink thong. Just black on white, no frills, only a logo of two intertwined top hats. Belinda looked at the name of the publisher, Hatto & Hatto, and snorted. Those losers famously hadn't got two pennies to rub together. Hardly surprising, if this was the kind of stuff they were churning out.

'Sucking Stones *by Henry Moon. Published by Hatto & Hatto, price £12.99 hardback. Dreams, drama and dysentery; the pursuit of a personal challenge by the last of the gentlemen explorers. A journey of discovery in search of a forgotten people . . .*' Belinda yawned. Well they could stay forgotten as far as she was concerned. Hatto's bloody PR woman had been on to her about this five times already. She seemed incapable of understanding that when Belinda Black said 'no', she meant 'no'. More than that, she meant 'no, never, not ever and why don't you just kill yourself while you're at it'. She picked up the next release. Those bloody top hats again.

'Our Mam *by Euphemia Ogden. Published by Hatto &*

Hatto, price £12.99 hardback . . .' Hatto certainly picked their authors, thought Belinda, squinting at the release. '*The touching tale of a poor, working-class Newcastle childhood . . .*' Poor, working-class and, for Christ's sake, *Newcastle*? Were there three words in the language more calculated to turn her off ? She read on. '*From the day she came into the world, one of thirteen children of a one-legged miner, Fanny knew her destiny was to be a writer . . .*'

After *Our Mam* had gone the way of her predecessors, there was only one press release left. She needed something for Tea Break. Would this do? Probably not. For there, once again, was the Hatto & Hatto logo.

'Napkins & Niceties: Modern Manners For A Modern Age *by Lady Cylindria Slaughter. Published by Hatto & Hatto, price £12.99 hardback. Covering everything from meeting Her Majesty to dealing with the dustmen, this indispensable handbook is in its third reprint . . .*' This job, Belinda thought, raising her eyes to the strip-lit ceiling, is more dead end than an abattoir. Her eyes slumped back to the Lady Cylindria press release. '*Ever wondered how to address an archbishop*?'

Ever wondered how to fill a newspaper column? thought Belinda. Call it desperation, but there might well be something in this. Besides, the Editor's fondness for the famous was matched only by his passion for the posh. '*For further details, call Ellie Renton at Hatto & Hatto.*' Scowling, Belinda prepared to do just that.

* * *

Wriggling her plump bottom on Sheekey's leather bar stools, Euphemia Ogden scanned the menu greedily. She ordered a dozen Colchester oysters and the same number of langoustines before declaring herself a martyr to her metabolism. 'I must have fish, fish, fish,' she announced. 'The freshest and the best. Nothing else will do. Champagne.'

The last word was an order rather than a suggestion, Grace realised. So, fortunately, did the barman. Two frothing flutes were quickly forthcoming. 'That's better,' Euphemia said, knocking back the first and grabbing the second. Winking at Grace, the barman slipped another glass in front of her.

'Happy with the book jacket quotes?' Grace asked her author.

Given that most past assessments of Euphemia's oeuvre were extremely unflattering, Grace felt she had done a creditable job selecting 'Praise For The Author' quotations for the back of the *Our Mam* book jacket. There were, admittedly, a couple of the 'a dark and quirky read' variety that Grace vaguely suspected was code for 'crap' among book reviewers in the same way 'flamboyant' was a euphemism for 'homosexual' among obituary writers. But there had been little other choice.

'Extraordinary, amazing even, how any publishing house was ever persuaded to accept such drivel', had been the frank view of the *Guardian* book pages. Well, that was easy enough to convert. 'Extraordinary' read the *Guardian* quote the *Our Mam* jacket. There was no quote from the *Independent*. Contemplating that paper's verdict on Euphemia, Grace had wondered whether she had the balls to drop the second, third, fourth and fifth words from 'Incredible how bad this is'. She had decided, on balance, that she hadn't.

Grace watched Euphemia as she read, and tried to guess how old she was. Or how much older, to be precise, than the forty-five claimed by her biographical details.

Euphemia wore head-to-toe red and a commanding expression. Two suspicious dark eyes crowded together beneath imperious brows at the top of a long sweep of nose. Her hair rose in an artfully bouffed wave glinting with the reddish tint Ellie had uncharitably christened menopausal auburn, while her chin plunged straight downwards into a collar of waxy fat. Her fuchsia lipstick clashed loudly with the vermilion, gilt-buttoned suit in which she was trussed more tightly than a stuffed quail ready for baking.

'And the front cover?' Grace asked next. In her opinion, *Our Mam*'s jacket image, a painting of a large lady in curlers staring challengingly out of what looked like an outside lavatory, was not one of the best. But better by far than the mournful girl in a patterned headscarf who had featured on the cover of Euphemia's last novel, *Pease Pudding Polly*.

It had been a hard morning. Accompanying Euphemia on the *Our Mam* promotional round as she swept into bookshop after bookshop with a hauteur that made

Cleopatra look sloppy had not been the easiest of tasks. And that had been before the Jenny Bristols incident in Selfridges' book department.

'Er, Jackie?' hazarded Euphemia, making a great show of pretending not to know her fellow author. A brave try, Grace thought, considering the other woman sat at a table signing a vast pile of novels on which the name Jenny Bristols was printed in huge pink letters.

'So *lovely* to see you,' Jenny purred, her eyes, to Grace's amazement, apparently blazing with sincerity. 'I'm so glad, because I've always wanted an opportunity to thank you for all the pleasure you've given me. I just don't know how you keep producing them so brilliantly, year after year.'

Euphemia's chest swelled like an opera singer about to burst into a particularly demanding aria. 'And which of my books did you enjoy most? *Coal Pit Kate*? Or my Number Three bestseller, *Pease Pudding Polly*?'

'Haven't read either, I'm afraid,' Jenny trilled, scribbling away with her Mont Blanc. 'I was actually talking about the wonderful display of yellow roses in your front garden. I live just down the road from you, you see.' With a vicious grin, she closed the book and picked up another.

Grace's heart palpitated afresh at the memory. Still, this lunch marked the end of her duties with Euphemia. Moreover, four glasses of champagne and a haul of oysters, prawns and langoustines that would have lasted Rick Stein for a fortnight seemed thankfully to have shut the great scribe up. Temporarily at least.

'So,' Euphemia boomed, plunging a small silver fork into the quivering heart of an oyster. 'Got me in the *Daily Telegraph*?'

Grace took a deep breath. There had, in fact, been a call from the *Telegraph*, but not one she intended to tell Euphemia about. 'I want to ask Ms Ogden,' the sniggering journalist had said, 'what, as an author considerably lower down the pecking order, she feels about the enormous advances being dished out for books like Sassy Jenks's *Shooting Up*.'

Euphemia looked outraged. '*The Globe* then? The Mo Mills Interview?'

'Well, I tried, as you know, Euphemia . . .'

'I thought of a marvellous idea for the photograph,' Euphemia boomed, ignoring her. 'I could lie on my chaise longue with Fulham and Putney on my knee.' Fulham and Putney were Euphemia's shih-tzus. 'In a short skirt, obviously.' Euphemia looked complacently at her calves. 'I'm terribly lucky,' she simpered. 'I've always had the most marvellous legs. My ankles, in particular.' Grace obediently examined the thick, white, blue-veined expanse of what looked like Stilton which connected each of Euphemia's legs to her tightly shod little feet.

'They're marvellous, Euphemia. But unfortunately, Mo's . . .' Grace hesitated. 'Turned you down flat' would obviously not go down well. 'Mo's apparently arranged all her interviews for the next two months or so,' Grace said, crossing her fingers behind her back.

'Well, what about that stupid little Tea Break thing then? I mean, obviously it's way beneath me, but . . .'

'I've tried that,' Grace said, wincing as she recalled the forthright response of Tea Break's editor. Although, much to her and Ellie's surprise, there had been an interview request from Belinda Black only yesterday. For, of all people, Lady Cylindria Slaughter, the least-requested writer of the entire Hatto stable, apart from the Hon. Greville Goodtrouser DSO, whose *Ginger's Bought It: Memoirs of a World War II Fighter Pilot* had not been doing as well as anticipated. Not as well as Adam Knight had anticipated, that was, although every bit as badly as Ellie had. A shame, as Sir Greville was a darling, really.

'*Our Mam*,' Euphemia told her, cracking a lobster claw for dramatic emphasis, 'has got to go straight to the top of that bloody bestseller list. I won't settle for *Our Mam* being under John le Carré.'

'Of course not,' murmured Grace, a giggle bubbling in her throat.

'I want *Our Mam* on top of Patricia Cornwell. On top of John Grisham, even.'

'Right.'

'So what about some really creative PR?' demanded Euphemia. 'I read in last week's *Bookseller* that Ptarmigan get their PR staff to do all sorts. One was painted gold and streaked naked down the touchline at Twickenham to promote something. Got an award for it, as well.'

'Really?' Grace would, she thought, need an OBE at least

before contemplating anything similar on behalf of *Our Mam*.

'*And* they send out all sorts of presents with their books,' Euphemia complained, pulling out the lobster flesh with thick, fishy fingers. 'Like pink neon thongs and chocolate willies.'

Grace raised her eyebrows. Neither struck her as particularly suitable accompaniments to *Our Mam*. It was hard to say what would be.

'*And* they have launch parties in pole-dancing clubs,' Euphemia added with her mouth full. 'They launched a Caribbean food book recently where the writer wore nothing but bananas – a bunch over both tits and another over her front bottom.'

Grace boggled, imagining Euphemia in such an outfit. 'But Ptarmigan have all that American money behind them,' she hedged. 'Hatto is . . ' How exactly could she put this? Less financially robust? Skint?

'All these women getting nine hundred thousand pounds for first novels,' Euphemia grumbled. 'By that reckoning, as *Our Mam* is my tenth book, I should be getting advances of five million.'

Whatever else Euphemia might be, Grace thought, she was certainly feisty. While you couldn't keep a good woman down, a bad one, it seemed, was still more irrepressible. You had to admire her fortitude. Her sixty-tude, possibly. Grace wondered again how old Euphemia really was.

Stuffing yet another bivalve into her pink-purple mouth,

Euphemia snatched up an *Evening Standard* that lay on the bar.

'Look at this,' she snarled, stabbing the books page. 'Even this effing history of food canning gets more column inches than I do.' She looked at Grace in contempt. 'You lot couldn't get coverage for a bloody duvet.' She drained her glass and slid off the bar stool. 'Well, I can't waste any more time with you. I have an appointment with my trainer.'

Watching her bustle out of the restaurant, Grace tried to guess what Euphemia's trainer could possibly be training her for. Anything of an athletic nature seemed unlikely. Perhaps she lay on her back while he threw her seafood.

Grace paid the bill, a sum representing her entire expenses bill for the next quarter, and reflected that, however taxing a morning with Euphemia was, it at least kept her mind off more difficult matters.

Such as her several recent exchanges with Henry Moon. There had been a couple – polite, work-related conversations in which he inquired after her health and Grace replied sharply that she was fine. Did he think she was always hungover, or something?

He made no suggestion of a date, though. Henry seemed to be sticking by the rule he had made, that she should alert him to any change in her situation. If things changed with Sion, in other words. Which she would not. Because they had not.

That the weekend at Janavid had done nothing to draw them together wasn't a change, as such. That Sion had barely shown his face in her flat all week was hardly new. Similarly, his uncontactability on his mobile was frustratingly familiar, and that his department at the University of Penge, seemed not to have seen him for some time was quite normal as well. You couldn't, Grace supposed, teach an old dogma new tricks. Yet, amid all this one thing had definitely changed. If Henry Moon asked her again whether she was happy, Grace was aware that she might have a different answer.

'But why don't you see Henry?' asked Ellie, who viewed the entire business, so far as she was aware of it, with a robustness bordering on the muscular.

'I honestly don't know why you're so embarrassed. Getting pissed and shagging someone happens all the time, believe me. Take Gordon from last night. Said he was in the SBS but it turned out he wasn't talking about the Special Boat Service. He meant the Special Bus Service. You know, the one that takes you between stations when the Underground breaks down?' She pulled a face. 'Great undercover operator though, if you know what I mean. Could definitely have made the Special Bed Service . . .'

Grace did not smile. For once, Ellie's accounts of amorous misadventure failed to hit the spot.

'Not worried about Sion, are you?'

Grace pulled a face. 'Maybe.'

Ellie's mascara'd eyes narrowed. 'You're mad. All he cares about is himself. Yet all he has to do is call you and you go running like a lovesick teenager.'

Grace did not have the heart to say that Sion had not called. But Ellie was right, she knew. Humiliating though it was to admit it, there was something irresistibly sexy about Sion's cavalier treatment of her. Even his Kettering tantrum, viewed in retrospect, with the memory of his lean and handsome face twisted in pouting irritation, had an unreconstructed charm. It was, she supposed, to do with deprivation. You wanted what you could not have. If absence made the heart grow fonder, absence of sex made it positively rampant. If you looked at it that way, what had happened with Henry was practically Sion's fault. But the sex, of course, was only half the story. There was also the affair of *The Clitoris Chronicles*, the Rolling Stones and the Spiegeltent. The publicity disasters, quite apart from the personal ones.

'Well, you'll just have to get over it.' Ellie said briskly. 'Henry's your author and you're doing his publicity. Haven't you got some bookshop signings with him next week?'

Grace nodded. 'But I was hoping . . .'

'That I might do them instead? Forget it,' Ellie said, laughing. 'You can't go on avoiding him.'

Standing in the tea queue, averting her gaze from an even larger quantity than usual of earplugs in the cheeseplants, Belinda jumped as a voice behind her butted in on her boiling thoughts.

'Belinda, isn't it?'

Mo Mills, Belinda recognised. Having spent the entire morning dwelling bitterly on her professional misfortunes, she was ill-prepared to see *The Globe*'s celebrity interviewer *extraordinaire* in person. And Mo Mills looked, Belinda thought, pretty bloody *extraordinaire*. Fringed skirt, Birkenstocks, centre-parted (greying) hair, patchwork suede handbag, Indian silver jewellery rattling from every orifice and a maddeningly good-natured beam all over her stupid round face.

'You're Tea Break, aren't you? Fancy joining me for a, um, *coffee break*, ha ha?'

Belinda hesitated. Fraternising with the enemy was not in her current battle plan. What was, she wasn't entirely sure. The precise nature of the transforming miracle by which she got Mo's job was still eluding her.

'Come on,' Mo urged kindly. 'You look as if you need a perk-up.'

A few minutes later, Belinda watched from over her watery cappuccino as, across the sticky table, Mo unloaded a cup of lemon and ginger herb tea and a plastic container of brown rice with a helping of grated carrot. 'I always have this about now,' she smiled. 'I got into the whole rice scene when I went to interview Yoko's mother in Japan in sixty-nine. Such a wise woman,' she added dreamily, fishing into the patchwork handbag, producing some chopsticks and stirring the carrot into the rice. 'Terence Stamp gave me these. He's very macrobiotic.'

Belinda wondered how Mo had got so fat on brown rice and grated carrot. Then again, you never saw a thin sumo wrestler.

'They're very good, your interviews,' Mo said, rapidly shoving gloops of rice into her mouth. 'You're very talented. A bit sharp sometimes. A bit raw, even. But talented, definitely.'

Belinda's sweet smile revealed nothing of the molten fury churning inside. Patronising old *walrus*.

'You know,' Mo continued, 'some of your stuff reminds me of myself at your age.'

'Really?' Belinda's face was misleadingly calm.

Mo beamed. 'Oh yes. That one you did last week with Bob Monkhouse was *so* similar in spirit to one I remember doing with the young Bob Monkhouse in sixty-seven. Same jokes, everything.'

'How interesting,' Belinda said, her voice slightly strained. Just when she had thought her career couldn't slump any lower, the Monkhouse interview had proved her wrong. She had arrived at the interview venue to discover the encounter was not, as she had imagined, just herself and the veteran comedian. It was herself, the veteran comedian and a whole gaggle of showbiz reporters from other newspapers who had turned up to cover what was, in fact, the launch of the ITV autumn schedule.

'As you would have realised, if you'd read your invitation properly,' remarked the uppity ITV PR girl.

Belinda had swept straight out. There was still a Tea Break to fill, however, so on returning to *The Globe* she had gone to the library, got out Mo Mills's interview with Bob Monkhouse and copied it – with the odd judicious omittance – word for word. No one, she reasoned, would remember something first published over thirty years ago. Would they? 'You've got an incredible memory,' Belinda remarked carefully.

Mo's jaws, working through the last of the brown rice, split in a grainy beam. 'I never forget a thing, my dear.'

That figured, Belinda thought, appraising the outline of Mo's billowing body. Elephants didn't.

'I never get a fact wrong. That's my proudest achievement. Forget the Moptop Interviews, forget Jagger's Mussels Marinara recipe even, it's getting all the ages, names and places right that means the most in the end. There's so much inaccuracy about these days.'

'Absolutely. The subs are appalling. They never check anything.'

'Oh, I don't leave it to the subs, my dear. Hardly fair. I check everything myself. The writer should be ultimately responsible for the facts.'

Belinda gulped on her cappuccino. The *writers* get their facts right? Was the woman mad?

'Enjoying it, are you? The interviewing?' Mo's one-hack-to-another grin made Belinda's skin crawl.

'Not really,' she said shortly. 'It's a bloody nightmare, since you ask.'

Mo looked taken aback. 'But why?'

'All those nonentities I have to deal with. I never get near anybody *really* famous. Not like you do. You've had an incredible career.' Though God knows how, Belinda added silently.

Mo nodded, picking a rice grain dreamily out of her prominent front teeth. 'Oh, the times we used to have. Skinny-dipping with the Kinks at Cromer. Beachball with the Beatles at Bognor. The country house weekends and the games we used to play. Like Hide the Chocolate Bar. Marianne – Faithfull, obviously – used to be very good at that—'

'Yes, *yes*,' cut in Belinda crossly. 'But what's your secret? How do you get to these people in the first place?'

Mo looked at her in surprise. 'But there *is* no secret. The only secret is persistence. It's not rocket science. I'm banging off the interview request letters just like you are.'

'I don't write letters,' Belinda said contemptuously. 'I don't have to. I get inundated on a daily basis with non-entities desperately seeking publicity.'

'Well, in that case you're lucky. *I* have to write hundreds. Usually in triplicate, to the star's US press office, the UK press office, the press officer for the perfume company they're a Face Of, the charity they're a patron of. Then there are the delays, the endless fobbing off, the chasing up . . .'

'But it can't be all that bad,' Belinda argued. 'Just look at the people you get. You did Madonna a couple of weeks ago.'

'Yes, but it wasn't easy. And she didn't say anything interesting. No one ever does, these days.'

'But surely all you have to do is push them. Trick them into saying things.'

'Some of them won't be pushed. And they're the ones with the tricks.'

'They *are*?'

Mo nodded. 'New tricks, subtler ones all the time. Take Joseph Fiennes, who I did the other week—'

'Yes, I saw,' Belinda cut in. 'You were very nice about him,' she added, acidly.

'Bland, you mean?' Mo looked at her searchingly. 'Well, it shouldn't have been. We got on like a house on fire and he told me lots of interesting things. But when I came to play back the tape, I realised that he'd dropped his voice so low when he was saying anything controversial that the tape simply didn't pick it up. On purpose, obviously.'

'Well, couldn't you just paraphrase what he said? Make it up, even?' Belinda tried to keep the contempt out of her voice. Honestly, talk about grandmothers and egg-sucking.

Mo looked horrified. 'How can I? I've got a reputation for absolute accuracy to keep up. I think if I ever got a fact wrong, I'd just . . .'

'What?' Belinda pressed.

'Oh, I don't know,' Mo smiled ruefully. 'The shock would finish me off, probably.'

Finish her off? At the back of Belinda's mind, something stirred. 'Would it? Would it really?'

'Oh yes. Take the interview I did this week, with the Duchess of Thanet . . .'

Belinda leaned forward eagerly. 'That one who's incredibly anti-privilege, lives in a council house, cleans for a living and sends all her children to the local primary?'

Mo nodded. 'That's her. She's very litigious. Sued one newspaper recently for saying she was wearing a Jaeger cardigan when in fact it was BHS and from a jumble sale.'

'No!' exclaimed Belinda in mock-horror. Inwardly she coursed with excitement. Had she finally stumbled across the answer to all her problems?

'Absolutely. So just imagine what would happen if I'd made even the tiniest mistake in the interview!' Mo was shaking her head and chuckling.

'Just imagine,' Belinda chortled, her fists curling into balls of glee.

CHAPTER SEVEN

Behind his bookshop signing table, fiddling with his chewed ballpoint, Henry Moon was looking resigned.

'Roll up, roll up,' he croaked bravely at a couple of spotty-necked office juniors whose garish nylon rucksacks cut into the shoulders of their badly fitting suits. 'You look the outdoor type. Read about some real-life adventure.' They looked at him in disgust as they passed into the 'Fantasy' section.

'Not exactly Salman Rushdie, is it? Or even Jeffrey Archer.' Henry glanced despondently at the small pile of unsigned books beside him. 'To be honest, it feels rather optimistic to have brought a pen.'

Grace felt her face riot with colour. It had been a light shade of beetroot since her rendezvous with Henry outside the shop – the first time they had met since the return from the St Merrion. She had bridled at first at his lateness; proof positive, she imagined, of the low esteem in which he held her. She had brightened as the delay progressed, entertaining hopes that he might not turn up at all.

With an unpleasant shock to the stomach, she finally recognised Henry Moon approaching her. She braced herself for the knowing look and the suggestive grin. As he neared, however, she saw his expression was carefully neutral. Politeness, Grace wondered, or lack of interest? An angry determination welled within her. She longed, somehow, to impress him, to do something right, for her professional self-esteem, if nothing else, *she'd* show him. With a set face, Grace led Henry into the bookshop.

There seemed little professional initiative to be regained here, however. The showcards in the window advertising Henry's appearance – 'Meet A Real-Life Explorer!' – had obviously spectacularly failed to have the intended effect. No ancitipatory queue of punters stood before the signing table piled with copies of *Sucking Stones*. Grace glanced at the queue divider that had been placed before it. An arrangement of slender chrome pillars linked by black ropes, it was the sort that bent restive lunchtime bank queues into neat zigzags to convince them the line was shorter than it really was. For Henry, however, the line could not be shorter. There was no one there at all.

'There could,' Grace said bravely as Henry took his seat, 'be a rush on at any minute.'

It was true that a good signing session could significantly boost sales. Particularly good ones could move an author up the bestseller list. Although Grace had not expected Henry's to do the latter, she had hoped for some variation on the former. She watched miserably as the bookshop assistant loped over and pointedly removed the queue divider.

The assistant's name, Damien, was printed below the slogan 'Passionate About Reading' on a large and colourful badge directly over his left nipple. He did not, Grace thought, look particularly passionate about anything. But she was determined to make him work up some passion for Henry. And, in doing so, regain that all-important professional initiative and show Henry just what mountains she could move when she tried.

'You could always sign the books anyway,' Grace muttered, to Henry, a few punterless minutes later. 'Shops are usually happy for you to sign copies that they have in stock. And you know what they say. A book signed is a book sold – the shops can't return them to the publishers after you've written in them.'

Leaving Henry thus engaged, Grace went in search of Damien. He was in the children's section, slapping 'Signed By The Author' stickers on a pile of the latest Harry Potters. Judging by the Empire State Building-sized heap awaiting stickering beside him, J.K. Rowling had evidently been busy.

'Oh, look,' Grace said brightly, pulling a volume out of the 'Society' shelf opposite Damien. 'How nice. *Napkins & Niceties: Modern Manners For A Modern Age* by

Lady Cylindria Slaughter. A wonderful writer. She's one of ours, actually.'

'That figures,' Damien grumbled, reaching for another Harry Potter. '*They*'re not exactly going like hot cakes either.'

Grace was several shelves along now. 'And I see you've got some Euphemia Ogdens. She's our bestselling author.' Bending below shelf after shelf of neon-spined Jenny Bristols, she dragged out a paperback whose cover was dominated by the legend *Pease Pudding Polly* in swirling yellow script, and the painting of the headscarfed girl carrying a bucket of coal. Next to it were copies of three of Euphemia's other works. Marian's departure, Grace was relieved to see, had evidently not affected distribution as badly as had been feared. '*This* was a bestseller,' she said proudly, waving *Pease Pudding Polly* at Damien.

Damien looked disbelieving. 'We sell about one a month these days.'

'But that's great,' exclaimed Grace. Surely one a month wasn't a bad average? After all, if every bookshop in the country sold one a month, that added up to quite a few.

'Henry's book,' Grace persisted, judging this a sufficient triumph on which to introduce the subject, 'is just wonderful. It's a completely thrilling account of a journey to find a lost tribe. People will love it.'

In reply, Damien flicked an eloquent glance towards the book-signing table, which implied the absence of punters spoke for itself. Henry, still seated there, did not seem unduly worried about this. In fact, he seemed to have found another pile of books from somewhere and was signing away contentedly. His table, Grace noticed, had been positioned in the 'Horror' section of the bookshop. Damien's idea of a joke?

'But it might be a surprise hit,' she urged. 'You know, a slow-burn word of mouth. Like Louis de Bernières. Or J.K. Row—' Glancing up at the towers of Harry Potters piled up beside Damien, Grace checked herself. Perhaps that was being a *bit* optimistic.

Damien, however, was suddenly no longer stacking Potters. He was suddenly heading across the shop floor to where Henry was still writing merrily in his pile of books. Scuttling behind him, Grace tried to comfort herself with the fact that she had heard of worse stock signings. Such as that of the hell-raising Scottish author who, shown a pile of his works awaiting autograph, whipped out his penis and hosed them with urine, roaring, 'That's mae fuckin' signature.'

Henry was completing his own signature with a laborious loop as Grace and Damien arrived at his side. 'The unsigned ones are far rarer, by the way,' he grinned at the assistant, patting the pile of books.

No they're not, thought Grace sadly.

'Actually, those are Jilly Coopers you've been writing in,' said Damien. 'I'm afraid you're going to have to pay for them now.'

* * *

When the bill had been settled – bang went the rest of the year's entertainment budget – Henry and Grace stood outside awkwardly on the pavement. Grace, at least, was awkward.

'Would you like some lunch?' she asked, aware that a Pret à Manger wrap – which in itself might bankrupt Hatto – would do little to raise her in his estimation. There were a couple of 2 for 1 Burger King deals she'd noticed that might be worth looking into, though. On the other hand, why was she bothering? It was a lost cause. They all were. The book, herself and Henry Moon.

'I'm sorry,' she muttered, staring miserably at the flattened-out black circles of chewing gum on the pavement.

'Doesn't matter,' Henry said. 'Ritual humiliation is obviously nine-tenths of book promotion. It was quite funny, really.'

Grace looked at him sharply. His wide mouth was stretched in a grin. Funny, was it? *Funny*? Was he laughing at her again?

Henry glanced ruefully at the battered copy of *Sucking Stones* he held in his hand. 'Oh well. Onward and ever downward.'

'Oh, *don't* say that,' Grace burst out, anguished. 'You make me feel *terrible*.'

Henry shot her a look which, to Grace's fretful state of mind, could have meant anything from sympathy to sarcasm. 'Sorry.' He shuffled his large feet on the pavement. An uncomfortable silence fell.

Grace clenched her fists at the end of her downstretched arms. Why didn't he just go? The sooner he made his excuses and left, the better.

Yet he lingered, kicking slightly at a nonexistent stone on the pavement. 'Come for a coffee?' he suggested mildly.

Grace calculated rapidly. This was Covent Garden, after all. Would the budget stretch that far?

'At mine,' Henry added. 'I only live round the corner.'

A wave of panic swept over Grace. Alone with Henry Moon again. Could she risk it? Might he say something about the sex? Or the Spiegeltent? Or both? And what would his coffee be like? He didn't look the type to have fresh milk in the fridge. On the other hand, as Ellie said, she had to get over it. Coffee – whatever it was like – would be a good first step. 'OK,' she muttered.

Henry's tiny flat, on the sixth floor of a red-brick Edwardian mansion block, was much tidier than Grace had expected. As well as more interesting – an apparent repository for whatever Henry had brought back from his travels, it reminded her of the basement of Liberty's. Coloured rugs covered the sisal, cheerful Indian-print curtains billowed softly at the open window, and carved ebony statues and painted masks were dotted about, all thoroughly cleaned and polished. On the small circular dining table, there was even a vase of peonies. 'It's so nice,' Grace said, looking round. 'So *clean*.' She reddened, realising how rude that sounded.

Henry grinned. 'It is now. You should have seen it a few

weeks ago. But now I've finally got a cleaner. The Domestos Goddess, I call her. Best thing I ever did. Do sit down, by the way.' He gestured at a big, red and very comfortable-looking sofa. 'I'll go and sort out some coffee.'

He re-emerged with two mugs emblazoned with airline logos. As he passed one to Grace and their hands touched, a faint electric shock bolted up her arm. Had he felt it too? Glancing abruptly down at the swirling brown coffee, Grace saw that he did indeed have fresh milk in the fridge. Unlike Sion, who chucked in week-old curds that then desiccated horribly on the surface of any brew he made. Grace forced away the memory and the problems that went with it and forced a smile at Henry. There were, after all, enough problems here to be getting on with. 'So,' she said, intending to ask how his new book was going and whether, as formerly intimated, he had hit on a new subject and style. 'Last time we met . . . ' She stopped, blushing. *Damn*. Why, of all things, had she said that?

'Last time we met . . .' Henry prompted, smiling delightedly.

'You said you might try writing about something else, not travelling,' Grace cut in. *Just don't get any ideas*, she thought, staring at him challengingly.

Henry nodded. 'Yes I am. And it's going quite well.'

'What is it?'

'A bit of a departure from *Sucking Stones*,' Henry's buoyant grin had suddenly faded. He looked very serious.

'I'm not sure whether it will work just yet,' he continued.

'It's difficult to say at this stage whether I'll get it off the ground.' He looked at her suddenly, his gaze resolute and unwavering. 'But I *hope* it will work out,' he said, apparently with meaning.

There was a silence in which Grace felt the pounding of her heart. Was this doublespeak? Was Henry referring to a project other than his book? She swallowed.

'There are a few obstacles in the way though,' Henry added softly, still looking at her. 'It's not going to be easy. But I'm going to keep trying . . . oh sorry,' he exclaimed in alarm as Grace, shifting in her seat, plunged unexpectedly downward into a hole between the sofa cushions.

'It's a bit ancient, I'm afraid,' Henry said apologetically.

His gaze, Grace saw as she scrambled up, lingered on the inches of bare thigh exposed by her rucked-up skirt. She felt indignant. Had he made her sit there on purpose?

'You were saying,' she snapped. 'About your *book*?'

Henry looked startled. 'Oh yes. I'm leaving the adventure stuff for the time being. No point flogging a dead Land Rover, ha ha. And most of them were pretty dead when I'd done with them.'

'I bet they were,' said Grace, neutrally.

Henry glanced at her. 'And so, I have so say, were my . . . relationships.'

'Were they?' Grace returned, in tones intended to convey that she was not surprised and that, really, she didn't want to know.

'Travelling's ruined my love life.' He was looking at her searchingly again.

'Has it really.' Grace's voice was flat. Why exactly was he telling her this? Did he expect her to care?

'Well, you can't get anyone to go with you, for a start. Dropping your only torch down an Ethiopian loo isn't most women's idea of fun.'

'No,' Grace said. 'But you could have gone somewhere else. Somewhere your girlfriends –' she emphasised the word with as much distaste as she could muster – 'might actually have wanted to go?'

'Easier said than done,' Henry said. 'One girlfriend . . .'

One girlfriend. As if there had been *millions* both before and after. Funny he had such contempt for Lad novels considering, Grace thought indignantly, he practically was one.

'. . . was completely opposed to the idea of anything remotely adventurous. So I told her she could pick where we went. She picked Southern Italy.'

'Lovely.' Despite herself, Grace wondered what this woman was like. Blonde? Dark? Fat? Thin? Prettier than her – not that that would be hard.

'Well, if you like that sort of thing, it was the sort of thing you'd like,' Henry said doubtfully. 'Sun, sea, Italian food, sightseeing – we were near Pompeii – all that. Perfect. Except,' excitement entered his voice, 'the volcano – which had apparently been grumbling for twelve months – started throwing out ash the morning after we arrived.'

'*No!*' Grace imagined rivers of lava.

Henry chuckled. 'Yes. We were sitting having breakfast on the veranda, looking out over the ocean, when this great grey cloud rolled into view. The next thing we knew, the volcano was erupting and we all had to be evacuated. So,' his eyes sparkled mischievously, 'that was our relaxed Mediterranean holiday.'

'And what did your – um – girlfriend think of it?'

'Dumped me the moment we got back to Heathrow.' Henry's wide mouth curled in a smile that hid his eyes entirely in creases. 'Like I said, I'm a romantic disaster.'

Grace wondered how she could make her excuses. 'I'd better go,' she said awkwardly.

'OK,' Henry said quickly. Too quickly, Grace thought confusedly. Had he just been passing the time, waiting to see the back of her?

Neither of them moved. Silence fell again.

'I was just thinking,' Henry mused. He was now by the window-sill, the expression on his face unfathomable as he stood with his back to the light.

'What?'

'That now the launch is over, there won't be anything happening any more.'

Grace moved to head off what she interpreted as an attack on her professional abilities. 'Not at all. There are bound to be a few extra things cropping up. The odd interview. A spot as a talking head on one of those current affairs programmes. And I could always drum up a few local radio things.'

'Good. We'll see each other again soon, then.' He was moving towards her from the window, but his face remained difficult to read.

'Still happy, then? With the boyfriend?' His voice was low, intimate. Excitement stabbed through her body.

As Grace stared back at him, there came from her handbag the grinding ring of her mobile. She willed her hand to be still, not to shake; not to answer; yet the wretched instrument kept on ringing. Demanding, shrill, unbearably loud in the silence.

Happy? Well, not exactly, obviously, but . . . The mobile rang on, unignorable, loud as a road drill. She looked helplessly back at Henry. Was it as simple as just admitting that she wasn't? What would that lead to? Perhaps she should say the word and find out. She opened her mouth.

Henry looked away and back at her. He pressed his hands together, fingers spread wide, in a gesture of impatience. 'I just wondered,' he muttered.

'Yes?' Grace croaked.

'Whether you'd like to . . .'

'Mmm?' She barely dared say anything, so fragile was the moment.

'. . . answer that?'

'Oh. Yes. Right.' Grace felt as if her entire body, whistling downwards, had made rough and sudden contact with the earth. Heedless of her nails, she crashed her hands into her handbag and dragged out the offending instrument.

'Darling!' shrilled maternal tones undiminished either by distance or the transmitting mechanism.

'Oh,' Grace said, flicking an embarrassed look at Henry. 'It's you.'

Face closing, Henry got up and disappeared abruptly into the tiny kitchen, taking the airline-logo mugs with him.

'Darling, I'm having rather an important dinner at the Consulate soon . . .'

In the kitchen, Henry was loudly rattling crockery.

'Mother!' Grace was exasperated. Lady Armiger really picked her moments for talking through menus, discussing the implications of various shades of table linen or whatever else she intended to witter on about. 'I'm a bit tied up just now. Can't we talk about this later?'

'Not really, darling.' Lady Armiger's tone was steely. 'I'm doing my *placement* at the moment. If you're coming, I need to know soon.'

'*If I'm coming?*' Grace echoed, aghast. 'But you're in Venice. Why would I be coming?'

Quite apart from the distance aspect, her mother's official dinner parties were the most genteel form of torture imaginable. The terrifyingly delicate antique china. The heavy unwieldy silver. The interminable dullness of making polite conversation for course after course, all under the eye of her mother. Being Italy, too, this meant more courses than most.

'Because there's someone I want you to meet,' trilled Lady Armiger, unrepentant, on the other end. 'A man. He'd be perfect for you, darling. Much better than—'

'I don't want another man, you know that,' Grace cut in loudly, as Henry, looking tense, returned to the sitting room. 'Look,' she muttered into the mobile, 'I'd better go. We'll talk about this later. Love you too. Bye bye.'

'Sorry about that.' Grace put the phone back in her bag and noticed a muscle in Henry's cheek working agitatedly.

''S'all right.'

She smiled at him sheepishly, feeling nervous. Could they pick up where they had left off? 'You were saying? Before we were so rudely interrupted? About . . . whether I was happy . . .' she prompted.

'Oh, that.' He looked neutrally at her. 'Well, you seem to be.'

'Oh. Right.' The atmosphere felt suddenly sombre. Yet, minutes earlier, it had been thick with suggestion, pregnant with possibility. Now it was taut with awkwardness. What was going on? What sort of a game was he playing?

'I'd better be going then,' Grace said, getting to her feet. This would test his mettle.

'Yes.' He made a movement towards the door.

'Thanks for the coffee.'

'You're welcome.'

'Good luck with the new *project*, Henry,' Grace said, looking hard into his eyes.

'Thanks,' Henry said politely. 'I should have a few chapters finished soon.'

Including this one, Grace thought dejectedly, going out

of the door without another word and descending the bleach-scented stairs.

Then, quite out of the blue, as she reached the ground floor, it struck her.

(Indignant) 'I don't want another man, you know that.'

(Furtive) 'Look, I'd better go. We'll talk about this later. Love you too.'

Of course. Henry had been crashing around in the kitchen during the middle of the conversation. From the little he had heard, he must have assumed she was talking to Sion. Grace's hand gripped the balustrade as she looked back up the stairs.

'Henry,' she called, just as, six floors above, the Moon flat door clicked shut.

Back at the office, Grace dejectedly pushed open the paint-flaked door of the Hatto & Hatto press department to find Ellie in horribly upbeat mood.

'Seen my new boots?' she demanded, leaning back on her seat and flinging a leg into the air. The entire lower half of her calf was a vision in purple snakeskin, from the base of which projected a long, thin, silver heel reminiscent of a radio aerial. 'I'm getting in touch with my inner slapper.'

'Last night went well, then?' Trust Ellie's love life to take a turn for the better just now.

'Went well? You must be joking. I must have been mad.' Ellie emitted a hollow groan. 'Blind dates. Been on so many I should get a free dog.'

'What happened?' Grace tried to keep the relief from her voice. 'I thought it was a perfect match.'

'Well, he does the same job.' Ellie sighed, tossing her hair as if to shake out the unpleasant memory. Streaks ranging from burgundy to white blonde flashed in the morning sun. 'He's in PR. I'm in PR.'

'So?'

'So, nothing. Apart from the fact we spent the evening discussing ways of getting more publicity for the brand of verruca cream he represents. He told me he wouldn't rest until he had made it the country's number one foot fungus treatment.'

'Oh,' said Grace, feeling, somewhere in her cheerless depths, a smile stir.

'It's my fault,' Ellie told her. 'I should never have agreed. Subconsciously, I knew something was wrong the very first time I spoke to him on the phone.'

Grace nodded. Ellie's subconscious had often sensed similar things in the past. Always retrospectively. 'Some little thing you couldn't quite put your finger on?'

'Not exactly. More a big, wide thing that I could put my whole hand on.'

Grace's eyebrows shot up. 'What do you mean?'

'It was a disaster from the moment I asked him how I'd recognise him.'

'Why?'

'He said he'd be wearing a tie with teddies printed on it. I laughed like a drain. Thought he was joking. But when I turned up, there it was. And there *they* were too. Big yellow bears with little red jumpers on.'

'But couldn't you just disappear. Run away?'

'No, because I'd told him what *I* had on as well. And, unfortunately, no one else in Sloane Square Tube station at that particular moment was wearing an unfeasibly tight red suit and green high-heeled mules.'

Grace snorted. Ellie's misadventures at least had the advantage of taking her mind off Henry Moon and the fact that, after an embarrassing morning and confusing lunchtime, a moment of apparent promise had come swift and sweet, only to become mired in misunderstanding. Would there ever be another such moment? Possibly she would never see him again. Possibly this was a good thing. So why was it that she felt some celestial hand had turned down the dimmer switch on her existence?

'Actually,' Ellie broke into her thoughts, 'there's been some good news while you've been out. A date's been set for Cylindria's Tea Break interview with Belinda Black. So that's now definite.'

Grace nodded, trying to work up some interest in what genuinely was an unprecedented coup for Hatto & Hatto's press office. Why, then, did it seem so insuperably dull. 'Great.'

'And – you won't believe this – but the *Guardian* Questionnaire have called to say they want to do Henry Moon!'

'Oh!' Grace's heart leapt in a flame of excitement which

died out as soon as she realised this would not involve her. Henry would be faxed the questions and send them directly back to the paper. But just as well, really. Much better never to see him again. Much, much better.

'What's more, Radio Gainsborough have called to say they want to do an interview about *Sucking Stones*.'

Grace frowned. 'A radio interview with Henry? In a studio?'

Ellie nodded. 'But you can take him to the studios in Broadcasting House though, and do it from there. You need to be there by ten.' Ellie winked. 'Another hot date with Henry Moon, eh?'

'Shut up,' Grace tried to subdue the glow in her eyes. Was this another chance?

The light from the computer screen glowed on Belinda's face. All around was darkness and silence, apart from the distant rumble of traffic outside. As her mobile shrilled into life, shattering her deep concentration, she looked furiously at the office clock. Half past bloody eleven. Who the hell was calling her at this time of night? She glanced at the display. Che Guevara, for God's sake. Damnation. How bloody dare he? That boy had the neck of a gang of brass giraffes.

'You free tomorrow night? There's a solidarity disco at the Wanstead Flats Mechanics Institute. Fancy it?'

'Like I fancy putting my hand in a blender.' Belinda stabbed irritatedly at the keyboard. What the *hell* was

Mo Mills's password? From 'musselsmarinara' to 'maharishimaheshyogi', she'd tried every sixties, Mo-related thing she could think of.

'That's a no then?'

'You heard.'

'Where are you?'

'At work.' Fuck. Why had she let *that* slip? She really must be tired to be so off her guard.

'Work? *The Globe*, you mean?'

''Course not,' lied Belinda. 'In my spare room at home.'

She'd taken great pains to make sure no one knew she was here. Had even hidden in the loos while the office cleaner came round. Had probably got piles from spending all that time on the plastic O. But it was essential. The risk of being spotted and connected with the deed was otherwise too great.

'Doing what?'

'What's it to you?' Belinda snapped. 'How's my interview with Cherie going, by the way?' she asked sneeringly.

'She's given it the green light,' came the utterly unexpected reply.

In the dark silence of the office, Belinda did her best not to squeal. '*What*?'

'Except,' added the voice on the other end of the telephone, 'Tony's kicking up a fuss. Smarmy bastard likes hogging all the limelight himself.'

'So . . . Cherie's *not* doing it?' Belinda's voice was acid. Of course Cherie bloody wasn't. How could she have believed otherwise? *Again*.

'I'm working on it, babe. Meantime, why don't you do something about me? My thesis, *Why New Labour Are Bastards*, deserves a much wider audience. Definite bestseller potential. Penge are very excited about it—'

'Piss off,' snarled Belinda.

'Alastair Campbell's going to write an introduction for it.'

'Is he now? That'd be the Alastair Campbell who works for the Inverness Tourist Board, would it? Because I'm not sure I believe you've ever met the other one.'

The voice on the other end sounded concerned. 'Hey, babe. We need to talk. Why not come round to my flat later?'

His flat? That disgusting boxroom in Catford which stank of the kebab house beneath it, shook to the bass speaker of the white rasta next door to it and featured a mattress as crumby as the bottom of a breadbin? 'I'd rather kill myself.'

'Ba-abe!' His voice was chiding. 'I'll cook you dinner.'

This was the last straw. Belinda's throat closed at the memory of the congealed mass of yellow and orange that had slid onto her plate on their last date, accompanied by a sea of sour fat. He had actually been *proud* of this revolting concoction. Had even said it could have been worse, as the fridge's only other contents were cream and sardines.

'Sod off,' she snarled, pressing the end of call button. Come *on*, she silently urged the computer. Twiggy. Stonesinhydepark. Iwannaholdyourhand. It shouldn't be so difficult. Once she was in, she could call up the piece about the litigious duchess, do a few tweaks and the rest would be history. Mo Mills certainly would be.

Christ, she was tired. No one appreciated just how exhausting this sort of thing was. With eyes like ball bearings and lids like sheet metal, Belinda keyed in one final, desperate combination, the last she could think of. Nothing, at first. Then, miraculously, that long-awaited welcome message on the screen. Belinda suppressed the urge to shriek with joy. Mo Mills's computer had finally capitulated.

'Davedeedozybeakymickandtitch' had hit the spot.

CHAPTER EIGHT

Henry Moon had arrived so late at Broadcasting House that there was no time for Grace to say anything about their last meeting, let alone give any of the explanations she had spent the night composing in both long and short versions. That it had been her mother on the mobile phone and that Sion was not necessarily a permanent fixture. And that she was far from happy – with either of them.

But there had only just been time to rush across the marbled BBC lobby, shove a pass badge at Henry and bundle him up the stairs to the London Control Room and its tiny studios that could link up to any local radio station in Britain.

'Stand by,' said the Radio Gainsborough studio engineer through the microphone.

Across the table, Henry, who had darker shadows than usual under his eyes – had he been burning the midnight oil? Had he been alone in burning it? – adjusted his headphones, bent nearer the large red foam-covered microphone, grinned, and stuck his thumbs up. He seemed perfectly relaxed; obviously, Grace thought, the events in his flat had not worried him overmuch. The thought stung rather.

The loud voice of the presenter, booming suddenly in her ear, made her jump and knock her tea all over herself. 'Hey, hi, how ya doing? Andy Twort here, Radio Gainsborough.'

'Hello, Andy,' Henry said, watching Grace try as discreetly as was possible to wipe a large tea stain off the front of her bra.

'Sorry to hold you up,' yawned Andy, in a mid-Atlantic drawl that implied the complete opposite. 'The exclusive about the talking sheep went on longer than scheduled. Guess none of us expected it would have that much to say, huh?' He gave a professional laugh, in reply to which both Grace and Henry found themselves grinning sycophantically.

'Just hang on in there, guys, while I do this next item,' instructed Andy in his cartoonishly contorted tones. 'Then we're ready to roll. Not to mention rock, ha ha.'

'This next item' comprised an excruciating fifteen minutes during which Andy, amid much fake laughter and contrived astonishment, quizzed a Scotswoman from

Troon about her duties as President of the National Husband-Carrying Association. Having elicited an association badge and tie – 'on its way to ye, Andy, and can ye say a big hello to ma husband?' – Andy finally turned his attention to Henry and Grace.

'Now listen, guys, I've kinda got to admit something.' Andy confided off air. Henry and Grace leant closer to the microphone. 'Haven't read the book. Time, you know. Never enough of it, huh? Anyway, Harry—'

'Henry,' said Grace and Henry in unison.

'Henry. *Woah*. Sorry. My mistake. Just so much going down in this studio, y'know? Anyway, I'll introduce it, and then you can do the talking about the book. Yeah? That cool?'

'Cool,' Grace said firmly, as Henry looked confused.

'Stand by,' said the studio engineer again.

'Radio GainsBUR-ERRRR,' trilled the jingle.

'*Aa-annd* our next guest,' Andy said smoothly, now obviously addressing his listeners, 'is a man who's written a book on a very interesting subject indeed.'

Henry looked gratified.

'*Sucking Toes*, it's called. So, Harry, sorry, *Henry* Moonie, what exactly was it that attracted you towards writing a biography of the Duchess of York?'

'I'm *terribly* sorry, Henry,' Grace said, fifteen minutes later, her face throbbing with shame. 'I can't believe how unprofessional Andy Twort was.' Let alone myself, she added silently. It was uncanny, really it was. While her life as Hatto's Head of Press hadn't generally been a bed of roses, she had never before had an author for whom so much went wrong. For whom every single PR effort ended in ignominious disaster.

They were sitting in the bar of a large luxury hotel across the road from the BBC. In front of them on the table were two champagne cocktails. 'Good for shock,' Henry had said as he ordered them. He seemed, Grace saw miserably, completely unfazed. His well-travelled worldliness? Or the fact that, with her in the equation, he hadn't expected any other outcome?

'It should be me buying these for you, not the other way round,' Grace wailed, though aware the entertainment budget would not permit it.

Henry shrugged. 'Doesn't matter at all. My pleasure. It's nice to see you again.'

The strong alcohol certainly had a soothing effect. She was halfway down her glass already and the events of the morning were beginning to assume a comfortable distance. Emboldened, Grace wondered whether to resume the discussion interrupted by her mother in his flat. She'd switched off the mobile. If only she could switch off the jangling of her nerves.

'Um . . .' she began.

'Um, how are the other authors from hell?' Henry asked at exactly the same time. 'Lady Cylindria and the rest of them?'

'Fine.' Grace rallied at the memory that Cylindria, for one, was benefiting from Hatto's PR efforts. 'Actually, Cylindria's doing an interview with Belinda Black in *The Globe*.'

Henry's face paled. 'Belinda Black, did you say?'

'Yes. Great, isn't it?'

'Not really.'

Grace looked at him, surprised. 'What do you mean?' Was Henry going to turn all jealous and competitive on her now?

Henry's lip had curled slightly. 'Belinda Black is one of the most unpleasant women in Fleet Street.'

This was not without some truth, Grace knew. In the few conversations she had had with her, the journalist had not exactly distinguished herself by her politeness. For example, having established that *Ginger's Bought It* did not concern the shopping habits of Fred Astaire's dancing partner, she had been very uncomplimentary indeed about poor Sir Greville Goodtrouser, DSO. As for what she had said about Euphemia . . . but Grace could forgive her that.

'The woman's a human steamroller,' Henry was saying. 'Poor old Lady C. Talk about lamb to the slaughter. Or Slaughter to the slaughter.'

'But Cylindria's book is about *manners*,' cut in Grace, mildly panicked. 'You can't get more uncontroversial than that. What could Belinda Black possibly do that is so awful?'

'She'll find something, don't worry.'

'But how do you know?'

Henry sighed. 'A writer should never reveal his sources. But seeing as – as far as most people seemed to be concerned – I'm not a writer, I'll tell you. Belinda used to go out with a friend of mine. Editor of *The Globe*'s travel pages. Very handy for cheap flights and luxury holidays, as you can imagine. When he got sacked, she dumped him like a hot brick. It was a tactical fuck, if you know what I mean.' He raised a conspiratorial eyebrow.

Grace swallowed. How would she know what a tactical fuck was? The one at St Merrion had been the exact opposite. Was he teasing her again?

But Henry's expression was serious. 'Belinda uses and abuses people, particularly men. And she's worse than ever now, according to my old mates on the paper. Takes advantage of any poor sod that looks deep enough into those Venus flytrap eyelashes of hers. Got an academic on board now, of all things.'

'Really?' Grace decided to play devil's advocate. 'Perhaps she's changing a bit. Becoming a bit more thoughtful.'

'I doubt it. I think the attraction has something to do with the fact that Belinda's got a column to fill and this academic's apparently got brilliant political connections.'

'Really?' Grace sighed. Academics with political connections. Then she flushed, suddenly unable to meet Henry's direct hazel gaze.

'Know someone like that, do you?'

Grace cleared her throat. 'A bit. At least, I know an academic who's very well connected to New Labour.' So he says, she added silently.

Grace had always had doubts about the strength – the entire veracity, even – of Sion's ties to the governmental great and good. But as they were not the reason she was with him – whatever that was – her doubts hadn't been significant.

'This bloke sounds as if he was camping up his contacts a bit, though,' Henry mused.

Grace nodded, remembering a particularly far-fetched claim of Sion's, about Cherie Blair's keen interest in his PhD.

'Told Belinda he'd get Cherie Blair to do a Tea Break. Apparently she's very interested in whatever he's studying. So as far as Belinda was concerned, it was lust at first sight – for the interview, of course.' Henry took another sip of coffee.

Grace's stomach lurched. What was it Sion had said last weekend at Kettering? *I'm shagging an ambitious nymphomaniac hack with huge tits who wants me for my brilliant political connections* . . . 'What does Belinda look like?' she asked, voice slightly shrill.

Henry shrugged. 'Dark hair. *Huge* – I mean,' he corrected himself, looking uncomfortable, 'quite large, um, breasts.'

Grace felt the sweat bead on her forehead.

Warming to his subject, Henry rattled cheerily on.

'Turned out to be all gong and no dinner, though. Obsessed with some campaigning New Labour pamphlet he'd written. Hardly Belinda's scene . . . Grace, you're looking a bit green. Are you OK?'

'I'm fine, honestly,' she mumbled. 'How long have they been together?'

'Not long,' Henry chortled. 'It never is with her. About two weeks at the most.'

Two weeks, Grace thought. She hadn't seen Sion for what seemed like two months, but was most probably just over a week. Since the return from Janavid. Could this woman be the reason why?

'Hilarious, isn't it?' Henry slapped his thigh with mirth. 'Apparently the last straw was when he asked her to dinner.'

Relief swept Grace so powerfully that she almost fell off the bar's striped sofa. *Not* Sion after all. He never took anyone to dinner.

'She got dressed up to the tens, thinking they were going to Nobu, but it turned out to be dinner at his flat.'

'*His flat?*'

Henry nodded. 'And you'll never guess what he cooked her.' He was guffawing now. 'Even I could do better, and I've eaten pigs' eyeballs and yaks' penises in my time, not to mention sucked stones, of course . . . *What* did you just say?'

'Carrot omelette,' Grace muttered. 'He made her carrot omelette.'

'That's *incredible*. How on earth do you know?'

'Excuse me,' Grace choked, getting to her feet and rushing out of the bar.

Belinda was even more deliberately late for work than usual the morning the Duchess of Thanet interview appeared in the newspaper. Only idiots, after all, were present at the scene when the crime was discovered.

The first intimation that all had gone perfectly was when she found the chief sub Laura sniffing in the loos.

'It's just dreadful,' Laura gulped, eyes watering. 'None of us can understand what's happened.'

'What *has* happened?' Belinda's eyes batted innocently in the mirror.

'You haven't heard? About Mo?'

Belinda lowered her eyelashes to hide pupils dancing with expectation. 'I've only just got into the office.'

'Oh, it's just awful,' Laura wailed. 'There were the most horrendous mistakes in the Duchess of Thanet piece. No one on the subs desk saw them.'

No change there, then, Belinda thought, pressing her lips together to prevent a smile. Her entire plan had relied on Laura's sloppy foot soldiers neglecting to check anything. They had not let her down, bless them.

'Such an easy mistake to make, anyway . . .' Laura stroked Boots mascara onto the stubby lashes of reddened eyes.

Wasn't it just, thought Belinda. The act of changing the name of the Duchess's son from Stan de Montfort to Satan de Montfort had been the work of seconds. As had the various additional, invented remarks about her curtains, ornaments and the bad behaviour of her children.

'Because, of course, Mo's copy is always perfect and never needs checking. She's never made a mistake before. Not in thirty years. So the subs desk had relaxed their guard a bit.'

'Of course.' Belinda smiled reassuringly at her colleague.

Laura sighed. Laura, however, did not look reassured. 'They say that Mo won't be out of hospital for months.'

Belinda stifled a yelp of delight. 'Hospital?'

Laura stared at Belinda in the mirror. 'You've not heard? Had a massive coronary in her local newsagents when she saw the piece. She's had a weak heart for ages, apparently, but wanted to keep it secret. You know what a pro she is.'

Hospital. Belinda wanted to cancan. A better result than she could ever have dreamt of.

'Tragic, isn't it? And it hardly helps that the Duchess is suing both Mo and the paper for libel. But then again I suppose that "Satan by name, Satan by nature" stuff about the boy kicking his mother and breaking the windows went too far.'

Perhaps, Belinda thought, she had got carried away a bit, but at the time, with the piece on the computer screen before her, half measures hadn't seemed an option. And the news that Mo Mills was in trouble with the legal department was almost more significant than the news about the hospital. Making large libel payments seldom went down well with newspaper proprietors. Kevin Grayson's immediate predecessor, Belinda remembered, had surrendered the keys to the executive washroom following a bizarre and, as it turned out, untrue incident involving Swarfega, an iguana, a nun and a Premiership football player. All had sued and won, apart from the iguana.

'I suppose the problem now,' Laura went on, clipping back her greying hair from either side so her ears stuck out like wing nuts, 'is to find someone to stand in for Mo.'

'Oh,' Belinda tried to keep the triumph out of her voice. 'I don't think *that's* a problem.'

She made her way directly to the features desk, her delighted grin somewhat at odds with the atmosphere of gloom around her. You'd think someone had died. If only they *had*. That really would have been perfection.

'Fran,' Belinda called to the Features Editor. 'You know that window of opportunity we talked about if Mo ever went away?'

Fran looked up resignedly.

'I think it's opened,' said Belinda exultantly.

Belinda Black, the voice in Grace's head jeered as she marched along Portland Place. So, as she had suspected, there *had* been someone else. The only surprise was that Sion had not been cheating on her with one of the Penge Apparat-chicks, nor even with one of the lovesick Saturday morning bucket-rattlers. He'd been doing it with the most unpleasant woman in Fleet Street. A woman of such vaulting ambition, by the sound of it, that she made Madonna look modest. A tabloid journalist who worked on a newspaper representing everything Sion claimed most to despise. He'd changed his tune, obviously, when he thought *The Globe* might further his career – although by the sound of it Belinda Black had been using him as much as he was her.

'S-sorry,' Grace gasped, cannoning into two tourists outside the BBC Shop. They looked at her in amazement – deranged Englishwoman talking to herself. As well they might, Grace thought. Mad is exactly what she was. Or must have been. To put up with all Sion's no-shows, his rudeness, his sponging, his playing on her middle-class guilt, his policing of everything from her conversation to the person who cleaned her flat. She would even have said he had brainwashed her, except that it was hard to imagine Sion washing anything.

Furiously, Grace beat her fists hard against the sun-warmed wall of Portland Place, imagining it to be Sion's face. She felt too cross to cry.

How could she a) have been such a fool, b) have not realised, and c) have been so wrong when everyone else had been right? Grace's stomach clenched at the thought of what Lady Armiger would say when she found out. *If* she found out. But she had a way of divining these things; no doubt the news was at this very moment on its way over to Venice in the diplomatic bag.

Grace's phone shrilled in her handbag. *If this was her*

mother. Ringing up about her wretched dinner party again . . .

'Yes?' she said brusquely.

'Ah, hi, babe.'

'Sion.' Grace could hardly believe it. Of all the bloody timing. Of all the bloody *cheek*. Anger flooded her, followed by confusion. What the hell did *he* want?

His voice was casual. Relaxed, even. 'Yeah, sorry I haven't been around for a while. Busy, you know.'

'Yes,' said Grace through gritted teeth. '*I* know.'

'Had a lot on.'

'So I understand.' Grace recalled the description of the full-breasted Belinda Black.

'Over the worst of it now, though.'

Now she's chucked you, you mean, thought Grace, beginning to get the picture. So this call was no mere coincidence. He just thought he could come back to her, did he?

'So I just thought . . .'

'What?' Grace snapped, daring him to continue.

'Well, that you might be free tonight.'

'Free? As in inexpensive?' Despite the circumstances, she felt a glow of pride at this line.

Sion, however, ignored it. 'I could come round, you could cook, we could watch a vid. Spend some time with each other again. It's been a while . . .' His voice was low, caressing.

'You said it,' shot back Grace. About a month, at least, she calculated. Once, her stomach would have surged expectantly, gratefully even, at the thought of sex with Sion. Now it only felt tight and sour.

'Piss off.' But already she felt weary, rather than angry.

'Oh, OK. Well, if you don't fancy that, there's a solidarity disco in . . .'

'It's over, Sion.' Saying the actual words felt oddly calming. It was with almost a steely sort of gentleness that she added: 'Never call me again.'

She pressed the red button, Call Ended. *All* ended. When she got home, she'd throw everything of Sion's into a binbag and take it to Oxfam. Even though most of it had come from there in the first place.

Grace slipped the mobile back into her bag, feeling as if she had been suddenly thrown to shore from a stormy sea. Tired, but peaceful. The angry rushing in her ears had stopped. The sunniness of the day suddenly struck her.

She started back down the road. *Henry*. She had to tell him. After all, there were no obstacles now. She could go back to the hotel bar, explain everything, clear up the misunderstanding. Perhaps, then . . . Grace walked faster until, approaching the hotel, she was almost running, rushing past the top-hatted doormen, up the red carpeted steps, into the bar. But Henry Moon had gone.

'Great news,' Ellie announced cheerfully, as Grace returned glumly to the office.

'Oh yeah?' The only good news Grace could imagine at

the moment was that Sion was swimming with the fishes in the Thames. In the *Godfather* sense, obviously.

'Yeah,' said Ellie, giving her a questioning look. '*Weekday Night Live* – you know, that current affairs debate programme – called while you were out, wanting talking heads for a show at the end of the week. I suggested they take Euphemia. Incredibly, they agreed.'

Grace felt vaguely relieved. An Ogden publicity opportunity at last. On TV, no less. Whatever other disasters had recently struck, at least Euphemia would be off her back.

'Less happily,' Ellie continued, 'is the fact that I've had another call from Belinda Black. Who no longer, unfortunately, wants to do an interview with Cylindria.'

'Why not?'

'Because,' Ellie sighed, 'she's not doing Tea Breaks any more. She's taken over the Mo Mills slot until Mo Mills gets better. The Mo Mills Interview needs big fish, apparently. Cylindria isn't big enough. Or fishy enough, presumably. Because guess who Belinda's doing instead?'

Grace shrugged. 'Who?'

'Champagne D'Vyne.' Ellie groaned. 'Pathetic, isn't it? Britain's very own It Girl superstar, friend of the royals turned upmarket model turned columnist turned actress turned film star . . .' She pulled a face. 'Famous for being famous. Remember how the *Sun* used to call her "Stars In Her Thighs" because she only went out with celebrities?'

Grace nodded. She might have known Belinda Black would dump Cylindria. She was a woman Grace had never met, yet who, bizarrely, now seemed hellbent on ruining her career after having done the same to her relationship with Sion.

'She went to LA,' Ellie was saying. 'Went with that film producer after she broke up with Matt Locke.'

'Casting couch.' Grace remembered the column inches concerning Champagne's move to America. Column miles, even. The woman was a magnet for publicity; everything she did attracted attention. Which, Grace had to admit could hardly be said for poor old Cylindria with her sensible tweeds and firm grasp of how to peel a banana with a knife and fork.

'Casting wheelchair, more like,' Ellie said acidly. 'The producer was about ninety. He was going to make Champagne big, she said. Not that he needed to. She's big enough already – at least in the upper torso. Don't you remember?' Ellie inquired, looking down at her own, artificially enhanced cleavage, 'Champagne was always saying she wasn't an A-list celebrity, more a DD-list one.'

'So why's she coming back?' Grace was losing interest.

'Got a part in that new Guy Ritchie film *Concrete Boots*. The one Red Campion's supposed to be doing a cameo in, playing some gangster or something. Madge and Guy are her new best friends, apparently.'

Grace was not listening. She was lost in a haze of self-hatred. What a sap Henry Moon must think her. As well as displaying obvious instability, she had presided over a series of PR disasters that had made the Countess of Wessex look surefooted. Much better for both of them if she never saw him again.

'Oh, almost forgot to say.' Ellie jumped with a splash into her miserable musings. 'About *Weekday Night Live*. They wanted more than one person, so I suggested Henry Moon. Hope you don't mind taking him with you to the studio as well. There should be room if Euphemia breathes out.'

CHAPTER NINE

I've done it, Belinda thought exultantly. Got the Mo Mills job. For as long as it takes the old bag to recover. Only, Belinda vowed, she won't. Not once she sees what I'm doing with her column. She'll probably have a fit a fortnight from now on.

Shifting her slender thighs slightly apart under the waffle duvet, Belinda dipped an exploratory finger into her own warm and ready wetness. Running her tongue over her lips, she began to rub softly at the slippery warmth of her clitoris, arching her back slightly as her palm skimmed over the soft mound topped by her scrupulously neat Brazilian wax. Her landing strip. All she needed now was someone to land on it. Someone with a private jet, preferably.

Until then . . . Belinda gasped slightly as the familiar,

delicious tension began to build. Not long now before she landed the rich man of her dreams. Someone fantastically famous, financially free and fabulously single. Just as well – the last letter from her bank manager had not exactly pulled its punches. Well, she'd go and see him and give him the shock of his life. He was always asking questions about the development potential of her job; he had understandably regarded Tea Break as not very promising. Well, it was a different kettle of fish now, Belinda thought, rubbing away. Big fish, hopefully.

The possibilities were endless. Had not Clint Eastwood married Dina after she'd come to interview him? Had not Keeley Shaye first met Pierce Brosnan when she quizzed him on television? Even Tim Henman had married a journalist, for Christ's sake. And Paula Yates had got it together with Michael Hutchence after she interviewed him for television, although perhaps that wasn't the best of examples.

Excitement welled up in her. At last, the days of champagne ideas and lemonade money were well and truly over. Well, almost. The champagne ideas were certainly set to continue. Literally. Belinda's lips twisted. It was impossible to think of anyone she wanted in her slot less than Champagne D'Vyne, especially as the opening interview. A woman whose fame – not to mention her ego – was in inverse proportion to her talents. A woman who, since first bursting out of her blouse at a polo match in front of Prince Charles, had enjoyed a success whose upward curve had almost rivalled that of her famous breasts. The story of her rise to fame was nothing more than a tale of two titties. Was there anything more irritating than a woman who had got to the top by unfair means?

And if this were not enough, Belinda had had the hell irritated out of her that afternoon by reading American articles describing how the once-obsessed-with-fame Champagne D'Vyne had found spiritual harmony in LA. How she had now put her wild days behind her and gone spiritual. How she had swapped carnal indulgence for reincarnation, and mind-expanding drugs for mind-expanding spiritual awakenings. 'My proudest achievement these days is to make a small difference in a stranger's day,' she gushed. 'I have been studying kabbalah for over a year now and its teaching has provoked enormous changes in my mental outlook.' Mental, Belinda thought, was the word.

And yet, even now, Champagne's profoundly annoying run of luck had continued. Had she not, for example, landed this part in the new Guy Ritchie film? Not only that, but the Guy Ritchie film in which the whitest, hottest name on Belinda's celebrity wish list, actor-of-the-moment Red Campion, was slated to play a cameo role as a gangster. And was there not, given Champagne's track record as a celebrity consort, a very good chance that they would end up in bed together? The thought made Belinda burn with jealousy. And, no doubt, explained why Champagne's much-heralded return from Hollywood had got Kevin

Grayson's Y-fronts in a twist. He had demanded Belinda get an exclusive.

The exclusive, moreover, was first thing tomorrow morning. Belinda groaned. To think she had escaped Tea Break and the likes of Stinky Cheshire only to open the batting in her new slot with a piece about arch-nonentity Champagne D'Vyne. A woman who made Stinky Cheshire look like Germaine Greer. She felt the excitement between her legs suddenly subside. The thought of Champagne D'Vyne could put her off sex with anyone. Even herself.

Next morning, Belinda sat in the foyer of Garage, the achingly fashionable West End hotel opened a mere few weeks ago in a conflagration of hype. It was here, according to Champagne's PA, a woman called Brandy with a rasping, masculine voice, that her mistress had billeted herself whilst the vast Notting Hill townhouse she was rumoured to have bought was renovated.

'Notting Hill?' Belinda had probed, ever hot on the scent of money. 'That's pretty flashy.'

'I'll remind you,' snapped the PA, 'that Miss D'Vyne's US career was very successful. Her guest appearance in *Friends* being the highlight—'

'Oh yes. Of course. Actually, I want to talk to her about that. They cut her contract short, didn't they?'

'Nodadall.'

'But wasn't it originally for an entire series? And then, in the second episode, Chandler accidentally backed into her in his car and ran her over. Why was that, exactly?'

'She doesn't want to talk about her career. The point of this interview is to talk about her spirituality. Miss D'Vyne is a very spiritual person these days.'

Perhaps 'spiritual', Belinda thought sourly, was a euphemism for 'late'. Even though – in point of principle – Belinda had herself been some fifteen minutes behind time in arriving at the interview, Champagne, to her fury, was still later.

Why oh why, Belinda thought bitterly, was she not now sipping a margarita on the patio of Elton's Nice mansion, or driving round LA in one of Tom Cruise's three identical Bentleys? She should have been talking Gwynnie with Madonna, and Madonna with Gwynnie. Not sitting in a hotel lobby like an abandoned suitcase.

Belinda contemplated without enthusiasm the concrete pillars, intended, according to the brochure, 'to bring the classic ambience of seventies multi-storey carparks' to the foyer. In her view, the long nylon curtains covering every window gave the place more of a chapel-of-rest feel. The only pieces of furniture were the purple satin-covered chaise longue on which she sat, a Perspex daybed, a large and deliberately kitsch portrait of Elvis in a decorative gold plastic frame and a vast fish tank apparently doubling as the reception desk. Behind it, an anorexic woman wearing a headset sat looking bored.

Belinda reluctantly returned to the perusal of an

American interview in which Champagne described how her new-found faith in ancient wisdom had encouraged her to reform her famously spoilt old ways. 'Instead of completely losing it, expending tons of energy ranting like a loony, I now stop to ask, "what can I learn from all this?" '

Belinda stood up. She walked across the miles of 'ironic' lino tiles to examine the menu of Caff, Garage's cutting-edge restaurant. Staring at a listing including fish and chip risotto, bangers and mash tagliatelle, dry-cured Spam in a ketchup coulis and Wonderloaf and margarine pudding, Belinda, who had not had breakfast, suddenly found she did not mind quite so much.

As the quarter hours dragged by, Belinda had even been reduced to drafting the introduction to her piece:

> Of London's five or six seriously hip hotels, Garage is currently the seriously hippest, targeted unashamedly at the so-called Five Ms – Media, Music, Movies, Modelling and Money.

Better make that Six Ms, Belinda thought suddenly. There were, after all, Morons as well.

> Every room features a futon suspended on ropes above a circular Zen garden, vintage AppleMac computers hanging from the ceiling and projections of the Dalai Lama and select porn movies flooding the blue glass

walls. Even the doors are the epitome of ironic chic – based on those in Victorian prison cells and bearing the names of classic Grange Hill characters. Somewhere above me, in the hotel's presidential Trish Yates suite, is Champagne D'Vyne, recently returned to the capital to take part in the eagerly anticipated new Guy Ritchie flick, *Concrete Boots* . . .

'Can I 'elp you, madame?' Belinda looked up to see a young man of about twenty-five wearing yellow aviator sunglasses and a goatee beard, grinning at her with what she decided was oleaginous over-familiarity. Partly due to the powerful wafts of aftershave he emitted, she had been vaguely aware of him gliding back and forth across the foyer, trying to catch her eye. She scowled at him in dislike. She had her new plunging Versace leather mini-dress on didn't she? Her new Choo stilettos, teamed with the latest in fishnets. Did he think she was a prostitute or something?

'Everything's fine,' she snapped. Apart from the fact that she should have been halfway through the interview by now and hadn't even been called up to Champagne's suite yet, things were tickety-boo.

'You are a journalist, non?' He flashed two rows of persuasive teeth. 'I am Olivier, ze deputy manager. Maybe, while you wait, I can show you round ze hotel a leetle beet? You might theenk it useful, for background?'

'No time,' Belinda said, giving him a freezing glare.

Greasy little creep. He could sod off trying to promote his hotel through her interview. If Champagne D'Vyne was furthering anyone's career, it was *hers*.

Olivier flashed his teeth again. 'Such a shame,' he said silkily. 'I am dying to show you my wunnerful 'otel. I am obsessed with eet. Everytheeng ees perfect. All lighting is MI5-approved and mood-adjustable. Each light bulb is an individual work of art and 'and-made by a team of artisans working in Vienna's 'istoric Bratwurst district. We offer guests a twenty-four hour sushi menu developed in conjunction with the Fylingdales early-warning seestem . . .'

'Doubtless even the loo flush is developed using technology from the Son of Star Wars anti-missile defence programme,' Belinda drawled.

Olivier looked startled. 'Eet is. 'Ow did you know? Zat is a trade secret.'

'I'm psychic on my grandmother's side,' Belinda told him, remembering one of her cleaner's most irritating lines. Bloody woman seemed to think she had magic powers for some reason. 'Well I'd prefer you used them in the bathroom,' Belinda would snap. Some people would say anything to sound interesting.

Olivier began again. 'OK, well, ze beds use ze latest in smart weapons technology to adapt zemselves to your shape as you sleep. I've slept in all of zem. Ze chairs use ze principle of nuclear fission to ensure you get ze most comfortable seat anywhere in ze world and I 'ave tested all of zem. I 'ave eaten from all ze plates, drunk from all ze glasses . . .'

'Is that so?' Belinda purred, flashing her most dazzling smile. 'In which case, I've yet to hear a more off-putting fact,' she added crushingly, then watched with contempt as Olivier, shrugging, bowing and with his smile still intact, glided away.

Belinda glanced at her watch. What the *hell* was going on up there? Forty minutes had now passed since she had first arrived in the lobby. Did Champagne D'Vyne not realise that time, tide and Belinda Black of *The Globe* waited for no man? Let alone woman.

Belinda leapt up and strode over to the fish-tank reception. The words 'Could you possibly find out . . .' had hardly formed, however, before a biting American voice from behind her cut in. A voice Belinda thought she recognised.

'I have a serious. Complaint. To make.'

She definitely recognised it. Brandy. Champagne D'Vyne's gravel-voiced PR. Before Belinda could say anything, however, there was a whooshing sound like the beating of wings, followed by a wave of powerful aftershave. Olivier had returned to the lobby and was standing in front of Brandy.

'What ees the problem, madame?'

'I have a serious. Complaint. About Miss D'Vyne's suite.'

For all the size and masculinity of her voice, Brandy, in the flesh turned out to be a tiny assisted blonde in spike heels and her early twenties. She was raking Olivier up and down with eyes as hard as marbles.

'A *serious* complaint?' Olivier's expression radiated amazement. Sightings of the Virgin Mary in the lobby, it implied, were more frequent.

A serious complaint? Belinda's ears were on stalks. This could be interesting.

'If you can call it. A suite,' snarled Brandy.

'But what ees wrong with eet?'

The blonde's stare was Arctic. 'An ironing board.'

'An ironing board?' Olivier soothed. 'But *every* room has one. Even ze suites. You 'ave looked in ze closet?'

The blonde nodded with threatening emphasis. 'I have looked in the closet,' she repeated in a sarcastic monotone.

'So, you 'ave an ironing board. And an iron?' Olivier rubbed his hands in relief.

'We do.'

'Oh.' Olivier looked as dumbfounded as his suspiciously wrinkle-free brow allowed. 'You mean,' he added, as inspiration struck a few beats later, 'zat zey do not work?'

'They work.'

'So what ees wrong with them?'

'What's wrong with them,' spat the blonde, in her snappy sing-song, 'is that. They should not be there. In the first place. Champagne D'Vyne. Does not do. Her own ironing. She resents. The suggestion that she does. She's very. Upset. About it.'

Belinda's brain clicked and whirred, remembering. 'Instead of completely losing it, expending tons of energy ranting like a loony, I now stop to ask, "what can I learn from all this?" ' Was Champagne D'Vyne's transformation, Belinda wondered, not all she was claiming?

It seemed not. 'Madame,' Olivier was whispering urgently to Brandy. 'We 'ave already bent over backwards for Mees D'Vyne. We 'ave replaced ze carpet in 'er suite with beech floorboards so, when she does 'er yoga, she does not 'ave to greet ze rising sun on our signature shagpile. We 'ave filled ze room wiz white sofas. We 'ave asked ze church next door to stop ringing its bells as zey interfere with 'er spiritual 'armony—'

'Yes,' retorted the personal assistant. 'Which was all fine until room service sent up those prawns. Which were not, as requested, all *exactly* the same size . . .'

'Thees morning,' shot back Olivier, 'ze chef he send up four deeferent room service breakfasts at ze same time because no one in her hontourage can guess what she wants to eat. And zen zere was houtrage because ze milk was not 'ot enough.'

'. . . *And* the complimentary champagne. Was the wrong brand . . .'

Belinda's fingers itched for her pen. This was all sounding less spiritual by the minute. Perhaps the Champagne D'Vyne interview would be more enjoyable than anticipated. Perhaps, come to that, she'd better get up there and do it. Enough time had been wasted.

'Zen we 'ad to move ze ozzer guests down to ze next floor because Mees D'Vyne's ambience co-ordinators tell us to turn ze air conditioning off.'

Before Brandy could reply, Belinda stuck out her hand and smiled her most winning smile. 'We spoke earlier. I'm Belinda Black of *The Globe*. I'd arranged to come and talk to Miss D'Vyne?'

Brandy turned on her a pair of cold eyes, lids half-lowered. 'So where the hell have you been?' For possibly the first time in her life, Belinda was too surprised to reply.

Brandy said nothing as she and Belinda ascended to the Trish Yates suite. The lift, Belinda recalled reading in the brochure, had glass walls whose different colours apparently reflected the moods of the passengers. She could remember some of them – black for sulks, yellow for happiness, red for wicked thoughts. Belinda was concerned to see that while on Brandy's side it was the expected thunderous black, her own side, accurately interpreting her interview intentions, glowed a suspicious vermilion. She tried to cover up as much as she could with her body and was relieved when the lift stopped at the designated floor.

'Belinda Block,' announced Brandy, opening the prison-style door opposite the lift.

'Black,' snapped Belinda, her eyes streaming as a powerful wave of jasmine incense, rearing tsunami-like from the suite entrance, sent her reeling backwards. She blinked wetly in the brilliant daylight bouncing off the expanse of white sofa and blond wood floorboard. Everything within was so pale it was initially impossible to make out any inhabitants. As her eyes accustomed themselves, Belinda could just about make out what looked like a shining figure dressed entirely in white sitting in the middle of the blazing floor.

Champagne D'Vyne, however, was not merely sitting. Her eyes were closed and her slender hands were pressed together. One long, white-clad leg was bent up behind her elbow and head to rest across her shoulders. The contortion looked extraordinarily uncomfortable, and yet the expression on Champagne's face was serene. A beatific smile played about her lips.

Jealousy rose within Belinda like bile as she registered how absolutely beautiful, if absurdly positioned, the other woman was. Champagne's body was as long and lithe as a dancer's, apart from the famously voluminous breasts, a good size bigger than Belinda's own and with no visible means of support. Yet, astonishingly upright, they rose from her narrow ribcage like a pair of footballs. She was dressed in baggy white combat trousers and a close-fitting white vest top which strained over the breasts and stopped a good twelve inches above the waist, revealing acres of muscled brown tummy and a flat navel pierced with a silver ring.

She had rings on her fingers – some intricate and silver, others sparkling in a way which suggested there were serious limits on giving goodness back to the world – and also on her toes, which gleamed with small silver hoops. Her ice-blonde hair flowed in a pale stream over her shoulders and her face was flawless – a perfect, cream-skinned, high-cheekboned oval without line, shadow or spot – apart from the small diamond positioned between her brows. She possessed, in short, the kind of looks Belinda had only previously imagined possible through extensive retouching on a computer. Worse, they looked as natural as they were effortless. From this distance at least, Champagne seemed irritatingly innocent of even a scrap of make-up.

'Go and siddown,' grated Brandy. 'You got ten minutes.'

Ten minutes! And she'd been promised forty! Belinda turned to argue and then thought better of it on seeing Brandy's set face. She clomped furiously across to one of the sofas.

'Not there,' Brandy growled. 'There.' She pointed at the floor opposite Champagne. Belinda, who hadn't sat on the floor since primary school, scrambled downwards, bare knees cracking against the floorboards, ungiving leather mini-dress digging painfully into her thighs. She hoped she wasn't expected to put her leg behind her head as well.

Champagne's eyes were still closed. Was she, Belinda wondered sardonically, really lost in contemplation of universal truths? Or simply unconscious, knocked out by the almost overwhelming combined aromas of the incense, the flickering scented candles dotted here and there about the floor and, on every window ledge, the huge vases of powerfully perfumed white lilies.

Struggling to cope with the sensory overload, Belinda

searched for an opening question. 'Miss D'Vyne. May I ask you . . .'

Champagne's eyes flicked open. Belinda felt her entire body scrutinised in seconds by irises as green and glowing as lasers before a slight sneer lifted the perfectly cut lip. 'Yah?'

'. . . why you've got pebbles between your toes?'

Champagne's eyes widened in amazed contempt. 'Because I'm Sprit, of course.'

'Sprit? What's that?'

'Spi*rit*,' Champagne groaned, rolling her eyes impatiently. 'I Am Spirit.'

'Oh.' Belinda smiled nastily. 'I see.' *For Christ's sake*. The woman was *ridiculous*.

'And this,' Champagne continued, flexing the leg behind her head, 'as I would have thought was *obvious*, is my Native American Hot Stone treatment. Although actually,' she added in an outraged honk, 'they've gone pretty bloody cold. Petsy!' She clapped her hands sharply. From an adjoining room, which Belinda could now see milled with people dressed in white, a small, dark-haired girl with hands covered in henna tattoos rushed forward and started plucking the pebbles from between Champagne's toes. As she did so, tears began unexpectedly to roll down Champagne's cheeks.

'Does it hurt?' Belinda inquired with fake solicitude. 'Or is it hay fever from the flowers?'

'Of course not,' snapped Champagne. 'Surely you

know that weeping cheers up your chi and makes the heart happy?'

Belinda thrilled inwardly. Champagne was far better, or far *worse*, than she had dared to hope. After some cursory questions about Champagne's diet – which seemed to consist mainly of ludicrous allergies – Belinda turned her attention to the people in white in the anteroom. 'Who are they?'

'My staff, obviously,' Champagne yawned. 'Nail guru, yoga guru, hair guru, holistic guru, kinesiology guru, feng shui guru, style guru, personal growth guru – that's the one who waxes my legs . . .' She yawned. 'Oh, and my guru guru.'

'*Guru* guru? What does he do?'

'Gives me advice about all my other gurus, of course,' Champagne said scornfully.

Belinda shifted uncomfortably on the floor. 'Tell me about your spiritual awakening. About your discovery of kabbalah.'

'Yah.' Champagne's hard green eyes were now melting pools of earnestness. 'Look, I want you to get all this down. I'm a very spritual person, you know. *Very* spritual.'

'Yes, yes, yes. Is it true that Madonna introduced you to it?'

'Yah. Good old M.'

'How exactly did it happen?' probed Belinda.

Champagne stretched both long, graceful arms. 'We were chatting one day – might have been at Skibo, now I come to think of it – and I asked her if she knew any good cobblers.

Next thing I knew, I was in LA being told about my tikons.'

'Tikons?' Australian for tokens? Belinda wondered. 'What sort of tokens?'

'*Tikons*,' Champagne snapped, 'are corrections we must make, carried over from our last life, to allow us to evolve and grow.'

'Oh,' said Belinda. '*Right*.'

'One of my tikons is that most things are out of my control . . .'

Belinda flicked a glance over to the retinue. In the light of so many servants, lack of control was evidently a relative thing.

'. . . and I must stay at all times free and light . . .'

It was with a sarcastic lift of the eyebrow that Belinda noted this down. Champagne had no doubt got her hotel room gratis, after all. And she was certainly light – about seven stone, although those breasts must weigh at least four pounds each.

An assistant stepped forward with a small bowl. 'Your hot oil treatment,' she whispered, rubbing it into Champagne's miraculously smooth forehead.

Belinda decided on a change of tack. 'You've been away for some time, Miss D'Vyne,' she simpered. 'How do you think Britain sees you these days?'

Champagne tossed her hair dramatically in reply. 'I left Britain a celebrity,' she declared. 'But I came back . . . *a star*.'

The woman's ego was almost beyond belief. Damn her. Belinda could feel the very soles of her feet itch with envy.

'And of course you've got the part in the new Ritchie movie,' Belinda spoke through clenched teeth.

'Yah. I'm very excited about it.'

'And you'll be acting opposite . . . um,' Belinda jealously forced the words out, 'Red Campion.'

Champagne smiled smugly.

Belinda narrowed her eyes. *Bitch.* 'Is it true,' she asked sweetly, 'that the technical crew on *Concrete Boots* have had to sign contracts agreeing not to look you in the eye?'

'What?' screeched Champagne. 'How bloody dare you? I'm a deeply spritual parson. I believe everyone is equal. No one is better than anyone else. Making a small difference in a stranger's day is a cornerstone on the path to spritual enlightenment.'

'So it's *not* true,' pressed Belinda triumphantly, 'that you've already got problems with the film because one of the other actors has been given a bigger trailer than you?'

Champagne started with shock, causing the bowl to slip. 'You *bloody moron*,' she screeched at her assistant. 'You've got hot oil on my Third Eye.'

'Interview over,' Brandy declared, as Belinda gathered her things and scrambled to her feet. 'The *Vogue* photographer's outside,' she added to Champagne, who greeted this apparently encouraging news with a series of loud raspberries. 'It's good for plumping lips up,' Brandy said tightly, showing Belinda to the door.

'And you'd better not forget to mention,' Champagne

ordered, pausing between farting noises, 'what a deeply spritual parson I am.'

'Don't worry,' promised Belinda. 'I won't.' After all, she thought, clomping down the metal stairs with their fire-escape ambience, Champagne had fulfilled in abundance one of the central tenets of her new-found spiritual awareness. She had certainly, Belinda thought gleefully, made a difference to *this* stranger's day.

As yet another enormous crash shook the flat, Grace rushed into the kitchen to assess the damage. Maria was having one of her off mornings.

'Madam Grace . . .'

'Grace. Just Grace. Please . . .'

The picture of abject regret, Maria was standing, wringing her hands, in the midst of a circle of striped china shards. The remnants, Grace recognised, of a particularly ugly dip bowl Sion had once given her – still bearing its Oxfam sticker. With its central indent for chopped vegetables and depressions round the edge for the sauces, it had always irresistibly reminded her of a large porcelain verruca.

'It doesn't matter. Really, it's fine.'

Employing a cleaner, Grace had discovered, was rather more of an emotional commitment than she had anticipated. It seemed to have made life, although tidier, much more complicated.

Maria's insistence on answering the telephone had resulted in a number of messages so garbled it was impossible to understand what they meant. Whether any calls from Henry Moon were among the indecipherable scrawls Grace occasionally found tucked under the telephone, she had no idea. But it seemed unlikely. At Grace's request, Ellie, amid much argument, had agreed to ring and tell him about the forthcoming *Weekday Night Live* date. Ellie had, however, refused to accompany Henry and Euphemia to the studio on the grounds that she had a date. 'They're your authors,' she told Grace.

The only messages Maria ever reported with one hundred per cent accuracy were those from Lady Armiger, who called frequently, demanding to know whether Grace was coming to the dinner in Venice. Grace, whilst inwardly resolved that she would rather stick needles in her eyes, did not yet feel strong enough to tell her mother this. Still less face the argument that would follow. Thus far, therefore, she had avoided speaking to her.

Allowing Maria to fit in the cleaning she did for Grace around work for other clients had also led to complications. Maria now turned up at the most unexpected hours, often when Grace was at home. Not that this was too much of a problem. Maria was oddly comforting to have around: a cheerful, whistling, polishing presence at times when it might have been tempting to brood on the failures, disappointments and let-downs of the past few weeks.

In addition to being appealingly quirky – today, for example, a neon orange streak blazed down the side of the platinum crop – Maria was scrupulously honest and generous with her time. She had a tendency to stay rather longer than Grace paid her for, to talk, to clean one last cupboard or basin, to tidy one last drawer – and she was a demon with a duster. If she had not quite yet washed that man right out of her hair, Grace thought, all traces of him had been expunged from her flat. Maria, indeed, had seemed to divine what had happened without being told. Shortly afterwards, she had taken appropriate action. The photograph of Sion throwing eggs at Princess Margaret had been the first to disappear, followed by the Support the Striking (Fill in Here) placards. What Maria had done with those, Grace could not imagine.

Looking up now from the smashed bowl, Maria's expression was one of intense relief. Her face flushed and her eyes watered. 'I thought you might take heem off my wages.'

'*What?* Of course I wouldn't do that. Surely nobody does . . . *do* they?'

As Maria, glancing away, dropped to her knees and began picking up the pieces, Grace remembered what Ellie had once said about Maria's less appealing customers. *Got some woman who's absolutely vile to her at the moment, no matter how hard she tries. Pays her peanuts, shouts at her . . .*

How dreadful this other woman must be. Grace policed herself vigorously for any sign she was pulling rank on her cleaner. She was scrupulously careful about any behaviour, any remark, even, that Maria could possibly interpret as evidence she was considered inferior. Maria, on the other hand, vigorously continued her campaign to pair Grace up with one of the single men she cleaned for. No visit was complete without a homily on behalf of 'my client, he verray kind, he perfect for you'.

'Actually, Maria,' Grace would reply, trying not to sound tense, 'I'm staying away from men for a while.'

Maria would look shocked. 'But you so pretty. My client, he handsome. *Why* stay away?'

'Coffee?' Grace said loudly.

As the rapidly diminishing packets in the cupboard attested, the cleaner loved nothing better than black coffee, heavily sweetened. As Grace crossed to the counter to switch the kettle on, she heard Maria, behind her, pause in her gathering activities.

'Meesees Grace. You work weeth books, no?'

Grace turned and smiled. 'In publishing, yes.'

'I wanna show you book. Good book.'

Grace expression turned to amazement. 'You've written a book?'

It was not the first time it had happened. One of the occupational hazards of working for publishers – even one as unsuccessful as Hatto & Hatto – was the endless stream of people, usually the faintest of acquaintances, asking if she would pass on their book to Adam Knight. Grace would try in vain to explain that anyone passing anything on to Adam would get an identical effect by flinging it straight into the nearest dustbin. This deterred no one: the whole world seemed to think that not only did they have a novel in them, but a novel that would net them tens of millions of pounds and a film deal into the bargain. It came as some surprise, however, to find that Maria apparently thought this too.

Maria pulled out a brown A4 envelope from her bag and handed it to Grace. 'Not me. My client. He verray nice man. Very handsome. The man I tell you about.'

CHAPTER TEN

'This way please,' said Belinda's bank manager's secretary in a high-pitched, nervous voice. 'Mr Vignoles won't be long. Can I get you anything?'

'Well, a glass of Cristal champagne would be lovely.'

The secretary erupted in hysterical giggles. 'Ooh, Miss Black! You are funny.'

Belinda folded her arms crossly. She hadn't meant to be funny. She was one of the country's top celebrity interviewers, wasn't she? This was a private bank, wasn't it? If champagne for the clients wasn't part of the service, then it bloody well should be.

The woman hovered. From the faint, wringing motion of her hands, Belinda detected suppressed excitement.

'Hope you don't mind me asking, but . . .'

'But *what*?'

'I just wondered,' stammered the secretary. 'Are you the Belinda Black who writes for *The Globe*? I think I saw something by you this morning . . .'

'You did,' Belinda said triumphantly. That morning's edition of *The Globe* had devoted no fewer than four pages to her interview with Champagne D'Vyne.

'It was very funny,' ventured the secretary, lingering in the passage outside Vignoles's vast office. 'Hang on, I've got it on my desk.' She darted back into her cubbyhole and emerged waving a newspaper. 'ABSOLUTELY LUDICROUS', read the headline, 'HOW CHAMPAGNE WENT GA GA IN LA LA LAND.'

'Amazing, isn't it, how she went to Hollywood and got all weird and faddy,' giggled the woman. 'All that stuff about how her fruit juice has to be poured through a funnel and she has to have daily acupuncture on her bottom to relieve the stress. And that her favourite drink is a water cocktail . . .' The secretary wrinkled her brow. 'What was it? Three parts Badoit to two parts Evian or something? And that she sometimes sleeps with a haddock on her face to feed her pores, but the cat attacks it in the night . . .'

Belinda grinned. Probably not exactly what Champagne had meant when she explained that fresh fish was an important part of the health and beauty routine prescribed by her food allergy guru. But everyone knew misunderstandings sometimes crept in.

'And that story about how she's into cabriolet . . .'

'Kabbalah,' corrected Belinda sweetly. 'It's an ancient wisdom that offers rules for living. People try and trust in the lessons learnt, rather than the selfish inconvenience of the situation.' With a sarcastic smile, she wondered how Champagne might be feeling about that this morning.

'And that she's got some ridiculous celebrity disease called Yogamortis, when your body seizes up entirely because you've done too much yoga . . .'

Belinda's smile tightened slightly. Champagne may have hoisted herself by her own petard, but it hadn't stopped a few spicy stories of Belinda's own invention slipping in.

'And how she's heavily into the afterlife,' the excited secretary continued. 'That story about her presenting a work on reincarnation to a dying cancer victim, when she'd written "Better luck next time" on the flyleaf . . .'

Belinda's tight smile turned to a grimace. Had she gone a bit too far with that one?

'And her acting career!' The secretary clapped her hands. 'Her taking her dog along to an audition and the director saying the dog was a better actor than she was. Hilarious!'

'Mmm.' Belinda's smile was all but invisible now. Still, given Champagne's undoubted lack of thespian talent, that particular addition would no doubt qualify under the 'fair comment' rule in the legal department.

The secretary was wiping her eyes. 'And I loved all that about wanting to make a difference to a stranger's day. It's certainly made a difference to mine. I haven't laughed so much in my life. As for that plastic surgery stuff at the beginning . . .'

'Look,' Belinda cut in. 'I haven't got all day. Where the hell's my bloody bank manager?'

The secretary scuttled off, leaving the newspaper on the coffee table. Reaching for it, Belinda re-read the first paragraph.

> *I arrive to find Champagne and her assistants poring over what sounds like a menu. Words like 'loin', 'thigh' and 'breast' come floating over, punctuated by periods of apparent deep thought; the recommendations, I assume, from Champagne's personal food guru. After a while I realise that what she is actually perusing is a list of the latest treatments from a leading Hollywood plastic surgeon and it occurs to me, as I look at her now, that never before have I seen so much cleavage and collagen under one roof. Her lip implants are so big she looks like Donald Duck. All apparently something of a contradiction to her much-expounded embracing of ancient wisdoms. Doesn't this quest for outer perfection, I ask Champagne, make a nonsense of the pursuit of sagacity? 'Certainly not,' she snaps. 'It's all about stopping sagging, in fact.'*

Well, Belinda thought defiantly. No doubt it *was* true. Someone, *somewhere* must say things like that. Anyway, what was important was that the mission had been accomplished. Champagne D'Vyne's reputation – such as it was –

now lay in smoking ruins. She looked a fool in the eyes of the world. And, when he read it, hopefully in the eyes of Red Campion too. Plus, the interview was hot; so hot the smoke almost came off the paragraphs in places. No wonder a delighted Grayson had given the piece four pages.

Belinda smiled with renewed self-satisfaction. She'd certainly taught the stupid spoilt bitch a lesson. That no one – but *no one* – got the better of Belinda Black.

Clicking away at his laptop files, Mr Vignoles stared intently at Belinda's account details. 'Things aren't looking too good, Miss Black.'

Speak for yourself, thought Belinda. Her bank manager might be small, plump, bespectacled and dome-headed, but she herself was looking her best ever. She had celebrated the new job by completely updating her wardrobe, and if she'd bashed the plastic a little bit too hard, what did it matter? She'd be as rich as hell soon. She smoothed the jacket of her Versace suit, flicked her glossy black hair back over her shoulders and treated the manager to her best showbiz smile. He did not return it. But then, Vignoles probably didn't have a showbiz smile.

Although Belinda's meetings with the manager had once taken place amid the informality of his in-office 'sitting room', an arrangement of leather sofa at one end and armchair at the other, she had more recently found herself facing him across this ominous expanse of desk. Moving her neat rump in the small hard chair, she swung one sheer-nyloned knee over the other. The main advantage of the 'sitting room' had been the opportunities it offered for Vignoles to view her legs. Still, the desk wasn't entirely devoid of seductive opportunity. Ramming her elbows together and leaning forward so her cleavage squeezed almost up to her throat, Belinda ran a finger along her bottom lip and suppressed a yawn as Vignoles lectured her on ISAs.

'You need a plan for a secure and wealthy future,' her bank manager told her. Belinda yawned. Did he not realise she was about to join the ranks of media superstars? 'Taking into account your incomings and outgoings,' Vignoles added, 'the sum I suggest you aim to live on weekly is . . .' He then named a figure so small it made Belinda gasp. It would, she thought savagely, hardly keep her in eyeliner. 'But what about my new salary?' she yelped.

Vignoles sighed. 'The sum I suggest takes your new salary level into account.'

'Is it fair to say, Miss Black, that you have, *ahem*, been spending rather a lot recently? On clothes, particularly?'

'A bit, perhaps.' Good tactics to give him an inch. 'But generally I've been trying to economise.'

Vignoles looked doubtfully at her over his glasses. 'Your hairdressing bills, Miss Black. Must you patronise that particular salon?'

Belinda arranged her glossy raven mane protectively on her shoulders. 'Absolutely. Riccardo Milano is the only salon to be hooked up to AP and Reuters so I can plug in and keep up with what's running on the news wires.' Not that she ever actually did.

'And are you still spending twenty pounds a day on taxi fares?'

'I charge a lot of them to expenses,' Belinda snapped. 'And anyway, twenty pounds a day is a bargain when you see what commuters from Surrey fork out for season tickets. I can't afford to travel on the Tube, anyway.'

Vignoles raised an eyebrow. 'Why not?'

'Well, imagine it. If I ruin my best Chanel on a dirty seat, Ken Livingstone's not going to cough up, is he?'

'Really, Miss Black. You should be thinking about investments. About pension plans. About investing in property even.'

Belinda stretched out one long, smooth leg (£45 per waxing, per month) and flexed long manicured fingers (£40 a session). Beneath her dress she imagined her neatly-trimmed bikini line (£25 every two weeks) and the swell of her breasts (free, so far). *Investing in property. Pension plans.* Didn't Vignoles realise that what she spent on herself was entirely, if indirectly, aimed at securing the best property around? That her perfectly kept appearance was her plan for a secure and wealthy future?

Vignoles took off his glasses and rubbed his eyes. 'Miss Black. May I suggest to you that you are living utterly beyond your means?'

'And may I suggest to *you*, Mr Vignoles,' Belinda spat,

'that I am about to become one of the best-known journalists in Fleet Street?'

Vignoles's gaze was steely. 'May I suggest a little self-denial?'

Belinda's nostrils flared. 'And may I suggest that I've cut everything back to the bone? What the hell else could I possibly economise on?'

Vignoles drew a deep breath. 'Let's just get an idea of what your weekly spending is like.' He squinted at the screen over his glasses again. 'Let's start with your smallest outgoing, shall we? This weekly cheque payment of twelve pounds . . .?'

'The cleaner,' Belinda told him. 'Three hours at four pounds an hour.'

Vignoles raised his eyebrows. 'I am glad,' he observed with light irony, 'that even though you obviously take taxis everywhere and spend six hundred pounds on a Gucci jacket without a second thought, you are still able to pay your cleaner almost the minimum wage.'

His sarcasm was lost on his client. 'What do you mean?' Belinda demanded. 'Four pounds is pretty cheap, isn't it? *Isn't* it?'

An hour later, Belinda opened her front door. *Excellent.* There was nothing like char-baiting after an afternoon being lectured by Vignoles. As she had hoped, the cleaner was still there.

Only just, though. Flustered sounds from the direction of the bathroom door indicated she was getting changed out of her cleaning clothes into her daytime ones. Not that you could tell the difference, Belinda thought nastily.

So what had she broken this time? Belinda's malign gaze rolled about the hall. A tiny white chip of indeterminate age could be seen on the corner of the red-painted skirting board.

'What the hell have you done to the walls?' Belinda shrieked triumphantly. 'You've been smashing the bloody Hoover into the skirting boards again.' She grinned at the frightened whimpers from beyond the bathroom door and shouted, 'If I have to get them repainted, it's coming off your sodding wages.'

The bathroom door swung open to reveal the terrified-looking cleaner. 'Oh, Belinda. I sorry. I not mean to make bang.'

'Madam Belinda,' corrected Belinda. 'Or just Madam, if that's easier for you to remember.'

Her lip curled at the sight of the cleaner's peroxide shock of hair which, for some bizarre reason, sported a neon orange streak down one side. Last week it had been blue. The explanation, Belinda knew, was that a friend's daughter was training as a hairdresser. 'Yes, but when does she start?' Belinda had asked crushingly.

'Don't you think your hair's a bit, well, Eastern Bloc?' she purred now, flashing the cleaner a brilliant smile. 'Bit Domestos, darling. We don't have hair like that in London, you know. Why don't you go to Riccardo Milano? He's very reasonable.' Belinda rummaged in her clutch bag. 'I think I've got his price list. Here.'

As Belinda had intended, the cleaner's face went grey with shock at the sight of Knightsbridge salon prices.

'I see you've used up all the bleach again,' Belinda complained, striding into the kitchen and peering under the sink. What did the woman do with it? Drink it? Do her bloody roots with it?

'I sorry, um, Madam Belinda. But the toilet, he is very dirty,' faltered the cleaner.

'Lavatory,' corrected Belinda. She was on a roll now. Which reminded her. 'You're supposed to keep the loo paper stocked up as well. I'm down to my last three, I notice.'

Why couldn't the woman ever remember *anything*? Amazing, given all that bullshit about having been a businesswoman before some bloody civil war destroyed her company. Talk about a pathetic excuse. Some people would say anything to disguise their own incompetence.

As for those clothes! The woman's market stall wardrobe was enough to make one cry if it didn't make one laugh so much. Like today. Those deliberately white-streaked denim flares were obviously a tilt at trendiness, albeit one, in Belinda's view, that missed its target by several hundred miles.

'Really, you shouldn't clean in your best clothes,' Belinda advised in mock concern. 'You've got bleach all over your trousers.'

'Thees ees not my cleaning clothes,' stammered the cleaner. From underneath trembling eyelashes, she shot her employer a chiding look.

Belinda's lips stretched in a nasty smile. Did the woman need yet another lesson on who was boss in this house?

'By the way, I need to talk to you about your wages,' she said airily, taking a bottle of the Food Editor's best Chablis from the fridge and sloshing herself a large glassful. She shot a suspicious look round the kitchen for evidence that the cleaner had been making herself cups of coffee, a practice Belinda had specifically forbidden.

The cleaner looked at her with frightened eyes. 'My wages?'

'I'm afraid things are going to have to alter,' Belinda announced, reaching for a knife and cutting off a piece of the pâté de foie gras stolen at the same time as the wine. She stuffed it between her scarlet and shining lips. 'I'm economising,' she announced, mouth full. 'From now on, you're being paid three pounds an hour.'

The cleaner's face grew pale. 'Three pounds! But Madam Belinda. I ham good cleaner. I always work longer than you pay me. Today, for hexample, I clean your bedroom. Under bed. Put all your clofes away.' She gestured through the open door at the end of the hall.

The bedroom, Belinda saw, had indeed been transformed. Gone was the talcum powder covering the carpet, closed and tidied the half-open drawers over which tights had been dangling like the Hanging Gardens of Babylon. Put away were the Versace dress and Gucci jacket, stored out of sight was the new suit from Joseph, and sitting neatly in a row in the wardrobe, no doubt, were the two pairs of shining new Manolos. Gone, even, was the grubby bra that had, for several days, been hanging drunkenly from the bedside lamp.

Belinda slid a glance at her Rolex. Half past six. The cleaner had worked an extra half an hour over her allotted three hours. What a fool. And if she thought that meant that she was going to be paid extra, she had another think coming. 'Bank manager's orders, I'm afraid,' Belinda trilled. Vignoles had told her to economise, hadn't he?

'Meesees Belinda—'

'*Madam* Belinda.'

'Madam Belinda, I . . . ham . . . a weedow,' pleaded the other woman.

Belinda folded her arms and looked the cleaner sceptically in the eye.

'Three pounds for a hower, Madam Belinda. Eet ees not merch.'

'Like it or lump it.' Belinda turned on her heel and walked out of the kitchen.

The cleaner followed her into the hall, her large, worried eyes full of water. For a hopeful moment, Belinda thought she was going to cry. Disappointingly, however, the cleaner rallied, swallowed and tipped her chin slightly into the air.

'Hokay. Three pounds it is. Eef you can not hafford more, I hunderstand, I ham poor woman too.'

'Good,' Belinda said, satisfied. 'That's settled then.' Walking down the hall, she slid a finger along the dado rail and looked at it. Not even the slightest speck of dust showed on the whorls on her fingertip. 'And do the bloody dusting before you go, will you? It's enough to give me bloody asthma.'

'Madam Grace?'

Grace leapt back from the bathroom mirror, where she was paying more than usually close attention to her make-up.

'What is it, Maria?'

The other woman beamed. 'You remember, Madam Grace, I geeve you book . . .'

Grace felt a stab of guilt. The rather grubby brown envelope Maria had given her – several days ago now – was lying, she remembered, under a pile of Sunday newspapers on the kitchen counter. Except that, Grace now saw in the reflection, it wasn't any more. It was dangling accusingly from Maria's rubber-gloved hand.

'Oh. Yes. Sorry, Maria.' Grace frowned as the eyeliner brush, which apparently had a will of its own, jerked upwards, giving her an Audrey Hepburn flick on one side that was not echoed on the other. Why was applying eyeliner so difficult? And why was she bothering anyway? It wasn't as if she was going on *Weekday Night Live* herself. Or as if Henry Moon, who was, would notice any special effort on her part.

'You have not read?' The envelope swung back and forth between the Marigolded fingers.

'I'm sorry. *I will* read it. I promise. It's just that I haven't really had a chance to look at it . . .'

Maria bit her lip and raised both arms from her side in a gesture of disappointment. 'Ees very good book, Madam Grace,' she said, chidingly.

'Of course it is.' Grace let her eyes slide from the cleaner's reproving gaze.

'My client, he very disappointed. He ask me every day eef you haf read eet.'

It was on the tip of Grace's tongue to ask why Maria's client hadn't just approached her directly, instead of making Maria do all the running. Was it, she wondered, the bullying client who treated her badly? No, it couldn't be. That was a woman; the would-be writer was a man. A verray handsome man, as Maria had emphasised. And one, Grace thought acidly, with all the spine of your average garden worm. *Men*. She twisted her lips and looked at her watch. 'Oh God. I'm late. Maria, just leave it on the table will you? I'll read it when I get back.'

No time even to finish my bloody lipstick, Grace groaned as she dashed through the puddles towards the Tube station, praying for the Central Line for once to be working. She was ten minutes late for the Euphemia rendezvous as it was.

Euphemia had received the tidings that *Weekday Night Live* required her services in typical style. 'Well of course I'd be perfect for *Question Time*. It will be so nice to see *dear* David Frost again. I've always rather expected to bump into him at one of his parties, but perhaps the invitation gets lost in the post.'

'Well, it's not exactly *Question Time*,' Grace had ventured. 'Which I don't think David Frost does in any case. That's David Dimbleby.'

'Same bloody difference,' snapped Euphemia. 'I'll still have to cancel my yoga teacher.'

'It would be wonderful if you could make time for the show, Euphemia,' said Grace, trying to imagine Euphemia greeting the rising sun in a leotard. 'The studios are quite a way away and it'll take some time to get back.'

'Who else will be on the panel? My very good friend Ann Widdecombe?'

'I'm not sure about Ann Widdecombe, but there's another Hatto writer on it.'

'Who?' demanded Euphemia sharply.

Grace swallowed and crossed her fingers. She had not seen, nor spoken to Henry Moon since the scene in the cocktail bar. Things couldn't get worse, so they had to get better.

A successful TV appearance by Henry would give her a chance to redeem herself professionally, and possibly in other ways as well. And what could go wrong with a trip to a debate show as formulaic as *Weekday Night Live*?

Halfway up the rain-lashed motorway en route to the studios, Grace felt less optimistic. Henry, unusually inscrutable, had hardly spoken when they had met. Rather than angling to sit next to her in the back as she had hoped, he had insisted on the front, where he was listening, with the driver, to a football match on the radio.

Beside Grace, Euphemia had promptly fallen asleep and

was snoring an open-mouthed, flappy snore. Grace watched as a dribble of saliva navigated a course through the *Our Mam* author's thickly applied foundation and ran into her neck. Euphemia had clearly pulled out all the stops for her television appearance, not to mention all the make-up drawers. She also sported a large jewelled necklace and a top ablaze with gold sequins sewn on in the shape of a butterfly. Completing the ensemble was a fur coat of a thickness and vastness that Dr Zhivago might have considered excessive.

The Charlton TV studios were in a grey Lubyanka on the outskirts of a large Midlands town. Immediately after arriving, Euphemia disappeared in search of a loo; Grace and Henry, meanwhile, contemplated the cheeseplants in awkward silence until, to Grace's relief, a leather-jacketed production assistant appeared. She announced that her name was Darcy and her mission was to take them to the *Weekday Night Live* Green Room.

Darcy had a strong Liverpudlian accent and a face poised exactly between male and female. 'Are you familiar with the programme?' she was asking as Euphemia bustled importantly back in the foyer, sequins ablaze.

'Never seen it in my life,' declared Euphemia.

'Ah.'

'I understood it was like *Question Time*.'

'Well, there are questions.'

They followed Darcy's leather-clad back through what seemed like miles of grey, shiny, hospital-like corridor before stopping before one of many identical grey doors. 'Here we are,' Darcy announced. 'This is the Green Room.'

'Ah, the Green Room,' boomed Euphemia, with the air of one who had been in more than even she cared to mention. 'An essential stop-off point,' Euphemia added theatrically, 'for the seasoned television performer before finally being thrown to the lions of the audience.'

'Absolutely,' grinned Darcy. 'You get the idea. The audience are in here. Come and meet them and have a drink.'

As Darcy pushed the door open, Grace heard Henry exclaim softly, 'My God. I've faced Mujahedin less scary than this.' The knot in her stomach tightened. Had coming here been such a good idea, after all?

Before them was a large, windowless room across whose bright green expanse of carpet a great many crisps had been scattered. Standing around in groups were a number of extremely large individuals of belligerent appearance. Many held a pint in each hand, while others were helping themselves liberally to the packets of complimentary cigarettes which lay around on the tables running down the side of the room. Tables which, in addition, bore something with a vague resemblance to a buffet. But a buffet after a tornado and a herd of stampeding elephants had done their respective worst with it.

The belligerent individuals turned to stare at the newcomers. Their stare was not a welcoming one. Catching the suspicious eye of a large, red-faced woman with scraped back hair, thighs bulging out of her leggings and no eyebrows to speak of, Grace quickly dropped her gaze to a stray cocktail sausage trodden into the ground near her feet.

'Good heavens,' declared Euphemia, in a loud, amused voice. 'Who *are* these people?'

Grace sensed the atmosphere turn a couple of shades uglier.

'I feel like Marie Antoinette as the mob approached Versailles,' Euphemia continued, rattling her bracelets, apparently oblivious to the resentful looks being flung in her direction. And where the looks led, Grace suspected, vol-au-vents and cocktail sausages would soon follow. Her heart sank further at Darcy's next words.

'We bus them in from the local council estates and let them loose on the free booze and fags,' the production assistant explained, *sotto voce*. 'They go for it in a big way and by the time we're recording the programme they're very, um, lively. Very lively indeed. But it all makes for good viewing.'

'What, you mean they join in?' Henry asked. His carefully neutral voice made Grace more anxious than ever.

'You bet they do,' Darcy grinned. 'The show *is* the audience, in many ways. They shout – I mean, they ask lots of questions of the panellists. They make their own views heard. Very much so.'

Despite her growing panic, Grace felt a pang of pity. What a life, being stuck on a Midlands council estate, the only fun to look forward to being bussed out, pissed up and encouraged to shout abuse on television.

Henry's face was set. 'What are our chances of coming out of this alive?'

Darcy snorted. 'Oh, they're all right really. Get them on your side and you're laughing.'

Henry looked unconvinced. 'Think Russell Crowe in *Gladiator*, in other words? Or Red Campion in *Legionnaire*?'

'Ha *ha*, no, it's not that bad, anyway, now you've met the audience, come over and meet some of the other panellists.'

'Absolutely,' Euphemia trilled, still unaware of the murderous looks raining like arrows from a group of large ladies in roomy neon tracksuits. 'Lead me to civilisation. Is dear David – Frost, of course – here? Or Ann – Widdecombe?'

'They were a bit busy this week,' Darcy said, her sarcasm going straight over Euphemia's head.

As, swathed in furs, sequins and diamonds, a superior sneer on her face, Euphemia trotted past what were quite literally the seething masses, her empathy with Marie Antoinette, Grace thought worriedly, could end up closer to the truth than she imagined.

'When am I going into Make-Up?' bleated the creator of *Pease Pudding Polly*. 'I need to touch up my foundation.'

Darcy's leather jacket squeaked as she beckoned to another minion. 'Stacey, can you take this lady to Make-Up, please.'

'Hasn't she been done?' Stacey peered at Euphemia's powdered mask. 'Actually, you're right. We probably need to remove some of it.'

'Do they have Kanebo?' Euphemia demanded as Stacey

led her, furs rustling, towards the exit. 'Although I suppose I could rough it with Christian Dior . . .'

'Come and have some food.' Darcy led Henry and Grace to a pile of sandwiches somewhat past their prime. Exuding sweaty, congealing lumps of lurid yellow grated cheese, they lay, crusts curling, against a grease-stained bed of red paper napkins.

'What particular aspect of current affairs is being discussed this week?' Grace inquired in an unnaturally high voice as they passed a group of huge beer guts with arms and legs attached. The fact that the subject matter seemed moderately respectable was the straw of hope to which she was clinging.

Darcy looked puzzled. 'Current affairs. That's what it's about.'

'Yes, but what *sort* of current affairs?' asked Henry. 'Education, the Health Service, immigration, that sort of thing?' He flicked a glance towards the drinking, smoking crowd, amongst whom, Grace could see, the spirit of debate had already gained firm hold. Some of the beer guts were squaring – or rather squashing – up to each other in a distinctly threatening manner.

Grace felt the apprehension in her feet spread upwards to her calves.

'No,' Darcy grinned. '*Current affairs*. Just what it says on the tin.'

'I don't understand,' Grace said. Was she missing something?

'What celebrity's shagging who. You know. Newspaper kiss-and-tell exposures, that sort of thing. Hang on, I'll get some of the other panellists to come over.'

Grace felt her spine freeze. She turned horrified eyes to Henry, then ducked as a cocktail sausage came flying over. The debate between the beer guts had been joined by a number of their wives as well.

'I'm so sorry,' she whispered desperately. 'It's my fault, absolutely. I didn't check it out properly. My colleague took the original call . . .'

Henry's only reaction was a slight shrug.

'I mean,' Grace continued, stammering, 'I knew what sort of programme it was, but when my colleague said current affairs I didn't realise . . .' Damn Ellie. It was obvious, in retrospect, she had been trying to matchmake, to get Grace and Henry together, however unsuitable the programme. *Current affairs*, indeed. Ha bloody ha. But damn herself too. She, after all, had let it happen. Not bothered to check.

Henry poked at a stale sausage roll. Under his eyes, the bags looked heavier than ever. His new writing project was clearly claiming a great deal of his energy. Or was it another kind of project? Grace wondered. A woman project. That would explain his air of detached boredom. His lack of interest in her. The fact that his store of good-humoured tolerance for everything from his cancelled talk at St Merrion to his encounter with Andy Twort of Radio Gainsborough seemed finally to have run out.

Grace felt torn between despair and defensiveness. Was it her fault she had had such a run of bad luck? Yet, as Darcy returned with two of the strangest-looking people Grace had ever seen, she had a sudden, sick feeling it was about to get worse.

'Your fellow panellists,' Darcy announced. 'This is Mandi. She's just kissed and told to the *News of the World* about her affair with a Leeds United footballer, haven't you, Mandi?'

Mandi nodded proudly. Tanned deep orange from head to foot, with blonde hair in curls which had apparently been fried, she was a truly awesome sight. Organ-stop nipples poked through a tight neon-pink top on which the word Babe was emblazoned in swirling glittery letters. Her feet towered a good eight inches above the floor in a pair of white plastic platform mules. Her only other item of clothing was a neon-green mini-skirt of a brevity that implied it did part-time work as a hair band. From between her pale pink lips, outlined in a much darker colour, dangled a cigarette.

''Sright,' said Mandi, without moving the cigarette.

'And this is Nicorette,' Darcy continued gesturing at the other girl. 'She's here to talk about the time she spent a night of passion with a certain famous fifty-something pop star. She can't say who, because it would be indiscreet.'

'It would, I suppose,' agreed Grace, surprised these girls had such scruples.

'Especially when you're in negotiation with the *Daily Star* to tell your story. Right, Nicorette?'

'Right,' said Nicorette, who had solid, muscular legs propped up on black spiked heels, and breasts the size of beach balls.

Grace's nostrils suddenly filled with a familiar, powerful perfume. 'Here I am,' announced Euphemia, bustling up, face still thick with powder. 'Has Cecil Parkinson arrived yet?'

Nicorette and Mandi stared at Euphemia with unconcealed amazement. Euphemia stared back with unconcealed disgust.

'Your fellow panellists,' Darcy explained.

Before Euphemia could respond, Mandi butted in.

''Ere,' she said to Euphemia, drawing hard on her cigarette and frowning. 'Don't I recognise you?'

Euphemia looked marginally less disgusted. She thrust out her jewelled and befurred chest. 'Well, yes, no doubt you do. After all, I *am* rather famous.'

'Fort so. You're the woman 'oo shagged that Paddy Ashdown. Aren't you?'

Pointedly, Euphemia had chosen to sit in the front for the return journey and not, as before, in the back next to Grace. She had been cold with fury after the encounter with Nicorette; even more so since the debate had ended, unable to see why her assertions that single mothers only had children to get council houses were offensive to an audience composed mainly of single mothers living in council houses. While relieved not to have to suffer the immediate proximity of Euphemia's frozen silence, Grace was hardly more cheered to have Henry Moon as a neighbour in the back. That he had been disgusted by the events of the evening and her part in them could not have been more clear. His brow was riven with frownlines and he kept passing a hand across his eyes in an exasperated manner.

What made Grace feel worse was the memory of how hard Henry had tried to exercise a civilising influence on the proceedings. His take on kiss and tell had been an eloquent presentation of the arguments for press freedom, which, lucid though it was, had had little impact on an audience raging with self-righteousness and free alcohol. So little impact, in fact, that he had every right to be as furious with her as Euphemia had been.

And boy, had Euphemia been furious. As the wet motorway sped by, Grace cringed at the recollection of how, as the last drunken heckler was hurling his final abuse at the panel and the end-of-programme credits were rolling, Euphemia had been on her feet screaming abuse at Grace. Having her professional abilities roundly condemned before a TV audience of millions had not been enjoyable. After Euphemia's assessment of her character as a 'useless, brainless, snotty cow' had been taken up with enthusiasm by several particularly inebriated members of the audience, Grace felt her professional career had very possibly reached its nadir.

Between Luton and Staples Corner, Henry fell asleep and remained so until the car pulled up before Euphemia's Fulham home. Slamming the car door with a ferocity to rattle every window in the area, the author swept furiously and, for once, wordlessly, off into the night.

'What was that?' asked Henry, waking with a jolt.

'Don't ask,' sighed Grace.

Henry smacked his lips and rubbed his baggy eyes, looking round in surprise. 'I feel a bit better now,' he muttered. 'Had a thumping headache before.'

He grinned at her in the orange glow of the passing streetlamps. 'I've been to some bizarre places in my time, but that,' he gestured a thumb back up the motorway, 'beats just about anything. Anthropologically speaking, as well. As a study of tribal habits, the whole thing was riveting.'

'I'm glad to hear it,' Grace said tightly. Was he laughing at her again?

'I mean, you couldn't make it up.' Henry's voice was shaking. *Definitely* laughing, Grace thought furiously. She swallowed hard. However disastrous her efforts, at least she had tried. She deserved more respect, surely. Even after what had happened at the St Merrion Festival. If only it hadn't happened. If only she'd never met Henry Moon . . .

Beside her, Henry was laughing harder. 'So much,' he snorted wetly, 'for the glamorous life of the author.'

Suddenly, Grace snapped at the driver to stop.

'I'm getting out,' she said, voice wobbly. 'Goodbye, Henry. It's been fun – obviously.'

She slammed the door even louder than Euphemia had done. As she stormed down the road, her last sight of Henry was of his surprised face looking back at her out of the window. Her very last sight of him, she vowed.

Entering her flat, exhausted and footsore, some forty minutes of walking later, Grace saw the answerphone flashing madly in the hall. Six messages. Her heart leapt unexpectedly – Henry ringing to apologise? She pressed the button.

'Darling!' Her heart subsided as Lady Armiger's tones floated commandingly into the hall. 'About this dinner. You really must let me know. I've got the most wonderful man for you to sit next to. Handsome, charming, staggeringly rich – and a Count, too. Just perfect for you, darling.'

Grace scowled. Then she became thoughtful. Was she being over-hasty, condemning the prospect out of hand? Venice, although it contained her mother, was still one of her favourite cities; should she get the odd hour here and there free from Lady Armiger-imposed duties, there were plenty of old friends to see. The Tintorettos in the Scuola Grande. The tomb of Monteverdi in the Frati. The mosaics in St Mark's, including the one of Noah and the Flood that Grace especially loved. Then the more everyday splendours – riding the Grand Canal vaporetti and meandering through the trestle tables at the Rialto fish market, watching the filleting blades of the fishmongers flashing in the sun.

Grace knew, however, that there was a good chance of

none of this happening. Her mother would take the maximum advantage of her presence; the dinner would be only one in a string of social engagements. The melancholy churches and treasure-stuffed museums, the squares with their pink-tinged lamps, the pert little bridges, the perfect vistas round every corner, the general stunning theatricality of the most romantic city in the world would be reduced to mere glimpses before she was stuffed through the entrance of yet another smart hotel to attend yet another reception as 'Have you met my daughter? She's in publishing you know.' But even that, Grace reasoned, had its advantages. The busier she was, the less time there would be to think about recent events in London. Not to mention those at a certain Midlands TV studio.

And miracles occurred. Grace doubted that the Count her mother was so desperate for her to sit next to would be anything other than the usual disappointment. But you never knew. There might yet be an upside to being young, free and single. An evening of being outrageously flattered in the candlelight of her mother's dining table might be fun, if nothing else. What did she have to lose, Grace thought, lifting the receiver.

CHAPTER ELEVEN

Belinda would have died rather than admit it, but attracting A-list celebrities to the column was not proving as simple as expected. Nowhere near as simple, in fact. There seemed no rational explanation for this. She'd had no problems raking in the Z-list for Tea Break. The A-list should have been even easier.

Adding to Belinda's frustration was Fran's glee at her failure to hook a megastar.

'Is it Judith Chalmers this week?' she would demand in a louder voice than necessary. 'Lynsey de Paul? Lesley Joseph? Jim "Nick Nick" Davidson? You need to let me know. Grayson's bound to ask me at the editorial conference.'

Belinda, to whom the toe-curling prospect of interviewing a *Big Brother* housemate – and an early-eviction one at that – was becoming increasingly real, merely scowled in reply.

Belinda had lost no time in commandeering Tarquin, the new assistant meant to be helping *The Globe*'s entire features desk, as her own personal slave and writer of interview request letters. Star journalists of her magnitude, Belinda had decided, didn't do their own admin; the fact that Mo Mills had for some ridiculous reason written all her letters herself had, Belinda reasoned, probably contributed more to her heart attack than any unscheduled additions to her piece about the Duchess of Thanet. So far, however, Tarquin's hit rate had been low. Nonexistent, in fact. Which was ridiculous. Going stellar should not be a problem.

'But Stella McCartney's said no,' Tarquin protested feebly. 'And you told me Stella Tennant was *so* five minutes ago.'

Even more ridiculous in Belinda's outraged view, was Tarquin's apparent belief that she was somehow to blame. That her interview with Champagne D'Vyne had put people off. Talk about an over-reaction, Belinda thought. She'd only made a few jokes about haddock, for Christ's sake.

'They all think it was a hatchet job,' Tarquin said. 'A deliberately nasty piece.'

'But it got four pages,' blazed back a furious Belinda.

'I think that was part of the problem.'

Well, Belinda decided, stalking into the office that morning, she'd had enough of these bloody excuses.

'I'm not entirely satisfied you're approaching this in the right way,' she snapped at Tarquin. 'Show me the letters you're sending out.'

'I send everyone the same one. It's a template. I just fill the names in.'

'Show me it.'

Tarquin obediently passed it over. Belinda screwed up her eyes and began to read.

The Globe
London

Date

Dear
I am writing to inquire whether your client, X, would be interested in being interviewed by our newspaper. *The Globe* is one of Britain's leading tabloids and has a readership of over 4 million. We look forward to hearing from you.

Yours sincerely,

Tarquin Cusk

pp Belinda Black
Celebrity Interviewer

Belinda screwed up the piece of paper and looked at Tarquin in disgust. 'Call that a request letter? On the interesting scale, that rates slightly lower than a reminder from the sodding dentist's.'

'I'm sorry,' Tarquin said huffily. 'It's just that no one told me what to write, so . . .'

'Well I'm telling you what to write *now*,' shouted Belinda. She threw herself dramatically back into her ponyskin swivel chair (on indefinite and reluctant loan from the Homes Editor), took a deep, shuddering breath and closed her eyes. In the ensuing silence, broken only by the hum of the office in the background, Tarquin, hovering with a pencil and pad, thought he could actually hear the rusty gears of Belinda's brain grinding and squeaking. The eyes snapped open.

'Right,' Belinda ordered. 'Take this down. First, the address. It should go like this.' She paused, flared her nostrils and declaimed:

'From the Desk of Belinda Black

'Celebrity Editor in Chief

'*The Globe*

'Globe Towers . . .'

Tarquin's eyes boggled slightly.

'And now the letter itself,' Belinda declared.

'Dear Celebrity Publicist! Congratulations! The day of which you have long dreamed has arrived. The Belinda Black Interview, the most prestigious slot in British journalism, has come to lay itself at the feet of your luminous client . . .'

'Um,' Tarquin interrupted, 'do you really mean luminous? It's just that at least one in every two people I write to have just come out of rehab—'

'Then you're right,' Belinda pronounced briskly. 'Luminous is *not* the word. Put "radiant" instead. Everyone looks better once they're out of the Priory.'

Tarquin sighed and scribbled this down.

'The Belinda Black Interview, the most prestigious slot in British journalism, has come to lay itself at the feet of your radiant client,' Belinda reprised, looking delighted with herself. 'So fiercely is this slot competed for by leading megastars that Meg Ryan and Sandra Bullock once came to blows over it . . .'

'Did they?' Tarquin's eyes were wide.

'Of course not,' snarled his boss. 'But there's no harm in saying so, is there? Now, the end of the letter . . .' She took a deep breath again. '*The Globe* is Britain's leading newspaper with a circulation of over ten million . . .'

'Erm,' Tarquin interrupted, 'I'm not sure that figure's strictly accurate. No newspaper in the country has a circulation that high.'

'*Accurate?* Who the hell cares about *accurate*? Do you want to get famous people in the paper or don't you?' Belinda shouted. 'Now, where was I? Oh, yes. Circulation of over ten million, no, make that fifteen. No, with a circulation of over *twenty* million. And your radiant client is of course safe in our hands . . .'

Safe, thought Tarquin, in whose ears the furious screams

of an outraged post-interview Champagne D'Vyne were still ringing. Her bloodcurdling shouts for vengeance were, in fact, starting to colour his dreams. What made matters worse was that Belinda, who had avoided taking any of the calls herself, feigned amazement that he was finding the situation difficult. 'But it's so *simple*,' she had exclaimed. 'Champagne said she wanted to make a difference to a stranger's day, and she gave a laugh to the entire nation. Next time she loses her rag, all you need to do is remind her of what she said to me. That she should trust in the lesson, rather than looking at the selfish inconvenience of the situation.' As a direct result of Champagne's hysterical reaction to this, Tarquin had developed tinnitus.

'Safe?' murmured Tarquin, fearfully. 'Are you sure?'

'No, you're right. That's *not* true.' Belinda wrinkled her brow before continuing. 'Your radiant client is *more than safe* in our hands. Because, unlike our competitors, we offer our interview subjects full copy approval . . .'

'But we *never* do that,' Tarquin interjected. 'Fran says that no one we interview must *ever* see the piece before it goes in.'

Belinda looked at him as if he was stupid. 'Well *obviously* they mustn't. And they *won't*. But there's no harm in telling them they will.' She cleared her throat and carried on. 'And full picture approval, naturally.'

A stab of terror pierced Tarquin's bowels. Of all the aspects of the interview to have angered Champagne D'Vyne, what had made her most furious was the photograph of her, breasts lolling out of her dress, eyes rolling as she sipped a glass of yellow liquid the caption claimed was her own pee. Gathering all his courage, he mentioned this.

'Well of *course* there was full picture approval,' Belinda stormed. 'Champagne herself may not have seen it, but the Editor approved of that picture very fully indeed. Look,' she added furiously. 'I'm not impressed with your attitude. Let me repeat, do you want this job or don't you?'

Tarquin swallowed. It was at times like this that he wondered whether his 'escape' from his former job on a glossy magazine to what he had imagined to be the 'real' world of newsprint was any more than an illusion. He had left *Fabulous* magazine because of an inability to face interviewing yet another entrepreneurial male aristocrat dressed up for a 'witty' shoot in a basque and fishnets, or writing yet another feature on why Padstow was sexy.

Now, however, the time his glossy mag Features Editor had made him beg, face smeared with a burnt champagne cork, first outside a fashionable London restaurant and then outside a leading merchant bank to see where he made £100 quickest, seemed like cutting-edge investigative reporting. With Belinda, Tarquin felt he had jumped from the frying pan into the fire, although admittedly, frying pans featured very little in either Belinda's world or that of the glossies he had left. From the vegetable steamer into the rice-cooker, perhaps.

Belinda, meanwhile, was ripping out a handful of glossy

magazine pages depicting stars at a film awards ceremony. 'Try writing to that lot next,' she commanded, thrusting it at him. 'Red Campion's top of the list, obviously.'

'Red Campion?' Tarquin looked disbelieving.

'Yes. Red Campion.' Belinda settled into contemplation of her favourite daydream. What an interview with him would do for her career.

Having greedily read the Campion cuttings file in the newspaper library, Belinda now knew the actor's story by heart. Entire paragraphs had lodged in her head: '*Campion shot to fame as the Roman soldier who rose from rank and file obscurity to the status of general in* Legionnaire, *the box-office-busting Roman epic which, like* Gladiator *before it, catapulted its gruff-voiced hero to international stardom. Life quickly imitated art; the enormous success of the multi-Oscar-winner catapulted Campion, the New York born actor with the melting eyes, from sitcom bit-part obscurity to being one of the biggest, brightest stars in the Hollywood firmament . . .*'

A faint sweat beaded Belinda's brow. She began to pant.

'*So many women fell hook, line and sandals for Campion's sad-eyed celluloid general that the condition was even given an official diagnosis: Legionnaire's Disease . . .*'

Legionnaire's Disease, Belinda mouthed rapturously to herself, as more remembered newspaper paragraphs unrolled in her mind.

'*The secret of his success? According to one film reviewer "a screen presence the combined equivalent of Cary Grant, Sean Connery and Leonardo di Caprio." Another dubbed Campion "the best-looking actor in a skirt and sandals – male or female – since Russell Crowe".'*

Russell Crowe. There was a problem there, Belinda remembered. According to another cutting: '*Campion famously resists comparisons to the Oscar-winning Kiwi heart-throb for reasons which some suggest stem from a belief in the superiority of his own acting and which others claim to be the result of simple jealousy* . . .' She must be sure that if – when, rather – she and Campion met face to face, she didn't mention Crowe's name. The only other potential pitfall was that Campion, apparently suspicious of the press, rarely gave interviews, although there was a rumour one had recently been done with a new American film magazine. As long as it was not with a British publication, that was not a problem.

Otherwise, Campion's press-shy antics were a positive advantage. The only thing better than an interview with a superstar, Belinda thought excitedly, is an interview with a superstar who never gives interviews. She'd turn on all the charm; he'd be unable to resist her.

Belinda thrust her breasts forward, ran her tongue round her lips and felt her nipples screw slowly out like concealed missiles on a Bond car. She *had* to get him. Or, rather, Tarquin had. She and Red were clearly made for each other. If *only* she could get near him.

'What exactly did Red Campion's office *say*?' she bellowed at Tarquin a couple of days later.

'N-n-nothing,' Tarquin stammered. His arms were twisted defensively round each other, his skinny legs were plaited together with anxiety. 'I've tried about ten different offices and I can't get an answer out of any of them.'

'You've tried the British PA, US PR, the Brit PA's PR and the US PR's PA, I take it? Following up each one with faxes, phone calls and emails? Yes? Ditto with the various agents, and the film PRs, and the PRs for the aftershave, shoes, shirts, dog food, semi-automatic rifles and whatever the hell else he's endorsing?'

'Everyone. Although, c-c-come to think of it, I haven't tried writing to his mother yet.'

'Don't be so bloody sarcastic.'

Tarquin blinked in surprise. 'I wasn't being.'

Belinda's fingers tingled with the urge to slap him. She resisted, however; Tarquin would only leave and then she would have to write all her letters herself.

'Oh, and stick in this picture with the letter, will you?'

Opening a drawer, Belinda pulled out a pile of prints and handed them to Tarquin. He stared at the image of a skimpily dressed woman, long dark hair tumbling over her tanned shoulders, limbs spilling endlessly out from a pair of Barbie-sized denim shorts. The woman's generous mouth was open in a laugh showing a row of teeth as large and white as fridges in a showroom.

'Is this you?' Tarquin asked, surprised. Belinda wasn't a bad-looking woman, but despite her best efforts with blusher, she didn't have cheekbones you could abseil off.

Her teeth, in addition, seemed to have worsened since the photograph was taken. 'You look like the young Cindy Crawford,' he added, diplomatically.

'That *is* the young Cindy Crawford,' Belinda snapped. 'Everyone says I look like her, so why waste *my* precious time posing?'

The two socialites, one dark and one blonde, faced each other across the snowy damask of the Consulate dining table. It wasn't, Grace saw, the candelabra alone that flashed in their diamonds. It was the light of battle, too.

'You have just the *two* nannies, then?' the brunette said in pitying tones. 'Really, I don't think we could cope without three. A day one, a night one and an extra one.'

Across the table, the blonde smiled pityingly. 'Yes. But in the summer we really don't need any more. We have two yachts, you see. One for us and one for the children.'

Grace watched as the brunette's perfectly manicured fingers tightened round the stem of her champagne glass. This particular dinner party of her mother's was proving livelier than most. Even though the Count she sat next to had as expected, been a let down.

Primed by her mother, Grace knew her neighbour to be possessed of wealth, a vast wine estate, several popes in his ancestry and so many names that his place card was the size of a postcard. His grooming was similarly impeccable – his clearly costly suit looked almost moulded to his back, and expensive cufflinks flashed whenever he lifted his glass. A signet ring shone on his plump little finger and he wore his thickly woven silk tie in a wide and complicated knot. His gleaming black hair was ploughed with comb marks and his cologne, whilst having the peppery whiff of Jermyn Street, exuberantly contradicted the Jermyn Street rule that perfume should whisper, not shout. Yet, as prospective son-in-law material went, Grace suspected Count Giancarlo Eugenio Albinoni Graciosi di Sforza y Visconti might ultimately prove a disappointment to her mother.

For one thing, he had not spoken a word throughout the first course. Now, as the second was served, he rolled his eyes theatrically, chewed, winced, then laid his fork discreetly beside the plate of osso bucco. Paling beneath his tan, he swallowed hard, moaned gently and dabbed at the corners of his mouth with a huge linen napkin.

Finally, and seemingly with difficulty, the Count spoke. 'You are enjoying yourself in Venezia, no?' he observed uningeniously. 'Very useful, your parents being at the Consulate. Lots of opportunities for sightseeing.'

Grace suppressed a sigh. Today, she had spent lunchtime in a darkened palazzo, her back firmly turned to tempting glimpses of the Ca'D'Oro across the Grand Canal while she listened to a lengthy account of the Third Secretary's mother's hip replacement. Tea had passed in the company of a fretful FO Under Secretary discussing the impossibility of getting Earl Grey east of Harwich.

'Oh yes,' Grace replied carefully to the Count. 'I've certainly seen some sights.' She paused, trying to think of some original observation to make. 'This afternoon, for example, I noticed how those thick wooden tripods in the water look exactly like bunches of asparagus.'

Incomprehension furrowed the Count's smooth olive brow. 'Ze *briccoli*, you mean?'

'Yes, I think so. Those poles that the boats sail between. Showing where the deep bits are . . .'

'Such an *active* imagination, Count, don't you think?' Lady Armiger called from down the table. 'We're all certain Grace is going to be a *very* great writer. The next Martin Amis, we're quite sure.'

Grace blushed furiously. Her mother couldn't – or wouldn't – understand that working in publishing didn't necessarily mean you wrote books.

The Count lifted his fork carefully to his mouth once more and slid it between his small, red lips. His face immediately creased in agony. Puzzled, Grace prodded the unyielding surface of the osso bucco. It seemed fine to her. No worse than usual, at any rate. 'Thees Martin Amees you are talking about.' The Count spoke urgently.

'Yes?'

'I am interested in heem. I admire heem very much. Hees enormous courage.'

Grace nodded. 'He's certainly never afraid to tackle controversial topics. His autobiography, for instance—'

'No, no. Not ze books.' Grinning manically, the Count gestured agitatedly at two rows of wonky molars. 'As you see, I am very scared of ze denteest. I admire Amees very much for having all zat work done on his tith.' The Count then launched into an eye-rolling, hand-waving account of the dental agonies he had suffered in the recent past: '. . . and then my dentist he say, just sit there while I grind down your stump. Grind down your stump! Can you imageen?'

Grace had never been so glad of her mother's custom of making guests change places for pudding. After the stomach-churning description of the Count's orthodontal sufferings, it was almost a relief to spend dessert next to an NFT representative called Howard who'd been attending the Venice Film Festival.

'How glamorous!' Grace exclaimed. 'Didn't I read somewhere that Red Campion was going to be there?'

From behind thick Buddy Holly spectacles, Howard's eyes narrowed. 'Logistical nightmare, apparently.'

Grace was intrigued. 'Really? Hundreds of screaming girls throwing knickers, that sort of thing?'

Howard sighed dramatically. 'All that. But the real problem, of course, was the fact Russell Crowe was there as well.'

'Why was that a problem?'

Howard looked aghast. 'You mean you don't know?'

Grace reddened. 'Know what?'

'Campion can't stand Crowe. It's Hollywood's worst-kept secret. I thought *everyone* knew.'

His know-all air was intensely annoying. 'But why not? He was wonderful in *Gladiator*.'

'That's the problem,' Howard flashed back smartly. '*Legionnaire* did well. But *Gladiator* did better.'

'Seems like splitting hairs,' Grace observed. 'Red Campion's hugely famous, after all.'

Howard pursed his lips superciliously. 'Not famous enough, obviously.'

'But isn't Campion supposed to hate all that Hollywood superstar stuff?' Grace vaguely remembered reading something of the sort somewhere.

'They all say that,' Howard replied crushingly.

'Well I enjoyed *Legionnaire* very much,' Grace said determinedly. Although, now she came to think of it, doing so had been just as hard fought a battle as any Campion had been involved with on the screen. Beside her, throughout the film, Sion had tutted and muttered frequently and disapprovingly about Roman militarism and empire-building.

Howard sighed patronisingly. 'It was OK, I suppose. Could have done with an edit, though.'

'Did you meet Red?' Grace asked excitedly.

Howard looked shifty. 'Not exactly.'

'What? Not at all?'

'He was off to London almost immediately,' Howard returned defensively. 'To film that new Guy Ritchie movie, *Concrete Boots*. But he's impossible, anyway.'

'How do you know?' demanded Grace. 'Considering you haven't met him,' she added wickedly.

Howard looked furious. 'No, but I've read the *Trailer* interview.'

'What's *Trailer*?' asked Grace.

'New American film magazine. Surely you've heard of it?' Howard looked at her pityingly. 'No? The first issue's got an interview with Red in it. Very dodgy stuff – all about dumping his wife by email and being a sex addict.'

'I can't believe it,' Grace was surprised at how shocked she felt. Red's grave screen soldier had, when she had been allowed to concentrate on the performance, seemed the model of courage and probity. It was impossible that the actor who played him didn't share at least some of the same qualities.

Howard smiled a superior smile.

Grace speared a strawberry, noticing, as she and Howard lapsed into silence, that the two elegant women were still at each other's powdered throats.

'I love your little Dior bag,' called the blonde piercingly to the brunette. 'I've got one exactly like it.' She paused to pat her perfect chignon before adding, patronisingly, 'But they're rather too small to carry things in, don't you find?'

'Put things in?' The brunette's capped teeth glittered pitilessly in the candlelight. 'What an extraordinary idea. Who needs to carry anything anywhere when you have a limo?'

They seemed, Grace realised, to be vying for the attention of the man sitting on the other side of her, to whom, so far, she had not spoken. Feeling guilty, she turned and smiled at her neighbour. The women's interest in him seemed surprising; there was nothing, on the face of it, to suggest he knew anything about limos, yachts or any of the other trappings of wealth that so obviously motivated them.

Grace's neighbour was, not to put too fine a point on it, *huge*. He looked both too large and too long for the tiny gilt chair on which he perched like a drum on a pea. He was clearly not a man for whom appearance was a priority; his hair, as thick as a dog's coat, badly needed a trim, while his eyes, fringed with pale eyelashes, were almost entirely hidden behind a scrubland of sandy brow. His bull-like forehead was coloured a deep brick red and split by wrinkles as wide as ruts. He looked, in short, like someone who spent a great deal of time outside. His place card, bearing just the two words, was similarly unpretentious. Bill Duke, it said.

Grace wondered what he did for a living. Her mother, rushing from kitchen to boudoir all afternoon, had not drilled her on anyone apart from the Count. But usually with her mother's guests, occupation guessing was not difficult. Signet rings, old school ties and absence of chin generally meant junior Foreign Office recruits. Wandering hands meant visiting MPs. But Duke offered no clues. His huge red hands were not only innocent of a wedding or signet ring, but stayed firmly clasped round his eating irons. Professionally speaking, he looked almost exactly poised between a building site foreman and a council waste operative.

'So you write for a living,' Bill Duke remarked, returning her smile. He spoke, she noticed, with a Texan drawl.

Both blonde and brunette, Grace sensed, had stopped trading insults and were watching her closely.

'Um, no, not exactly.' Grace realised her voice sounded thick. Perhaps she had been hitting the wine rather hard. As always, her mother's admonishments to drink as little as possible 'on duty' had had the opposite effect. But you needed lubrication to tolerate the likes of Howard and the Count. The experiences of recent weeks, moreover, had receded pleasantly in the face of some fruity red.

Duke met her eye with a stare like a blowtorch. 'So you're *not* a writer?'

'No, I'm not,' Grace admitted, rather crossly. After all, it wasn't she who had made this claim for herself. 'I work for a publishing company though.'

'Publishing, huh?' His perfectly round, bright eyes were fixed on hers.

'Called Hatto & Hatto.'

Duke took a sip of water. 'Never heard of 'em.'

Grace was unsurprised. It would have been amazing if he had. People in London had no idea the firm existed, and Duke was a Texan.

'I never read books,' said Bill Duke.

'Really? Why not?'

'They're pretty dull.'

'But what about the way books distil experience?' she demanded, woozily outraged. 'Travel, for instance. And romance . . .' Grace stopped. Publishing, after all, had brought her little of that. Down the table, the two listening women stiffened. Their diamonds glittered agitatedly in the candlelight.

'Numbers have a romance of their own, y'know,' Bill Duke was saying.

'But would you deny that books take you places emotionally and imaginatively that you never thought you would go?' She had to stand up for her trade, Grace felt. No matter how bad she was at it personally.

Duke drummed thick fingers on the table. 'In mah experience, money has taken me much further than any book could.' There was a rustle from the women at this. 'Ah'm not, in any case, all that interested in other people's experiences. Unless there's a way Ah can make money out of them.'

'Not everything boils down to money, you know,' Grace said, feeling suddenly cross. 'Some things are much more important.' The blonde and brunette exchanged astonished looks at this.

'Sure they are.' Duke spooned up zabaglione.

'Of course,' Lady Armiger interjected from down the table, 'the real reason Grace went into publishing was to mix with the stars.' She beamed encouragingly from Duke to Grace.

'That true?' Duke looked surprised.

'No,' Grace said, exasperated. 'We're very small and specialised. We have a tiny office in Bloomsbury. London,' she added. Duke did not look like someone familiar with the celebrated literary stamping ground.

He raised an eyebrow. 'I know it.'

'Oh, but I'm sure you meet *some* rich and famous writers,' Lady Armiger called.

'Not really,' snapped Grace, reddening with embarrassment and alcohol. 'Hatto & Hatto don't really *do* rich and famous. We specialise in obscure and unsuccessful – I mean, authors with a more selective appeal.'

'But why?' Duke asked.

Grace felt irritation well within her. Could this philistine not understand anything unconnected to profit? 'Because we're *literary*,' she exploded. 'We try to publish quality,' she added, trying not to think of Euphemia Ogden.

'Darling! You're just making excuses. Tell Mr Duke which well-known authors you look after,' instructed Lady Armiger sternly.

Grace suppressed a groan. She took a slug of wine. 'There's Euphemia Ogden,' she muttered to Duke. 'I suppose she's our best-known one.'

'Euphemia Ogden!' The blonde and brunette giggled and sipped at their wine.

'*Euphemia Ogden?*' Duke rolled the name round his tongue. '*Hell* of a name.'

'Yes, and she's a hell of a – I mean, she's quite a personality.' I really should stop drinking this, Grace thought, taking another sip of wine.

'She successful?'

'Well, she's written a bestseller. Called *Pease Pudding Polly*.'

Duke's eyes widened. At the end of the table, Lady Armiger's head was bobbing encouragingly up and down like a toy dog on a dashboard.

'Who else?' Duke demanded.

Grace sighed and reached again for her glass. 'Inigo Thongsbridge? He wrote a book called *The Curate's Ego*.'

The light of speculation seemed to gleam, somewhat unexpectedly, in Duke's eye. 'What's that about?'

'It's a sort of satirical reworking of the Dead Sea Scrolls based around the martyrdom of Joan of Arc who is inhabiting the body of an artist in residence at . . .' Grace paused. Had she got that right? It sounded odd, but then, everything about Inigo Thongsbridge was odd.

'It win any prizes?'

'Not as such,' Grace said carefully. 'But his *The Cortina Monologues*, an account in four voices of the journey of a back-seat driver through the Argentinian pampas, was shortlisted for a prize.' She was determined to withhold the fact that the laurels in question were the Ford Cortina Fan Club Lifetime Achievement Award.

'Who else, darling? Come on,' urged her mother.

There was really only one left. The very man she had come here to escape. Did she really have to mention him? She cleared her throat, blinked and tried her best to sound casual. 'Er – Henry Moon? Author of *Sucking Stones*?'

There was a pause. Sucking *what*?' asked Duke.

'It's an autobiographical account of a journey to discover

a forgotten tribe who sit round in circles with pebbles in their mouths. He's the last of the gentlemen explorers . . .' Grace stopped her automatic gabble, realising that, actually, she didn't consider Henry Moon much of a gentleman any more.

'Maybe you've heard of Tenebris Luks?' Grace added, struck by sudden inspiration. How could she have forgotten *him*? 'Author of *A Humorous Look At Pain*?'

Duke's eyes bulged slightly. 'Tenebris . . . *who*?'

Grace felt a wave of envy. The blessed ignorance of not knowing who Tenebris was. 'Luks,' she repeated.

'Wow,' said Duke. 'Go on.'

Grace gritted her teeth, wishing desperately she had never mentioned him. Until now, she had managed successfully to blank out the memory, of the one and only time she had accompanied Tenebris to a bookshop reading.

'This guy Tenebris,' Duke prompted. 'Is he handsome?'

'Er . . .' Possibly handsome was *not* the word. It had been a shock for Grace, who had not met Tenebris in the flesh before, to realise that the deranged-looking middle-aged man with undone flies, bottle-bottomed glasses and a tea-cosy hat pulled over his face, who had emerged from the bookshop audience ten minutes after Tenebris Luks, apparently not yet present, was due to have started his reading, was in fact Tenebris Luks. The bookshop manager had not been impressed.

'I'm sorry,' Grace had gasped. 'These authors. They're . . . um . . . artists, you know.'

'And I can tell you exactly what *sort* of artist as well,' snarled the manager.

'Tenebris is . . . um . . . *interesting*-looking,' Grace told Duke now.

'And what's he like?'

'Um . . . eccentric.' Grace shuddered as the details of Tenebris's performance sprang effortlessly back to mind. How he had grabbed a copy of *A Humorous Look At Pain*, thrown it up into the air, let it crash on the floor and started to read from the opened page. Upside down, Grace noticed.

'Let's fuck,' Tenebris had screeched at the audience, and in particular at a couple of old ladies in the front row resting their legs during a shopping outing. To Grace's horror, a protracted sex scene then followed, involving repeated use of the word c**t and punctuated for dramatic emphasis by frequent thrusts forward of Tenebris's open-flied crotch. After what seemed like years, the reading was over and a silence like a pall descended on the audience. The old ladies staggered out, one distinctly blue around the lips.

'He's original,' she muttered to Duke, who, from the close way he was looking at her, seemed to be divining something of her thoughts.

'And you do the publicity for these guys?' he mused.

'Yes, I do.' Grace answered defensively.

'Must be pretty tough.'

'It's a challenge. But I like challenges.'

'Like challenges, huh? I take my hat off to yuh. What

you do must be about as thankless as publicity gets. How the hell do you do it?'

'This zabaglione's delicious, isn't it?' Grace said, changing the subject with all the subtlety of a car passenger suddenly grabbing the wheel to avoid crashing into a lamppost. She was surprised when Duke, taking the hint with a speed and sensitivity she would not have credited him with, began immediately to talk about Italian food. About which, even more surprisingly he seemed to know rather a lot. Certainly more, Grace guessed, than her mother's cook, whose store cupboards, disconcertingly for a professional Italian chef, contained tinned spaghetti.

Five minutes later, however, Duke returned to the attack.

'So you don't have any famous authors?' he asked. 'None at all. No Martin Amis? Zilch, zip, nada?'

Grace shook her head wearily. 'As I've said, Hatto & Hatto don't do celebrity authors. We're old-fashioned. Publishing as it used to be, if you like. Our office is small, eccentric, and in Bloomsbury. Not a hideous, vast multinational with a plate-glass palace, thousands of staff and TV, film and advertising arms as well as the publishing one. We select our writers for the sake of their work, not their profile.' Well, she had believed it all once. She drained her glass of Friuli with a reckless air.

Duke signalled for a refill. 'What's the boss of Hatto & Hatto like?'

Now heartily sick of the subject, Grace picked up her

wine and explained baldly that the owner of Hatto & Hatto was an octogenarian who spent all his time on the French Riviera. No one in the London office – the only office – had ever seen him. She was surprised to see Duke's eyebrows shoot into his hairline.

'What about board meetings? Who runs it day to day?'

Grace took another slurp of wine and told him about Adam Knight.

Five minutes later, she was still talking. Duke's brows were still pointing skywards. They went intergalactic after she mentioned Adam's habit of leaving manuscripts on buses. But why? Why did he give a damn? Grace was, however, too tired and too inebriated to find out.

The coffee was handed round and the evening began to draw to a close. Bill Duke was one of the first to leave, his departure adding a bitter edge to the internecine struggle between the blonde and brunette. 'Of course *I* know it isn't true, darling,' Grace heard one gushing to the other as they wrapped their cashmeres about them in the hall. 'But I think you need to put a stop to those rumours that your staff are so badly treated they've formed a support group.'

Having closed the door on the last guest, Lady Armiger rushed back into the drawing room and threw her small, compact body into an armchair.

'You should have *seen* it,' she gasped. 'It was *huge*. Black. Thick. *Disgusting*.'

'What was?' asked Grace's father.

It was then that Grace learnt that the Notes To Staff criticisms concerning the evening in her mother's entertaining diary would read as follows: *Primo Piatto* – Pasta Primavera (Not Drained Properly. Peas Hard); *Secondo Piatto* – Osso Bucco (Tough. Plates Cold); and, most damning of all: *Dolce* – Zabaglione (Found A Moustache Hair!!!).

Grace hid her smile behind her hand. Her father, meanwhile, turned his back for significantly longer than usual whilst throwing some ice cubes into a whisky glass.

'Oh God!' suddenly exclaimed Lady Armiger. Horror-struck, her small, round face bore an astonishing resemblance to a surprised boiled egg. 'The most appalling thought's just struck me. Imagine if the Count had a moustache hair in *his* zabaglione as well. Now I come to think of it, he didn't look very impressed with the food. Hardly ate anything.'

'I'm not sure he's got grounds to object to the food, darling,' said Sir Anthony, reasonably. 'Actually, *I* wasn't entirely convinced about the drink. I know the Albinoni Graciosi di Sforza y Visconti vineyards have been in the family for over six hundred years but quite frankly it tasted as if the wine had as well.'

Lady Armiger's eyes widened in horror. 'But darling, we absolutely *have* to keep buying it.'

'Why? That Friuli practically took the lining of my throat off. Expensive, too.'

Lady Armiger drummed her fingers excitedly on the chair

arm and lowered her voice to a conspiratorial hiss. 'Because the Count's very interested in *Grace*, of course.'

Grace was indignant. 'He's not.'

'He *certainly* is. You got off to a slow start, admittedly.' Lady Armiger pressed her lips together. 'But at the end he was eating out of your hand.'

Well, he certainly wasn't eating from anywhere else, Grace thought.

'He was obviously trying to impress you. Darling, don't look at me like that.' Lady Armiger's little eyes were burning with excitement. 'And the family's so much grander than I thought! Of course, I knew about the popes and everything, but, my dear! The Count was talking to you for *hours* about having a new crown fitted.'

'Mum! He meant his *tooth*.'

'*Oh*.'

It was not often, Grace reflected, that she saw her mother lost for words. She was quick to press home her advantage.

'Look, I'm not really his type, Mum.'

'Of coursc you are, darling.' Lady Armiger's tone was determined. Blinking her eyes innocently at her daughter, she ran her thumb backwards and forwards behind her pearls.

'Apart from anything else,' Grace argued, 'the Count was quite obviously a friend of Dorothy.'

Lady Armiger looked astonished. 'But your Great Aunt Dorothy hasn't left Eastbourne for thirty years. Where on earth would she have met the Count?'

'She means he's *gay*, Annabel,' Sir Anthony sighed from behind his newspaper.

'*Oh.*' Disappointment flickered for a few moments in Lady Armiger's small bright eyes before her countenance blazed once again with intrigue.

'But did you enjoy meeting Bill, darling?' she questioned Grace eagerly. 'Quite a chap, isn't he?'

'I suppose so,' Grace said neutrally.

'What did you talk about?'

'Books, that's all. And publishing.'

Lady Armiger nodded, pleased. 'Very good. He would have liked that. And he did, you could see. Lady Thicknesse and the Countess of Thyn were furious. They were *dying* to get their hands on him. Tongues practically hanging out. Not to mention everything else they had.'

'Yes, I saw that. But why?'

Lady Armiger looked at her daughter in amazement. '*Why?* What do you mean, *why*? I explained to you before dinner, didn't I?'

Grace shook her head. 'You were too busy briefing the staff. I hardly saw you . . .'

Lady Armiger closed her eyes and groaned. 'You mean to tell me . . .'

'What?'

'. . . that you didn't know?'

'Know what?'

Lady Armiger's eyes were still shut. 'That, after the Count, Bill was the person I most wanted you to meet?

Why else do you think I sat you next to him for pudding?'

'But *why*?'

'Because,' Lady Armiger wailed, crashing both fists against her chair arms like a disappointed child, 'Bill Duke is one of the fifty richest men in America. He's just divorced his third wife . . .'

'*Ah*,' said Grace, understanding.

'Darling!' Her mother had caught the sarcasm in her tone. 'Just because someone is rich is no reason to dislike them. If rich people are dull, poor people can be duller. As I think you've probably discovered.'

'So what does Bill Duke do then?' asked Grace, determined to change the subject.

'He's a media mogul, darling.' The wail had returned to her mother's voice.

'What?'

'We first met him as editor of one of the local Washington papers when we were posted there. Then of course he bought it, expanded the business and now he's president of a multinational.' Lady Armiger paused and sighed. 'Offices all over the world,' she moaned softly. 'Plate-glass palaces, apparently, with literally thousands of staff.'

Grace felt uncomfortable. Her own words came back to her. *Our office is small, eccentric, and in Bloomsbury, not a hideous, vast multinational with a plate-glass palace, thousands of staff . . .*

It was a little embarrassing, but that was all. Duke ran a newspaper company. Just as well it wasn't anything else. In retrospect, his questions about Hatto & Hatto had been both detailed and interested; her answers possibly fuller than strict politeness demanded. If Duke had turned out to be involved in book publishing, it might have been cause for concern.

'So Duke's a newspaper baron?'

'Amongst other things.' Her mother sounded anguished now. 'The company has lots of other interests. TV, film and advertising arms, of course. He was here at the Film Festival in connection with the film side of it, in fact . . .'

. . . *Thousands of staff and TV, film and advertising arms* . . . Oh God, Grace thought . . . *as well as the publishing one* . . .

'And of course there's a publishing one,' said Lady Armiger.

'Publishing?' Grace repeated in muffled tones.

Lady Armiger's mouth was a thin, unhappy line. 'Oh yes. Several publishing houses, all over the world. Darling, what's the matter? You don't look at all well. In fact, you look rather green . . . Darling? Perhaps you ought to go to bed?'

CHAPTER TWELVE

It was better than nothing, Belinda supposed. Nonetheless, it was a disappointment that her new, improved interview request letter, plus photograph, had elicted a yes from only one person.

'Brian Stone, of the Brian Stone Experience?' Belinda had yelled in disgust when Tarquin had given her the news. 'That old sixties scarecrow? I thought he was dead.'

'Not at all,' Tarquin assured her.

'*Looks* dead, at any rate.' Belinda scrutinised what claimed to be a recent newspaper clipping of a wizened, prune-faced man with a stringy mullet and tight leather trousers, his arm round a girl who, under her clear plastic dress, wore nothing but the tiniest of thongs.

'He's one of the great rock and roll survivors,' Tarquin

told her breathlessly. 'His latest greatest hits album, *Balls Out*, went double platinum . . .'

Belinda looked back at the photograph thoughtfully. He might look like a superannuated weasel, but Stone would certainly have a million or so salted away. If she could keep the contents of her stomach down, it could be worth a punt. 'Give me the address,' she snapped at Tarquin.

And so it was that, for Belinda, the Brian Stone Experience began in a drawing room distinguished by a sea of blue shagpile carpet in which was woven the rock star's initials in bright yellow. It was here that Stone's butler had left her after revealing, in a dignified monotone, that his master was delayed because 'sir decided his hair needed to be bigger'. A faint growling sound, as of an industrial-strength hairdryer, could be faintly detected in the house's upper echelons.

Belinda busied herself by making notes about the drawing room décor. Every window had leaded panes, the diagonal diamonds looking exactly as if a pair of giant fishnet tights had been stretched over the aperture. *Striving for Middle Eastern opulence*, Belinda scribbled spitefully, *but falling some two thousand miles short of it near Felixstowe*. What else could be said of the souk-style white drapery at the windows, the scallop-backed sofas piled with gold-festooned cushions, the brass trays crammed with thin-spouted coffee jugs, the bunches of onyx grapes and, most of all, the model yacht in a glass case, complete with tiny Jacuzzi and named *Tits Out For The Lads*? On the other hand . . . What on earth was she thinking of? Belinda stopped. Stone would no doubt take her frank assessment of his décor personally. This would not necessarily help her cause. Besides, when she was mistress of what, for all its decorative shortcomings, was an eminently acceptable Chelsea townhouse, she could make whatever changes she liked.

Growing bored, Belinda wandered through to the dining room. Here the overwhelmingly fake Tudor mood was set by a long baronial table apparently laid for a banquet. A pile of plates topped by a napkin mitre marked each place setting, accompanied by a crowd of thickly cut glassware. Spreading out either side of the dishes was at least a foot of silver-gilt eating equipment, including grape scissors. Each piece bore the initials BS in flowing letters.

'Hey, babe.' A gravelly voice, part Cockney, part mid-Atlantic, suddenly addressed her from behind. Belinda, whirling round, saw, lounging in the doorway, a skinny man in a too-small red silk robe festooned with dragons. This hung open to reveal a chest covered in medallions. The hairdresser, she noted, had done a good job. Or, rather, a thorough one. Above a knot of tanned and wizened features, backcombed spiky locks dyed a determined shade of black rose like the top of a coconut to double the height of his head. They streamed down over the red silk shoulders almost as far as his elbows.

'Yer don't look much like yer phodograph,' drawled Brian Stone in his nasal Leytonstone-LA hybrid. 'Yer look older.'

Belinda struggled to rein in her temper. The cheek of the

man. For Stone himself had obviously made strenuous efforts to keep the march of time at bay. Up close, he had had so many face-lifts he almost looked Chinese.

But Belinda forced a dazzling smile across her face, nevertheless. She hadn't come here to find fault. She had come here to find a rich husband. She rammed her elbows together, forcing her cleavage upwards.

'Cam and siddown.' Stone beckoned her through into the drawing room. 'Like the yacht?' he asked, as they passed *Tits Out*. 'Bewdiful, isn't she? Cost me millions. Disco, health club, cinema and everything. Ten state rooms. Three swimming pools. Only wish I could remember where I'd moored the bloody thing.'

Belinda's eyes bulged. Was this a joke? Must be. No one lost yachts. Especially not yachts as big as this. Privately, she thought *Tits Out* resembled nothing so closely as a huge, hi-tech training shoe. But that was hardly the point. She tried to think of a witty response. 'Didn't Ted Heath,' she asked him, 'compare sailing to standing under a shower tearing up five pound notes?'

This seemed to ring few bells with Stone. 'Hundred pound notes, more like. And 'oo the hell's Ted Heath, anyway?'

Belinda stared. 'But you must remember him,' she blustered. 'He was Prime Minister in the sixties, I think . . .' Her voice trailed away, suddenly not entirely sure. Had it been the seventies? Or the fifties?

Stone shrugged. 'Babe, I can't remember a bleedin' thing

about the sixties. Or about anything else come to that. You know the saying, if you can remember the sixties—'

'I know,' Belinda smiled knowingly. 'But everyone says that.'

'Yeah, but in my case it's true. All one big blur to me. Stone by name, stoned by nature. Why do you think I've got me bloody initials everywhere? I'd forget 'oo I bleedin' was, otherwise. It's true, isn't it, er . . .?' Stone turned to the butler who had just shimmied back across the monogrammed carpet.

'Benson, sir,' said the butler. His slight martyrish air hinted they had this conversation several times a day.

'I forget, don't I . . . er . . . Benson?'

'You do, sir.'

'Have me name everywhere,' Stone added. 'Even in the bottom of me swimming pool, if you look outside.'

Belinda looked outside. An immaculate green lawn stretched away before her, into the middle of which a swimming pool had been set. Swirling in yellow script across its blue mosaic bottom were indeed the inevitable letters, although it was not this that attracted Belinda's attention. The pool, long, straight and ending in a round pool at the top, was the exact shape of a penis. With, at the very top of the round pool, a busily foaming Jacuzzi.

'Only pool shaped like that in the world,' Stone told her.

'I can imagine.'

'No one else has got a microphone-shaped one. No one. Have they, er . . .?'

'*Benson*,' said Belinda and the butler in unison.

'Want to come upstairs?' Stone asked Belinda.

Belinda, of course, wanted nothing more. Yet she could not quite prevent a feeling of repulsion as she followed the thin, fuzzy-haired legs beneath the flapping bathrobe up the stairs. She checked the tape recorder in her pocket was working. It was, although given the state of Stone's memory, Belinda suspected that it would be largely useless. What was needed here was a medium, not a journalist.

Stone showed her into a room that was evidently his den. Two large leather chesterfields stood facing each other across yet more wastes of monogrammed carpet. Six electric guitars stood along one wall, while the one opposite was dominated by a large black painting.

'Picked that up for millions years ago,' Stone remarked.

Belinda was interested. 'Who's it by?' Someone famous, and valuable, hopefully.

Stone looked at her in amazement. 'How the hell should I know?'

Belinda looked at the next picture, a view of a yacht-stuffed port. 'Is this Monte Carlo?' she asked.

Stone shrugged. 'Might be. Think I lived there with one of the wives. Sod that though. Come and look at my walk-in wardrobe.'

Belinda followed him through a door at one end of the den into a small room crammed with garish stage suits. 'I'd like to be remembered for my fashion sense,' Stone declared, pulling out a lime-green jacket of dazzling brightness and a fuchsia suit encrusted with rhinestones.

Belinda laughed loudly, until she realised he wasn't.

'Oh, I think you will be,' she assured him, trying to avert her fascinated gaze from the pair of tiny gold shorts he wore beneath the Japanese robe.

'I'm very keen on fashion,' Stone added. 'I like to look sharp. I'm a stylish dresser.'

Belinda noticed, as he spoke, that Stone's latest operation had been on his eyelids. It did not seem to have been entirely successful. He was completely unable to blink.

She followed Stone back into the den. He pointed her in the direction of one of the chesterfields before quickly locking the door and pocketing the key. 'Don't want intruders, do we?' He grinned wolfishly. 'Might disturb me memory flow.' His medallions clanked like wind chimes as he leant close to her. 'Tell me,' he drawled, 'what turns you on about interviewing stars?'

Belinda tried to keep her sudden-leaping nausea under control. 'Because I hope some of their magic will rub off on me,' she murmured, hoping nothing of Stone was going to rub off on her. At least, not until the engagement ring was on her finger.

His eyes gleamed. 'I used to be a bit of a stud, you know.' Belinda swallowed. From where she was sitting, the only studs visible were those on the leather chesterfields.

She lunged desperately for her notebook. 'So, you began life in a back street in Hackney. You've come a long way since your childhood.'

Stone raised his eyebrows resignedly. 'Hey, where I grew up we were so poor we couldn't afford to pay attention. Or so I read in everything that's ever been written about me . . . Look, do we really have to talk about it?'

Belinda dredged about for some sympathy. 'Not if it's painful for you,' she murmured, eyes wide with hastily summoned understanding.

'It's not that. More that I can't remember any of it. But now you mention pain . . .' Stone's face suddenly contorted in an expression of agony. Belinda watched amazed, as he began yelping and clutching his thigh.

'What's the matter?' Belinda, terrified, was suddenly assailed with images of headlines of the MYSTERY ROCK STAR DEATH – GIRL HELD variety. Much as she longed to make the front page with a rich and famous man, this was not ideally how she imagined it happening.

'It's me bleedin' groin,' gasped Stone, his hand now plunged between his tiny gold-shorted legs. 'Always happens when I try and remember something. Ow. Ow. *Ow!*'

Belinda watched in fearful horror as, continuing to clutch the affected area, Stone dragged himself across the monogrammed carpet to a small cupboard where, after frantic rummaging, he produced a bottle. 'This is what we need,' he muttered, staggering back towards Belinda and thrusting the bottle into her hands. She stared as, on the floor next to the sofa, Stone slowly lowered himself; more to the point lowered the gold shorts.

'Yer know what to do,' he told her, wincing.

'I don't,' Belinda said hoarsely.

'Yer bleedin' well do,' Stone growled.

'I don't,' she yelped.

Stone's eyes snapped open. 'Rub in the bleedin' oil,' he barked urgently.

'Rub it in where?'

Slipping his shorts past his hips, Stone exposed his veiny, brown and wrinkly penis, coiled in the mass of grey hair like a bald and newborn gerbil. 'In there!' he said triumphantly.

After a momentary hesitation, Belinda gritted her teeth and stuck a finger in the ointment. Whoever had said that sleeping your way to the top was the easy option? This had better be worth it.

As the seatbelt sign bonged off, Grace waved away the stewardess's offer of champagne. If only, she thought ruefully, she had waved the wine away at her mother's dinner. It was obvious now why Bill Duke had been so keen to fill her glass.

How pathetic Duke must think her, working for a company with so little idea of what it was doing. How Hatto must pale and shrivel beside his own can-do, no-shit, balls-out, ambitious and successful business. Small wonder, listening to her spelling out Hatto's managerial philosophy, he had looked so surprised. Amazed even.

She shifted uncomfortably in her seat, piercingly ashamed of her disloyalty. Hatto & Hatto might not exactly be listed in the Footsie, but they *had* had the good manners to give her a job when few other firms – *no* other firms, in fact – had been similarly inclined. Surely they deserved more from her than a stream of red-wine-fuelled invective delivered to a complete stranger? She wondered uneasily what he would do with her information. Inside information, moreover, which he had got, if not quite on false pretences then certainly without being entirely straight. But was what had happened entirely his fault?

Grace closed her eyes and groaned. What was done was done. The in-flight magazine looming uninvitingly, she rummaged in her bag in the hope of finding something other than old taxi receipts to read.

Her fingers brushed against something thin, wide and bent in half – ah yes. Of course. The dreaded brown envelope. Containing the story by Maria's client, the verray nice man. Which, for all her promises, she still had not read.

Grace drew the envelope out. Bound to be crap, of course. Unsolicited manuscripts almost always were. Although normally they were better presented at least, usually in clear plastic folders full of well-spaced typescript. As receptacles for genius went, Grace thought, examining the creased, stained and battered A4 envelope covered with mysterious East European postmarks, this one looked unlikely.

Still, the sooner she read it, the sooner she could tell Maria why Hatto could not publish it. Fortunately, there wasn't much of it – a mere couple of chapters, Grace noted with relief. Obviously a work in progress. Well, after this it wouldn't progress much further.

She cleared her throat, sighed slightly and let her eyes drift unenthusiastically over the first page.

THE NEDS OF TWINKY BAY: *A story for children.*

A *children*'s story. Aimed at possibly the most competitive area of all. Grace knew, as did everyone in publishing, that since the staggering success of Harry Potter the children's book market had become saturated with authors dashing off books about young wizards. Hatto & Hatto, however, had had almost less success in children's literature than in any other area, impossible though that seemed.

There was probably no point in reading further. But she had promised Maria. And, somehow knowing she would never hear the end of it if she didn't, Grace propped her chin on her hand and started to read it.

When I was a child in Ireland, we lived near Twinky Bay. It was a place of magical power – and magical people. Every night, a family of Irish gypsies, the Neds, would be jigging up and down on the sand, dancing by the sea. Every adventure began in the same way. Lying, sleepless, in my little white bed, I would hear the music from their violins winding up through the darkness. It seemed to be calling me. I would slip out of bed and, tiptoeing past the sleeping cat, whispering 'Hush' to the wakeful dog, I would slink through the garden as stealthy as a fox.

Grace furrowed her brow. Hmm. Not bad. Quite sweet, really.

> *. . . down the tiny, winding steps at the end that led to the beach. Within seconds I would be with the Neds on the shore. Once at Twinky Bay, I would join in the dancing, which would get faster and faster and wilder and wilder until eventually we would all be whisked off the ground altogether and be hurled into the air. Then the real adventures began . . .*

This would never be published. And even if it were, it would never sell, not in the crowded children's book marketplace. An unknown author. A first book. And yet, reading on, Grace felt the tug on her imagination. She felt herself floating over the rooftops with the little boy in his pyjamas and the charismatic band of flying gypsies taking him to faraway lands. She found herself laughing, then, on the next page, felt the sudden sting of tears. Whoever had written this was a gifted storyteller. A true spinner of yarns. It seemed incredible that in reality he was a bald single man in a vest with a crippling lack of self confidence. After lingering, regretfully, on the last page, Grace folded the manuscript and put it back in Maria's envelope. Which incidentally, looked rather more like a receptacle for genius than it had done before. Then she sat back and thought.

Her fingers softly tapped the greasy manila. The story

was obviously a long way from finished. Just as obvious, however, was that it was something out of the ordinary.

Grace thought about Ellie. What would she make of it? No doubt, Grace thought, I'm wrong about this manuscript being any good. But there would be no harm in showing it to Ellie, surely? Ellie, after all, was constantly combing Adam's slush pile for undiscovered works of genius, saying it had been around for so many years there was probably some unpublished Shakespeare in it.

And of course, if a miracle occurred, if Ellie *did* like it, if the story *was* published, then, Grace thought, she would have atoned in some small way for her recent indiscretions. For if there was ever a time when Hatto needed her help it was now. Morale had hit an unprecedented low. Ellie was becoming ever more cynical and despairing and Adam had even left Euphemia Ogden on the bus the other day. In manuscript rather than flesh and blood form, but once the novelist returned from her annual Tuscan break, there would be hell to pay. Inigo Thongsbridge and Tenebris Luks were agitating for more money, despite barely selling into double figures between them. Gladys the secretary, meanwhile, was relishing her favourite role of prophetess of doom. 'I've seen bad times at Hatto,' she would say. 'Very bad. But none so bad as now.'

Things were, if anything, worse in the sales department, whose latest Head, a furtive ex-teacher called Philip, was still reeling from the fact that his first call on his first morning had been to the manager of the bookshop electrified by Tenebris Luks. Gladys had since reported several sightings of Philip scouring the *Times Educational Supplement* with a haunted expression.

I *must*, Grace decided, try harder. If she redoubled – *retripled* – her efforts in the PR department it *had* to make a difference. She hadn't rolled with the punches lately. She'd indulged in despondency over the smallest details, so, now, she would simply have to be tougher. More out there, less inhibited. Enough time and energy had been wasted, on stupid incidentals like Henry Moon. No longer. She must think positive from now on. Even the Duke experience, instead of being an excuse for yet more toe-curling regret, could be put to good use. She would regard it as her wake-up call. The sign that she should pick herself up and get on with things. Things for her employers, especially.

She should, for a start, stop letting her personal life cripple her professional one. Sion and Henry were to be bundled into a box marked 'Forgotten' and the lid firmly shut. From now on, Grace resolved, her career was coming first. Of course, there would be difficult moments. PR was full of difficult moments, as she had found to her cost in the past. But from here on in, she'd cope better. Every cloud had a silver lining, after all. Even if, she thought, peering out of the plane window, the one they were in at the moment had an interior of unrelieved grey.

'Champagne, madam?' The hostess was leaning over her with the bottle again. 'Of course you're going back Club Class, darling,' her mother had insisted. 'Airlines always bow to diplomatic privilege. And you never know, you might . . .'

'Meet somebody?' Grace snapped, before dissolving into sudden giggles. 'Oh, Mother, you never give up, do you?'

'Certainly not,' said Lady Armiger sternly. 'Someone's got to have your best interests at heart.'

Grace grinned at the champagne-proffering stewardess. After all, she had something to celebrate. A new attitude. A better future.

'Yes, please.' She smiled, raising her glass in a silent toast. To me, she thought. And to *The Neds of Twinky Bay*.

'This manuscript is great,' Ellie announced, a few days later dropping a sheaf of pages on her desk with a tremendous air. 'I'm incredibly excited about it.'

Grace looked up from her press release in delight. 'It's really good, isn't it? You can tell from the first chapter that it's fantastic.'

Ellie nodded. '*Completely* fascinating.'

Grace felt like clapping her hands. Her editorial instincts confirmed.

'All about how to make someone mad about you,' Ellie continued.

Grace blinked. 'You're not talking about the children's book I gave you?'

Ellie shook her head. 'Sorry. Haven't had a minute to read it yet.'

'But you could be sitting on the next Harry Potter,' Grace urged. Seeing Ellie raise her eyebrow in a 'let-me-be-the-judge-of-that' sort of way, Grace decided to let the subject drop. The more she pushed Ellie, after all, the more she would resist. And then the longer Maria – already beside herself at the news that Grace liked the book and had passed it to her publishers – would have to wait. 'So what's this other manuscript you're talking about?' she asked Ellie reluctantly.

'Love spells,' beamed Ellie. 'How to magic someone into falling for you.'

Grace looked doubtful. 'Do you really think people are interested in all that loons and runes stuff?'

'Not people, *women*,' Ellie said confidently. 'Take us two. Women like us are sick of being single in bars, slurping Chardonnay. We want to take things into our own hands. Get the power back.'

Grace winced. She disliked Ellie's habit of cheerfully roping her in with herself and all the other unattached women in the world. Her single state, after all, was now neither here nor there. Following the lecture she had given herself 20,000 ft up in the air, her career was now everything. Being unattached was therefore a positive blessing. Still, it was politic to seem fascinated, for the Neds' sake if nothing else.

'What are the spells?' she asked. If only there was one to make editors – and wannabe editors – read manuscripts.

'Well there's this: "Let your ex forget" one. I was thinking of trying it with that Premiership footballer I went out with the other day. He's very keen and keeps ringing me.' Ellie grimaced. 'I think when I told him if he kept playing things the way he was he was bound to go down, he thought I meant something other than the First Division.'

Grace snorted. 'How does the spell work?'

Ellie's finger followed a passage of the manuscript. ' "Standing round a campfire at sunset, we took some bulbs, exposed them to the four elements and chanted, 'As I wish it, so mote it be.' Then we burnt our emotional baggage." '

I'd need a whole carousel for mine, Grace thought despondently. But – silver linings, she reminded herself. There were lots of good things about not having Sion around, for instance. Her flat was cleaner. The brown envelope recently received from Janet containing a freezer bag with her knickers inside no longer had the power to embarrass.

'Needs a bit of editing though,' Ellie was muttering. ' "Standing skyclad under the stars" – what on earth does that mean? Oh, I see, *naked* . . . "we scattered glitter and rose petals over a Tube map and said, 'From north or south, east or west, let him come who loves me best.' " Isn't that sweet?'

'Adorable,' said Grace, sarcastically. She did not believe in magic, although Maria seemed to have something of an obsession with it, constantly telling her she was from a long line of white witches. Domestos goddesses, perhaps. She smiled. Wasn't that what Henry called his cleaner? But she wasn't thinking about Henry . . .

'And here's a good one for you, Gracie!' Ellie exclaimed

suddenly. ' "To freeze a bad relationship out of your life, put the name of your lover on a piece of paper, stick it in a jam jar full of water and put the whole thing in your freezer." '

'Very useful.'

'This would be a sort of *Bridget Jones's Spell Book.*' Ellie ignored Grace's tone. 'Or even better,' she added, eyes alight, 'we could call it *Spells And The Single Girl.*'

'We *could,*' Grace said without enthusiasm. 'Don't you think all that single stuff is a bit over now, though?'

'*Over?*' Ellie's brilliant gaze swung into her own. 'Look at me. Look at *you*. Does it look like it's over?'

Grace frowned and rattled crossly at her keyboard.

'Well, *does* it?' pressed Ellie. 'You didn't meet anyone in Venice, did you?'

Grace blushed, reluctant to be reminded of the dinner party, much less her mother's revelations afterwards. Silver linings, she told herself, aware of Ellie's mocking-curious stare.

'You *did* meet someone,' she said accusingly, with an incredulous grin.

'He was an awful philistine,' Grace began. 'Thought the only point of books was to make money out of them.'

'I agree with him. If Hatto & Hatto did, we'd be in a better position than we are . . . oh don't lose your rag,' she grinned, as Grace's face went tight with annoyance. 'I promise I'll read that book you gave me. I'll do it tonight. How about that?'

CHAPTER THIRTEEN

Belinda slammed down the telephone and sat at her desk in a fury. The Brian Stone interview had been a blow. In every sense of the word. The bile rose up her throat at the memory of those scratchy grey pubes against her nostrils, that ridiculous tattoo of a snake that had straightened itself out as the organ extended. She had performed the required exceedingly unpleasant function in the belief that it would be the first step to, if not exactly a beautiful relationship, then certainly an attractive one financially. Yet now, the day after, when she had called to confirm the rock star's parting offer, she had been blanked. Snubbed, even.

'What do you mean, he can't fucking remember who I am?' she had roared at Benson the butler who had answered the phone.

'I am afraid, Modom, that the events of yesterday have somehow slipped Mr Stone's mind,' intoned the functionary.

'What – everything?' fumed an incredulous Belinda, wishing desperately that the same could be said for her. As it was, she feared Brian Stone's gold shorts would haunt her dreams for a long time to come.

'It appears so, Modom. I informed him of your presence on the telephone and your identity did not seem to register.'

'But that's impossible,' Belinda yelped. 'I mean, I know he took so many drugs that his septum fell out in the supermarket, but surely he must remember *some* things?' Me, for example, she thought indignantly.

On the other end of the telephone, the butler cleared his throat politely.

'Look, he said he'd fly me to Cap Ferrat this weekend in his private jet, for God's sake,' howled Belinda, aware of excited stares from the subs' desk.

'If I may say so, Modom, that would be highly unlikely.'

'Would it now?' sneered Belinda. 'Not good enough for him am I?'

'I did not mean to imply that, Modom. Merely that Mr Stone's sense of direction is not what it was. Furthermore, I regret to say, mystery has for quite some time surrounded the exact whereabouts of his private jet.'

'Oh, sod off,' Belinda shouted before crashing the telephone back into its cradle. She was now glaring at Tarquin who, judging by the apprehensive expression on his face, had just successfully persuaded another celebrity not to take part in the Belinda Black Interview. 'Well?' she snapped.

'Sharon Stone's said no again,' Tarquin confirmed, replacing the receiver. 'Her people said the Champagne D'Vyne interview put her off.'

'*But I told you not to write again to anyone else called Stone*,' Belinda screeched, even though she had in fact given no such ultimatum. 'No Oliver, no Rolling and certainly no bloody *Sharon*.' She threw back her chair and began to stalk about the office in her perilously high heels. Christ, what a lot of queeny divas these celebrity females were. The bloody Queen being the queeniest of the lot. According to Tarquin, HM never talked to journalists and had never been interviewed, which was downright *ridiculous*, Belinda thought, when you reflected how much the old trout needed the publicity. Her Maj's loss, Belinda told herself. A shame, though. It would have been a great opportunity to ask if those huge grey curls in the front of her hair were, as Che Guevara had once told her, rocket launchers in disguise and the centrepiece of Britain's anti-nuclear defence programme.

'Anyway,' Belinda snapped at Tarquin, 'I told you I wasn't interested in women, full stop. The only interview requests from now on were to be with wealthy, famous and, um, *available* men.'

'*Available* men?' asked Tarquin cagily. 'Available in what sense?'

'Available in the sense that they want to do an interview, of course.'

'You mean like Terry Wogan?'

'No. Not like Terry Wogan.'

'Jimmy Savile?'

'No,' shouted Belinda. '*Not* like fucking Jimmy Savile. I want hot men. Famous men. Big men.'

'I've tried Marlon Brando twice already,' Tarquin ventured. Belinda flicked her assistant a suspicious, narrow-eyed glance. Was the jumped-up lickspittle toerag actually making fun of her?

She drew a weary hand across her carefully made-up eyes. The strain of keeping the pressure up on Tarquin was incredible. Did anyone else in the world have to cope with such incompetence from their inferiors? Still less such ingratitude? It was infuriating, his lack of appreciation for the efforts she was making on his behalf. Training him up was bloody hard work; work, more to the point, that went unrewarded and unacknowledged. On the contrary, Tarquin had actually had the cheek to look upset on the occasions she had insisted he stay late to chase up by phone the letters he had sent to people in LA, eight hours behind London time. *Ungrateful bastard.*

Belinda sighed deeply. No one realised how lonely it was at the top. Have I, she wondered, reached the summit of the mountain – and Mo Mills had definitely been a mountain – to find the view just as dull as it was from down below? Have I got somewhere and found I've got nowhere at all?

She scowled. Hell, she sounded like Champagne D'Vyne at her worst.

'Men like Red Campion of course,' she howled at Tarquin. 'For God's sake, just get him, will you?'

That night, Belinda slept badly. And the next day did not start well. Before she even left the house her nerves were stretched to breaking point. As if she didn't have enough to put up with, the bloody cleaner had put her purple silk duvet and pillowcases *together* on the bed, instead of contrasting them with the pink for a fashionable clashing effect. Didn't the bloody asylum-seeking moron know anything? And yet again the woman had forgotten – *defied*, rather – the rule to hang up her dresses in colour spectrum order after bringing them back from the dry cleaner.

Belinda had had no option but to reduce the cleaner's wages yet again. 'This hurts me more than it hurts you,' she had told her dejected employee. The wretched woman had to learn somehow. She was doing her a favour, really.

Reaching the office, Belinda shot through the various departments like a hunted animal, determined not to bump into either Kevin Grayson or his deputy Warren Street and have to answer awkward celebrity-related questions. Luckily, neither Street nor Grayson seemed to be about. She had managed to avoid them yesterday too, both having been detained in day-long negotiations with a family of Leicester Pakistanis who apparently possessed an aubergine bearing the face of Mohammed. Hopefully the improbable vegetable season would run and run. Belinda was determined to evade all inquiries about what the hell was going on with the next interview.

Finding, as she swept up to her desk, Tarquin lurking with a stupid grin on his face did not improve her mood.

'What are you looking so bloody pleased with yourself about?'

'I've got the perfect interviewee for you,' Tarquin announced. 'Famous and unmarried, just what you asked for.'

'Russell Crowe?' Belinda's voice was hoarse with hope. 'George Clooney?'

'Think younger,' grinned Tarquin. 'It's Stan,' he proudly revealed.

'Stan?' Belinda's eyes shot almost out of their sockets. 'Who the fuck is *Stan*?'

'Only the hottest DJ of the moment,' Tarquin informed her, affronted.

'A *DJ*?' spluttered Belinda. 'What, like Simon Bates or something?'

Tarquin's expression was one of extreme patience. 'Not that sort of a DJ. It's all moved on a bit since then. DJs these days do remixes of other people's stuff and put them out on their own labels. They make millions. People like Fatboy Slim, Pete Tong, Paul Oakenfold – and Stan. They're the new rock stars.'

Belinda felt slightly mollified. She had, after all, had quite enough of the old rock stars.

'Everyone on the indie music scene thinks he's a god. U2 think he's a genius. Madonna's been begging him to do her remixes.'

'*That* washed up old tart,' Belinda cut in. Feeling undermined by Tarquin's unexpected grasp of the music scene, she was eager to display her superior knowledge of the subject. 'Talk about yesterday's woman. The trouble with her is that she can't reinvent herself.'

'Stan caused riots when he played Glastonbury,' Tarquin continued. '*And* he's just won two Grammys, three Brits, a soundtrack Oscar and sold millions of copies of his last album. He makes a fortune. Sixty thousand pounds just for two hours' DJ-ing in Ibiza the other week.'

Belinda's eyebrow curved upwards. This sounded . . . *interesting*. Much more like it.

'A nice guy as well. Very modest and shy, apparently.'

Much, *much* more like it, Belinda thought, remembering Brian Stone's swimming pool. Brian Stone's everything, come to that.

'Stan's the hottest, hippest thing out. Everyone who knows anything knows about him.'

'That's bloody impossible,' Belinda stated imperiously. '*I've* never heard of him.'

There was a diplomatic silence from Tarquin. 'Anyway,' he added, 'the other great thing about this interview is that it's an exclusive. Stan's never given one before.'

Belinda coursed with excitement as the taxi drew up at the

designated address. By early evening she should be well on her way to three homes around the world, a fleet of Bentleys and a Gulfstream with an inglenook fireplace.

She looked, she knew, a million dollars. Walking up and down before her bedroom mirror that morning, Belinda had awarded herself the full five stars. Her legs on their spindly heels were long, flawless and gleaming with moisturiser. Her nails were perfect. Her hair swung about her slim shoulders like a glossy black cape and she had spent the entire previous afternoon having her face massaged and plucked to perfection. Beneath the designer shirt-dress, her breasts swung free, pert and perfectly brown. In deference to chic-fashionable-casual, the dress was almost entirely unbuttoned to show the maximum cleavage and leg.

The taxi had driven past the address she had been given five or six times before Belinda realised that it was, as Tarquin had assured her, a hotel. It just wasn't the sort of hotel she had been expecting. This place did not exactly suggest two Grammys, one Oscar, millions of album sales and £60,000 for two hours' work.

Belinda had imagined Number 20, Earl's Court Road, to be a smart townhouse hotel in the Blake's and Hempel mould, the sort with matt black baths, four-posters swathed in fuchsia muslin and minibars designed by Ronnie Wood. Or, failing that, a modernist boutique hotel with a Zen spa, Mongolian lambskin bedspreads, wenge washstands with agape basins and sixties Finnish leather loungers.

In reality, Number 20, Earl's Court Road fitted neither

description. However you looked at it, the only suitable description was – not to put too fine a point on it – *scruffy*. It was one of an identical row of scabby white houses fronted with cracked and sinking porticos whose peeling pillars revealed an entire genealogy of improbable colours of paint. Its front window, again identical to the others in the row, featured a couple of kettles and a milk carton pushed up against the grubby pane.

The only respect in which the building she was visiting differed from its neighbours was that while the others bore names such as 'Princess Hotel', 'Palace Hotel' and 'Shangri-La Hotel', the owners of Number 20 had clearly either been too honest or too lazy to attempt such euphemisms on its behalf.

In the front window, the sign 'Vacancies' hung above the chilling legend 'Backpackers Welcome'. To Belinda, to whom backpackers barely counted as human, the concept of an establishment that actually welcomed them was beyond her comprehension. Still, as within these unpromising walls resided her best hope of wealth and fame, she had no choice but to put her best Manolo forward.

There were, of course, other reasons to be cheerful. The interview was that rare thing, an exclusive, although Belinda secretly considered this a bloody inconvenience. The lack of previous interviews with Stan in the library files had made it impossible for her to find out about and therefore feign sycophantic interest in his hobbies. This was, she knew, a method which had served several gold-digging actresses well.

Some, she was aware, had even acquainted themselves with the dismal mysteries of golf to ensnare rich husbands. Belinda was entirely prepared to do the same, despite imagining a mashie was something you served with haggis. But Stan did not sound the golfing type.

One of the few facts she had managed to grasp about him was that Stan was not his real name. He had, on some package holiday – *package holiday?* – before he was famous, apparently been mistaken for someone called Stan and had taken the name as a joke. Why he preferred this to his real name, Crispin, Belinda could not imagine.

The review of Stan's latest album, *Child B*, only confused matters further. 'With *Child B*, Stan has pushed out his rock trolley into deep space and come back with something so complex it makes the Rosetta Stone look like graffiti on a chip shop,' opined the *Guardian*'s rock critic. 'While most of his peers seem content with punting their pop Puntos around their local ringroad, Stan has constructed a crazy intergalactic rock roadster out of the Obscure Jazz section at Virgin Megastore and he's driving it to Mars.' Belinda was not sure whether this was praise or condemnation.

Still, at least Stan was rich. That was clear from the cuts Tarquin had dug out. They had provided reassuring reading about the album sales and confirmed that Madonna, Courtney Love, Geri Halliwell and Robbie Williams were all desperate to secure Stan's skills. Stan was also, Belinda noted, gratified, extremely good-looking. His lean and peaceful face, a serene smile playing about his mouth, stared back out of the pieces of newspaper at her. Seducing him would be a pleasure – were it not for the surroundings. Why the hell, Belinda wondered, walking into the foyer and trying not to wince as the sticky carpet adhered to her foot, wasn't Stan staying at the Berkeley? Why wasn't she meeting him in that hotel's celebrated Blue Bar, hang-out of everyone from Fergie to Christy Turlington?

'I'm here from *The Globe*,' she announced in her best jump-to-it tones to the yellow-faced man with the untidy black hair, grey nylon trousers and grubby diamond-patterned jumper who sat in a cubbyhole at the entrance.

He nodded enthusiastically. 'And I here from Kosovo. Ees very nice here.' Belinda wrinkled her nose in disgust. She'd put money on this being, if not her cleaner's actual husband, then at least one of his relatives.

'Where's the concierge?' she demanded. The man in the diamond-patterned jumper shrugged helplessly.

'They don't have concierges here.'

Belinda turned suspiciously at the sound of the soft voice, a voice with a laugh in it. 'Who asked you?' she snapped, before realising, a split second later, to whom she spoke. Stan's head was just as satisfactory as it had appeared in the photographs, but the rest of him was decidedly below par. In Belinda's view, an aubergine-coloured fleece, creased grey combats and a pair of clearly very experienced trainers hardly implied wealth and fame, still less £30,000 an hour. The only type of rock he suggested, she thought crossly, was geology student.

Stan grinned shyly. 'Shall we talk in the foyer?' He waved a hand vaguely at an area before them. As foyers went, Belinda considered, it was hardly the New York Four Seasons. Hardly even the local Posthouse. A number of old-people's-home chairs stood haphazardly about on a puke-coloured carpet, a few sick-looking fish limped around a stagnant tank and the ailing sign of a large Coke machine flickered manically on and off. All around the walls, bulging backpacks stood like sentinels.

'Let's go to your room,' Belinda purred, trying to sound seductive rather than disgusted. 'It would be better,' shooting a suggestive glance from beneath her eyelashes, 'to be alone.'

Through a curtain of fine mousy hair Stan blinked at her doubtfully with large, long-lashed eyes. Belinda rested a long-fingered hand on his arm. 'It's just that I find one-on-one much more . . . *intimate*. Don't you?'

'Sure.' Stan flashed impeccably white teeth. 'But there's a problem with my room.'

Belinda dimpled, thrust her breasts forward and batted her eyelashes so hard her contact lenses almost fell out. 'Oh, I understand. You're worried that the hotel will disapprove of you taking a stranger upstairs.'

Stan looked uncomfortable. 'Oh, it's not that. More that the room's not mine. I'm sharing it with two Australian backpackers, a temporary secretary, a student nurse and a South African barman who works night shifts and has a few gastric issues.' He shot Belinda a grin. 'It's, well, kinda *rich* in there at the moment.'

Belinda felt a sudden fury surge within her. *Not* the kind of richness, she realised, that she had bargained for. Let alone *dressed* for. Even the most hopeless subject of her least inspired Tea Break had never occupied farty hostel bedrooms. What the hell was going on?

'Why aren't you staying at the Berkeley?' she flung at him.

Stan gave her an angelic smile. 'All kinds of reasons,' he said in his gentle voice. 'Posh hotels make me feel cut off. All that air con and bellhops and VIP stuff. I don't need that in my life.'

Belinda stared stupidly. Had she heard him properly? How could *anyone* have a problem with VIP stuff? 'I get it,' she gasped as inspiration struck. 'Invasion of privacy and all that. Oh Stan,' she breathed huskily, 'it must be *dreadful* for you. People just don't understand how difficult it is to be a celebrity.'

Stan grinned. 'Man, that's so overrated. I walk around just as I please and no one ever bothers me. Those people who go around with forty bouncers, they're just asking for attention. David Bowie told me that a pair of sunglasses and a copy of a Greek newspaper is all he ever needs to go anywhere.'

Belinda blinked. What was wrong with this guy? How could she massage his ego when he had no ego to massage? And without massaging his ego, how could she move on to massaging any other area?

'But there must be *some* mad fans . . .' she pressed, desperately.

Stan gave her a relaxed, happy smile. 'I have a good relationship with my fans. In fact, I consider myself privileged to have any. I'm on to a good thing and I know it. You won't ever find me acting up about it.'

Was that, Belinda wondered, swallowing, a *cockroach* running along the bottom of the Coca-Cola machine? 'But you're a star. You're supposed to be all about bad behaviour and drugs and *sex*.' She pouted at him, slightly desperately now, and inched the shirt-dress a few inches further up her thigh. She had come out sans thong; would a Sharon Stone flash now clinch the deal?

'I know,' Stan replied calmly.

'But what about your famous friends?' Belinda was trying hard to contain her panic. 'You must go to lots of celebrity parties . . .'

Why aren't I surprised, she thought sourly as Stan shook his head. 'No. I'd rather write my diary and go to sleep. People are always telling me I missed a great time, that Madonna was there, Tom Cruise was there. But in my experience all that happens at these things is that you go, you stand around, you have a drink, and then you leave. They're boring.'

Boring? Hobnobbing with the kind of people it took her – or rather Tarquin – months of ardent faxing to get even a *refusal* from?

Stan giggled at her expression. 'Really, most celebrities aren't very interesting. Most of them are horribly insecure and lead pretty sad lives.'

Belinda tried to control her urge to get Stan by the neck and shake him. How could what he had just said *possibly* be true? Everyone knew that being famous was the most wonderful thing in the world.

'You're a multi-millionaire,' she said at last, thick-voiced. *That* should provoke a reaction. Rich people always hated talking about their money. No one ever admitted to how much they had.

'What about it?' Stan asked, his eyebrows raised in polite inquiry.

Ha. He wasn't denying it, was he? 'Yes. How much have you got?' Belinda demanded, deciding to go for broke. As it were.

'Probably two to three million right now.'

Two to three million. And he looked about fifteen. Belinda bent over as far as she could without falling off the chair in order to flash as much cleavage as possible.

'You OK?' asked Stan. 'You're doubled up.'

'I'm fine,' snapped Belinda. 'So. This money of yours. What do you spend it on? Lear jets, private islands, racehorses, yachts and so on?'

Stan shook his head. 'None of that interests me. I'm not very into material possessions . . .'

Oh God, thought Belinda. Like bloody Champagne D'Vyne all over again. Only much, much worse. Because this guy obviously meant it.

'. . . I get around in my old Peugeot 106 just as well as I would in a hundred thousand pound Ferrari.'

Belinda felt her lip tremble. She wanted to burst into tears at her own bad luck. Only an assistant as spectacularly useless as Tarquin could set her up with the one millionaire star in the whole goddamn world whose idea of a good time was an old car and an Earl's Court hostel with cockroaches. Why wasn't she talking to Rod Stewart?

'You see,' Stan said, fixing her with a beatific smile, 'the reason I make records is nothing to do with money. It's because I love making records. And I DJ because I love DJ-ing. And if it earns money that's fine, but not the main issue.'

Oh Christ. What was the point? She was getting nowhere. Belinda turned off the tape recorder abruptly.

Stan looked relieved. 'Is that it, then?'

'Yes,' Belinda snapped.

'Brilliant.' Stan grinned. 'You see, I've never done an interview before. I always turn them down but my manager says I should do at least one, so you were it. Thanks for being so easy on me.'

Belinda gathered up her things in a silent sulk. And thanks for being so bloody hard on *me*, she thought furiously. Thanks for making me return to the office with nothing to show for my efforts. Not even a snog, let alone a date. Not even a story worth writing. *Thanks a lot.*

'You see,' Stan continued, 'I was afraid you might ask about my background. My manager said it was about time I opened up about it. Told someone and got it off my chest. Came clean . . .'

Belinda stifled a yawn. His background? Sorry. He was evidently confusing her with someone who gave a damn.

'. . . about how I'm the Old Etonian son of a prominent cabinet minister . . .'

Belinda continued to shove everything back in her bag. Her ears rushed with fury. It was impossible to hear anything but her own hot, thwarted anger.

'. . . and how I got sick of him cheating on my mother with various male members of the Royal Family and so I moved to London and went through a really bad drugs phase. Then I was a prostitute for a bit before I murdered someone quite famous and went to prison before I escaped and assumed a whole new identity. And then I changed it again. But hey, all that's past. No one's interested.'

'No,' Belinda snapped tuning in just as the roaring in her ears stopped. She decided against getting Stan to repeat whatever he had just said. Judging on past form, it was hardly likely to be worth hearing. She rose to her feet.

Stan grinned in relief. 'My manager seemed to think it would cause a sensation. I'm so glad he was wrong.'

CHAPTER FOURTEEN

It seemed to Grace that ever since she had decided to look on the bright side of professional life, events had conspired to plough Hatto & Hatto's fortunes still further into the dust. She rubbed her eyes and stared at Ellie. 'I can't believe it.'

'Well, at least it explains his shakes,' Ellie said. 'Not to mention his books. It was better stocked than a branch of Oddbins in there. There was even booze in the wastepaper basket. His favourite drink seems to be Wild Turkey, which is apt, considering how many of them he publishes.'

There was, Grace noticed, a note of glee in Ellie's voice. Personally, she did not share her colleague's delight at the discovery that Adam Knight's Dunkirk spirit owed less to an unshakeable belief in his own editorial judgement and the company's publishing integrity than to the spirits piled behind heaps of paper in his office. For Grace, the discovery was depressing in the extreme. As was the realisation that Ellie, despite apparently having suspected the problem for some time, had said absolutely nothing about it to her.

'I just thought you had enough on your plate,' Ellie explained now. 'With Sion and, um, the rest of it.'

Grace looked at her sharply. Did 'the rest of it' mean Henry Moon?

Evidently.

'I must say,' Ellie said casually, 'I do think it's odd Henry hasn't even called you. There's been radio silence for weeks.'

Grace reddened furiously. 'I don't want him to call me. How are you getting on with the new Inigo Thongsbridge, anyway?' she added, determined to return to professional matters. 'That press release for *Not Of Woman Born*?'

'Thongy's new book?' Ellie cast about on her desk and fished out a piece of paper. She cleared her throat. ' "A tale of the manipulative monster of vulgar rapacity," ' she declaimed. ' "As changing fortunes put a strain on a family already buckling with internal tensions, each one of them must make sacrifices to overcome the crisis. What has really happened to Charlie? Who is the victim or the guilty party? Will the truth ever come out? Will anyone live happily ever after?" '

'Lot of questions there,' Grace said doubtfully.

'Yes, but the plot's completely incomprehensible. Apparently it made sense when viewed through the bottom of a whisky glass darkly,' Ellie explained, 'but now Adam's sober he's got no idea what it's about. That's why it's called *Not Of Woman Born*. All he's sure about was that it was written by a man.'

Grace suppressed a grin. 'You've made it sound pretty gripping,' she conceded. 'Especially that bit about the manipulative monster of vulgar rapacity.'

'Well, Thongy really is the most appalling lech,' Ellie said, pulling a disgusted face. 'Even though I'm pretty sure he has a wife. I once asked him point blank if he was married and he said, "Only when I'm in Hertfordshire." '

'Adam!' sighed Grace.

'I only really began to suspect,' Ellie resumed, 'when I saw his Christmas cards from the Queen's Head, the Skinner's Arms and Sharon and Mahmoud at the local off-licence. But, you know,' she added grinning, 'it's a huge piece of luck, really.'

Grace stared. 'And how exactly do you figure that out?'

'Elementary, my dear Armiger. Adam knows I know his secret. I've promised not to tell anyone – apart from you, of course – on condition that he goes to AA meetings. Last Chance Saloon.' Ellie grinned. 'Except that he isn't to go near a saloon bar ever again.'

'But why will that transform the company fortunes? Rehabilitation's a slow process.'

'But you haven't heard the other condition,' Ellie said

eagerly. 'The deal is that I won't tell anyone about his, um, *problem*, on condition that he goes to AA meetings *and* lets me help select future manuscripts for publication. Lets me be properly involved. What's more, he's agreed. I'm Deputy Fiction Director. By hook or by crook,' Ellie finished triumphantly, 'I've got my job in editorial.'

'But what about your job in publicity?' Grace asked, pointedly.

Ellie threw her a dazzling smile. 'Well, it's not as if it's so busy that I haven't got time for anything else, is it? Honestly, Grace, it makes sense. I know I can pick out books that will sell and that's got to be good news for the company. Adam's agreed to rush *Spells And The Single Girl* – you know, that book about love spells I showed you – into production. It's going to be massive, I know.' Ellie's face glowed and her eyes shone. Grace, by contrast, felt flatter than ever.

Ellie seemed to spot this. 'Which reminds me,' she added, more gently. 'I've been meaning to tell you. I've read the first part of *The Neds Of Twinky Bay* at last.'

Grace looked up. It had been several days since her last inquiry after the manuscript. She regarded Ellie without enthusiasm, knowing the news was bound to be bad. Had she been the least bit interested, Grace knew, she would have devoured the manuscript instantly. She would not have had to be bullied into reading it. 'And?'

'And,' Ellie said, 'I think it's just brilliant. You're right. It's *incredible*. I want to see the rest of it as soon as possible.'

'In which case,' Grace said, scrabbling in her bag excitedly and handing over the latest instalment, 'you'd better have this.' Her heart had sunk on seeing it waiting for her on the kitchen table when she had arrived home the evening before, together with a note from Maria informing her she had run out of bleach. Grace had spent the rest of the evening lying on the sofa, so lost in the world of the flying gypsies and the little boy that even the thought of dinner had not occurred to her. 'It's even better than the first part.'

'Fantastic!' Ellie snatched the envelope out of Grace's hand. 'I'll read it tonight.'

After work, Grace fairly raced to get back and tell Maria the good news. To reach the Tube quickly through the home-going crowds, she hurried down the road, rather than the pavement, dodging spluttering buses and cursing cyclists as she went. Having almost fallen down the escalator in her haste to get to the bottom, she then fidgeted on the platform as the train was – inevitably – delayed. Having – again, inevitably – mislaid her ticket when she reached the barrier, she rummaged desperately in her bag, tipping everything out on the floor in her frustration. Finally released, she sprinted from the Tube station to the flat, arriving, chest heaving, bright purple in the face.

Grace burst through the door and dashed into the kitchen where Maria, on hands and knees, a teacloth slung over her shoulder, was sweeping up a mass of broken glass. She looked up guiltily.

'Madam Grace!'

'Just Grace,' gasped Grace. 'Please.'

'What has happen?' demanded Maria, scrambling to her feet, eyes wide with concern at her out-of-breath employer. 'Sometheeng terrible?'

'Not exactly,' grinned Grace, heart racing like a whippet, leaning against the counter and breathing heavily. 'Something rather wonderful, actually.'

Maria picked up a glass from the draining board and began to polish it with the cloth. Her face blazed with pleasure. 'Madam Grace! You haf new man?'

Grace burst out laughing. 'Much better than that, Maria.'

'What you mean better?' scolded the cleaner. 'Nothing ees better. You so pretty, Mada – Grace. Ees wrong you are without man.'

'Maria, stop talking. I've got news for you. My publishers. I think they're really going to publish that book. *The Neds of Twinky Bay.*'

Maria's reddened hand stopped rubbing the glass. It was with a certain sense of inevitability that Grace watched her fingers loosen round it and the vessel smash to the floor.

Maria, however, had not seemed to notice. 'They publeesh?' she asked, half croak, half whisper. Her eyes were widening, filling with water.

Grace nodded, a responding lump rising in her throat. 'I mean, nothing's been signed, but it's looking good. So you can probably tell your client. After all, he's the one who wrote it.'

Maria gave her a dazzling smile. Her eyes had a wicked look in them now. 'No, you tell heem. He want to meet you very much. He tell me. He lonely. He by himself. He very handsome . . .'

'No, Maria,' Grace interrupted, recalling the alarming image of the bald man in a vest. Was there no situation whose matchmaking potential Maria did not immediately weigh up? In some ways, she was worse than her mother. 'You tell him.'

Maria's face was sober again. 'You theenk they really publeesh?'

'I'm pretty sure they will,' Grace reassured her gently. 'In fact,' she added, throwing caution to the winds, 'I'd stake my job on it.'

Grace appeared at work next morning tense with the expectation of tremendous news from Ellie. What she did not expect was to find the offices buzzing with tremendous news of an entirely different nature.

'They've been spying on us for *ages*,' Gladys the secretary told a Grace poleaxed by the revelation that Gervase Hatto had, seemingly overnight, signed his company away to an American company called Omnicorp.

'What makes you think that?' Grace asked.

'Obvious.' Gladys's face was flushed with the drama of it all. Her eyes behind their bifocals bulged. 'They must have been spying. How else would they be so well-informed about how we operate?'

'Omnicorp is one of the biggest media companies in America, apparently,' Ellie announced, rushing excitedly into the room. 'Interests all over the world. A real go-ahead, can-do ass-kicking conglomerate.'

'Stop,' Grace groaned, putting her hands to her ears and remembering Bill Duke. Not another. Hadn't she heard enough of US media companies recently?

'Why? Aren't you glad? It's thrilling, isn't it?'

'But I'll be sacked,' Grace wailed. The possible consequences of the takeover were beginning to dawn on her. Given her disastrous professional performance over the last few weeks, what go-ahead, can-do, ass-kicking conglomerate would consider a Head of PR with her track record?

'Stop being the Dame of Doom. That's not going to happen.'

'But how do you *know*?' Grace challenged.

'Adam told me all about it. The Americans have bought Hatto & Hatto to add prestige to the rest of their businesses. They want us to stay exactly the same – apart from sharpening up our act and making a profit of course,' Ellie grinned. 'So just as well Adam turned out to be a dipso. I'm not sure Tenebris Luks was going to do it for Omnicorp. Let alone Inigo Thongsbridge.'

'But . . .' Grace faltered.

'But nothing. It all sounds wonderful. We'll have profit targets, proper budgets and so on, but everything else stays the same. Oh, apart from the fact that Philip's apparently getting an assistant or two in the sales department. He'll have people to be Head of, at last. Can you believe it?' Ellie said, eyes sparkling. 'The Americans actually want to sell books!'

'But—'

'Don't worry. Nothing's really going to change. Except for the better. There'll be health care plans. Pension schemes. Come on, Grace. The nearest Hatto & Hatto came to pensions before were the salaries themselves.'

Grace opened and closed her mouth, trying to keep up with the speed Ellie was dispensing information. 'But what about the authors?'

'Ah. Now you're talking,' said Ellie, grinning even more broadly. 'As it happens, there *are* going to be a few changes to Adam's – I mean *mine* and Adam's – list of authors.'

'*What?*' Grace's eyes were wide with shock. 'Who?'

Ellie frowned for the first time. 'It's the strangest thing,' she said. 'I've no idea how they know anything about them. But sources very high up in the organisation are apparently strongly recommending that Tenebris Luks and Euphemia Ogden be dropped from the list.'

'*What?*'

Ellie shrugged. 'Amazing, isn't it? But they're keeping Thongy for the time being, though, as they quite like the title *Not Of Woman Born.*'

Tenebris Luks and Euphemia Ogden were being dropped? Grace tried to work up a sense of outrage at such a marked degree of corporate interference in Hatto's creative independence. She failed. There was, after all, little that was creative, much less independent, about Euphemia Ogden or Tenebris Luks. Grace felt, in fact, as if a huge weight had tumbled from her shoulders. Which, in the case of Euphemia it most certainly had. Her delight, however, was followed by the sober realisation that the benefits of this would be enjoyed by a PR director other than herself. 'And, um, Cylindria?'

'Fine. Americans love that British manners stuff.'

Grace's forehead felt moist. Henry Moon would be dropped, almost certainly.

'Don't you want to know about Moonie?' teased Ellie. Grace looked at her crossly. Why did Ellie never miss an opportunity to mention Henry? What, in any case, did *she* care?

Nonetheless, Grace's stomach twisted and the inside of her palms pricked with sweat, as Ellie announced the verdict.

'He's been given a reprieve on the grounds that he stops banging on about exploring and tries something else. They're impressed with his writing. But not with his sales.'

Grace, trying to look unmoved, was annoyed at the irritating rush of relief she felt. As if it made any difference to her.

'We – that is, Adam and I – are apparently going to concentrate on building up a whole new list of writers,' Ellie was saying. 'We're being encouraged to find good new manuscripts – throw our net as wide as possible. *Spells* will be exactly the sort of thing they'll love. As for *The Neds* . . .'

She grinned happily at Grace. 'That second bit was brilliant. You were right. Even better than the first.'

Instead of feeling the excitement flare within, Grace felt only the backs of her eyes stinging. The worst of all this takeover business was that, having brought the manuscript to Hatto she would not be around to see *The Neds* brought to their triumphant, published conclusion. Still, she thought miserably, Maria could always keep her up to date on her cleaning visits.

'The only problem,' Ellie sighed, 'is that apparently we're not moving from these revolting old offices. Retaining that whole old-fashioned Bloomsbury shit is part of the new plan. The nearest we're getting to a plate-glass palace with forty-nine floors and air conditioning is a looking glass in the loo and some wild talk about fans. And we're keeping the name. Hatto & Hatto.' Ellie grinned. 'So bad they named it twice.'

'*A plate-glass palace?*' Grace repeated slowly. Somewhere in the troubled depths of her brain, a bell was loudly and insistently ringing. *The American film arm* . . .

'What's the matter? You've gone all white.'

'Who's the chairman of the company that's taken over Hatto & Hatto?' Grace whispered, her voice barely above a croak.

'Oh, didn't I say?' chirruped Ellie. 'He's called Bill Duke.' She picked up her ringing phone.

Bill Duke. There was a dull thud somewhere in Grace's head. Like a door closing or a bullet being fired. She had wondered what he would do with all that information she had so freely given him. Now she had her answer. But how he must despise her for her disloyalty. No doubt, by now, he was fully aware of how bad she was at her job as well. No doubt, too, he had decided he did not not want the likes of her in his company, whether he knew her parents or not. A woman who couldn't hold her drink, still less keep her mouth shut.

Damn it. Damn it all.

'That was the human resources department of Omnicorp,' Ellie said brightly, putting her receiver down. 'They're sending me my contract.'

Grace looked bleakly back at her.

'Why are you looking like that? Human Remains will ring you any minute, obviously.'

'No they won't,' said Grace.

Nor did they. 'Well they've probably got a lot of names to work through,' Ellie suggested at the end of the afternoon, as she shrugged on her new cream peacoat. 'The whole alphabet.' Grace did not point out that her surname began with A.

She trudged home, her heart in her boots. Under her boots. What made matters worse was discovering, on the kitchen table, another experienced-looking envelope from Maria. Another instalment of *The Neds* – she must have dropped it in during the day. Grace picked up a creased brown corner and let it flop down. What was the point of reading it? She needed to detach herself from the project, not get further involved. She would give it to Ellie in the morning. *The Neds* – and Hatto – were no longer anything to do with her.

The telephone in the hall shrilled. Grace shuffled reluctantly to answer it.

'That Grace?'

Grace swallowed hard. Her stomach yo-yoed frantically. She knew that voice.

'Yes.'

'Y'alright?'

'Yes thank you Bill – I mean, Mr Duke.'

'Come and see me in my office tomorrow,' growled the other end of the line. 'We need to talk.'

CHAPTER FIFTEEN

Whooshing upwards like a launching rocket in the lift to Duke's office, Grace suppressed her condemned prisoner feelings as best she could. The lift was glass-sided; she could see the cityscape of London flattening and widening beneath her. It was, she decided, rather like the Bridge of Sighs. The Lift of Sighs, perhaps. There was Tower Bridge, there St Paul's, Westminster in the distance and, just below, the pewter flash of the river.

The Omnicorp building – a plate-glass palace, Grace noted with a sinking feeling – rose from the midst of a city of plate-glass palaces. Bill Duke's UK headquarters occupied one of the newest parts of the Docklands development and its shining walls reflected the dancing Thames, the clouds and the ever-circling aeroplanes. Grace eyed the aircraft longingly, wishing she, too, was en route to a glamorous destination. Just as long as it wasn't Venice. She'd had quite enough of that place for the moment.

'Great view, isn't it?' she observed shyly to the assistant who had come to fetch her from the downstairs reception desk.

'It is.'

Her easy-going tones, instead of relaxing Grace, flooded her with awkwardness and apprehension. It was all right for her to be so calm. During the preceding fitful night, Grace had worked out exactly why Duke wanted to see her. To sack her. But as a friend of her father's, he was at least doing her the courtesy of informing her of her fate himself.

'Here we are,' said the assistant, as the lift doors sprang open and Grace found herself in a glass-walled space into which light poured from all sides. From above, too; looking up Grace spotted the still blades of a helicopter through one of the panes.

The beautiful blonde receptionist sitting behind the front desk smiled and picked up a telephone. 'Miss Armiger for you, Mr Duke.' She put the receiver down. 'He says go straight in. Down there on the left.'

Grace padded down the short, wide corridor indicated and tapped gently on a thick, blond-wood door.

'Come in,' boomed a deep Texan voice.

Grace went in, bracing herself for the sight of Duke

staring at her from an executive leather swivel chair. Yet executive leather swivel chair saw she not. Nor executive desk. Of executive trappings in general, there was no sign. No brass-and-green glass desk lamps, no tooled leather in-tray, no gold-plated PC with silver Tiffany mouse, even. The walls, furthermore, were innocent of the smallest corporately purchased Old Master.

These walls, though wooden, were not the anticipated corporate walnut. They looked like cedar, and roughly hewn, cabin-style cedar at that. An entire menagerie of animal-skin rugs cluttered the floor and Adirondack chairs sat expectantly about.

A rumpled, quilt-covered daybed had been pushed against one wall; opposite it, on a sofa covered in sheepskins, Bill Duke was slumped, chin on chest, talking into a small silver mobile. He wore jeans, and a checked shirt. His cowboy-booted feet were propped up on a stuffed leather pig. More extra from *Oklahoma!*, Grace thought, than billionaire head of a multinational corporation. Was this his usual style? It must have been an enormous concession to wear a suit to her mother's dinner. No wonder he had looked so uncomfortable in it.

Gesturing to her to sit down, Duke swept his torch-like stare appraisingly over her. Grace, whose only source of confidence was her smoothly ironed white shirt and knife-creased trousers, sent up a prayer of thanks to Maria. 'I'm just talking to my estate manager in Montana,' he hissed in a stage whisper before returning to his conversation. Grace sensed tension. Duke was clearly irritated about something. Was it her?

'You don't know what to do, Joe?' he boomed into the mobile. 'Well, I'll tell ya. The local farming syndicate don't want me to buy that ranch, huh? Well, just you listen to me. You go along to their next meeting, say you're speaking on mah behalf, and tell them that I sympathise.'

There was a pause, during which, Grace guessed, the distant Joe was expressing his surprise at this.

'Oh, I sure do sympathise,' Duke boomed, raising his long legs above the pig on which they were resting. 'I really do. And you can tell them that. And tell them as well that if they really want to stop me, mah advice to them is to go off and work like hell, save up sixty million and buy the ranch themselves. Heh, heh, heh.'

He flicked the mobile off. 'Sorry about that. I'm just about to buy another ranch, and the locals are kicking up rough.'

'Oh, right.' Fascinating though this glimpse into his personal concerns was, Grace wondered what it was all leading up to. If the knife had to be stuck in, she would prefer it done so as quickly as possible.

'Anyways, Grace . . .'

'Yes?'

'How are the folks?'

'Oh. Fine. I spoke to my mother only this morning, in fact. She was, um, much the same.'

Duke looked at her sharply. Had the circumstances

not been so serious, Grace might have thought he looked amused.

'That was a mighty good dinner of theirs. A great success.'

Grace nodded. For some, certainly. For Duke, the upshot had been acquiring the last of the quirky British publishers at a no-doubt knock-down price to add up-market patina to his media empire. A success indeed.

'Surprised to hear I'd bought the company, were ya?' he fired suddenly, evidently reading her thoughts.

'Well, yes.'

Duke reached over with his long checkered arms and poured himself a cup of coffee from the percolator. 'Want one?'

'Please.' The cup rattled against the saucer as Grace took it in her trembling hand. She looked angrily at her treacherous knuckles.

Duke slapped his hands up and down on the exposed leather sofa arms. 'Know what I was doing in Venice when I met yuh?'

'You were at thc Film Festival,' Grace muttered, remembering her mother wailing something about this.

Duke nodded. 'You know Omnicorp's got film interests, right?'

TV, film and advertising arms as well as the publishing one . . . Grace nodded. She knew all right. What she still didn't know was where the conversation was going. What did the Venice Film Festival, or Omnicorp's film arm, have to do with *her*?

'Well,' Duke drawled, 'an actor on contract to us was there, promoting one of our pictures. So it was the perfect opportunity to firm up a little deal he and I had been talking about. And now it's all signed and sealed.'

'I see,' Grace said politely.

'Which is why you're here. I'd like you to look after his project.'

Grace's mouth dropped open. Look after his – anyone's – project? Was Duke joking? Was all this a horrible tease? 'I thought you'd called me up here to sack me,' she blurted out before she could stop herself.

Duke's face was momentarily obscured by a swirling blue cloud of cigar smoke. '*What?*' he choked. '*Sack* you?'

Face burning, Grace nodded.

Duke mopped his streaming eyes. 'Hell, no. For a start, I wouldn't dare upset your mother. She's the only woman that scares me enough to make me wear a suit.'

Grace grinned, knowing the feeling. She'd asked herself a hundred times since why she'd gone to Venice. Of course. That was why.

'I want you to work for me,' said Duke. 'It's obvious from what you were telling me at your mother's dinner party that you can handle publicity for anybody. Because if you can take those loony tunes authors you've got there . . .' He rolled his eyes and whistled.

Grace swallowed. 'Yes, but . . .' Did Duke not know that her recent professional life had been a catalogue of PR disasters? Given that, inevitably, sooner or later he would find out, it seemed unwise to hold back the fact that she was the Mr Bean of public relations. 'Well, to be honest,' she mumbled, 'I'm not sure I have handled them all that well. My track record's pretty bad,' she added.

'All that Henry Moon stuff?' Grace started at the unexpected mention of the name. She felt the crimson rise in her cheeks. Duke smiled. 'That don't matter. Most people would hardly have bothered with him . . .'

If only, thought Grace, *I* hadn't.

'. . . the fact that you threw everything you had at him says everything about you . . .'

Doesn't it just? Grace mused despondently.

'. . . that you kept trying to get him coverage even when every newspaper in the country was saying no, not to mention every TV and radio station. That you cared that much about *Henry Moon*.' Duke shook his head wonderingly. 'Awesome, really.'

'More fool me,' Grace shrugged, purple now with embarrassment.

'No. *Good* for you. Way beyond the call of duty.'

Grace twisted her hands in her lap. You could say that again.

'That's what I like. Tenacity. And I've also heard great things about you from your colleague, Ellie.'

'Ellie?' Grace was round-eyed with surprise. Ellie had not mentioned meeting the new boss.

'Great girl.' Duke cleared his throat abruptly. 'So. If you

can handle all that, you can handle a Hollywood star, no problem.'

'A *Hollywood star*?' If she had been barely able to cope with Z-list writers, surely an A-list celebrity – even a B-list one – would be way beyond her capacity? 'I'm not sure I have the . . .'

'Experience? Sure you have,' breezed Duke. 'If you can deal with that dame – whazzername – Euphemia Oswaldtwistle – you can deal with Red Campion. Easy.'

Grace stared. '*Red Campion?*' she croaked.

Duke swung his legs off the pig and sat up. 'Hey, what's the problem? You told me you like challenges.'

Grace put her cup down on a ponyskin rug. She steadied her hands by clasping them firmly together. She heard her own voice at the Venice dinner table. *It's a challenge. I like challenges*. Her brain rushed with panic.

'But . . . but . . . what about Omnicorp's film arm? Won't the studio PRs be handling any project that Red Campion's involved in?'

Duke looked puzzled. 'Why in Gawd's name would *they* be handling it?'

'I don't have much experience of film promotion . . .'

'It's not a goddamn *film*. Red Campion's signed to write his first *novel*. And Hatto & Hatto will be publishing it.'

'A *novel*?'

Duke nodded. 'He's always wanted to write a novel. What's more, he wants to have that novel assessed on its own merits and be nothing to do with goddamn screaming women, Oscars, or Legionnaire's goddamn Disease. So, I figured, with Hatto's reputation for uncompromising quality, they were just the babies to publish it. And you do their publicity. Right?' He looked at her quizzically from under his brows.

'Oh,' Grace said slowly. 'Right.'

'So now all that's sorted out.' Duke looked at his watch and stood up so his big head almost hit the ceiling. 'I've gotta get on. Red'll ring you.'

'Ring me?' Did people as famous as Red Campion just pick up the telephone and dial? And, of all numbers, hers?

'Well, you're going to have to talk to him, obviously. And meet him.'

'What – go to LA?' croaked Grace, excitement and terror batting for possession of her vocal chords. She had never been to LA.

'No need. He's in Paris at the moment, doing a few bits of post-production. Re-recording some of the dialogue on his new film.'

'Um, fine,' Grace squeaked, only half listening. Excitement had bulldozed her doubts. *Red Campion was going to ring her!* Just wait until she told Ellie. Her feet itched to run back to the office.

'Just one thing,' Duke drawled. 'All this here's a secret. Say nothing to anyone, right? Not even Ellie. She's brilliant at ideas, but I'm not sure about how good she is at keeping secrets.'

Grace smiled faintly, remembering some of Ellie's no-holds-barred stories of her amorous encounters. The 'Italian Tripod' had been the latest. 'Think about it,' Ellie had said, dissolving into laughter. Duke was right. Her colleague had many talents, but discretion was not one of them.

After all this, the fact that the following day ended with no word from Red Campion was something of an anticlimax. As the next, and the one after that passed untroubled by any celebrity phone call, Grace started to wonder if the whole episode in Duke's office hadn't been a dream.

Whether Ellie suspected anything was another matter. Given her colleague's talent for cross-examination, Grace had dreaded letting anything slip. Fortunately, Ellie, for the past few days, had been flat out reading the proofs of *Spells And The Single Girl*. 'So if you make an altar with two red candles and write on a red card underneath the name of the someone special you want to fall in love with you . . .' Grace heard her muttering. Utterly absorbed, she seemed to have no interest in anything else.

Grace was therefore alarmed to enter the office one morning to find Ellie bouncing delightedly in her chair and shouting, 'Have you heard?'

'Heard what?' Grace trembled, aware her face had gone white. How had Ellie found out? Would Duke, she wondered, blame *her* for the leak?

'About Sassy Jenks and Jenny Bristols?'

'Oh.' Grace felt herself deflate with relief. She tried

to concentrate on Ellie's story. It concerned an unfortunate Ptarmigan PR who, in an effort to kill two publicity birds with one stone, had persuaded Jenks to take part in a 'My Writing Friend' feature with her stablemate Jenny Bristols.

'The idea,' Ellie giggled, 'was that each of them was meant to wax lyrical about the invaluable support the other is during the creative process. It seems that the magazine suspected they might be the victims of some PR trick when Sassy and Jenny refused even to share the same room during the interview and flatly refused to be photographed together. All hell broke loose, apparently.'

Grace nodded absently. She was, she realised, faintly disappointed that Ellie had not guessed her secret. For Ellie to know would make it fact. Reality.

But, even if she'd had no calls from superstars, there was plenty to be thankful for. She still had a job, at least. And a much better one, too. A fresh new spirit was coursing through Hatto & Hatto; and one nothing to do with a screw-top bottle. Ellie was champing at the bit for as much *Neds* as Maria could deliver; further evidence of her industry lay in the brilliant pink bound proofs of *Spells And The Single Girl* on Grace's desk this morning.

'It's almost finished!' Grace exclaimed, picking it up.

Ellie nodded proudly. 'Yes. Thought you'd like to see it. Actually,' she gestured at the bright pink Post-It flags sticking out of it, 'I've marked a few spells for your particular attention.'

Grace turned to the first page. 'A Spell To Make Him Declare His Love'. She flushed angrily. Was this meant as a reference to Henry Moon?

> To make him declare his love, place a £1 coin between your palms and ask for love to rise in a great wave and flood your life. Imagine your beloved's face in the coin. Place the coin in a circle of pink flowers, leave there overnight during the full moon, then find some way of giving it to your beloved. Once it has left their hands, a gesture of deep affection should be forthcoming.

Grace snorted. 'Honestly, Ellie.'

Ellie turned on her a look of radiant innocence. 'Thought you might find them useful.'

Grace felt her temper fray. 'Useful? This is hen-party stuff. Completely irrelevant to anyone's real life.' She riffled scornfully through the pages. Then, suddenly, she stopped. Something had caught her eye. 'A Spell To Make Him Telephone You'. It was all rubbish, of course. But, given that she was expecting – admittedly with dwindling hope – a rather important phone call, the topic held a certain interest.

'Found something?' Ellie inquired sweetly. Reading on, Grace ignored her.

> Make your beloved telephone you by sitting in a tepid

> bath with acorns, oak leaves and a circle of fresh rose petals in it . . .

That *sort* of made sense. People always waited until you were in the bath to call.

> Hold a photograph of him in one hand and lie in the water, looking at it for ten minutes and allowing your thoughts to fill with him and nothing else. After the ten minutes are up, toast him with cider and chant, 'Pick up the phone and give me a call; there's nothing stopping you at all.'

Oh, but that was just too silly. Ludicrous, in fact. 'Nothing,' Grace muttered, shoving the bright pink book in her bag.

CHAPTER SIXTEEN

Belinda could not believe it. That *unutterable* drip Toby Brooke, whom she'd interviewed for a Tea Break ages ago, had become a superstar. According to this morning's newspapers, he had a part in the new Tom Cruise film. Not only was it ludicrous, but also went to show how Z-list the A-list was becoming.

She'd tried that line on the Editor. He hadn't gone for it. On the contrary, he had demanded to know when her own exclusive with Brooke was going to run. Well, frankly, and as she had yet to tell him, it wasn't. Not that this was her fault, as the Editor would hear. The PR company, for some stupid reason, had refused to play ball. Toby Brooke was with an up and coming PR agency; the very same up and coming PR agency, Belinda remembered, who had tried to flog her that dwarf Jim Friedlander. Unfortunately, Belinda had only remembered this after she had put in the call to Amber. Amber had, in fact, helped to remind her. It had all been very embarrassing, Amber had not neglected the opportunity to point out that Jim Friedlander was now the second hottest Brit ticket in Hollywood. After Toby Brooke, that was.

Belinda ground her teeth in irritation. Only that morning she had read in a rival newspaper how, 'having captured the hearts of the TV-viewing nation as the deserter in *Shot At Dawn*, Brooke has consolidated his success with a blistering performance as baby-faced psychopath necrophiliac pathologist Tom Carver in the new series *The Mortuary*'. She would have lost her breakfast, except that she hadn't eaten any. Her stomach had been surging with bile ever since the night before, when she had read, in the *Evening Standard* media pages, that Mo Mills – apparently, incredibly, on the road to recovery – was up for a Lifetime Achievement gong at the forthcoming *What The Papers Say* awards. To be presented, moreover, by Paul McCartney. Belinda's fury was tripled by the discovery that she hadn't been entered for any awards herself.

And now this.

Belinda felt the rage rise within her. Why wasn't she getting *her* just deserts? Why was nothing turning out the way she had planned it? She'd been in charge of Mo Mills's column for weeks now and she was no nearer bagging someone rich and famous than she had been when she started.

'Why haven't you got me Red Campion?' she screamed at Tarquin.

'I've written to him fifty times,' Tarquin answered. 'He's said no to every single request.'

'So what?' Belinda snarled. 'The fifty-first might just break the camel's back.'

It struck Belinda that perhaps she was setting her sights too high to expect both wealth *and* celebrity. The results were maddeningly slow in coming. In order to speed things up, it might be an idea to settle for one or the other. In which case, merely rich would have to do. For the moment.

'Start looking in Debrett's,' she bawled at Tarquin. 'I want a list of all the peers of the realm by first thing tomorrow.' Tarquin sighed and shuffled off to the library.

A bright fire now burned in Belinda's breast. If this didn't work, nothing would. Peers were notoriously susceptible to journalists anyway; there was that story about the gold-digger who'd met every château-owning marquis in the Loire by pretending to be a BBC researcher. It was, Belinda mused, a good idea. Why the hell hadn't she thought of it herself?

Next morning, Tarquin presented her with the list. Scanning down it, Belinda scowled as she realised most of the peers on it seemed to be married. 'This one,' she snapped, her red-painted fingernail pausing by a name. 'Peregrine.' She pronounced it to rhyme with ear and wine.

'Peregrine,' corrected Tarquin, pronouncing it to rhyme

with cherry and bin. 'Peregrine Oscar Herringbone Somerville. Yes, he sounds a good one. The son of a thousand earls. Stands to inherit half of the Midlands. His father is Lord Whyffe of Swaddling.'

'*Is* he now.' Belinda was interested.

'And he's single.'

'I *see*.' Very interested.

'Thought you'd be pleased.' As relief irradiated Tarquin's long, pale face, Belinda narrowed her eyes. If he was fishing for compliments, he could sod off. Did *she* ever get thanked? Did she even *expect* thanks? Of course not. She was a professional.

'Never forget that it's *my* name on the bottom of those letters you send out,' she snapped. 'It's me who swings the interviews. You just lick the bloody envelopes. And don't just stand there! Find out about the bloody train times, will you?'

Belinda, flushed with excitement, vowed to lose no time in getting up there and surveying the rolling acres. Rolling in the acres with the son and heir, even better. The only tricky bit, Belinda knew, would be getting her subject past the Editor. But then, would it be so difficult? *The Globe* loved stories with lashings of patrician colour and eccentricity, with a few four-posters, noble oaks and oxbow lakes thrown in. And what was this bloke's name again? Peregrine Herringbone Oscar something? Well, that settled it. If pressed, she could say in all honesty that her latest subject had an Oscar. He was A-list, too, if by that one meant Aristocrat list.

Belinda smiled to herself. Lady Whyffe of Swaddling. It had a certain ring to it. And it was her business on this visit to make sure it was a large antique diamond one.

Tarquin had arranged for the Hon. Peregrine to meet Belinda at a branch-line station called Swaddling Close and drive her to the house. It was therefore an unpleasant surprise, to detrain and be greeted by no one at all. Twenty boring minutes passed before a gangling, uncoordinated figure appeared round the corner of the closed and rotting waiting room.

'Blinda?'

The Hon. Peregrine gave, Belinda thought, a whole new meaning to patrician high colour. Two feverish magenta spots burned in the upper corners of his cheeks. His clothes, by contrast, were the colour of sludge at the bottom of a pond. His hair was white-blond, his scalp was pink, his eyes were sloping and watery blue and his shoes had apparently been exhumed from the garden after the best part of a century.

'Sorrybladdycarconked out,' the Hon. Peregrine gasped. It wasn't only his shoes, Belinda thought, that had been buried for a hundred years. His accent had as well. Still, this was what upmarket types were like. Everyone knew that. It was just that he was more so than she had expected. The son of a thousand earls, Tarquin had said. Now she came to think of it, earls were not noted for their pulchritude at the best of times. And Peregrine seemed to combine the least attractive features of all of them.

Belinda was mollified, however, by his obvious appreciation of the great honour she was doing him by her presence. 'You're a sillibrity interviewer!' he yelped as they juddered along in his ancient open-top car. 'It must be *virry* rewarding. All those rich and famous people you meet.' He was, she realised, looking at her rather expectantly. 'I mean, you must move in such illivated circles.'

Belinda was puzzled. What more elevated circles could there be than his? Then she realised; no doubt this was the famous aristocratic charm at work. 'Well, quite elevated,' she admitted. There had, after all, been several pairs of built-up shoes in Brian Stone's wardrobe.

Peregrine nodded eagerly. The magenta spots on his cheeks burned with pleasure. Or with hypothermia, possibly. Feeling the chill wind screaming past her ear, pulling her hair and blasting her face, Belinda clutched the collar of her thin, tight, short leather jacket to her neck and prayed for the ride to be over. And that they would arrive in one piece. Peregrine seemed to believe the white line in the centre of the road was meant as a guide to drive down.

Belinda comforted herself with the thought that the experienced-looking Peugeot was merely the four-wheeled equivalent of Peregrine's wardrobe. Scruffy in the manner so typical of the upper classes, according to that book of Lady Cylindria Slaughter's, Belinda had briefly considered the Way of the Barbour herself before reading, in *Napkins & Niceties*, that a creakingly new waxed coat, just-bought corduroys and a headscarf with a discernible pattern ran the risk of being viewed as irredeemably naff and common.

Naff and common being the last thing Belinda intended to be, a tight leather skirt, high heels and a push-up bra formed the central thrust of the all-new outfit in which she intended to stun Peregrine Oscar Herringbone Somerville.

As they rattled over a cattle grid and into the park, her heart soared higher and faster than a clay pigeon at a corporate shoot. This was more like it. This was what she had come to see. Before her, two great classical wings positively bristling with urns and goddesses stretched either side of a vast, central, domed rotunda. Swaddling was *Brideshead Revisited* and then some. As they paused to admire the view, Belinda was planning her revisits already.

'Trimindis, isn't it?' Somerville said now, looking proudly from Belinda to the building spreading before them. 'Marv'lous domes,' he added, his glance lingering briefly on Belinda's breasts. 'It's famous for its frontage.' Belinda pushed her own out and smiled seductively. This was going to be a walkover. In high heels on his back if he wanted.

She refrained from commenting on the house, however. Lady Cylindria Slaughter's *Napkins & Niceties* had warned that, 'as very grand people cannot conceive that everyone doesn't live in the same privileged circumstances as themselves, admiring remarks about their houses are deeply non-U.' Was Somerville, Belinda wondered, testing her? Staring, poker-faced, at the spreading mansion before her, she was determined not to jeopardise her chances.

'Not bad, is it?' Peregrine urged.

The look Belinda turned on him was of amazement mixed with scorn. Did he really expect her to fall for such an obvious trap?

Looking disappointed, Peregrine drove the car forward over a balustraded bridge and past an ornamental pond. Watching the reflection of the house's celebrated frontage sliding slowly through the water, Belinda thrust her breasts out still further.

'Come in,' Peregrine said as the car expired, rather than stopped, on the sweeping drive before the house.

'Nort thait way,' he called as Belinda tripped proprietorially up the steps to the vast front door. His voice was almost lost in the icy wind that slapped around their faces. 'They hivn't been opened since Quin Victoria left. Round the back.'

The fact that the vast front entrance doors had not parted company since eighteen whatever seemed to Belinda no reason why they should not open for *her*. Until Peregrine explained the risk, due to age and lack of maintenance, of their collapsing outwards and crushing anyone attempting to enter. Oh well. Plenty of time when she took over the estate to sort that out, and the disgusting smell in the damp back kitchen passage, where something fishy had clearly long ago died a protracted and hideous death.

'It's a bit nippley . . . I mean nippy,' Peregrine remarked, trying to avert his gaze from Belinda's cold-stiffened chest.

He was right. Her nipples were scraping like frozen peas

against her shirt. Perhaps layers of wool and tweed in pond-sludge brown had their merits. These temperatures would be considered extreme atop the Matterhorn. As for that chilly gloom filling the main hall, it looked suspiciously like freezing fog. But it *couldn't* be. This was *inside*. Those *couldn't* be icicles on the end of her lashes. Could they?

Realising that she could no longer feel her feet, Belinda found herself struck less by Swaddling's space and magnificence than by the fact that she could actually see her breath.

'Bladdy freezing, in fact,' Peregrine elaborated, rubbing his hands briskly.

Belinda shot him a look. Was this another test? Stately homes were famously bracing; no would-be chatelaine could afford to comment on the cold. 'Not at all,' she breathed seductively but visibly from between hammering teeth. 'I'm fine.'

'Fine? But you've got goosepimples like molehills.'

'I wouldn't have expected anything else.' Belinda stretched her near-rigid features into a smile. She could hardly get a facial muscle to move; still there could be advantages even in this. After all, it was cheaper than Botox.

Peregrine looked relieved. 'Good. So glad you understand.'

'Of *course* I understand.' Belinda smoothed her red-nailed hands suggestively down her leather-clad hips and flicked Peregrine a come-hither from under her eyelashes.

'Money's a bit tight, you see.'

Belinda wanted to laugh. *That* old chestnut. Everyone knew that the richer the person, the more desperate they were to deny they had money. And of course the Whyffes had money. With a house this size and land as far as the eye could see? *Puh*-leese. It was obvious Peregrine, not to mention his parents, was rolling in it.

'Are your parents here?' she asked suddenly.

'Oh yis. The rentals are rattling around samwhere.'

'Rentals?' Belinda repeated hollowly. What could possibly be *rented* in an ancestral home whose occupants had, according to Tarquin's research, possessed it in unbroken line from the reign of George III?

'Oh, sorry. Parentals. Rentals.'

Belinda felt inwardly scornful. Upper-class slang and nicknames irritated her. *Napkins & Niceties* had had a whole chapter entitled 'Busty, Bumface, Basher And The Rest Of Them.'

'They're looking forward to meeting *you*. Virry much,' Peregrine told her as they entered another gloomy passageway. 'They love high spotties.'

'High spotties?'

'House parties,' enunciated Peregrine, carefully. 'They like having young people about.'

Belinda, exasperated, forced herself to keep her mind on the big picture. There must be a couple of large Gainsboroughs *somewhere* in this house.

'We're beneath the rotunda now,' Peregrine said as they emerged from the passageway into a vast, circular, marrow-freezing hall. 'The dome,' he added, as Belinda looked blank. Through the huge windows she saw the ornamental lake, and the avenue of trees they had driven up; saw, too, that the panes had condensation on the outside rather than the inside. No wonder the upper classes had blue blood. No one with anything warmer could survive.

'I'll take you up to your room,' Peregrine said, blowing on his hands.

Belinda's face fell as far as her frozen features allowed. *He* was taking her? So where were the servants? If the maids weren't going to unpack her bags, what had been the point of making that useless bloody cleaner wrap *everything* – down to her knickers – in scented tissue paper?

On the other hand, she thought as she followed Peregrine down a sequence of endless corridors, they would be alone in a bedroom together. What better opportunity to make the first move?

'This is your room.' Peregrine paused before an enormous door upon which the paint was heavily cracked and blistered. 'You need to give it a little push. And be careful of the paint, it's coming off slightly. I get round how awful it looks by telling myself it's the sort of fashionable distressed effect I'd pay a fortune for on Sloane Street.'

Distressed? Belinda thought, almost dislocating her shoulder as she tried to move the mass of solid wood. Inconsolable, more like.

Her spirits improved on seeing the interior. This was more what she had been expecting. As cat-swinging facilities went, her own flat offered less than the ideal; here, however, you could have rotated a lioness with ease. That someone might well have done so was evidenced by the several animal skin rugs upon the floor. The murderous snarls of the attached heads reminded Belinda irresistibly of Warren Street, Deputy Editor of *The Globe*.

Visible in what little light managed to force its way through the bevelled, if grimy, windowpanes was a huge four-poster bed. Its red-fringed canopy swept upwards to a surmounting crown of atrophied feathers. Spotting her opportunity, Belinda clacked over to it in her high heels and, throwing one tanned, goosepimpled, leg over the other, sat on the edge, stroking the coverlet seductively. She sneezed violently as thick clouds of dust leapt into the air, accompanied by one or two moths.

'Bliss you,' said Peregrine pleasantly. Eyes streaming, nose in desperate need of a wipe, Belinda dug her nails viciously into her palms. This wasn't quite going the way she was expecting.

'Hisahinky.' Digging into his pocket, Peregrine thrust a large, ragged red piece of material in her direction.

Belinda rolled her eyes in despair and saw the ceiling. It was, she noticed, covered with figures – possibly naked – frolicking in murky gloom. This struck her as apt. 'Bit of an orgy going on up there,' she grinned at Peregrine suggestively.

'Yis,' Peregrine sighed. 'Mount Olympus. Terribly dirty, I know.'

'Yes, well, the pollution in Athens *is* terrible,' Belinda offered before stopping herself. Making flip remarks about

Swaddling wasn't the best way to join the chatelaine classes. The cold must be affecting her brain. 'Where's the ensuite?' she demanded.

Peregrine looked blank.

'Toilet,' Belinda said impatiently, then stopped in horror, remembering *Napkins & Niceties*' list of U and Non U-speak, 'Lavatory, rather.'

'Oh, right. The nearest bathroom's just ten doors down, but unfortunately the loo's on the next floor, round a corner, up some stairs and then about five hundred yards down the corridor. Be careful, the floorboards are a bit iffy. But if you don't want to bother, I'm sure my mother's got a spare chamber pot she can lend you.'

Belinda laughed heartily until she realised Peregrine's face had not moved.

'I'll leave you to have a rest, shall I?' Peregrine suggested. 'Then we could do the interview over dinner.'

Belinda's mind went momentarily blank. '*Interview*?'

'You're going to ask me all about . . . well, actually I'm not sure, really,' Peregrine smiled weakly. 'The letter wasn't terribly clear.'

'Oh. Yes. Actually, I think we can do it tomorrow,' Belinda said decisively. 'Why spoil a lovely evening with work?'

'Righty-ho. Well, I'll see you later. I expect you want a nice rilixing bath,' Peregrine disappeared into the gloom towards the door. 'Dinner's at eight in the dining room.'

Belinda nodded. A nice relaxing bath was *exactly* what

she wanted. After that, she would get her battle armour on. In the Bottega Veneta luggage dumped unceremoniously on its side by Peregrine was a pinched-from-the-fashion-cupboard Versace evening gown as tight and shiny as the scales on a mermaid's tail. Swinging her Jade Jagger sponge bag as she walked down the corridor, Belinda remembered with satisfaction the cleaner's awe at the sight of the dress.

'Ess wunnderful, Belinda,' she had breathed, as she wrapped it reverently in tissue paper.

'Madam Belinda,' snapped Belinda. 'And it bloody well should be wonderful. Worth your wages for ten years, that is.'

The bathroom with its huge claw-footed bath delighted Belinda. In accordance with the *Napkins & Niceties* rules for the ideal tub size, seven-foot-tall man in a top hat could easily have lain down in it. Filling it, however, was a different matter. Turning on the taps full blast, achieved only a lukewarm trickle in an offputting shade of yellow, accompanied by a faint sulphurous smell. In which case she'd put *all* the bath salts in. Belinda accordingly added the entire contents of a rusty canister that stood beside the tub. Only after getting in did she realise that the faded, rust-eaten lettering on the canister side said 'Ajax'. Afterwards, itching unpleasantly, she returned to her room. Here, the flowered, crack-glazed receptacle newly arrived by the bedside confirmed that Peregrine had not been joking about his mother and the chamber pot.

At ten minutes to eight, Belinda, still scratching despite sloshing on a whole bottle of Dr Hauschka moisturiser, stood alone by the enormous empty fireplace. Of all the rooms she had looked into during a long and tiring search, this seemed most likely to be the dining room. The rotting carvings over the fireplace seemed – originally at least – to have been birds and fish, and there was a table, albeit a very dusty one. Belinda passed the time trying to remember the table manners chapter in *Napkins & Niceties*. 'Tongs are wrong,' she muttered to herself. 'Asparagus is eaten with the fingers. All words derived from French are vulgar – so napkin, not *serviette*. And never pile up the plates after eating as it makes it obvious you're not used to having servants.'

Five to eight. No servant had yet appeared, still less any plates. Belinda had now moved on to contemplation of the long table. Despite its thick layer of dust, it was suggestive of hearty aristocratic meals with chandeliers glinting on ranks of Sèvres and silverware. No silverware, however, was in evidence, and the room's only illumination came courtesy of the dying day outside, although it was by now raining hard. Of the hearty aristocrats there was as yet no sign either, but surely the Whyffes must be on their way. Or did they get lost in the passages as well? 'Say Greens, not vegetables,' Belinda muttered to herself, wondering how one distinguished in that case, when asking to be passed the bok choi, rather than the broccoli. And was asparagus a vegetable or a fruit?

'Hoy thar,' Peregrine said, suddenly emerging from the gloom of the hall into the gloom of the dining room and placing a brown plastic tray – very BHS canteen, Belinda thought, surprised – on the table. She noted disapprovingly that he was not dressed for dinner. Rather, he seemed to be wearing the same clothes he had worn earlier, apart from the addition of a couple of jackets on top.

But of course he would, she realised with sudden relief. As son and heir of Lord Whyffe, he was part of what, according to *Napkins & Niceties*, was that top strata of society so grand they were above dress rules altogether.

'Drink?' Peregrine gestured at the tray. On it were three cans of beer and a glass of what looked like cloudy water. Across its surface, a raggy piece of lemon floated like a dead fish. 'I've brought you a gin and tonic. The rest of us drink beer, I'm afraid.'

'But why?' Belinda hated beer, just as she hated the whole working-class, dog-racing, hobnailed-boot culture she imagined went with it. 'It's horrid, isn't it?'

'Well, it's cheaper than wine and after a while you get a taste for it.'

Cheaper? Belinda raised an eyebrow. Change the record, she thought. The Whyffes really were mean. Quite staggeringly so. On the other hand, that was usual among millionaires – billionaires, hopefully – and something of a relief to have it confirmed. Only the Whyffes being wealthy tightwads, would, after all, explain a great deal that had been puzzling. The house's shabbiness. Its lack of heating.

The four circular raffia mats that, even now, Peregrine was dragging out of a chest. Out of a drawer came a rattling handful of plastic knives and forks, together with paper napkins and salt and pepper sachets.

'People pick these up for us,' he grinned apologetically. 'Saves a fortune on cutlery.'

Belinda nodded slowly. Upper class eccentricity, no doubt. And hopefully the food would be good. Jugged hare, game chips, chafing dishes, that sort of thing.

Just then, a woman appeared through the door behind them bearing a Pyrex dish and several serving spoons. She smiled broadly at Belinda, who frowned in reply. The cheek of it. When she was running the show, servants would smile when they were bloody well smiled *at*.

'Mum,' Peregrine said. 'This is Belinda. Belinda, my mother.'

Belinda's hand grabbed the table edge in horror.

'How do you do,' Lady Whyffe plonked her tray down. 'We've so been looking forward to meeting you.'

Belinda barely had time to recover before a stooping man in a ragged tweed jacket stumbled through the doorway. Two minutes ago, she would have assumed him to be the gamekeeper. Or perhaps the gamekeeper's gardener. But, as a shaking, blue-veined hand came out in greeting, Belinda found herself looking into a pair of streaming, lopsided blue eyes exactly like Peregrine's.

'My father.'

'Hello there,' said Lord Whyffe kindly. 'I must say, we've

been looking forward enormously to meeting you. A sillibrity interviewer! What a marvellous job. You must move in such illivated circles.'

'Absolutely.' Belinda was now familiar with this routine and in any case buoyed by the triple-strength gin and tonic. 'Lots of rich and famous people.'

The Whyffes' starry-eyed fascination with all the rich and famous people she must know was slightly puzzling. Weren't the landed gentry continually mixing with celebrities themselves? Jerry Hall was always staying at Badminton.

'*Terribly* rewarding,' Lady Whyffe nodded. 'Well paid, I mean,' she added.

'Oh, very. Hugely. Embarrassingly, in fact, ha ha.' The penny had dropped, as it were. Belinda could now see their little game a mile away. Being extremely rich and extremely mean, the Whyffes obviously wanted some reassurance she was going to contribute something to the household when she joined it. Better wait until after the wedding to tell them it was the ten pence a month left over after she'd paid off the instalments on all her other debts.

Peregrine had by now arranged the place mats round one end of the dining table. Sitting down, the dusty length of mahogany stretching away into the gloom in front of her, Belinda felt rather like a skittle in a bowling alley. Peregrine had set up what looked like a small bedside lamp, but it barely made an impression on the encircling darkness. It did, however, illuminate the dusty cruet set beautifully.

'I hope this is all right,' said Lady Whyffe, looking uncertainly into the Pyrex dish. It contained a chicken in what looked like a pool of clear grease. 'It said on the jar that you just had to throw it over the chicken but it looks a bit funny to me.'

Outside, the rain continued to dash against the windows. Unable to bring herself to address the lump of putty-coloured poultry on her plate, Belinda started to dig. She was determined to plumb the true depths of this family's riches. A good thing that digging was her living.

She nodded at the drips starting to come through the ceiling. 'Dreadful, isn't it, the way stately home owners have to pay VAT on all repairs,' she began, remembering the small bit of research she had done into patrician preoccupations. The demands of customs and excise versus the need to maintain the ancestral fabric was, she knew, a subject that exercised practically every landowner in the country.

'Not a problem for us,' replied Lord Whyffe, giving her a trembly smile.

Satisfaction swept Belinda. They must indeed be rolling in it in that case. Then, to her delighted amazement, Lady Whyffe turned to her and, between chews of her chicken, said something sounding like, 'We hope you like millionaires.'

'*Absolutely*,' Belinda assured her. She gazed adoringly at the woman who was to be her future mother-in-law.

'I'm so glad. Some people don't, you know.'

'Unbelievable.' Belinda's eyes were wide with genuine amazement.

Lord Whyffe nodded at her approvingly.

And so it was that, dinner over, Belinda found herself sitting with the Whyffes around a small convector heater in a corner of one of the reception rooms, watching *Who Wants To Be A Millionaire?* on a tiny, ancient black and white television.

'We never miss it,' explained Lord Whyffe. 'Olympia – my wife – writes endlessly to ask if she can be on it, but they haven't replied yet.'

Belinda blinked. Didn't you have to telephone to get on that programme? Or was this upper class humour? She racked her brains to recall what *Napkins & Niceties* had said on the subject.

'But we're living in hope,' Lady Whyffe added. 'It must be wonderful to be rich. Don't you agree?'

Tell me another one, thought Belinda.

'Of course, you'd know all about it,' said Lord Whyffe. 'Millionaire lifestyles, that sort of thing.'

Belinda sighed inwardly. For some reason, the Whyffes were looking at her like a group of eager hamsters. These people were obsessed. 'I know a bit,' she admitted.

'You're being modest, I know,' Lady Whyffe nodded. Belinda suppressed an indignant gasp. She had been accused of many things in her time. But never that.

'Caravaggio!' shouted Peregrine suddenly at the television. 'It's the right answer,' he added. 'The question was what Italian painter was famous for chiaroscuro? Caravannio, Caravaggio, Joe di Maggio or Cornetto. And it's Caravaggio.'

'We used to have one of those,' Lord Whyffe intoned wistfully. 'But we had to sell it.'

Belinda felt cheered. If there had been Caravaggios at Swaddling recently, might a Van Gogh or two still be knocking about?

'Peregrine tells us you have a very important job,' Lady Whyffe added. 'The paper would fold without you, he says.'

Belinda remembered that she had said something of the sort in the car. It was, anyway, absolutely true. The fold which got *The Globe* to flop open in its particular way was inserted by a machine somewhere in Peterborough.

The drips through the ceiling seemed to be intensifying. In the gloom of the corner of the room, Belinda could see the gleam of wetness; a positive cascade seemed to be sliding down the wall by the fireplace. It struck her as an ideal change of subject.

'Funny you've got so much water coming through the roof,' she observed, 'when so little seems to come out of the taps.'

'What do you mean?' Peregrine looked surprised. 'The baths at Swaddling fill in two minutes.'

'Not the one I was trying to fill.'

'Ah. Yes. Actually, the water supply *is* a bit erratic in your wing. It can be a trickle for ages, and then suddenly comes through the pipes with a tremendous surge.' He looked up at the ceiling, frowning slightly. 'I must say, you're right, though. The drips do seem to be rather worse than usual.'

Belinda remembered the taps in her bathroom, opened to their fullest extent in the attempt to coax even an inch of water into the bath. Had she turned them back off?

Peregrine's attention, thankfully, had returned to the television. '*Abdicate!*' he yelled. 'What word ending in ate did Edward the Eighth do when he resigned the throne? Agitate, ruminate, abdicate or masturbate?'

'Edward the Eighth came here once,' Lord Whyffe sighed.

CHAPTER SEVENTEEN

'Madam Grace. You are at home?' Maria's call echoed hollowly down the corridor of Grace's flat. She put her head on one side and listened. Nothing.

Maria glanced at her watch. Half past six in the evening. Grace was usually here at this time. *Something* was odd; she could sniff it in the air. The bathroom door was closed as well, which was unusual. 'Madam Grace?' she called again.

Grace could hear Maria. She was, however, unable to move. Getting out of the bath would disrupt the spell it had taken such ages to put together. 'Make your beloved telephone you by sitting in a tepid bath with acorns, oak leaves and a circle of fresh rose petals in it . . .'

It was, actually, intensely uncomfortable; the water was now stone cold, the leaves were scratchy and bobbing unpleasantly against her and dirt from the acorns gritted the bottom of the tub. The rose petals were not only waterlogged and sinking, but refusing to remain in a circle. And there were three minutes yet to go of staring at the photograph of Red Campion and allowing her thoughts to fill with him; the cider-toasting was still to come. The bottle stood on the side of the bath; Grace eyed it without enthusiasm. Of all her least favourite drinks, cider ranked near the bottom along with snakebite and advocaat. Then there was the invocation; the fatuousness of chanting 'Pick up the phone and give me a call; there's nothing stopping you at all'. It made Grace's toes curl. What sort of an idiot was she? On the other hand, Red Campion hadn't called yet. It seemed as good a way as any – apart from the heartsinking, I'm-a-failure option of going back to Bill for help. No, she'd stay in the bath. There was no way she was going to all this trouble again. The gathering of acorns and oak leaves alone had involved some very unpleasant poking about at the foot of the trees in the local park.

'Madam Grace?'

Determinedly, Grace ignored Maria calling in the corridor. She must think of nothing but Red, otherwise the spell would be no good. She stared hard at the picture of him she had carefully cut out of *Hello!* magazine.

'*Madam Grace!*'

Ten seconds to go . . . *damn*. The bathroom door was opening. And she hadn't even toasted him with cider yet. Grabbing the bottle, Grace stuck it in her mouth and threw as much as she could down her throat, swallowing manically, as some of it forced its way back up. As she did so, Maria's trademark peroxide hair – decorated, this time, with a slash of neon blue – came into view. 'Pick up the phone and give me a call . . .' Grace gabbled frantically.

'*Madam Grace!*' The cleaner looked in amazement, then horror, from the bottle of cider in Grace's left hand via the debris-filled bath to the photograph in her right. 'Ees everytheeng OK?'

'. . . there's nothing stopping you at all.' Grace gasped, drawing her knees up to cover her breasts. No doubt from now on Maria would think her an insane alcoholic. Not to mention one given to sitting in cold, dirty baths. Still, everyone knew the English were eccentric. And the picture of the film star was easily explained. Maria would just think she was an obsessed fan.

'Thees man,' Maria said, looking at the picture of Red.

Grace looked sheepish, ready to play the part of love-struck sap. 'He's a famous film star. I'm mad, I know.'

'He ees?' Maria shrugged. 'I know nothing about feelms. I never haf time to see feelms.'

She may not have recognised Red, but Maria had recognised instantly what was going on. She knew a spell when she saw one. And she knew this one: an odd but still recognisable variation on one her grandmother had taught her, whose aim was to draw a couple together. She hoped it would not work. Maria did not like the look of the man in the picture. He looked, first and foremost, very pleased with himself. Secondly, she'd never known a blond man be trustworthy.

But then, this spell wasn't either. It was notoriously unreliable. Had Madam Grace asked for her advice, Maria would have recommended the one where you pictured your beloved's face in a coin and put it in a circle of pink flowers. Then you buried it in sand, then somehow contrived to get the coin to the loved one. *There* was an invocation that got results every time.

A thought suddenly struck Maria. Perhaps there was someone else who could use it. Her writer client, the single man. If anyone needed romantic assistance, he did. His book might be almost finished and publication almost certain. But his real object, to get near to Grace, had not been achieved.

'Maria,' Grace muttered. Maria, however, was not listening. Her brain was whirring with possibilities. The coin spell. That was the answer. The book idea had been a good one, as Madam Grace worked in publishing. And it had been fun to supply her client with details of her own childhood, of her fantasies about the bay where she had grown up. He had, it must be admitted, woven a wonderful story round them. Yet the main plan, to bring them together, had not worked.

But the coin spell – that might. Maria's eyes gleamed. *He* would have to do the first bit and bury the coin. Then she would pass it on to Grace.

'Maria,' Grace repeated louder, faintly disturbed by the

cleaner's apparent trance. 'If you don't mind, I'd like to get out of the bath now.'

As Maria exclaimed apologies and scuttled out, Grace pulled the plug. She felt both silly and uncomfortable. She was cold, her throat felt sore; worse, she felt utterly certain that Red Campion was never going to call. All she would gain from this particular episode was flu.

But even as, miserably, Grace wrapped herself in a towel, the telephone shrilled in the hall.

'Madam Grace. What 'as 'appened?' Maria stood in the doorway of Grace's bedroom. Fifteen minutes ago, thanks to her ministrations, it had been an oasis of calm and smooth linen. Now, freshly ironed clothes lay scrunched all over the floor and spilled out of half-open suitcases. 'Eet looks as eef a bomb as eet it.'

Maria's past experiences, Grace knew, meant this was likely to be more than a figure of speech. 'I'm sorry, Maria. I've just got, well, rather an important meeting and—'

'You have date with man in picture?' Maria said disappointedly. She was puzzled. The spell Grace had cast rarely worked; why, of all times, had it chosen to do so now? But love spells, like most other love-related things, sometimes worked in mysterious ways.

Very mysterious in this case. She glanced again at the picture of the film star, now positioned on Grace's dressing table. He was handsome, certainly, although his face was too perfect, his features too regular, his jaw too arrogant.

Yet he looked familiar; where, Maria wondered, had she seen this man before? She had never seen him in a film, as Madam Grace evidently had, but she had seen him somewhere. Recently. But where? *Where?*

Ah. It was coming. In her mind's eye, Maria saw a dirty cup, a pair of holed stockings, a cigarette ground out into a plate. There was only one client who created so much disgusting mess and then expected her to have the whole place spick-and-span within three hours. And at half the rates anyone else paid. Maria's mouth curled with contempt. *Belinda*. Belinda had pictures of this man scattered all over her flat. Evidence for certain that he was not a man to be trusted. Madam Grace should not get involved.

'It's not a date, it's an important meeting,' Grace declared before she could stop herself. Damn, and the whole thing was meant to be a secret.

Maria knew now what she must do. She must cast the coin spell to counteract this as soon as she could. She would not be put off with excuses from her client, either. That was what had gone wrong with the book plot. If only he had heeded her urges to be bolder and had, as she suggested, turned up in person at Grace's flat to deliver his manuscript. But he had been adamant that, for some reason, she wouldn't want to see him. He had wanted to wait until the book was finished. It was obvious, now, that he had waited too long. Possibly missed his chance altogether.

Grace, on the other hand, felt the biggest chance of her life was imminent. It hardly seemed possible that the summons from Red Campion had finally come. Come as she was standing in the hall in a towel with Maria banging away at the skirting boards in the background. Fortunately, it had not been Campion himself who had made the call; instead, a personal assistant from Los Angeles had instructed her to present herself the following evening at six o'clock at the Meurice Hotel.

'I don't know the Meurice,' Grace had admitted after cudgelling her brains for a few seconds. 'Is it new?' she hedged. 'Is it in Park Lane?'

'It's about a hundred years old and it's in the rue de Rivoli.' Of course. Duke had said Red Campion was in Paris. 'Ask for Mr Valentino,' breezed the assistant, as if all this were the most normal thing in the world.

Grace had put down the receiver, heart soaring into her mouth. Going to Paris was thrilling enough. Going to Paris to meet a film star who was a lust object all over the world; now that was simply off the scale.

She glanced with irritation at Maria rubbing unhappily at the mirror over the dressing table. What on earth was wrong with her?

But Grace had other things on her mind. Pressing issues such as What To Wear. Something more than jeans and T-shirt would be required. Unless, of course, the jeans were Prada and the T-shirt Stella McCartney. Looking down at the floor and the combinations she had tried and rejected, Grace longed for something treading an effortless, elegant and expensive line between hip and chic.

She dragged out a pair of agonisingly high-heeled black ankle boots written off after one wear, along with ever going to shoe shops with Ellie again. Yet, standing before the long mirror in her bedroom now, Grace suddenly saw the point of them. They added at least a foot to the end of each of her legs – quite apart from the ones she already had. She was thinner too; the stress of recent weeks had made what were once standard-fit Silver Tabs almost into a pair of loose hipsters. Just as well, really. Because even if there had been the money, there wasn't the time for the casually fabulous haircut, the morning in Bond Street with the personal stylist, the Eve Lom facial and the full head-to-toe exfoliation that would make her even basically presentable. Grace looked back at herself. Not bad. Not bad at all. She smiled at herself before catching, in the depths of the mirror, Maria polishing away at the window, her face creased with disapproval.

It was only later that evening, after Maria had left, the clothes were packed and the Eurostar ticket booked, that Grace calmed down to the extent of realising that, actually, she knew very little about the man she was about to meet. Facts were what she needed, or at least a bit of insight. Shelving the idea of going to bed, she pulled on a fleece and jeans and set off for the late-night newsagents.

The shop was empty apart from the heavy-eyed Ethiopian who ran it. Under the painfully brilliant strip lights, Grace rummaged through the racks, thinking enviously of the information-packed newspaper-cuttings libraries on which journalists were able to draw. Had she been Belinda Black . . . but Grace pushed the thought away. All that was behind her now.

After a prolonged and unsuccessful riffling session, Grace had still found nothing with Red in it. There was an *OK!* paparazzi shot of him looking cross in an LA supermarket car park, but that hardly ranked as enlightening. Trust her to have picked the only week in UK publishing without a single piece about Red *somewhere*. Vaguely she remembered someone mentioning an article. Oh yes. Yes. That strange man from the NFT who she'd sat next to at the Venice dinner. What had the magazine been called? All she could remember was that the piece had sounded very sleazy. And, no doubt untrue. But beggars could not be choosers. It might give her something to go on.

'Have you got any *Trailers*?' Grace asked, remembering suddenly.

'Trailer? I've got a van,' smiled the newsagent helpfully. 'What you wan' it for?'

'It's a film magazine,' Grace explained helplessly. Had she got the name right? 'An American one,' she added.

Enlightenment flooded the man's brown eyes. 'Oh yeah. We got one lef', I think. Under the *Cosmopolitan*s.'

Under a pile of promises to have the best orgasm in the world ever, Grace eventually found what she was looking for. Red's tousled blond hair and electric blue eyes, plastered over with neon headlines. 'STARDOM, SEX

ADDICTION AND ME: CAMPION COMES CLEAN'. Uncomfortable under the newsagent's gentle gaze, Grace paid and left.

Back at home, coffee in hand, scanning the pages for the interview, Grace found her attention waylaid by *Trailer Trash*, the gossip section at the front of the magazine, A piece entitled 'Emails At Dawn: Is Ritchie Flick In Trouble?' purported to be an exchange between the head of publicity at the studio making the Red Campion film *Concrete Boots* and the publicist for one of the film's other stars, Champagne D'Vyne.

From: vicky *(vickymacfarlane@concreteboots.co.uk)*
To: cat *(catrogers@bigmouthpr.co.uk)*
Re: Champagne D'Vyne and 'Concrete Boots' publicity

Cat, I have a problem. You're asking us to put Champagne's name above the film title in bigger letters than anyone else, and also call her CDV instead of Champagne D'Vyne. We cannot do this!!!! Quite apart from being the least famous person in the cast (Red Campion is in it, remember), she signed onto this project as Champagne D'Vyne. We can't help it if she's decided to get a diva transplant.

From: cat *(catrogers@bigmouthpr.co.uk)*
To: vicky *(vickymacfarlane@concreteboots.co.uk)*
Re: Champagne D'Vyne and 'Concrete Boots' publicity

OK, I'm going to do you a big favour, Vicky. I'm not going to repeat to Champagne what you just said. But only because I don't want to see her go to jail FOR RIPPING OUT YOUR ORGANS WITH HER BARE HANDS!

From: vicky *(vickymacfarlane@concreteboots.co.uk)*
To: cat *(catrogers@bigmouthpr.co.uk)*
Re: Champagne D'Vyne and 'Concrete Boots' publicity

Hey. I thought she'd gotten into spirituality. Peace and love and all that?

From: cat *(catrogers@bigmouthpr.co.uk)*
To: vicky *(vickymacfarlane@concreteboots.co.uk)*
Re: Champagne D'Vyne and 'Concrete Boots' publicity

I simply can't believe the lack of respect here. Champagne D'Vyne is a pre-eminent female celebrity.

More than this, she is determined that being called 'Champagne D'Vyne' isn't where her movement is at these days. She is 'CDV'. If Catherine Zeta Jones is CZJ, Champagne is CDV.

From: vicky *(vickymacfarlane@concreteboots.co.uk)*
To: cat *(catrogers@bigmouthpr.co.uk)*
Re: Champagne D'Vyne and 'Concrete Boots' publicity

I'd like to see 'CDV' try to rip out my organs. I hear my liver would grow back anyway. Which is more than I can say for her movie career after these emails get out.

'Rumour has it,' the concluding sentence informed the reader, 'that Guy Ritchie has recently withdrawn his services as director in the troubled *Concrete Boots*. See Red Campion interview on p.15 for further info.'

Grace did just that.

CAMPION OF THE WORLD, announced the headline on page 15.

'Red Campion is most celebrated as the Roman soldier who rose from rank and file obscurity to the status of general in *Legionnaire*. Women round the globe thrilled to the celluloid soldier whose shyness and

> courage were apparently reflected in the actor's real-life, modest, press-shy persona . . .'

Grace was disappointed. She knew that much already. Apart from Sion muttering darkly beside her, what she recalled most about the film were the rows of shining eyes and flushed cheeks in the women's loos afterwards. On Sion's insistence, the cinema they had gone to had not been a Leicester Square temple to American cultural empiricism. It had been a Bloomsbury arthouse; the women in the loos, like herself, doubtless had pretensions to intellectualism and, just like her, had been fighting infatuation with the film's hero. Yet Campion had defeated them all, just as, in the course of the film, he had vanquished the various armies of Picts, Gauls and Goths. The introduction continued.

> 'Yet rumours of email wife dumping, sex addiction and Crowephobia imply the grave screen general might not be all he seems . . .'

Ah. The dirt was about to be dished. Grace was determined not to believe a word of what followed. She thought of the women in the cinema loos again. Campion had something that appealed to the thinking woman as well as the masses; a suggestion of intelligence and sensitivity below the almost blandly beautiful features. The fact he was now writing a book seemed to more than bear this out. And who else in the world knew about that apart from her, Bill and Red himself? Certainly not *Trailer*, Grace thought, triumphantly. Duke's rich Texan drawl floated into her head: 'He's always wanted to write a novel and have that novel assessed on its own merits and for it to be nothing to do with goddamn screaming women, Oscars or Legionnaire's goddamn Disease.' Red, in other words, was as modest as he was talented. And as talented as he was sensitive and handsome.

Magazines like *Trailer* had no idea what they were talking about.

Grace returned to the interview. After the fawning introduction, the questions started. She was surprised how relaxed Campion's attitude to his stardom seemed to be. He did not seem to take it seriously at all:

> Q: You've not always chosen your scripts wisely. Dare I mention *Zombie Vicars Must Die*?
> A: Hey, when I first became a movie star I was so amazed that I was one that I kept working on anything anyone asked me to do before they found out that I wasn't one. So by the time they found out I wasn't one, I was one.

Grace smiled. Red sounded refreshingly unegotistical. Just as she had hoped and believed. Yet, as the interview strayed into more personal territory, its mood turned darker.

> Q: It was rumoured that your marriage broke up because you were a serial skirt-chaser. Your wife, it is

said, finally realised the marriage was over when she came into your hotel room to find you *in flagrante* with one of the chambermaids. Mr Campion, are you a sex addict?
A: (tersely) Are you seriously suggesting that I dignify that question with an answer? What exactly makes you think you in any way have the right to ask it? That's what pisses me off most about celebrity. Punks like you thinking they can ask whatever they want, however personal.
Q: So why did your marriage break up?
A: My marriage break-up was due to press intrusion. People like you, poking around in it.

Good for him, Grace thought. Red was right. The line of questioning was *outrageously* intrusive. Pressed by the obviously unrepentant *Trailer* journalist, the actor was next forced into a denial of the rumour that he had dumped his wife by email.

A: Of course I didn't. Why would I? I have an excellent and very peaceful relationship with my former wife. We've reached a settlement that suits both of us and everything's fine. People always say these disgusting things about famous people just to provoke them into denying it and make a bigger story.

Poor Red. How *hideous* to have no protection – apart from,

in extreme circumstances, the libel laws – from any ill-natured scandal a journalist might wish to print about you.

Q: So you find press intrusion a problem. How do you cope?
A: I ignore it, usually. But you'd be amazed how persistent some of them can be.
Q: Long lenses, people bribing your neighbours to talk, hiding in your dustbin, that sort of thing?
A: Yeah. And endless interview requests. One English paper has sent the same request through fifty times. Fifty goddamn times. Unbelievable. I got the fifty-first only yesterday. It's still a no, though.
Q: But why?
A: Journalists are scum. They want to use you, that's all. Only last week I was being interviewed by someone who asked me to sign a photograph. I was happy to, until she asked me to dedicate it to someone who wasn't her. I asked why and she explained it was for her builder's wife. Her builder had apparently promised her a free wooden floor if she'd get a personal dedication from Red Campion to his wife. It's sick. It really is.
Q: OK. Let's change the subject.
A: I was hoping you might.
Q: How do you really feel about Russell Crowe?
A: (tersely) I have the highest admiration for him. Now can we talk about my new film release? Which

was, after all, supposed to be the purpose of this interview.
Q: Really? You admire Crowe?
A: (through gritted teeth) I repeat, can we talk about my new film release?

Grace felt indignant. The gritted teeth bit was so obviously made up. How unfair. Red's new film release, it turned out, was a World War Two Air Force drama in which he played a wing commander. Reading the dutiful synopsis of the movie plot, obviously hurriedly stuffed in at the end of the interview, Grace wondered if film could be a publicity opportunity for *Ginger's Bought It*. The character Campion was playing sounded remarkably similar to poor old Sir Greville Goodtrouser DSO.

Q: Can I ask you about the film you're slated to work on next? The Guy Ritchie film *Concrete Boots*. Is it true that Guy has refused to direct it because of difficulties with certain members of the cast, even though filming hasn't even started yet?
A: I don't want to comment on that.

Good answer, Grace thought. Why should he? Now she was about to meet Red Campion, she felt oddly protective of him. He was to be her new project, after all.

Q: Can you confirm for us the persistent rumour

> that, after having fallen for each other in preliminary meetings, you and Champagne D'Vyne are now . . .

Champagne D'Vyne? Fallen for each other! Grace's eyes widened in shock and surprise. Impossible, surely. This sensible, grounded, defensive-but-understandably-so man, having fallen for that ridiculous woman? *Surely not.* She was relieved when, as with the various rumours about his divorce, Red blew this one conclusively out of the water.

> A: The hell I am. Even if it was any of your business, which it isn't . . .

Quite right, Grace thought, deploring the *Trailer* journalist's deliberate policy of provocation.

> . . . There's been no woman in my life since I split with my wife. Right now, I'm dedicated to my art, and to a new and very exciting project I'm involved with. Something very different from anything I've done before.

The book! Grace was exultant. Surely he meant the book! And she was one of the very few who knew about it.

> Q: Can you tell us anything about that?
> A: No. But you'll find out soon enough.

The interview on his latest film ended by confirming that the actor would be going to Paris to do post-production; to re-record some spoken parts that hadn't quite worked during shooting. And, Grace thought, delightedly, to have a meeting with *me*.

No doubt about it, Swaddling was pretty creepy at night. Blundering around on her own in the dark was not Belinda's idea of fun. But she had a job to do.

Fortunately, the pale and mournful moon that had lately hauled itself into the sky was pouring weak illumination through the corridor windows. Trying determinedly not to think about ghosts, Belinda tapped and pushed irritably at serried ranks of locked doors. Where the hell was Peregrine's room? Reaching the vast staircase, she glanced up at the portraits. She could just about see the face of one of them, a dishy Cavalier type. Well, *those* genes had clearly disappeared from the Whyffe pool some centuries ago.

Belinda descended a level, cursing as the splinters slid into the balls of her feet. She was trembling with the cold and her own mounting fear. She clutched her Agent Provocateur baby doll nightie about her as the icy finger of terror slid slowly down her spine. The urge to return to the relative safety of her room was great. Greater still, however, was the need to find Peregrine.

Locating his room was like looking for a needle in a particularly large and loose haystack. The endless corridor twisted like a python, swinging abruptly left and right and then turning back on itself. Belinda had some time since surrendered the faintest idea of where she was. The freezing temperature, moreover, was doing odd things to her bowels. Or was it that truly disgusting chicken slop Lady Whyffe had cooked? Whatever the reason, Belinda was increasingly and uncomfortably aware of the pressing – very pressing – need for a lavatory. Not a chamber pot. Just then, as she came upon a door whose smallness and plainness hinted at a strictly utilitarian function, hope rose wildly within her.

Rattling the handle, Belinda realised it was not locked, merely stuck. Unopened for a number of years, very likely. After application of her now-practised shoulder, the door gave way to reveal – wonder of wonders – an ancient lavatory. The obliging moon shone on a floral china bowl and a patent name in inverted commas displayed on the cistern. Relief, Belinda thought. In all senses of the word.

Too late she realised that what the moon did not reveal was anything in the way of lavatory paper. The small shelf beside the loo was innocent of as much as a roll of Izal Medicated. Damn this bloody dump. What was she supposed to do, use her nightie?

There was only one item on the shelf. A small book. Some crappy old novel, by the looks of it. Belinda picked up the volume with its layer of dust and cobwebs. How long had this been here? Obviously no one had missed it – unsurprisingly, given how boring it looked. Further proof of its trash status was the fact someone had scribbled all over the inside front cover. As well as, she saw, flicking through it, several of the pages inside.

Belinda did not hesitate, and pulled out as many pages as were necessary to complete the act. Most of them, it turned out. That chicken dish had a lot to answer for.

She found her way back gratifyingly quickly to the main staircase, where the sexy but grimy Cavalier ran his eyes approvingly over her skimpy nightwear. Her first act after moving in, Belinda decided, would be to have the portraits cleaned.

Belinda suppressed a yelp as she tripped over something lying in the corridor. Looking down, cursing, rubbing her throbbing big toe, she realised it was a pair of shoes. Familiar shoes. Shoes that looked as if they had been buried in the garden for a hundred years. She felt a stab of optimism. If Peregrine was leaving his shoes outside to be cleaned, surely that implied at least *one* servant at Swaddling?

The door creaked open and Peregrine looked out. 'Hoy thar,' he said, looking surprised. 'Sorry you fell over my brogues. I only leave them outside because otherwise the mice in my bedroom would eat them.'

Belinda, shuddering, added Rentokil to her chatelaine's shopping list. But that was for later. For now, on the other hand . . . 'Time for the interview,' she purred. 'I thought one on one was best.' Pushing her naked breasts into Peregrine's pyjama'd chest, Belinda hooked one long leg round the back of his and began to grind herself gently against him. Her nails dug into his back as she kissed him, wetly, lengthily and loudly.

Peregrine staggered backwards in panic. 'I say,' he stammered.

'You drive me crazy,' Belinda groaned, gazing passionately into his terrified pupils. '*God*, you're big,' she gasped, sliding her hands inside his pyjamas and feeling about. Where the hell was it? Did he actually *have* one? Then her fingers closed over something small, cold and flaccid.

'God,' she exclaimed in mock amazement. 'You're *huge*.'

Peregrine blinked in surprise. 'Rilly? Always thought it was a bit on the small side myself. It never really recovered from the school matron hitting it with a cold spoon.'

'It's massive,' Belinda insisted, ripping open Peregrine's flannel pyjama top.

'You think so?' Peregrine's voice was rising slightly.

'Colossal. Masterful.' Belinda ran her tongue slowly round her lips as she pushed him gently back across what seemed like miles of rotting carpet. Eventually, they reached the large four-poster bed in the middle of the room.

'M-my last girlfriend said you could put a thimble over it,' Peregrine bleated. His tone indicated he was perfectly content with this assessment.

Belinda ignored this. As Peregrine's heels collided with the bed and he disappeared suddenly backwards, she fell upon him like a tiger, growling, scratching, licking. 'You're a god,' she murmured. Her face bumped against his protuberant ribs, skimming the sparse patches of hair on his belly.

'You're fantastic. Vast.' Belinda groaned. Her ardour was by now genuine, powered by the fact she was addressing, not its heir but the huge Swaddling estate itself. It was the house she was seducing, the park she was making love to, the ancestral aisle she was going down.

She moaned ecstatically as she rubbed herself against the surface of his still-up pyjama bottoms. The rough cotton was surprisingly stimulating. Peregrine's penis, unfortunately, was still only slightly erect. Like a crane long out of use, the flaccid organ lying limply alongside his thigh was rousing itself very slowly and rustily. It was, Belinda thought, writhing resignedly against him, like waking the dead. She was in the right position, but nothing much was happening. The only thing growing within her was boredom. 'Is it in yet?' she inquired finally, exasperated. Below her, Peregrine yelped in assent.

It was difficult to see and not to choke in the clouds of dust rising from the bed. And then there was the temperature. Forget love in a cold climate, Belinda grimaced. This was sex in sub-zero conditions.

And what was that noise in the corner? Drip-drip-drip – *more* bloody buckets, Belinda thought crossly, remembering the state of her bathroom when she'd gone back to turn off the taps. Some of the final scenes in *Titanic* had sprung to mind. On the other hand, what a wonderful opportunity to, once again, introduce the subject of the Whyffe family wealth. After all, she thought, clasping Peregrine's rather flat posterior, she was in the perfect position to get to the bottom of things.

She continued grinding herself determinedly against Peregrine's unresponsive penis. As this was obviously going to take some time, a little more probing into the Whyffe family fortune might be a good way to pass some of it. They'd get there eventually. Everything came to those who waited. Even Peregrine. In the meantime, what she wanted to know was simple. Did the Whyffes have billions? Or merely millions? 'Wonderful that VAT on repairs isn't a problem for you,' she remarked.

Peregrine's exertion-reddened face changed from an expression of fear to one of amazement. 'Well, I'm not sure about wonderful, exactly.'

'But it's *such* a problem for so many landowners,' Belinda pouted, wriggilng her bottom. 'Repairs and the VAT on them.'

'Yes, but the only reason VAT's not a problem for us is that we can't afford to do the repairs in the first place.'

Breasts cupped voluptuously in her hands, Belinda looked down at Peregrine in exasperation. How long was this charade going to go on? This ridiculous pretence that the Whyffes were poor? 'So what about the Caravaggio?' she demanded, pointing her thick purple nipples towards him like interrogators' torches. 'When did you sell it?'

'About a hundred years ago.'

'*Uh?*' Belinda stopped grinding. 'But what about all your other valuable . . .' What was the word? 'Whatsits?'

'Heirlooms, you mean?' Peregrine sighed. 'Well, there's the Austen of course. It's around somewhere. Only no one can find it.'

Belinda's lip curled. Austen? Caravaggio she knew – he'd painted the Mona Lisa, after all. Or had that been Van Dyck? But she'd never heard of a painter called Austen.

'What does the Austen look like?' she demanded.

'What do you mean, what does it *look* like?'

'Well, is it big, small, is it of a person, some countryside, or what?'

Peregrine blinked. 'It's not a painting. Jane Austen was a writer.'

That Austen. 'Oh. A *book*,' Belinda said in disgust.

'Quite a valuable book though,' Peregrine said mildly. 'A first edition of *Pride and Prejudice*.'

'What's so special about that?' Belinda's voice was cracking slightly. The image of the dusty brown volume she had found in the loo floated uncomfortably to mind. But it couldn't have been the Austen. Someone had scribbled all over it, for a start.

'Well, it's mostly special because she's written on it, apparently. Left lots of notes in the front and in the margins for an alternative version of the story. Lesbian scenes, alternative endings, the lot. But because it got lost here it never saw the light of day.' Peregrine sighed wistfully. 'It would be worth a fortune to scholars if we could find it. Hundreds of thousands, probably.'

Belinda felt a sweat break out on her brow. *Shit*. Literally. *Literally* literally.

'Would be terribly useful, a couple of hundred thousand,' Peregrine added longingly. 'You see, we simply can't sell Swaddling.'

'Of course not,' Belinda interrupted. 'It's your ancestral home. You're the custodians for future generations.'

'Well, it's not really that, actually. The fact is, we *can't* sell Swaddling.'

'*Exactly*.'

'What I'm trying to say,' Peregrine interrupted, 'is that no one will buy it.'

'*What?*' Belinda's spine froze with horror. 'Why not?'

'Obvious, I would have thought. It's in such a mess. You'd need a truly enormous amount of money to do the place up and make it habitable again. That's why my parents were so delighted when they heard *you* were coming to interview me.'

'Why?' Sliding one leg off Peregrine, Belinda frowned. Along with cramp she had the growing impression that, somewhere along the way, wires of some sort had been crossed.

Peregrine looked embarrassed. 'Well, um, besides the fact that you are a beautiful and charming young woman, you're obviously one of considerable means as well . . .'

Belinda leapt indignantly off the bed and yelled out in pain as she reeled into a washstand. Was she hearing right? The Whyffes thought *she* was rich? *They* were after *her* money? Fury welled within her. The outrageous bloody *cheek* of it. The unashamed, conniving, barefaced *cunning*.

'I just can't *believe* it,' she spluttered. 'How I could have been so . . .' she searched for the word. '*Deceived*. Are you really telling me the place is a ruin and you're all skint?'

'But I told you that as soon as you got here.'

'I didn't realise you actually *meant* it.' Belinda's voice was an agonised wail. 'No Caravaggio, no bloody anything? You've got no money and there's nothing valuable in this house at all?'

A hurt expression crept into Peregrine's sloping, watery eyes. 'Well, apart from the Austen, of course.'

'*Bugger the Austen*,' Belinda yelled. And bugger bloody Tarquin, once she got hold of him. Because, make no mistake about it, this was all *his* fault. She'd fallen hook, line and sinker for the whole lady of the manor line, only to find the manor was some freezing bloody aircraft hangar with buckets everywhere to catch the drips. Of which the biggest was undoubtedly Peregrine.

Swaddling. Home of the Whyffes. A family so cash-strapped that the nearest they got to money were the checks in their wardrobe. Blatantly after what they plainly thought were *her* millions and *her* smart connections. How dare they? There was a word for those sorts of people. Gold-diggers. That's what they were. *Bloody gold-diggers*.

CHAPTER EIGHTEEN

That the Hôtel Meurice was every inch the imposing establishment Grace had anticipated was confirmed when, twenty minutes after leaving the Gare du Nord, Grace found herself being deposited outside an arcaded, gilt and plate-glass façade opposite the Tuileries.

She was vaguely aware of a flurry of interest from a group of people brandishing cameras on the pavement. Tourists? Flunkeys rushed to open the car door. Seconds later she was ushered across a monogrammed mosaic pavement and into a lobby positively blazing with mirror, marble and chandeliers. It was enough, Grace thought, staring at the palatial interior stretching around and above her, to give anyone a gilt complex. This was the opposite of restraint. This was elegance with its corsets off.

'Madame?' The concierge looked at her inquiringly.

Grace hesitated. Oh God. Who had Red's assistant told her to ask for? Amid the fanfare of light, gilt and marble, she had completely forgotten The Name.

'Um,' Grace gasped, 'I've come to see Mr, er . . .' Oh no. It couldn't be true. 'Mr *Rudolf*!' she blurted in triumph. 'I've come to see Mr Rudolf.'

Incomprehension. Then light dawned on the concierge's smooth face. 'Ah yes. *Mr Valentino*. You are Miss Armiger? He is expecting you.'

Five minutes later, Grace, buzzing with a last-minute onset of nerves, emerged from the penthouse-floor lift into a thickly carpeted corridor. All was quiet, until the monied calm was suddenly shattered by a very loud and very angry female voice.

'Just tell your ex-wife to fuck off,' it shrieked. 'Ringing up at all hours, screaming about how you don't give her enough alimony. You've got better things to spend it on now. Me, for instance.' As the voice grew louder and closer, Grace shrank instinctively against the wall. '*I'm sick of it*,' yelled the voice, almost in Grace's ear now. Suddenly, round the corner, came the source of all the noise.

Stalking past Grace went a blonde, tanned and long-legged goddess dressed from head to foot in white, her tight vest top straining over her breasts and cropped to reveal at least a foot of caramel midriff. There was, Grace thought, something vaguely familiar about her, though identification was impossible due to vast blue mirrored visor sunshades the size and appearance of welding goggles. Most probably – definitely, to judge from the conversation – this woman was a high-class prostitute whose client was balking at the bills. It seemed amazing that, in such an exclusive establishment as this, screaming madwomen disturbed the peace. Had she been Red Campion, she would have made a complaint.

The penthouse suite's double doors were slightly ajar. Automatic opening, Grace assumed. Someone must have seen her approach through a surveillance camera. She pushed the doors open. From the vast central lobby sweeping away before her, several other rooms could be seen leading off. A soft cream sea of carpet rolled smoothly away into a landscape dotted here and there with tasselled and damask-covered sofas the size of cross-Channel ferries. A huge, wide-screen television looked almost inconsequential in the far distance; nearer to where Grace stood was a large, low antique table bearing a silver flower vase of apricot-coloured roses. To her left was a wall of pure light, made, she realised a second later, entirely of steel and glass. Glass so clean it was invisible; Maria would be impressed, Grace thought.

The silence was deafening. 'Hello?' Grace called, her voice thin and nervous in the humming, air-conditioned atmosphere.

She padded forward and put her head into the first room she came to. A bathroom, but not just any bathroom. The hugest bathroom she had ever seen in her life. Easily the size of her entire flat, it was covered in black and white marble from floor to ceiling. A pair of giant handbasins flanked a vast round Jacuzzi bathtub. There was a bidet, a loo-side telephone, a shower the size of a lift, towel rails cascading with thick, crested whiteness and serried ranks of very smart, full-sized and obviously complimentary toiletries. Sion's father, Grace thought, would have had a field day here.

'Mr Campion?' she called softly. The suite's emptiness felt strange. Not so much as a sushi chef seemed in evidence, let alone a chauffeur, masseur, secretary, florist, feng shui consultant or any other of the army of personal assistants that stars of Red Campion's calibre were reportedly unable to leave home without.

She hesitated before another half-open door. Peering in, she saw it was a bedroom and withdrew her head hurriedly, but not before taking in the rumpled, blue-damask-draped bed dominating the centre of the room. Backing away from the door, she recoiled as a blond man in a bathrobe came stomping agitatedly round the corner.

'Oh, back already are you . . . who the hell are *you*?' snapped Red Campion, his handsome features twisted first in a smirk and then in surprise.

'Grace Armiger,' Grace gasped, panicked. 'From Hatto, um, I mean from Omnicorp. I mean from Hatto,' she added, remembering the firm was to retain its name. 'About your book.'

Grace had read somewhere that film stars were

disappointing in the flesh. Smaller and plainer. Not in this case. Even standing in his bathrobe in his bare feet, Red Campion radiated blond-god handsomeness, sexiness, charisma, power – all those things, she supposed, that when mixed up made the potent cocktail called star quality. She felt almost sick with excitement.

He was smiling at her now, showing a row of brilliant white teeth. 'Yeah,' Red drawled. She was thrilled to see the famous blue eyes crinkling. 'I've been expecting you. Red Campion.' He stretched out a hand.

Grace shook it, dazed. Was all this real? His hand felt real enough. Strong and warm. A powerfully delicious lemon scent filled her nostrils; Campion evidently used the shower gel of the gods.

'Drink?' Red was looking at her, a smile twitching his precision-cut lips. Something seemed to be amusing him. 'Champagne?' he offered.

'No thanks,' Grace stuttered.

Red raised a well-practised eyebrow. 'Not keen on the stuff, huh? I get pretty sick of it myself.'

Campion's tanned chest was more visible than before now that the robe had fallen slightly open. She could see the thick chest hair, jewelled with beads of moisture from the evidently recent shower. 'I'd love a cup of tea,' Grace squeaked.

'Very English.' He grinned. 'I like English girls. So polite.' His brow creased suddenly. 'Well, some of them are, anyway.'

'Shall I order tea?' Grace offered, keen to demonstrate

she was one of the former. 'While you get dressed, I mean,' she added. She crimsoned immediately; was she speaking out of turn? Perhaps film stars lounged around in bathrobes all day.

Red showed his gleaming teeth again. 'Yeah. Guess I'd better slip into something less comfortable. There's a room service menu on the desk. Order away.' As he strode off, Grace devoured with her gaze the easy swing of his long legs, the breadth of his back, the trimness of his waist even through the thick towelling.

The twenty-four-hour room service menu made absorbing reading. Like *The Neds of Twinky Bay*, Grace thought, it opened up a fantastical nocturnal world in which anything was possible and all wishes were granted, however outlandish and no matter what time of night. Who, she wondered, ordered steak tartare at two in the morning? Or caviar? The drinks list kicked off with more than twenty different champagnes. Grace briefly treated herself to imagining Sion's reaction. Apoplexy, without doubt. The thought was heartening. She lifted the telephone and ordered tea for two.

Red Campion came back into the room accompanied by his delicious lemon scent and rubbing a towel over his shining blond hair, almost white in the light streaming through from the plate-glass windows.

Grace jumped slightly. Still, she realised, in a state of high-celebrity alert. She had to pull herself together. She was here to do a job, on her own merits not as winner of some 'Tea With Red Campion' competition.

She must be cool and professional. Red had changed, she saw, into freshly pressed sand chinos and a pristine T-shirt only rivalled for whiteness by his smile. Grace smiled back, trying to calm her thrashing heart.

'I'm dying to read your book,' she blustered excitedly.

Red's grin widened. 'Well, take a look,' he drawled, striding over to the desk and picking up the thick, white-bound volume Grace had assumed to be the telephone directory. 'It's just arrived from the printer,' he added, thrusting it into her hands.

Her wrists slumping with the weight, Grace stared uncomprehendingly at the book's cover. Partly because there was nothing to comprehend. The jacket was completely blank. Just white. Plainer than day. No title, no author name, no nothing. Grace struggled for a few moments. Then, thankfully, realisation dawned.

'Oh. This is the proof copy, is it?'

Red's exquisitely regular features radiated utter blankness. He pushed his full lips out slightly.

'The uncorrected early version from the typesetters before the final one is printed?' Grace smiled, feeling a gratifying twinge of superior knowledge. No doubt Red was a little vague about publishing terminology.

The actor drummed his fingers on the delicate marquetry desk-top. 'We didn't do bound proofs in case someone got hold of the story before we were ready.'

Grace stared. She should have known that. Why had Duke not mentioned it? Come to think of it, he had mentioned very little about the book in general. Her fingers clenched involuntarily round the volume in her lap. 'So this. . .'

'Is the final version,' nodded Red. 'There are fifty thousand of them in the Omnicorp warehouse right now.'

The doorbell rang. The tea she had ordered, Grace remembered. She watched, first in anticipation and then in dismay as a table the size and, thanks to the mass of white linen draping it, appearance of a double bed trundled into the room accompanied by a poker-faced waiter in a buttermilk jacket.

'Oh no. I just asked for tea. But they must have thought I meant *tea*.' There was cake of all descriptions, neatly arranged sandwiches and elegant miniature scones swathed in linen napkins. Clustered all round were teapots, cups, and silver containers filled with jam and clotted cream. Remembering the non-appearance of breakfast, Grace's stomach rumbled loudly. The sound echoed mercilessly in the swathed silence of the apartment. 'I'm so sorry.'

Red shrugged. 'Have something to eat.' He looked amused. Abashed, Grace reached for an egg mayonnaise sandwich.

Red was watching her. 'So what do you think?'

'Delicious.'

'Not the sandwich.' The smile faded; his eyes flashed. 'The Book.'

'Oh, sorry, yes, of course.' Grace put down her cup and

smoothed a hand over the dazzling white surface now weighing down her lap. 'Er . . .'

Grace realised she was not entirely sure what she had been expecting Red Campion to write a book about. A Hollywood kiss and tell, perhaps? A novel about an actor, possibly. But a volume the size of the phone book with nothing whatsoever on the cover? Not exactly. 'I suppose I was expecting to see your name on the cover,' she confessed eventually.

'Author identities are limiting,' Red announced sternly. 'Having my name on the cover would make people jump to far too many conclusions. This is an important book. A book people have to make up their own minds about.'

Grace considered this. Red had a point certainly. Having Dickens's name on a cover, after all, made people jump to conclusions. Generally positive ones, admittedly. But to have no name *at all*? 'You might have Anonymous on it,' she suggested. 'Like *Primary Colors*.'

As Red shook his head, Grace tried to find reasons to agree with him. Falling out with one of Hollywood's hottest properties at their first meeting would hardly impress Bill Duke. And perhaps Red was right; a *Primary Colors*-style Hollywood scandalfest couldn't possibly go wrong, whatever wasn't on the jacket. Once word got out that this plain white cover concealed some of the most colourful anecdotes published for years, it would sell like hot cakes.

But *Primary Colors* had at least had the advantage of a title. A title, moreover, that firmly hinted the book was a political drama. At the moment, all Red's book cover hinted at was a terrible mistake at the printers.

'Not having a title is . . . interesting,' Grace ventured.

'Yes, isn't it.' Red shot back immediately.

Grace found herself unable to hold his piercing sapphire gaze, hypnotic and flooded with light. She noticed he had sat opposite the windows – on purpose? The effect was certainly striking; Red looked even more handsome than on screen. His tanned, butter-smooth, indefinably wealthy-looking skin stretched over his delicate bone structure without a line. Grace started to feel dazzled again. 'Don't you think a title would help?' she stammered. 'To give an idea of what the book is about?'

'Doesn't need one.' Red spoke with steely nonchalance. 'Titles are limiting. This book has to stand on its own two feet, on its own terms.'

What on earth, Grace wondered, could this book be about? From the impassioned way he spoke of it, the Bible and the Koran combined were nothing in comparative importance. An odd way to look at a Tinseltown lid-lifter. Its revelations really must be seismic.

'People have got to approach this book in a free, untrammelled way,' Red added. 'It's a pure experience.' His glowing eyes were locked on hers. Grace felt her palms prick and the soles of her feet fizz.

But – what had he just said? Hollywood kiss 'n' tells weren't supposed to be pure experiences, were they? Trashy prurience, to be frank, was more the idea. Unless Red was referring to a heroine – or hero – whose innocence was destroyed during the course of the book. Perhaps that was it.

'This book,' Red declared, his voice low with urgency, 'is important. Something the world needs to know about. And I need to know,' he added, looking at her as intensely as the *Legionnaire* general looked at his trained and trusted troops, 'that you're up to the challenge of it. I think that you are.'

Grace thrilled. Weren't those the very words from the film? And like the troops in the film, she felt the take-on-all-comers desperate urge to please. To follow this man to the ends of the Earth. 'I'll do my best,' she gasped.

Like the celluloid legions, she was rewarded with a heart-stopping smile. 'And I'll drink to that,' Red cried rousingly. Now that they were both psyched for battle, she half-expected him to throw on a sheepskin cloak and stride off, but instead he strode over to the minibar. Not that there was much mini about it, she thought, as Red opened it to reveal a huge array of bottles from which he slid out one with a gold-foil top.

'We'll drink it outside,' he told her.

Outside, Grace soon discovered, was rather more than a mere balcony. Still less a peremptory projection from one of the windows. Bordered with a sage-painted balustrade, dotted about with plants and small trees and punctuated here and there with wooden garden furniture, its limits were that of the entire hotel roof.

'*Oh!* The *view*!' Grace gazed in awe at the 360 degree view of the city. Laid out below her were the Tuileries, with the great wheel at the end, its lights flashing in the gathering twilight and pierced by the obelisk before it. To her right was the Panthéon, and oh, yes, there was Notre-Dame, its solid towers gilded by the last of the fading sunshine.

As he handed her a gleaming glass of dancing bubbles, Red's fingers lightly touched Grace's. Ten thousand volts shot through her veins. She caught the faint, delicious lemon scent again and breathed deeply, eager to capture the moment in her nostrils.

'To the publication of The Book,' Red said softly, looking at her intently.

'To The Book,' Grace mumbled, dizzily lifting her glass. Could this really be happening to her?

'And to our partnership,' Red said in a thrillingly low voice that found an echo somewhere equally thrillingly low in her body.

'To us . . . I mean, to our partnership.' Grace gulped, realising that she still had no idea what The Book was about. Whatever lay between those covers was a mystery; nonetheless, she thought, her glance returning to his eyes, she was committed to it. Just like the *Legionnaire* legions had been committed to their leader.

Her every nerve end now trembled with the awareness of Red, opposite, lounging against the balustrade watching her. Behind and beneath him a million points of Parisian light moved and glittered in the growing darkness. She could trace the lines of streets, the moving red and white stripes of the Champs-Elysées. It was, Grace thought, almost ridiculously romantic. It had a heightened, unreal quality. Like being in a film.

All the more so as, opposite, stood a handsome film star. Grace sipped disbelievingly at her own golden glassful, as if alcohol might restore her to reality. She closed her eyes and opened them; Red was still there. And, behind him, the jewelled spider's web of the City of Light.

'This is wonderful,' she said.

'Glad you approve.'

'And the view's like . . . I don't know. A living guidebook. You can see everything. You can sit here and decide over breakfast which place you're going to visit. The Louvre over there. The Panthéon up there . . .'

'I guess so.' Red shrugged. He did not seem very enthused by the prospect.

'Where have you been today?' Despite her shyness she felt suddenly curious about his life. What *did* film stars do when they weren't filming? 'The Louvre?'

'Hey, very funny.' Red gave a short bark of laughter.

'I wasn't meaning to be funny.'

'You're serious?'

'Of course I am,' Grace said.

'Well, I've been here, mostly. I can't go out, obviously.' His tones were slightly petulant.

'Can't go out?' With the whole of Paris literally at his feet? 'Why?'

'I would have thought that was obvious as well.' Red rubbed his eyes wearily. 'You saw all those photographers at the entrance, right? I'd be all over the papers if I put a toe out of the door.'

Grace glanced back at the magnificent apartment. It was certainly a wonderful place to stay. But if you really *had* to stay there, all the time . . .?

On the other hand . . . her gaze swept admiringly back over the Parisian panorama . . . wasn't he being a bit, well, *melodramatic*? A tad spoilt, even? Her entire working life, after all, had been dedicated to interesting uninterested journalists in authors they could not care less about. It was hard, Grace thought, suppressing a smile, to imagine Euphemia Ogden having a problem with paparazzi.

'What are you laughing at?' Red demanded suddenly. The white of his teeth and his T-shirt glowed in the soft light from the suite windows.

'Oh, nothing.' Grace took a nervous gulp of champagne and felt her head start to swim. 'Is it really all *that* bad?' she said, braced. 'Being famous, I mean.'

Red grinned dazzlingly. 'Of *course* not. It's really *great*. I'm really flattered by the fact that nothing I do is too mundane to be photographed. And that a picture of me locking up a car or buying a burger apparently earns a snapper a few hundred bucks in some celebrity gossip rag. And as for a picture of me with a *woman* . . .' His eyes flicked over hers. 'It was press intrusion that broke up my marriage.'

Grace's blush, which had begun when she realised he was being sarcastic, deepened. She recalled the question in the film magazine about the divorce. What was his romantic status now? she wondered. The Champagne D'Vyne rumour was obviously ridiculous, made up by the magazine to sell a few more copies. It had to be; no one in their right mind could stomach the former Miss Stars In Her Thighs. And what was it Red had said, in addition, in the *Trailer* interview? '*Right now I'm dedicated to my art. There's been no woman in my life since I split with my wife.*'

Had his fingers been burned so badly he could not even think of trying again? As Red, looking down over Paris – city of lovers – gave a rather stagey sigh, Grace fought the urge to rush over and throw her arms round him. Despite his fame and fortune, he was vulnerable. Did the man the whole world was in love with lead a lonely sort of a life? Or had she simply drunk too much?

If that was the case, from the way he was looking at her, however, it seemed she wasn't the only one.

By the time the minicab wound its way up the long Swaddling drive it was nearly lunchtime. Dangerously near lunchtime, considering the standard of cuisine. Belinda was incandescent with fury. 'Where the *hell* have you been?' she hurled at the hapless driver.

'Taking a couple of my regular ladies to the factory outlet at Wetwang,' he replied, unperturbed. 'There's some wonderful bargains to be had.'

As Belinda opened and shut her mouth like an outraged mullet, Lady Whyffe appeared on the steps behind her.

'Are you sure you won't stay for lunch, dear?' she inquired mildly. 'There's actually quite a bit of chicken left over from last night.'

In reply, Belinda threw her luggage contemptuously into the boot.

'Steady on,' cautioned the driver. 'My suspension's not all it could be, you know.'

As they finally set off – the taxi lurching and swaying over the potholes in the drive – Belinda pointedly ignored the waving Whyffes on the steps. She switched her mobile back on and began to listen to her messages. A chill finger scraped down her spine as she recognised the voice of the Editor's secretary. 'Belinda? Amabel here. Can you call me?'

The second message was from Amabel too. It sounded slightly tenser than its predecessor and came straight to the point. 'Kevin wants you to ring him about who your next star interview is. He's getting a bit concerned about the people you've been doing.' Belinda drew a shuddering breath, feeling a nausea completely unconnected with Lady Whyffe's chicken dish.

'Belinda, where are you?' wailed Amabel in the third message. 'Kevin says to tell you he wants stars, stars, stars. Starting now.'

Belinda clenched her fists. The attempted seduction of Peregrine Somerville had probably been one of the most stupid mistakes of her career. Grayson's obvious fury at not being able to get hold of her would hardly encourage him to look kindly on her recent miserable run of luck.

Not that it was her fault Belinda remembered, faintly cheered. Of course it wasn't; it was that bastard Tarquin's. *His* useless letters. *His* pathetic ideas. *His* lack of initiative of any kind. Not to mention bloody Mo Mills. Selfish old bitch could have at least set up a couple of A-list interviews before she'd had her bloody heart attack. But oh no. *Far* too much to ask.

'Just get a move on, will you?' she snapped at the driver. Although they had by now reached the motorway, his fear of exceeding fifty was limiting their progress. Stuck in the back, Belinda watched the cars flash past them, ground her teeth and reflected that at least she could take it all out on the cleaner when she got home. And she'd take this cab bill out of expenses, damn it.

As Belinda, still shouting at the driver, finally drew up outside her flat, Maria was drawing dusty underwear from under Belinda's bed. How, she was wondering, could any respectable person live in such squalor? Not that Belinda *was* a respectable person, which possibly explained it. Madam Grace was untidy but not in the squalid way Belinda was. Grace, unlike Belinda, would not leave a smashed wine bottle in the middle of the kitchen floor for an entire week until she, Maria, came to clear it up. And Grace's sheets, unlike Belinda's, were not smeared with takeaway pizza, ash, cream, chocolate and other substances Maria didn't even want to guess at.

Straightening the pile of celebrity gossip magazines at the side of Belinda's bed, Maria noticed again that the topmost cover featured the man Grace had gone to see. And the cover beneath it, and the cover beneath that. That slickly handsome face beamed from all of them. That too-blond hair. Those horribly intense blue eyes. Maria could not rid herself of the conviction that there was something not quite right about this man. And certainly something all wrong about the fact Grace had gone to Paris to meet him.

But all was not yet lost. In the pocket of her jeans, under her apron, Maria felt the warm disc of the pound coin. The enchanted pound coin, moreover. She had explained the procedure to her client; though surprised and a little abashed, he had eventually performed the required rites and passed the coin back. Now all that remained was for Maria to put it in Grace's possession. Easy. She could put it in a pocket. Leave it on the kitchen counter. Or slip it in her purse even, although that poised the risk of being caught with Grace's wallet in her hands. Even kind, liberal Madam Grace might think *that* was going a bit far.

Maria smiled to herself and turned her attention back to her cleaning; wondering as she removed the drinks rings from Belinda's bedside table, why she, too, was so interested in this man.

Sitting down gingerly on the edge of the bed, Maria picked up the top magazine and studied the cover. WOMEN AND ME *by Red Campion*. She flicked to the story inside. Her English was poor, but she could make out something about a divorce. Something about an email. And lots of pictures of beautiful women; the biggest one, Maria noticed, being of someone called Champagne D'Vyne. Lots of others too; you didn't need perfect English, Maria thought, to work out that the handsome actor had a complicated love life.

Again she felt the coin in her pocket. Would a pound be enough to rescue Grace? Last night, her sleep had been disturbed by visions of Grace standing on a rooftop high above Paris, holding a glass of champagne and laughing. The penthouse suite. Maria remembered Grace's telephone conversation in the hallway. 'The penthouse suite of the Hôtel Meurice, rue de Rivoli,' Grace had repeated, writing it down on the back of a gas bill.

'What the hell's going on?' hissed a vicious voice from the bedroom doorway.

Terrified out of her wits, Maria gasped and leapt to her feet, dragging the duvet cover to her for protection.

'I pay you,' Belinda snarled, pacing forward, 'to *clean* this bloody flat. Not to sit around on your arse reading magazines.'

'I sorry, Belinda,' gulped Maria, shrinking back into the bedroom wall.

'*Madam* Belinda. And I'm afraid,' Belinda hissed, eyes glittering sadistically, 'that sorry is not good enough. Your behaviour is completely unacceptable and as a consequence your wages are going to have to drop by—' Her mobile suddenly shrilled out 'Diamonds Are Forever'. 'Bugger it,' Belinda cursed and snatched it out of the breast pocket of her black leather jacket.

'*Tarquin*,' she snarled, hearing the unwelcome voice of her assistant. 'What? *Dale Winton* has said yes? You thought I'd be *pleased*?'

Maria watched Belinda's eyes narrow to slits of fury. Her sympathies went out to the unfortunate creature on the other end of Belinda's mobile line. Not to mention her thanks – Belinda had looked about to hit her.

'Look,' Belinda spat. 'There's only one person I'm interested in getting for the Belinda Black Interview. And you know who that is.' There was a pause. 'Red bloody Campion, yes. And no, I don't care if he's turned down the fifty-*second* request. Just find out from the picture desk where the hell he is and I'll . . . I don't know . . . go and bloody *doorstep* him.'

Listening intently, Maria softly began to dust. So that was it. Belinda wanted the blond man for her newspaper.

'*What do you mean the picture desk don't know, you've asked them?*' Belinda shrieked. 'Of course they bloody know, the lying bastards. They just don't want to tell you.' She slapped her free hand hard against her forehead. 'Christ, where's the bloody team spirit on this paper?'

Maria dusted faster. Plans were forming in her brain. What was that English saying? Killing two ducks with one pebble?

'*Someone* must know where he is – *gaaah*. What's the

fucking use?' Belinda stabbed the call ended button so hard her nail broke. '*Fuckbugger.*' She threw a poisonous glare at Maria. 'And what the hell,' she yelled, 'are *you* looking so bloody pleased with yourself about?'

Maria drew a deep breath. It was now or never. The opportunity would not come twice, although, if she was in luck, if her new plans worked, *The Neds of Twinky Bay* writer's just might. 'Because, Madam Belinda, *I* know where Meester Campion ees.'

Belinda's snarling mouth dropped open in shock. '*You* do?'

'Yes. I tell you where.'

CHAPTER NINETEEN

Red Campion's eyes were coming towards her, his blue gaze so brilliant his eye sockets practically steamed. His mouth soldered to hers in a burning kiss that made her bowels turn to molten metal and fired a twenty-one gun salute in her gusset. He slipped something into her hand – yet another gleaming glass of chilled champagne.

Grace drank until she was giddy, the bubbles dancing on her tongue. Red led her out to the edge of a terrace where night-time Paris spread and sparkled; taking both her hands, he whirled her up, up and away, deep into the black spaces between the stars. And then, suddenly, she woke up.

Her eyes focused – not on the plate-glass and steel walls of Red's magnificent suite, but on the faded pink floral paper covering the wall directly opposite the bed. The same wallpaper that had been covering the bedroom walls of this small, cheap Parisian hotel for all the years she had been coming here. The small, cheap Parisian hotel she had booked herself into the moment the meeting with Red Campion had been fixed. American takeover or no American takeover, Hatto & Hatto rules about expenses – i.e. as few and as low as possible – had died hard.

Positioning her head carefully back on the bolster, Grace tried to re-summon the Jacuzzi, the silver, the mirrors, the acres of swirling black and white marble. The miles of carpet, the bed the size of a swimming pool, the waiters, the magnificent terrace. Perhaps it *had* all been a dream. Had she really drunk champagne with a film star with the whole of Paris at her feet? Had she really seen the Eiffel Tower bursting into a million points of dancing light?

She had. Oh God. She really *had*. From where she lay, Grace could see a large white volume the size of a telephone directory poking out from beneath a tangled pile of clothes. The Book. Red Campion's kiss-'n'-tell – even better, hiss-'n'-tell – Hollywood lid-lifter. Despite her headache, she felt a faint fizz of anticipation.

The phone on the wall beside the bed burst suddenly into life.

'Mademoiselle Armiger?' Grace recognised the voice of the friendly hotel owner.

She glanced at her travelling alarm clock. Quarter to ten, for Christ's sake. But then, she had got in very late last night. Now, no doubt, she was being called to be told she was about to miss breakfast. Well, that was fine. Grace moved her furry tongue around her mouth. She didn't much feel like breakfast.

'J'ai un appel pour vous. Ne quittez pas.'

Uh? Who could this be?

'Grace? Red.'

It was, Grace thought, just as well she was lying down already. She would certainly have collapsed with shock otherwise. Red Campion. Ringing her.

'Hello,' she squeaked.

'How ya doing?'

'Um, fine.'

'The limo got you back OK?'

'Yes. Thank you.' Obviously it had. If she tried hard, Grace could almost remember it doing so.

'No problem. You read The Book yet?'

The Book. She remembered now the relief she had felt last night when Red had announced further discussion of his masterpiece was pointless until she had read it. It had freed up the evening wonderfully.

'Um, not quite,' she admitted. 'But it's the first thing on my list,' she added brightly.

'Great. Want to make the second thing lunch with me?'

'Er . . .' She had been due to return to London today. The Hatto press office would not run itself and Ellie who, despite being now in editorial, still shared Grace's room, would be furious at having to pick up endless inquiries from journalists. But then again, given the press's habitual utter lack of interest in Hatto, how likely a problem was this? And how often did a film star ask you to have lunch with him anyway?

'That's settled, then. Come to my suite at lunchtime.'

Grace's hand trembled with excitement as she hung up the receiver. More and more of the evening before was flashing back now; she remembered the peck on the cheek as she left, a lingering look, which she might have imagined. Or had she?

Difficult to say. There had been times, during the evening, when Red had seemed almost bored, almost as if he was waiting for something. And others when she had caught him looking at her, a speculative expression on his handsome face. As the evening wore on, he had looked at her more often; had even pulled a lock of her hair once, admiring its dark gold. He had gone on to admire her skin, her eyes – and then, damn it, he had gone to answer the telephone. After which the evening took rather a different turn.

Grace could recall it all quite clearly now. The way his face had closed up as he answered, how he had turned away and muttered into the receiver. 'Back on again then, are we?' he had said, in tones which she had been unable to place exactly, but which sounded vaguely sarcastic. She'd thought, heart sinking, it was a woman for sure, but then he had ended the call, stood up and stretched and said, apparently regretfully, yet in a way that clearly meant business: 'That was the studio. The voice-over recordings are rescheduled for tomorrow. Better get my beauty sleep.'

Not a woman then, Grace had thought with mixed surprise and relief. Clearly Red was, as he had assured *Trailer*, dedicating himself to his art. He had moved swiftly into action, helping her gather her things together, arranging – yes, of course she remembered it now – a car to take her home, shoving into her arms as she left the large white volume which she had, embarrassingly, been on the point of leaving behind. She had clasped it to her chest with a guilty giggle.

Then came the peck, the intense stare that might have been imagined. Then the humming lift, the blazing foyer, the car that had glided soundlessly along the boulevards while she had tried to stay sitting upright in the back, but slipped down against the leather seats, her head fuddled with champagne and drink-loosened lust.

He wanted to have lunch with her. Idiot, she chided herself, it probably wasn't personal. No doubt he wanted to discuss her promotional ideas about The Book. In which case she'd better get on and read it. She slipped out of bed, picked it up and turned to the first page.

Chapter One

Dateline: The Future (it's closer than you think)

The President glided through as the sliding doors opened and shut before and behind him without a noise. This really was the White House . . .

Grace let out a slow breath of relief. Her hopes were justified. Red's book *was* about the rich and famous after all.

> . . . This really was the White House. It was a white house; everything a puritan, blanched expanse of untainted space. Once in his quarters, alone, he slumped on the slimline, functional couch . . .

Good, Grace thought. Behind-the-scenes intimacy. Insider detail gleaned, presumably, from Campion's own visits to the First Family. All politicians, even Presidents, loved associating with the princes of Hollywood.

> His face was streaming, not with sweat, but with a strange fluid. His pulse rate was increasing. He needed to be near water. 'Croak!'

Grace swallowed. She scanned the paragraph again. No, she'd read it correctly. '*Croak!*'

> An involuntary ejaculation deep in his thorax betrayed an inhuman characteristic. He hopped off the couch and now, squatting on all fours, his hands between his feet, he leapt in two bounds to the bathroom where he put the cold bath tap on full.

Grace's palms were clammy. A shudder ricocheted up and down her spine. This was not quite what she had imagined.

The President's skin was changing. From pink to grey-green. His eyes were beginning to bulge; webbing grew between his fingers and toes. He was already four-fifths amphibian. He hopped into the bath. 'Croak!'

Wild hope suddenly gripped her; perhaps it wasn't like this all the way through. The first sequence might just be a bit of script, a story within a story, unconnected to the rest of the plot. Or something like that. She took a handful of pages and turned over.

. . . Jed pulled his jet boots from their rechargers and zipped them on. Ready now, he leapt from his 100th floor kitchen window and powered through the air. 'Va-voom!' they went, those boots.

Jed had long suspected that the planet was ruled by a species of amphibian that appeared to be human but took all the top jobs, including the presidency. But no one had believed him when he warned them. The news that the King of England had confessed to being a toad was, Jed felt, the first chink in their slimy, amphibious armour. They had to be stopped. But how?

Oh God, thought Grace. How indeed?

As, several hours later, Red kissed her gently on the mouth

at the door of the penthouse suite, her insides plunged, then looped the loop. He looked so Hollywood, so film star, it took her breath away. If only his book had as well. Several seconds passed before Grace could rein in her helpless, galloping speculation about what he would be like in bed. Only to replace it with the dread anticipation of being asked whether she liked what he had written.

He took her out on to the terrace again where lunch was ready. The view was even more glamorous in daytime than it had been the night before. Below lay the ordered green and white carpet of the Tuileries gardens; beyond, gilded domes and golden stone shone against a sky of impossible blue. Grace felt thrilled but uneasy. Sooner or later the question would come.

She tried to forestall it. 'How were the voice-overs?' she asked.

Red looked blank

'You were recording some of the dialogue from your new film,' she prompted.

Red grinned quickly, a flash of white amid the tan. 'Oh yeah. The *dialogue*. Yeah, the dialogue was great, thanks. Very good.'

'I'm glad,' said Grace, impressed it should be remembered with such relish. Red was obviously an obsessive perfectionist who took pride in the tiniest details. Of his films, at any rate.

'Like The Book?' He was looking at her. His gaze was hot and melting. The casual air with which he spoke was, considering he was an actor, staggeringly unconvincing. Grace hoped she could do better.

She took a deep breath. 'The Book is, um, incredible. Very exciting.' She paused: was this enough? No: Red was looking at her expectantly; clearly, more superlatives were required. 'Um, *dramatic*. That bit when the President turns into a frog especially.'

'It's not a frog. It's a non-specific amphibian.' Red's blue eyes glinted icily.

Grace forced the laugh trembling on her lips back down. Of course, he couldn't be serious. But something warned her not to put this to the test.

'Oh. Right. Well, I think it's great, really I do.' Looking into the orange-flecked eyes, Grace felt her doubts melting. And that, actually, she meant it. She wanted to please Red; there was nothing she wouldn't do or say to make him happy.

'So you've got ideas to promote it?'

Grace took a deep breath and reeled off the fruits of her cogitations so far: a few names of literary editors she planned to approach; friendly reviewers she hoped to be able to whip in. She avoided mentioning features. Features were trickier. There was no obvious peg for a book lacking either author or title and about non-specific amphibians. Unless he *could* be persuaded to put his name to it . . .

She flicked him an assessing glance. He seemed relaxed. The champagne glass in his hand was almost empty, over his white-T-shirted shoulder the Eiffel Tower shone in the sun. Could there be a better time or place to try and persuade him?

'First novels, even ones *as good* as this one,' she ventured bravely, 'they need – well, not *need*, exactly, but it certainly helps – something to get them going. What Flaubert called a thunderclap. The fact that—'

'I'm a famous film star will help?' Red said, his eyes crinkling in a way that made her intestines knot.

Grace beamed gratefully. 'Something like that.'

Chips of blue ice gleamed above the crinkles. 'No can do. This book is important,' Red said, a frown flicking across his face. 'I don't want people approaching it with preconceptions about film stars.'

'But—'

He interrupted her. 'I want to exercise my right to remain anonymous, to be judged on the same level as everyone else.'

Grace felt nervous. 'You know,' she grinned, 'you won't believe this, but for some silly reason I thought your book was going to be a kiss and tell about Hollywood.'

Red eyed her sardonically. 'Well, of course, I *could* have done that. *Hollywood*.' His lip curled. 'All such crap. Getting paid millions for standing in front of a camera, reciting a few lines.' Grace said nothing. As crap went, it sounded fine to her. She had more sense than to say so, however.

'Not what you'd call art, exactly. And not,' he added fiercely, 'what I want to be remembered for.'

Grace nodded. 'But people are so interested in Hollywood stories,' she ventured.

Red shrugged. 'More fool them. It's all crap. But there are,' he admitted, 'millions of stories. Things that would make your sweet little hairs curl.' As, suddenly, the sun shone once again in his smile, Grace felt herself blushing.

'The whole actress thing, for example.'

'What actress thing?'

'Actresses these days aren't selected for their acting ability. They're picked for how thin they are. Talent's got nothing to do with it.'

'Really?' Grace's eyes were wide.

'You'd better believe it. Let me tell you something. I was on set with a world-famous actress not long ago and the director came up and started screaming at her. He said, "We're paying you twenty million dollars a picture to look like *that*? Look at you. You're flabby. You've gone all soft. What am I going to do? Shoot round you?" '

'That's terrible,' Grace intoned dutifully, thinking that it *was*, but it was also fascinating. Why hadn't Red written about this?

'You've heard of Lolliwood?' Red asked.

Grace shrugged. 'I've heard of Bollywood.'

'Lolliwood,' Red drawled contemptuously, 'means actresses known in the trade as lollipops because their heads are so much bigger than their skinny bodies. They take speed, diuretics and exercise for hours each day just to fit in a size zero couture slip dress. They look disgusting,' he added. 'No breasts. No ass.' His gaze flicked briefly over Grace's bust. 'They don't look like real women at all. They don't look like you,' he added, his voice suddenly low and throaty.

Grace's heart was thundering like bison across the plain.

'Hey, baby,' Red whispered, coming closer. Her nostrils caught the tang of lemon. And . . . was she imagining it, or was an international screen-star-cum-lust-object *really* pushing his hand up her shirt? 'I want you,' he breathed, his lips touching her neck.

Grace's first reaction was panic. Then self-loathing: She was crap in bed, she had the wrong underwear on, she was here for work, she hadn't shaved, she'd only met him yesterday . . . but really, did any of this matter? Grace felt her insides collapsing like ice-cream in the heat as someone more instinctive and self-confident than herself took charge inside her head. She could hear Ellie's scornful voice, picture her horrified face, when she told her she'd turned down Red Campion. '*Christ*, Grace. *But why*? What the hell for? I always thought you were mad, but now I *know*.'

'Go ahead,' urged the can-do voice of Ellie in her head. 'Seize the moment – and whatever else you can get you hands on. This is fantasy land, you're in a dream situation, none of this is remotely real. And if it is, even better. Making love to a film star. Being seduced by a box-office god. Why not? It's not as if you've any better offers. And you won't get one like this again. Let go, for God's sake. Stop trying to control everything. You're hopeless at it, in any case.'

As, gently, Red covered her mouth with his own, Grace felt every nerve end thrill with the power of his presence and the possibilities of what he was going to do to her.

In a dream, she followed him from the terrace into the apartment. In the cool, curtained darkness of the bedroom, he turned to her and drew her slowly into his arms.

There was about him no unwashed whiff. No garlic, no tobacco. Only that sharp scent of lemons with a faint undertone of vanilla. There was no wax in his ears, no ingrowing hairs. Nothing unpleasant sprouted from his nostrils. No bald patches formed firebreaks in his forest of chest hair. Dotted at regular intervals across his satin-smooth back, Red's very moles seemed grouped for artistic effect.

Grace had never found sex in films convincing. It was too perfect, too rapturous; all those mutual orgasms, no nails dug sharply into flesh, no hair knelt on, no embarrassing farty slapping noises escaped as skin encountered skin. No failed climaxes, no embarrassment. But this *was* perfect. From the moment when Red first took her stiffened nipples in his mouth to the moment when he slowly, wonderfully entered her swollen, wanting groin. None of the usual sharp, hot pain, only a wet and willing eagerness. There was no squashing, no heaving, no cramps. From the very beginning, Grace felt herself to be on a journey with but one rapturous conclusion. As, with the inevitability of a waterfall, she glided to the edge of the cliff and went over, the slow, electric shudder spreading exquisitely through her body. Grace, crying out, looked up at Red in wonder. Followed by mild amazement. It had been her most intense experience with a man ever, but it had literally been no sweat for him. Not a hair was out of place, apart from those looking as if they should be. She almost felt like clapping. Then the telephone rang again.

CHAPTER TWENTY

It wasn't often that Belinda thanked God for her cleaner. As a matter of fact, it was unprecedented. She'd found out Red's whereabouts just in time. The interview in *Trailer* magazine – which had finally made its way on to the Editor's desk – had sent Grayson into a why-didn't-we-get-that frenzy. Fortunately, *Trailer* was a US magazine, and not a rival British newspaper, but it was made clear to Belinda that she now had two options. Get an interview with Campion, or get a new job.

The *Trailer* piece lay open on her desk. Belinda read, for the hundredth time, Red's answer to the question 'Are you a sex addict?' Frankly, for what she had in mind, he'd better be. For *that*, she had decided, was her way in.

And the cleaner had better be right about where he was,

but Belinda was fairly certain about that. Anything but the truth would have crumbled by now. Telling the Home Office lurid and trumped-up stories about abused immigrant status; planting drugs in her cleaning materials; a mysterious death; an unmissed body and an unmarked grave – these were the least of the threats she had made to Maria should her information prove wrong.

Watching Fran get her comeuppance had been delicious. Belinda had bided her time to make the optimum impact – just before the weekly conference, when Fran was positively dancing from foot to foot with nerves at the prospect of telling Grayson what was on the features list. Including what Belinda had lined up for her interview slot.

'*Come on.*' Fran tapped her watch bossily. 'I'm about to go in. So tell me. Who's the lucky megastar? Lynda Bellingham? *Coronation Street*'s Tracy Shaw? TV's Su Pollard? Wilnelia Forsyth?'

'None of them,' Belinda replied in a tone of enigmatic smugness.

'Keith Chegwin? Bob Monkhouse?' Fran felt irritated by Belinda's superior expression. Her eyes were wide and shining; her mouth slightly open. She looked as if she had just seen the Virgin Mary over by the water dispenser.

'Tell Grayson,' Belinda breathed rhapsodically, lingering over every triumphant syllable, 'that Red Campion is next in the Belinda Black slot.'

'*Red Campion?*' Fran would certainly have fallen over with shock, thought Belinda, except that would be impossible in such sensible heels. In footwear as in everything else, she seemed to take her style cue from the Metropolitan Police.

'You mean *the* Red Campion?' Fran gasped. '*Legionnaire* Red Campion? You've got *him*? But how?'

Belinda tossed her shining black hair. 'A good journalist never reveals her sources.'

It was on the tip of Fran's tongue to snap that as Belinda was far from being a good journalist, this was irrelevant. She held fire, however. Unlikely though it seemed, if this was true Grayson would be delighted. Hopefully, he would even stop making the nasty remarks about the features desk that had made her last few appearances in conference so humiliating. The nightmares about losing her job might end. With amazed horror Fran realised, that she genuinely wanted Belinda to succeed.

'But – *how*? How did you do it?'

Belinda merely smiled in reply. No point explaining that she hadn't actually got the interview yet. But she was confident she would. Now that the elusive star had been located, the hard work was done. All that now remained was to get into his suite. Which was why she'd taken the extra precaution of booking herself into the Meurice. The cost would be astronomical, but so too would be the paper's circulation after she'd landed the story of the century.

'So I'll see you later,' Belinda flounced off down the office with what, Fran noticed, was a suspiciously familiar-looking travel bag. Was that not the silver ostrich leather scheduled for tomorrow's accessories shoot? If it was, Fran realised glumly as the door swung shut behind Belinda, it was too late.

Belinda stalked out of *The Globe* office glowing with triumph. The feeling, admittedly, was a novelty. 'Eurostar terminal,' she commanded the first taxi driver to stop. Her Tea Break days were at last well and truly behind her. The Belinda Black slot was about to welcome its biggest star yet.

It was quiet, very quiet when Grace awoke. Back, she realised, in the small hotel. Red had sent her home in a limousine, just as he had the night before. But not before he had made love to her no less than five times.

The dull throb between her legs was no trick of the imagination. Five times! More than Sion managed in a month. And yet she had got the impression that Red could have gone on for even longer. *Five times*.

She had, she remembered, wanted to stay in the glamorous apartment rather than return to her own room. The call of the bolster was not an enticing one. But he had insisted on sending her away; for her sake, he had told her, kissing her, otherwise there was a risk of long lenses through bedroom windows, of being splashed over the front pages as the latest blonde in his life. Was that, he had asked, nuzzling her neck, really what she wanted?

'Yes,' Grace had replied without hesitation. 'I don't mind the whole world knowing. Only joking,' she had added when Red's silence and tense face implied he felt the opposite.

'Ha ha,' Red had chided, smiling with annoyed relief. 'Believe me, I hate to send you away, honey. But I'm going to be up the rest of the night.'

'You are?' Grace blinked at him in surprise. Their lovemaking had, throughout the evening, been punctuated by telephone calls, involving occasionally agitated conversation. It had, as far as she could make out, revolved around some sort of a meeting, someone returning from somewhere. Surely that someone wasn't coming here to see him? Now?

'My dialogue coach again,' Red sighed, calming a host of unnamed fears with a few words. Don't be silly, Grace told herself. She was just being paranoid. Of course his work was important; the film must come first. She had no idea that post-production was so labour-intensive. Why hadn't they got it right the first time round?

Red had grinned when she asked this. 'Baby, there are some aspects of dialogue that just need to be done again and again.'

'You're such a perfectionist.'

His eyes crinkled. 'You got it. Guess I'm the kind of guy who's never satisfied.'

'What exactly does it involve?' Grace asked, anxious to demonstrate an interest in the technicalities of Red's world, as well as the glamour. 'Lots of deep breathing and rolling around on the floor, isn't it?' She had once read an article about voice coaching.

Red's eyelids flickered. 'Something like that.'

Grace decided to make a joke of it, to lighten the

suddenly tense atmosphere. 'I get it. You'll be getting some girls from the Moulin Rouge around just as soon as I'm out of here.'

The remark did not have the humorous effect she intended. Red's eyes narrowed; then, in a second, he had collected himself. 'Right as usual, honey. One or two of the female sound technicians did work on *Moulin Rouge*.'

The telephone by her bed shrilled. '*Ne quittez pas*.'

Grace's heart leapt.

'Red!'

'I gotta be quick,' Red told her. 'Meet me in the Meurice bar at lunchtime. One pee em.'

Grace blinked. He was coming *out* of the suite? Downstairs, to where people might recognise him? Was he feeling less suspicious of the outside world? Less hounded for some reason? Was that reason – Grace allowed a moment's ecstatic hope – *her*?

The receiver hung heavily in her hand. Despite her near-permanent state of stomach-churning excitement, Grace thought guiltily of the office. Ellie must be wondering what was happening.

Groaning slightly, Grace dialled the number. As expected, Ellie was in the office – since being moved to editorial, she had increased her working hours by at least a third. Also as expected, she was not best pleased at being left alone.

'But you can cope for a bit?' Grace pleaded. 'Nothing's happening, surely? Nothing ever does.'

'That's not the point,' snapped Ellie. 'What are you *doing* over there?'

'I'll tell you when I get back. Which will be soon, I promise.'

Grace made her way excitedly, if slightly guiltily, to Red's hotel at lunchtime.

The bar was a magnificent affair, painted sunset on the ceiling, painted château on one wall, ribbed with gilded pilasters and full of red leather chairs. All were unoccupied, apart from someone buried behind a newspaper in the corner.

Grace chose a chair opposite the main corridor so as to spot Red as soon as he appeared. Her eyes roamed the hotel's public areas. In the magnificent pink and gold reception room opposite, a blonde girl of about eight was running, laughing, arms outstretched, along the curving swags of roses woven into the carpet.

One p.m., Red had said. By the time her watch showed quarter past, some of the bubbles in her mood had evaporated. But of course, she reminded herself. He was never going to be on time. Stars famously weren't. He might not turn up at all. Something Might Have Happened; he was after all, an A-list celebrity. President Bush might have asked him to brunch. Madonna might have suggested they fly down to Juan-les-Pins for dinner.

'Madame?' The white-jacketed barman loomed before her with a silver tray. Snapping out of her daydream, Grace wondered how long he had been standing there.

'Nothing for me just yet,' she said firmly. 'I'm waiting for a friend.' She had ruled out anything on the bar menu after calculating that one Bloody Mary cost the same as her Tube travel for a fortnight.

The barman remained, however; Grace glanced up at him challengingly. Was he about to charge her for the nuts she had eaten?

'There's a telephone call for you, madame.' The barman proffered the salver, on which reclined a tiny state-of-the-art mobile.

Grace cast an embarrassed look around. To her relief, no one was watching. In the corner, the man was still buried behind his newspaper. 'Hello?'

'Hey there.' The low roll of his voice sent her stomach plunging immediately into her knickers.

Stop it, Grace urged herself, preparing for the inevitable disappointment. 'Where are you?' she asked. Madonna's Gulfstream, obviously. Just as she had thought.

'Not far.'

Grace looked around. There was no sign of Red in the room.

'I can't see you.'

'Keep looking.'

She arched her neck to peer around; had he somehow concealed himself behind the angle of a sofa? Under a table? Was he dressed up as one of the barmen? Impossible; they were half his height. In the lobby dressed as a bellhop? A quick tour of the corridor revealed nothing. Mobile still clamped hotly to her ear, she returned to the bar. Had Red been in and gone out again in her absence?

She looked round again. That man with the newspaper; had he noticed anything? She rummaged in her brain for the French required, found she had the basics and set her best foot forward.

'*Excusez-moi.*' As the newspaper lowered, Grace recoiled in amazement at the sight behind it. The shabby clothes, the filthy, woolly hat pulled almost down to the eyes. Christ, he looked like Tenebris Luks. Except that even Tenebris Luks did not have a face quite so dirty. The eyes that turned up to her under matted clumps of eyebrow were yellow and bloodshot; the grinning maw revealed blackened stumps.

'Hey!' said the apparition.

Grace froze. 'Red?'

'You got it.'

She could recognise him now. Beneath the grime, the stubble, the frighteningly realistic warts, she could make out that delicate jaw, the matted blond of his hair. Those unmistakable, if yellowed and bloodshot, blue irises.

'Why are you dressed like this?'

'Disguise, of course,' Red said easily. 'And it works. You should have seen the bar empty when I came in. I've had to stump up majorly in compensation.'

Grace was not surprised. Even for Paris, a city specialising in tramps, Red looked horrendous. 'How did you do it?'

'False stubble, false eyebrows, fake skin dirt, yellow eye-drops, false warts, wardrobe, and colouring in some of my teeth black,' Red recited triumphantly.

It had, he said, taken a couple of phone calls. One to the hotel manager, who could be trusted to brief certain staff not to throw him out. 'Although,' Red said, 'that would have been even more authentic. Really fool the paparazzi, that would.'

He grinned at Grace. 'So now I can have a normal day, for a change. Being anonymous.'

Red's ideas of normal, Grace thought, were clearly some distance from her own. But perhaps that was only to be expected. As for anonymous, every eye in the hotel, in the know or not, was currently contemplating Red in well-bred horror. 'Did you do your make-up yourself?' she asked.

He shook his head. It had been a film make-up technician he knew who just happened to live in Paris.

'Another *Moulin Rouge* girl?' Grace joked.

Red did not answer. Rather abruptly, he struggled to his split-trainer-shod feet and tugged his woolly hat down firmly with a grimy, black-nailed hand. 'Ready to hit the town? I thought we could do some sightseeing.'

'Are you sure?' Grace asked doubtfully. Red was quite enough of a sight himself.

'Sure?' The blue-red-yellow eyes rolled at her. 'Baby, with you I'm sure about everything.'

Grace followed him out, heart swelling with happiness.

* * *

Pinch me, Belinda wrote in her notebook. *I'm sitting in the foyer of one of the grandest hotels in Paris, awaiting an audience with one of the biggest celebrities in the world. Red Campion, star of some of the most successful action movies in action movie history, has breezed into town. And I, lucky girl that I am, have moved mountains to get an exclusive interview with the reclusive celebrity*. She paused. Well, there was no point in telling the truth, was there? That she hadn't got an interview at all, but was counting on Campion's fabled weakness for women to get into his room? Sooner or later he'd walk down the corridor and spot her; until he did, it was vital to get as much of the interview written as possible. Once in Campion's room she was hardly going to waste valuable time *talking*.

The plan clear in her head, Belinda had dressed to thrill. There was absolutely no chance Red Campion could miss any of her finer points. Or any of her less fine ones either. The ratio of exposed to covered flesh was approximately 70:30, and what cover there was consisted entirely of black leather. There was very little underneath – why put obstacles in the way? – and on top was a tiny black leather jacket that had cost a fortune in the avenue Montaigne. Vignoles would just have to regard it as an investment, that was all. Still, if all went according to plan, he'd be a very happy man.

'Can I 'elp you, madame?' Interrupted in her scene-setting scribbles, Belinda looked up to find herself staring into the sharp olive face of a man with persuasive teeth and oily hair. Yet another interfering hotel middle manager, like the one at that wretched bloody Garage place; hopefully, though, this was a good omen. The Champagne D'Vyne interview had been her first success. Her only one, in fact.

She scowled. 'I'm fine, thanks,' she snapped. 'I do have a room here, you know.'

'I know, madame. You are waiting for someone? Eef you tell ze concierge, they weel send your guests up to your room when zey arrive.'

'Just sod off, will you?' Belinda hissed, folding her arms aggressively. She had no intention of admitting that the person she wanted to see was in the hotel already. The sight of the handful of paparazzi at the door – so much for the bloody picture desk not knowing where he was – had increased the vital importance of apprehending Red Campion before they did. So far, however, he had not appeared.

Watching the manager trip off down the glittering hotel corridor, Belinda wondered how much longer she would have to wait. She had no idea doorstepping was this complicated.

A few minutes later, every vein in her body stiffened. Her eyes bulged, her palms fizzed and the hairs on the back of her neck stood on end. It was incredible; it couldn't be – but it was. As he came towards her, Belinda half rose from her chair . . .

What was that *revolting* tramp doing in a hotel of this quality? How had he got in? Why was it being allowed? One stayed in places like this to get away from that class of person. Belinda held the end of her nose pointedly as the shambling figure approached. Where was that bloody manager now she needed him? She'd a good mind to communicate her disgust to Reception. If she made enough of a fuss, she might be able to swing a discount at least. A free night's stay, even. On the other hand . . . Belinda sat down again, crossing one almost entirely exposed leg over the other. She didn't want to make herself conspicuous. Not in that way, at any rate.

She curled her lip as the tramp shuffled past. *Repulsive.* And who was that woman with him? His probation officer? His outreach worker? Was this one of those ridiculous resettlement of offenders exercises? Bit of a babe, anyway, in a gangly, blonde, English sort of way. Looking very pleased with herself as well, for some reason. Mad, obviously.

Grace was giggling inwardly at the ludicrously dressed woman holding her nose. How she could smell anything under her own eye-watering perfume was incredible for a start. Whatever it was filled the foyer to choking point. Red, in any case, had no smell, apart from the faint whiff of lemon cologne. Grace felt a pang of apprehension; might a sharp-eyed or sharp-nosed person notice his lack of trampish reek and be suspicious?

She need not have feared. The disguise worked like a charm. The photographers crowding the mosaic pavement outside the hotel hardly even looked up as they emerged. Red stumbled past them, grinning nastily with his black teeth, rolling his yellowed eyes. Grace followed, thinking that if any of the press hounds had been even remotely observant, they might, besides the lack of smell, have derived a clue from Red's slight but noticeable flinch on seeing his reflection in the polished lobby mirrors. Or from the way he punched the air triumphantly as soon as they got outside.

It was a perfect day. Once Grace had got over the shock of Red's appearance, that was, and once he had recovered from the shock of spotting a poster featuring Russell Crowe. So it was true, Grace realised, surprised. She took him to the top of the Arc de Triomphe; 'Great views,' Grace exulted, staring through the railings at the boulevards below. As car after car edged from the connecting roads to join the mad motorised ballet of the Etoile itself, she remarked that watching the traffic was more exciting than a movie. 'Whoops, I probably shouldn't have said that,' she added, smiling nervously.

Red grimaced.

'*Anything*'s more exciting than a movie. Words are where it's at. Right?'

Grace nodded. 'Right.'

His smile disappeared with the trill of his mobile. More dialogue? wondered Grace. Frowning, Red dragged it out, looked at the number and impatiently punched the switch-off button. 'Here,' he said, thrusting the phone at Grace. 'Keep this in your bag. I don't want to be bothered with it.'

They descended the Arc, the other tourists in the narrow stairwell keeping a safe and disgusted distance. There were,

Grace realised, advantages to accompanying someone so repellent-looking; crowds parted with the ease of the Red Sea before Moses.

'Hey. Look at us,' Red said, pausing in the window of a Champs-Elysées car showroom. 'Lady and the Tramp. No wonder everyone's staring.' He seemed oddly pleased at this, to Grace's surprise. He had wanted anonymity . . . hadn't he?

'And just think,' Red added with relish, 'how much more they would stare if they *knew*.' He chuckled like a child, delighted by his own cleverness. Grace smiled. Weird though it was to hear Red's voice coming from such a blackened, scrofulous-looking mouth, it was also wonderful to see him enjoying himself so much.

It was just that something within her, something horribly trivial and shallow no doubt, wished that Red wasn't in disguise. Wished he was out being himself and that she could therefore be stared at for reasons of envy and appreciation, rather than scorn.

Still, it was hard to be miserable in Paris, still less when you were out with a film star. Even if he looked like something out of *Waiting for Godot*.

They sailed up the Seine on a *bâteau-mouche*; she pointed out, in raptures, the enfilade of bridges and explained that the Pont-Neuf was actually the oldest one of all. He listened with a bewitching grin that would have made her heart flip had it not been surrounded with all that stubble and those warts. She took him to the top floor of Samaritaine, to the café where they sipped red wine, ate croque-monsieurs and looked down on the Ile de la Cité while she told him about Marie Antoinette's wretched last days in the Conciergerie. 'Sounds like the Oscars,' Red remarked darkly as Grace sketched out the execution scene – tumbrils struggling to get through the crowds, excited onlookers baying for blood.

They walked over the Pont-Neuf where Red's stuck-on eyebrows raised as she explained how expensive apartments in the Place Dauphine were. They sat, swinging their legs, on the stone prow at the end of the Vert-Galant island, watching the Seine divide and slide past them in a mass of heavy beige water. They visited the Sainte-Chapelle and stood in the queue, Red exclaiming in delight at the novelty of having to wait for something. Behind, a group of tourists from the West Midlands recoiled. Inside, necks cricked, they both stared at the windows exploding in colour and light.

'Man,' Red said, when they got outside. 'I'm having fun. This is *great*.'

Grace laughed. 'But we're hardly doing anything out of the ordinary. Just the bog-standard tourist things.'

'What next?' Red demanded.

'We could do some window-licking, as the French say.'

'What?' Red looked thrilled. '*Window*-licking?'

'*Shopping!*' Grace giggled. The street market at the rue Lévis was always fun, or maybe the one at the smarter rue Cler. Red would no doubt appreciate a chance to see the roast chicken revolving on spits, the different types of bread in the bakers, the wheels of cheese, appreciate the displays of the *traiteurs*. Even if, given his appearance, the *traiteurs* were unlikely to appreciate having Red in their shops.

'Great,' Red said. 'I could use some new Gucci.'

'Oh. Right.' *That* sort of shopping, Grace thought.

The vendeuses in the rue du Faubourg St Honoré boutique glanced in chilly astonishment as the filthy, dishevelled figure in cracked trainers entered their pristine establishment. Like antibodies expelling poison they rushed to annex him with a flurry of smoothly menacing inquiries.

'You need 'elp, monsieur?'

Red threw them a haughty do-you-know-who-I-am glare which was pure Hollywood prince. No, but we know what you look like, came the answering steely stares. He had, Grace realised, half panicked, half amused, forgotten he was in disguise. He began pulling garments from the rails as horrified assistants scurried everywhere. 'Monsieur?' they squealed.

'I am looking for something for Madame.'

The chief vendeuse's eyelids fluttered heavenwards. Grace nudged Red in panic.

'But I *can't*,' she hissed. Just one dress – probably one T-shirt – from here would wipe out her wages for months. Grace reddened as the immaculate vendeuse looked at her untidy hair, horribly aware of the fact that her shirt, despite hanging all night in the bathroom to de-crease, was still as wrinkled as a prune. It was clear that, in this place, they had no truck with shabby chic. Tramp chic, even less.

'Relax, baby,' Red grinned at her. 'It's on me. I want to dress you up.'

'Monsieur,' dived in the vendeuse, 'if there 'ees something in particular . . .' Grace almost felt sorry for her, stuck-up though she was. She had to protect her stock somehow.

Red ignored her. Pulling out a red leather trouser suit from a rack, he held it against Grace. 'You'd look great in this. Try it on.' The vendeuse's eyebrows skyrocketed.

Grace swallowed. Quite apart from being more flamboyant than anything she had ever worn before, the suit looked far too small.

'And this.' Red whisked a black corset dress from another rail. 'And this.' A close-fitting jacket in buttery suede.

'Thees way, madame.' Realising she had no choice, the assistant was waving Grace frigidly towards the changing rooms. Realising she had no choice either, Grace followed her direction. Her heart sank; she hated all changing rooms. The communal ones where you discovered you had on your oldest and greyest bra; the tiny boxes where your stomach pushed up against the mirror . . .

The ones in this shop, however, fitted neither category. Standing, alone, in a robing area the size of a garage, Grace stared at her reflection in the red leather trouser suit in awe.

Her mother, she reluctantly acknowledged, had been on to something. Lady Armiger had frequently stressed the empowering effect of good clothes; Grace, suspecting merely another smartening-up ruse, had never believed it. Until now.

Fluffing her hair about her shoulders, she sucked in her cheeks and left the changing rooms in search of Red.

'What do you think?'

He put his woolly-hatted head first on one side, and then the other. His gaze slowly climbed her body, then descended again. Grace felt her palms prick with fear; did she look dreadful after all?

'It rocks,' Red clapped his hands and flashed her a brilliant grin. Her stomach whirled like a washing machine on final spin.

'Baby, you've got *great* legs,' Red said. 'Let's see the rest. Of the clothes, I mean,' he added hurriedly, as the vendeuse pursed her lips.

Slipping into the black corset dress, Grace regretted that the great legs hadn't been exfoliated or moisturised much lately. Yet the way this dress was cut – in at the waist, stopping dead at the most flattering part of the thigh – made her look so impossibly curvaceous it distracted attention from anything else. Her waist seemed a handspan; over the corset top her breasts swelled and spilled like breaking waves.

'Fantastic,' said Red, as she sashayed – the waist was so tight, it was impossible to do anything else – around the marble floor of the shop.

From then on it was quick change after quick change. The jacket with its delicious cool silk lining was pronounced an equally great success; he threw in a crocodile-skin bag, a soft fawn pashmina, a white sleeveless top of breathtaking plainness made of some miracle material that didn't crease. Grace, having overcome her self-consciousness, started to enjoy playing the supermodel. The assistants smouldered at the back, scissoring forwards from time to time to hand over a garment in a different sizing – usually smaller, to Grace's great joy.

'But you can't possibly pay for all this,' Grace breathed, as Red finally slapped his credit card down on the counter. The vendeuse snapped him a look suggesting that this was her opinion exactly.

'Baby, relax,' Red said easily. 'I could buy this whole company if I wanted to.'

The vendeuse looked as if she were about to explode. She glanced without interest at the name on the card – if she recognised it, she clearly did not connect this R. Campion with his famous namesake. Disapprovingly, she tapped in the numbers for authorisation. The machine rattled joyously as what Grace estimated as several thousand dollars rolled from Red's account to that of the shop. The vendeuse would, Grace imagined, be on the telephone to the police as soon as they had gone, suspecting the card had been stolen.

They walked out. The carriers on Grace's arms dangled heavily. She felt like a walking, very expensive, Christmas tree.

'Now we need a cab,' Red said, sticking out a ripped, stained, raincoated arm. Taxi after empty taxi rolled by.

'Hey, what's wrong with those guys?' Red grumbled. He had, Grace realised, forgotten he was in disguise again.

Eventually, she took over the effort. When a taxi finally stopped, Red shoved every last bag in it and muttered to the driver.

'He's going without us,' Grace gasped as the cab sailed off. 'What about the clothes?'

'Being taken back to the hotel and put in the suite. We're going back on *public transport*,' Red said excitedly.

On the Metro they sat opposite a rival tramp whose degree of bedragglement was so extreme as to be almost magnificent. He exuded a rich, savoury aroma and rolled a rheumy, suspicious eye over Red before revealing, in a sudden jerk of the pelvis, that his flies were open and his penis was hanging out. Red was delighted.

'You know,' he grinned as they exited at Tuileries. 'That guy was the first person all day who didn't quite buy my disguise.'

Once again, not a single gentleman of the press raised so much as an eyebrow, still less a Leica, as Red and Grace re-entered the hotel. In the private lift to the penthouse suite, Red ripped off the filthy tea cosy hat, rubbed his hands through his matted blond hair, and plucked off the eye-brows. By the time they reached the door of his suite, he was looking vaguely like himself again.

'Drink?' he asked.

Grace nodded. 'Yes please.'

The door clicked open. Grace sighed happily as she surveyed the line of smart shop-carriers ranged along the wall by invisible hands. She could get used to this sort of service, to being waited on hand and foot.

Red, meanwhile, had gone immediately to the flashing answerphone, and was listening to the messages. His face neutral, he disappeared into the bathroom. He was in there for a while; she could hear him talking agitatedly on the telephone by the loo. More dialogue? But it could be anything. He had agents all over the world. PRs all over the world. Including, Grace thought with a stab of joy, the one here in his hotel suite. A great wave of happiness broke within her. The day had been perfect; Red had seemed so happy, too. Surely, even to him, this was special?

Her heart leapt as Red emerged from the bathroom. Although he was smiling, there were traces of irritation on his face. Without a word, he pulled her into the bedroom, pushed her back on the bed and ripped open her jeans. He was in her before she knew it; urgent now, rough. Grace gasped with mixed shock and delight. After their first, almost choreographed encounter, their subsequent sessions had had a thrillingly hasty, almost brutal quality. She had never been this needed before. It was terribly flattering.

Afterwards, she slipped into the bathroom and under the shower. Red followed her in, pressing her against the warm marble. 'You're gorgeous,' he murmured. Arching her back, tilting her face into the falling water, she gasped as once again he entered her, rigid against her softness. She wanted to giggle as his thrusts pushed her bottom in rhythmic slaps against the marble, but didn't; sex, she had learnt, was a matter Red took extremely seriously. The sudden starburst;

that now-familiar feeling of being turned inside out, and it was over. Or was it? He was kissing her wet nipples, then her lips and bringing her hand to where, below in the steam and heat, he was rising yet again. He wanted her so much. And she him. Could this, Grace tremulously, hopefully, wondered, be love?

CHAPTER TWENTY-ONE

Dressing up as a chambermaid had, Belinda decided, been a stroke of genius on her part. Even if the *Trailer* article mentioning Red being caught *in flagrante* with a hotel cleaner had given her the original idea. As he had not yet materialised to ask her himself, it fell to her own journalistic ingenuity to gain access to his suite. This was certainly the perfect disguise, although it involved buying a hideously unflattering white blouse, black skirt and shoes almost as flat and municipal as Fran's. Still, needs must, and now, dressed like every other drudge in the place, all she had to do was hang around looking industrious. As well as await the opportunity to slip into the private lift to the penthouse suite.

She had abandoned attempts to dust after a passing guest

gave her a questioning look. She looked back challengingly; what was so wrong with spitting on the mirror? How else did you clean them?

The discovery of the vacuum cleaner, standing unattended in the hotel corridor, had been useful. She could pretend she was about to give the penthouse suite a thorough seeing to and then move on to its occupant. Easy – until Belinda began to drag the machine down the corridor to the private lift entrance. The damn thing weighed a ton. Perhaps she *should* pay Maria more; on the other hand, the woman was saving herself a fortune in gym fees. It would be at least £40-plus per session to get this sort of workout from a personal trainer; Maria should think herself lucky.

Belinda ground the vacuum cleaner bad-temperedly against the carpet. She may be an investigating journalist on a hot story, but felt all this rather beneath her dignity. The dressing up, the ridiculous roleplay; it felt less Woodward and Bernstein than Morecambe and Wise.

Still, needs must. The pressure on her was intense. Damn Kevin Grayson. What did he want – blood? Stupid question, really; of course he did. Grayson was, after all, the man who had built his reputation on gory scoops. Not for nothing was his rule for front-page stories 'If it bleeds, it leads.'

But this assignment shouldn't be too complicated – once she got inside Red Campion's room, that was. Beneath her white blouse and black skirt, Belinda's underwear was on high alert. She sported her battle smalls – a silk split-crotch thong with a black lace trim and the matching silk bra with nipple holes that gave her a cleavage like the Cheddar Gorge. Red would almost certainly be unable to resist her. The mission that had taken her into the homes and hotel rooms of so many apparently promising celebrities, only to meet with disappointment, would be accomplished at last.

That was the initial plan. Her past experiences, however, urged a previously scorned tactic for Belinda – caution. As she was now aware, A-list celebrities rarely behaved the way they might be expected to. Nothing was certain. Even a sure-fire bet like appearing in gala lingerie before a rumoured sex addict.

Belinda had therefore taken steps to ensure that whatever was about to happen, she would not, as with Brian Stone, as with Stan, as with Peregrine bloody Somerville, emerge the loser. In the unlikely event that – incredible and impossible though it seemed – Campion was immune to her charms, Belinda had hit on what was to her mind a most ingenious method of making capital out of their encounter.

She had realised that an interview was unlikely. That involved asking questions, and she was hardly dressed for that. Pictures, however, were a different matter. They spoke a thousand words – thus freeing her from the effort of writing them – and sold millions of newspapers. Which was why, nestling between her breasts, was a small camera Belinda had bought – with considerable difficulty, given her limited French – that morning. She was fairly certain that she had the autoflash instructions right; completely certain, on the other hand, that if Red failed to warm to her immediately, all she needed to do was rip open her blouse, throw herself into his arms and have the camera record the action. Flash, bang, wallop, 'My Romp With Raunchy Red' all over the front page, Kevin Grayson's weeping gratitude and a job for life.

So she was ready. All she had to do was get into that private lift, up to that private floor and into that private room. Which meant she had to stay here, beside that relentlessly closed lift door, and wait for it to open. Until it did, the carpet outside was going to be vacuumed until it was bald.

In her room at her small hotel, Grace stared at the email the kindly manager had just brought her. It carried the address of the Hôtel Meurice; there was little doubt who it was from. Grace read again the bare lines:

> ATTN: Miss Grace Armiger
> Can't make our meeting today as a few things have come up.
> Will call soon.

Walking to the open window, still holding the email, she propped her elbows moodily on the tiny iron balustrade and stared up at the birds wheeling in the pale blue sky. She envied them their absolute freedom to take off and land. Including on Red's terrace, if they wanted. How unlike her. Today, for reasons she wasn't sure she quite grasped, she had been grounded.

There had been no hint of Red having business today during yesterday's shopping trip. Yet once again, he had not let her stay. After returning to the hotel, after the sex, he had packed her off once again in the limo with all her carrier bags. She had assumed that they would see each other the next day, that they would have lunch as usual. *As usual.* How quickly she had grown used to it all, the star life. Accustomed to his fame, his face and several other parts of his anatomy.

The breeze rippled the paper in her hand. *A few things have come up . . .* Grace wondered what, exactly. Sudden meetings, last-minute important arrangements, were no doubt par for the course when you were Red Campion. The eternal voice-overs, perhaps, the dialogue as he called it, those girls from *Moulin Rouge* again, ha ha. Odd how he had never seemed to find that joke particularly funny.

An email. An odd way to let her know. On the other hand, why not? No doubt he had not wanted to waste time, to let her know as soon and as accurately as he could. She must take it calmly, as a film-star girlfriend – for wasn't that what she was now? Grace felt a soaring excitement at the thought. After all, this was the kind of thing she would have to put up with quite a lot, if their relationship continued as it had started. And there seemed no reason to think it would not continue. After the day they had spent sightseeing, shopping and sitting on the banks of the Seine, the evenings on his terrace, the nights . . . well, part of the nights, in any case. It must be love. Mustn't it?

One of the best ways to express her devotion, Grace decided, would be to spend the day working on The Book. It had, after all, been a little neglected of late. Her heart sank slightly at the prospect, and yet why, when she had much to thank it for? Bringing her and Red together in the first place, most of all. How pleased Red would be when he realised she had been working on it. Making plans for it. No, the only real problem with The Book, Grace thought, was the suggestion it carried of London and Omnicorp. She had now completed her Parisian business. She had received her PR brief from Red Campion. No one had mentioned her doing any more. Still less doing what she had done.

After all she and Red had shared these last few days, he could not possibly want her to go back – yet. If ever. For who knew, Grace thought rapturously, what the future held? In the meantime, she'd better get on with some reading.

Reluctantly, she peeled herself off the worn wooden rail of the window. Something small and silver sat on top of the book. Red's mobile. The mobile he had given her to look after, and which she had forgotten to return. Of course. *This* was why he had sent her the email. He had been unable to call her – apart from the ten or so in-suite telephones of course – but he had already told her he didn't trust them. It was all crystal clear now.

What was equally clear was that she must return it. Grace lunged for the door before sense could stop her. Red would need his mobile, she thought, tripping down the worn wooden spiral stairs rather than waiting for the lift. It was an essential business tool, no doubt crammed with vital messages already. He was probably panicking, wondering where it was. He would not mind being interrupted to be reunited with it; on the contrary, he would thank her. She would return it now to the Meurice and save the day. Perhaps, as a reward, Grace thought jubilantly as she darted out into the sunlit street, Red would allow her to stay the night.

Belinda stood in the private lift and tried to look innocent, as if butter wouldn't melt in her mouth. Which it rarely did anyway – nasty, fattening stuff. She felt triumphant. The waiter had hardly noticed her slipping in after him; hardly noticed her at all, rather irritatingly. Far too busy admiring his reflection in the champagne bucket on his loaded trolley. Belinda complacently examined her own reflection. Even given the distortions of the silverware, even given her uninspiring uniform, it was hard to dispute how triumphantly, thrummingly, film-star-temptingly gorgeous she looked.

As the lift glided to a stop, Belinda followed closely behind the waiter, flicking busily about with the duster as she went. There was no doubt about where she was going; the penthouse suite, after all, was the only one. And who else but a film star would have ordered two chilled bottles of Veuve Clicquot, a dozen oysters, an entire dressed lobster and a silver dish of caviar at half past ten in the morning? For such were the contents of the trolley in the lift. The trolley she was now following down the thickly carpeted corridor.

Belinda watched as the waiter knocked hard on the pair of double doors at the end. The crucial moment was approaching. Red Campion – and with him her entire future – lay just a couple of inches of wood away on the other side of that door. She hesitated. If she dashed in after the waiter, would he try and stop her? Well, let him bloody well try. Belinda approached the doors determinedly. She was almost on top of the waiter now, close enough to see the boils on his neck. It was now or never. And it certainly wasn't going to be never.

To her horror and surprise, the waiter wheeled round and stared her straight in the eye. His expression registered brief amazement; Belinda, reeling backwards, immediately began to flick about even harder with the duster. Her heart was crashing like a teenage rock band – had he finally realised there was something suspicious about her? Even Belinda was aware that so inexpert was her dusting she looked as if she were performing a handkerchief dance and that, thanks to her underpinning, her bust stuck out three feet. Any normal chambermaid would probably find it got between her and the taps.

To her relief, however, the waiter merely murmured something polite and French before mincing off back down the passage. Almost unable to believe her luck, Belinda realised he had just told her of his instruction to leave the trolley outside the suite door. As he turned the corner and disappeared, Belinda instantly sidled up next to it. The perfect excuse for getting in had just fallen into her lap. Now all that remained was for Red Campion to do the same. As the door opened, she inflated her cleavage and unleashed her killer smile.

Grace fingered Red's mobile where it sat warm and silent in her jacket pocket. She had heroically resisted the urge to switch it on and listen to the messages. It was Red's mobile, after all. His business, his life. Nothing to do with her. *Yet*.

Grace's head had been so full of Red and how delighted he would be with her that it was only as she entered the hotel that she realised she might have trouble getting near him. His suite was, after all, on a private floor; hardly ideal for unexpected visitors. She could, of course, telephone to announce her arrival, but the sudden, face-to-face spontaneity would have gone. He might be cross at the interruption; worse still, he might send down a flunkey. What would Ellie do in this situation? Something bold and resolute without doubt.

Then the answer came to her. She must brazen it out, breeze past the Reception and look as if she knew where she was going.

It worked. The concierge, recognising her, gave her a cheery smile and Grace sailed by to the lifts. Striding confidently down the fifth floor passage to the private penthouse lift, she saw that, almost unbelievably, she was in luck again. A large number of expensive-looking carrier bags were being packed into the lift by a porter. Fortune, Grace thought, slipping gleefully in next to them, really did favour the brave.

'Mr Campion's expecting me,' she grinned at the porter.

Pushing the trolley in and her breasts out, Belinda entered the penthouse suite.

She licked her lips, ruffled up her hair and checked that the camera was still in her cleavage. Everything was ready. Wealth and fame, here she came.

Was Red alone, though? The suite was vast and silent, but if Belinda listened closely, could she detect voices in the distance? A frown rippled across her forehead. Yes, definitely voices; voices, moreover, that seemed to be getting louder. Two people, a man and a woman. A throaty, female British accent, interwoven with a male American drawl. A male American drawl that was unmistakably Red Campion's.

'Come on, baby. I want you. I've been so lonely without you. I've done nothing. I've been so *bored*.'

The woman squealed suddenly. '*You're insatiable*.' She sounded pleased. 'Missed me, have you?'

'Desperately.' His voice was lower, muffled, as if buried in something. 'Baby, I'm so sorry we had that row before you went. I know I've got to get the alimony thing sorted out. But I will, I promise you. I can't help it if my ex-wife's a loony tunes. Spreading rumours that I'm a sex addict when you know I'm a one-woman man . . .'

A sequence of gasping and groaning ensued, culminating in a series of piercing shrieks from the woman.

From her position down the corridor, Belinda frowned. The fact that Red Campion was obviously having sex – given the *Trailer* interview, she'd expected that – was not so much of a problem as having another woman around. This definitely complicated things. Thank Christ she'd made alternative arrangements. Time for Plan B. Her fingers hovered over her blouse buttons in order to rip them apart as soon as Red Campion appeared. She was ready for her close-up. The close-up, Belinda gloated, of Red Campion in a compromising position that would appear on front pages all over the world, that was. The margin for error was now practically nonexistent. She would have to fire fast and furiously with both breasts as well as the camera as soon as the man appeared. Alone, she hoped. Although, come to think of it, compromising photos of the three of them might well prove yet more useful.

'Go and get me a drink, would you, darling?' honked the woman. 'The trolley's just come. A bit like you. Har har har. Christ, I'm funny. Oh, and could you just check my shopping's come as well? I know you won't mind, darling, but I bent a bit of plastic on your account this morning . . .'

The famous blond head appeared above a bathrobe in one of the doorways. As he looked at her without interest, Belinda grinned in triumph, stepped forward and yanked her blouse apart.

Unbelievably, the buttons stayed together. Damn these

cheap clothes, Belinda cursed, tugging hard. Practically indestructible. That was the last time she'd buy anything in a supermarket. At last, with a loud rip, the buttons gave way. Belinda, breasts leaping forth like Olympic hurdlers, rushed towards the startled actor, rummaging busily in her cleavage as she did so.

'What the fuck's going on?' honked an indignant, throaty female voice. Finger on camera button, Belinda boiled and froze at the same time. *Oh God.* It couldn't be.

It was. Stalking into the hallway, surveying her with green-eyed contempt, came an imperious-looking blonde in skinny black leather trousers, unzipped to the crotch, and a tight, black, fur-trimmed top. A gold collar set with diamonds sat at the base of her slender throat; more diamonds, Belinda saw, flashed from the fingers pressing aggressively into the slender hips.

It was obvious from her appearance that Champagne D'Vyne's period of minimal spiritualism was over. Or had it been spiritual minimalism? At any rate, Belinda thought, it had certainly been minimal. As well as ridiculous. As she was uncomfortably aware of having told the world in wildly exaggerated and outrageously insulting terms. That Champagne had vowed to annihilate her, she knew. She had gathered from Tarquin's phone conversations, moreover, that Armageddon was nothing compared to the vengeance Champagne had vowed. And here she was, inches away from it.

Belinda's only hope was that Champagne had not

recognised her. She might be staring at her with a contemptuous expression, but that, Belinda suspected, was how she looked at everyone. It had been the way she looked at everyone in her suite at the Garage.

'So,' sneered the hideously familiar voice, evidently addressing Red. 'This is the slut you've been shagging while I've been away. Back on chambermaids, are we? I'd heard you'd had half the Moulin Rouge.'

Belinda willed herself to make a run for it, to escape. But she was too late, caught already in the bright green glare like a rabbit in the headlights. Champagne's gaze, surprised at first, narrowed to recognition before turning into glassy fury. '*You!*' she hissed, grinding the metal heel of a snakeskin stiletto meaningfully into the carpet. '*Belinda Black*, no less. Not content with trying to shaft my career, you shaft my boyfriend as well.'

Belinda gulped and attempted to drag the remnants of her blouse back together. Her gaze, beaten downwards by the murderous intent in Champagne's eyes, was tremblingly fixed on the long legs in their leather trousers now beginning to swing towards her. Unfortunately, the trousers' unfeasible tightness did not seem to restrict speed of movement in the slightest. Belinda's palms began to sweat. Her mouth opened and closed like a stranded guppy's. The hairs on the back of her neck stood more erect than Buckingham Palace guardsmen.

'*So.*' hissed Champagne, fury contorting her face. 'Absolutely Ludicrous, am I?'

Belinda's stomach pounded with panic. Oh God. That headline. 'I can explain,' she gabbled. 'I don't write the headlines. The subs do. Just calm down.'

Out of the corner of her eye, Belinda noticed Red Campion leaning against the wall, arms folded, apparently enjoying the spectacle.

Champagne's perfect white teeth bared in a terrifying snarl.

'Stop, stop,' yelled Belinda. 'The Editor made me change it all. *He* put all the horrid bits in.' She cringed before the blazing green eyes, the inflated chest, the furiously tossed hair.

'How *dare* you write those things about me?' roared Champagne, circling closer. 'You lying *bitch*.' She took a step forward, eyes narrowed, fingers clenched. 'Thought you'd get away with it, did you? *I'm going to kill you*.'

'Hwwhhww,' whimpered Belinda, backing into a chair.

'*No one* says things like that about me,' hissed Champagne. 'Let alone *writes* them.'

As, great teeth snapping, muscles flexing and white hair whirling, Champagne continued her terrifying approach, Belinda fumbled for the chair. Forming in her mind was the desperate idea that if the worst came to the worst and Champagne leapt on her like a blood-crazed lioness, she could fend her off with the furniture.

Opening her mouth in a war cry, Champagne charged. Belinda's sweating palms closed round the chair arms. Too late.

One mighty shove in the chest later, she found herself hurtling across the carpet and smashing, head first, into a console table. She yelled in outraged terror, trying to get to her feet but succeeding only in pushing herself round in circles like a beetle on its back. Champagne leapt voraciously on her, ripping off her skirt to reveal the split-crotch knickers. Now in fear of her life, Belinda fought desperately. Her flailing foot caught the trolley and pulled it over. There was a sliding sound, then, seconds later, a cascade of caviar, lobster pieces and a foaming river of Veuve Clicquot emptied itself over Belinda and Champagne, accompanied by a deafening crash and a shattering of glass.

'Want my fucking lunch as well, do you?' screamed Champagne. 'Well, take this.' Picking up a handful of lobster, she rubbed it hard into Belinda's face. Her fear now bottomed out, Belinda retaliated with a handful of Sevruga. As an amused Red, clad only in a bathrobe, watched, the two fell on each other, caviar eggs stuck to their bosoms, mayonnaise coating their hair, oysters squelching beneath their knees, snarling, punching, kicking and screaming. The action, as they rolled over and over the champagne-soaked carpet, was punctuated by occasional flashes from Belinda's breasts.

It was then that Grace, followed by the porter and the carrier bags, arrived brimming with happy expectation at the open door of the penthouse suite.

CHAPTER TWENTY-TWO

Grace stared dully out of the Eurostar window at the passing fields and wealds of Kent. No comfort there. The hills and valleys only reminded her of the force-of-nature curves of Champagne D'Vyne. So that was the way Red got his kicks. That was the business he had been engaged in. Sordid seafood wrestling bouts with women in split-crotch knickers. He, who had made himself out to be so different, so sensitive, so anti-fame, so unlike other stars in the huge Hollywood galaxy. So unlike the way rumour had him too – did she still not believe he was not a sex addict who had dumped his wife by email? Grace thought miserably of her own email, currently lying in a thousand pieces in the bin in a small Parisian hotel room.

This, though, was no longer the thing that hurt most. It

was difficult to say what was: stinging recollections were now coming thick and fast. The image of the two women wrestling on the floor not only replayed itself whenever she closed her eyes, but, increasingly, when they were open as well. Within a split second of arriving at the suite, Grace had realised that the *Trailer* interview had been right about Champagne D'Vyne and Red. Realised too the identity of the blonde in the huge sunglasses she had met on her way to her first meeting with Red. It was obvious – as so many things were – in retrospect.

So much for Red's whole 'press-broke-up-my-marriage', fingers-burned, bird-with-a-broken-wing routine. The blonde bird clearly didn't have a broken wing, or any damage to any other part of her magnificent anatomy. Whether the same could be said for the brunette was another matter. She had clearly been getting the worst of it.

Grace had no idea who the brunette had been. It was possible she really was from the Moulin Rouge. Or possibly Red's 'dialogue coach'? Grace snorted. The euphemism was obvious enough now. All that business about rolling around on the floor and heavy breathing. She would have felt angry, but she was too busy feeling upset. As well as embarrassed and stupid.

What an idiot she had been. Most of all, to have believed it could be otherwise. Red Campion *was* a film star, after all. If she had been incapable of motivating even Sion to monogamy, what hope, realistically, had there been with an international heart-throb? And, actually, her heart was throbbing. It hurt. She ached all over.

She'd run straight out of the hotel suite, of course. There had seemed little point staying. Red had not even noticed her arrival at first, so absorbed had he been in the caviar catfight, a lascivious look on the smooth, thick skin of his face. Not to mention the equally lascivious erection raising itself between the open curtains of his bathrobe. Grace remembered the email; *something's come up*. Too right. It bloody well had.

He hadn't even looked sorry when he finally saw her. But it was hard to look apologetic with a penis like a fire hose poking triumphantly out of your bathrobe. Even if you were a professional actor.

What Red's face had registered was shock. Unpleasant surprise, even. *Very* unpleasant surprise when, with a furious roar she had no idea was in her, she had dragged the mobile from her pocket, hurled it at Red and, throat aching with outrage and tears, stormed off down the corridor to the lift. Yet even here it had all gone wrong. The private lift was unboardable, still crammed with dozens of upmarket carrier bags. Bags not dissimilar to those from the shopping spree of the day before, which now seemed a thousand years ago. '*Excusez-moi*,' the porter had apologised at the exact moment Grace noticed that most of the bags bore a label bearing the words Mademoiselle D'Vyne, c/o Penthouse Suite, Hôtel Meurice. There were more and they were bigger. The winner, Grace recognised, had taken it all.

There being no other way to descend to the ground,

Grace was forced to wait and watch while the porter unloaded them all. She wondered what would happen in the event of a fire. And then, as a natural consequence, how one might start it.

Clenching her teeth, Grace stared out of the train window again. The sky seemed full of mist out of which ghostly trees and occasional houses loomed. It had started to rain; long streaks spattered across the glass in despondent diagonals. England looked grey, sodden, sunless, hopeless. Exactly, Grace thought bleakly, like me.

Matters were not improved by the Underground. But then, matters never were. Grace discovered that her arrival at Waterloo coincided with one of the Northern Line's periodic hissy fits. Obliged to undergo more changes than a Shirley Bassey spectacular, it was more than an hour later that Grace reached Archway station and made her way down the greasy, wet pavement of Tomintoul Road. A passing car swerved into a puddle in the gutter and splashed her from head to foot with dirty water. Squelching up the front steps to her door, Grace felt the welcome home complete.

Her flat, at least, was clean, even if it did smell strongly of bleach. And tidy. Grace, heading straight for the kettle, felt her ransacked soul ever so slightly soothed at the sight of the rows of mugs ranged neatly in the kitchen, the shining sink whose former brown stains, as mysterious as they were immovable, Maria had managed miraculously to banish. If only, Grace thought, rummaging in the cupboard for the tea bags, Maria could take up her sponge and scrubbing brush and erase all trace of Red Campion from her heart. Her lip trembling, Grace located the tea bags at last, noticing, as she put one in a mug, a pound coin in the middle of the kitchen counter. Something about the way it was placed seemed deliberate, different from the ad hoc piles of coins Grace tended to leave around. The money must be Maria's.

Grace froze suddenly. Had she heard something? The hairs prickling on the back of her neck and lifting slowly from the follicles of her scalp alerted her to the certain, instinctive knowledge that she was not alone in the flat.

Her back pressed hard against the kitchen wall, Grace fought the urge to scream as a shadow, backlit from the bathroom, moved slowly down the hallway. She settled instead for a terrified gasp as the figure, with hideous, slow intent, moved into the frame of the kitchen door.

'Maria!' How, Grace wondered, could she not have noticed that the door was on the latch? She really was losing her faculties. She felt very odd, all round. She sagged against the wall tiles, weak with relief and with the sudden realisation of how utterly worn out she was. She stared at the kitchen floor, whose monochrome swirls Maria had tried originally to rub to a uniform snowy whiteness before Grace pointed out that the black trails were not dirt, but were, incredibly, supposed to imitate marble.

'Madam Grace . . .?' said Maria.

Slowly, Grace sank to her knees before the fridge, her eyes as heavy as industrial ball bearings, her throat working hard to swallow. Level with the freezer, she stared hopelessly into the pan store under the kitchen counter, her shoulders heaving like a steam engine, the salty tears coursing slowly down her burning cheeks.

Grace howled. She clenched her fists, bowed her head, bent her back and filled the kitchen with a rhythmic keening of such volume she could scarcely believe it was her own. She could feel, in the pit of her stomach, where the sobs formed; where, higher up, they scorched in her throat; where, at the top, they pushed their way out.

'Madam Grace,' Maria crooned softly, stroking Grace's back as if she were a kitten. 'Why you cry?' Maria had a pretty good idea, however. She had not been wrong about the man in the photograph. The whole thing had, as she knew it would, ended badly for Grace. And yet, thankfully, much more quickly than she had anticipated. But the game was only half won as yet. What remained was for Grace to take that pound coin, the one her client had filled with his love, into her possession. Only then would the spell begin to work. She flicked a glance to where it still lay on the kitchen table.

Grace raised her head slowly, running a hand beneath her streaming nose. 'Maria, I'm sorry,' she sniffed, scrambling to her feet. This week's streak, she noticed, was fluorescent cyan. Despite herself, a smile tugged the corners of her mouth.

'You not well, Madam Grace . . .'

'It's nothing.' Her words seemed to boom in her brain.

She had pulled herself together with such an effort that every nerve resounded in protest. Her head swam slightly. Her bones ached.

Maria lifted an eyebrow. She pressed a cool hand against Grace's forehead. 'Madam Grace, you very hot,' she pronounced. 'You eel, I theenk.'

Her throat was swollen, Grace realised. A cold? Flu? Psychosomatic stress? Or, given Red's track record with women, horrors she couldn't even begin to guess at? 'But I'm fine,' she insisted weakly, as Maria grasped her firmly by the shoulders and started to gently push her forward. She felt lightheaded. How long was it, since she had eaten anything?

'How long seence you eat?' demanded Maria.

'Why are you fussing?' Grace croaked as, five minutes later, Maria had turned down an invitingly fresh set of sheets and gestured to her to get in. 'Really, I feel perfectly OK.'

As the cool linen pressed painfully against her twitching, burning limbs, Grace realised sleepily, through the fog gathering in her brain and the sudden weight of her eyelids, that she did not actually feel anything of the sort. All she could see, suddenly, was pink, and of a brightness that hurt her eyes. Ah, it was a book, on her beside table. The spine of a book proof. *Spells And The Single Girl.* Of course. Ellie's book. 'A Spell To Make Him Telephone You'. The bath filled with leaves. The cider. The phone call. If only she hadn't done any of it. If only she had left well alone.

'If only,' she murmured, 'there was a spell to take the

pain away.' Not to mention the embarrassment. But that seemed less important now.

After what could have been hours or merely moments later, Grace opened her eyes to find Maria standing by her. She was holding a glass in her hand.

'Dreenk.'

'Is it magic?' Grace muttered. The cool of the glass against her fingers was almost painful.

Maria nodded. 'This ees best spell I know for your sort of pain.'

'But it tastes just like whisky.'

Maria smiled, took away the glass and tiptoed to the door. 'I be back soon,' she whispered.

Suddenly remembering something, Grace raised herself on one elbow with difficulty. 'Maria,' she croaked. 'There's a pound coin of yours in the kitchen. Make sure you take it with you when you go.'

There was a sigh from the door and a 'Yes, Madam Grace.'

'Grace,' murmured Grace, sinking back, head pressing like a cannonball into her pillow, as the first of the nightmares began in which blonde women with large breasts rolled over and over in a sea of caviar and expensive carrier bags.

'Well, aren't you going to answer it?' Belinda barked at Tarquin as the telephone on her desk shrilled. Did he expect her to answer the phone herself or something? Especially when there were currently certain difficulties involved in reaching over. If her wrist was not broken – and the hospital had insisted it wasn't – then it certainly felt as if it was.

'The Editor wants to see you,' Tarquin reported, putting Belinda's telephone down. Belinda looked at him with loathing. Was that a hopeful note in his voice? Thought she was going to be torn off a strip, did he? Well he had another think coming.

'Well, what a coincidence,' she beamed. 'The very person I want to see most.'

Tarquin felt apprehensive. It was obvious that something extraordinary had happened to Belinda recently, and not only because she was covered from head to foot with bruises. Since she had limped into the office that morning, following an absence of several days, Belinda had been radiating smug triumph of a variety Tarquin was unfamiliar with. The fear that – incredible though it seemed – she actually had landed the story that would make her name was growing in him.

'Yes,' sighed Belinda happily. 'This story's going to grab Grayson right by the short and curlies.'

'Is it?' Tarquin croaked.

'Put it this way,' Belinda simpered. 'It involves a film star in a state of high excitement watching two naked women wrestling in caviar. All captured on film, naturally. The perfect family newspaper front page, not to mention several inside spreads. So to speak.' She grinned lasciviously, then her smile faded. *Damn.* She hadn't meant to give so much away. But then, what difference did it make? The entire world would know within twenty-four hours. Belinda patted the front of her bra – where more appropriate, after all, to keep the just-developed pictures from Boots? *Hilarious* that the woman at the photographic counter had not recognised Red Campion. Not commented as she had handed them over, even. But wasn't that the point of the story? Not many *would* expect it of Red Campion. Not everyone believed the rumours – the sex addiction, the email dumping and all the rest of the dirt that his moral-high-ground, all-journalists-are-bastards routine hid so well. Her fingers itched to plunge down her cleavage, get out the photographs and look at them, but she resisted. It would be *such* a treat to see reflected in Grayson's face the glow of the treasure she had brought home. That was why she had not even allowed herself to see them yet.

She felt her insides melt with glee at the thought of Grayson's grey, fishy face lit with jubilation, excitement – and admiration. Admiration for her. It would make everything worthwhile. The humiliation, not to mention the extensive physical injury, she had suffered at the hands of Champagne D'Vyne would be nothing, nothing, compared to what old Stars In Her Thighs would suffer when these pictures hit *The Globe*. If Champagne had thought the Belinda Black Interview was bad . . .

She'll learn now not to mess with me, Belinda thought with savage satisfaction as she pictured the headlines.

HOLLYWOOD STAR IN SEAFOOD SEX ROMP
Fishy business as naked women wrestle in Campion caviar

She could see the words so clearly. And the rest. The awards, the fame, the pay rises, the bidding for her services by every newspaper in the land. Kevin Grayson on his knees, begging her not to leave. 'You're the jewel in our crown, Belinda . . .'

Something of this had transmitted itself to Tarquin as, miserably, he watched Belinda limp off across the coffee-stained carpet. That one foot was in a stiletto and the other in a plaster cast would normally have struck him as hilarious, yet Tarquin did not as much as smile. That Belinda had actually landed a decent story was almost impossible to believe. If Belinda had any journalistic skills beyond bullying and shouting, Tarquin had yet to see them.

Belinda paused at the Editor's door and flashed a triumphant smile at Amabel. The secretary did not smile back. Jealous cow, thought Belinda.

'Go in. He's waiting for you.'

Belinda's newly repainted smile froze. That sounded slightly ominous, but then, Grayson at his most friendly – not that Belinda had ever seen it – was hardly effusive. On the contrary, he was renowned for his utter lack of expression.

She stumbled into the Editor's office with her assorted footwear; at the sight of the cast and stiletto Grayson's eyebrows flicked infinitesimally upwards.

'Sit down, Miss Black.' He sounded weary, she thought.

Flat, even. But no doubt he was merely being at his most respectful. Senior and valuable staff like herself had to be treated with care. Belinda settled herself comfortably on the sofa. The feeling of being at the pinnacle of power, in the engine-room of influence, gave her an almost sexual thrill. She smiled dazzlingly at Grayson, batting her eyelashes ferociously. Not with the slightest flicker of a facial muscle did he respond.

'Miss Black . . .'

'Belinda, please,' breathed Belinda huskily.

'I've asked you in here because I have something to tell you—'

'And I you,' returned Belinda, risking a small pout. Grayson was, she thought, quite sexy, in a frozen-fish-like sort of way. She took a deep breath, thrust forward her breasts, uncrossed her legs and – carefully manoeuvring the cast – planted them apart. 'Would a story involving a semi-clothed film star in a state of high, ahem, *excitement*, watching two naked women wrestling in seafood interest you at all?'

Grayson's eyelids lifted fractionally. Across his expressionless face crept the trace of an expression. His haddock-like lips pressed involuntarily together and there was a movement in his throat, as if of sudden swallowing. 'You got pictures?' he rasped.

'You bet.' Belinda's laugh was shrill, brassy – and triumphant. Raising one hand slowly to her bosom, delighting in the Editor's just-perceptibly-bulging eyes as she did so, she inserted her fingers down her cleavage and produced the packet of photographs. In one movement, Grayson had leant over the desk, snatched them and was riffling through them; so fast had he moved that Belinda was conscious only of the smarting of her injured hand.

As the Editor raised his head, a surge of irrepressible excitement broke thunderously against her chest wall. 'Great, aren't they? The biggest showbiz story *The Globe*'s ever run, I imagine.'

Grayson's excitement, she noted, did not quite match hers. But then, it wouldn't, outwardly. Although, no doubt he was leaping up and down inside, his face had regained its dour, haddocky aspect.

'What the hell's this?' Grayson snapped, holding up a picture.

'Red Campion, Champagne D'Vyne and myself,' grinned Belinda. 'All semi-naked and covered in seafood.' In the end, even Red had not been able to escape piscatorial plastering. 'Let he who is without sin cast the first prawn,' an enraged Champagne had yelled at her coolly watching lover, before dragging him into the fight.

Grayson waved the picture. 'You sure? Looks like a close-up of the bloody moon.'

'What?' Belinda leant forward and squinted at the glossy oblong the Editor held contemptuously between his fingers. Then she frowned, wincing at the reminder of the bruises on her face. It was impossible, there was obviously some mistake, but somehow, instead of the crisp images of Red

Campion's engorged penis, Champagne D'Vyne's vengeful breasts and shots of clearly identifiable, caviar-smeared flesh, the prints revealed nothing but blurred beige.

'You sure you've got the right shots?' Grayson asked sadistically.

Panic rose in Belinda.

Were they the right pictures? Had the woman at Boots made a mistake? Obviously. She'd bloody kill her, Belinda vowed.

Except that . . .

Leaning still closer, Belinda saw with a sinking heart that they *were* the right pictures. But they had come out all wrong. The beige was edged with what was unmistakably lace of her gala bra. Horror gripped Belinda. Could it be possible that the camera had been turned the wrong way round and she had taken photographs of her own cleavage?

'There must be some mistake,' she spluttered. 'They must have printed them wrong, the negatives will be fine—'

'There certainly is a mistake,' Grayson cut in, his voice as cold and sharp as the edge of a sword. 'The mistake,' he added, 'was in giving you Mo Mills's job in the first place. Which is actually what I asked you in here to talk about.'

Entering the loos before she went home, Belinda found Laura, the chief sub, applying her make-up. Although why, Belinda couldn't imagine. It wasn't as if it made any difference.

'Have you heard?' Laura gasped, meeting Belinda's eyes in the mirror. 'Mo Mills is coming back, apparently. Doing her old job again, so I hear.'

Aware of the mischief in Laura's oh-so-innocent stare, not to mention the anticipation in her voice, Belinda drew a deep, keep-calm breath. 'Of *course* I've heard,' she snapped, trying not to sound hysterical. '*Someone's* got to take over the slot now I've been . . .' she searched for the word, '. . . *promoted*.'

'Promoted?' Laura repeated. Belinda noticed with irritation that the chief sub was suddenly having problems with her mouth. She kept twitching the corners forcefully downward.

'Promoted, yes,' Belinda declared. 'To a specially created position as . . . ah . . . Roving Showbiz Party Reporter In Chief.'

'Roving Showbiz—' Laura suddenly dissolved into a fit of coughing. And it had better be genuine coughing, Belinda thought violently, and not because Laura had some ridiculous idea that being a roving showbiz party reporter was the paper's lowest of the low, little better than being a drone on the Diary pages, in fact. Because it wasn't. Not any more.

'I thought perhaps Mo was coming back while you recovered from your injuries,' Laura ventured. 'When you came in, we all thought you'd been in a war zone.'

'Injuries?' Belinda shrilled. '*These* little things? Scratches, that's all.' But putting a brave face on it was difficult when one eyelid hung half-closed and swollen over a blazing purple eye and the bruises on the other side were as yellow as autumn leaves. And the neck brace was never going to be a good look, even beneath the Wright and Teague collar she intended to bully out of the fashion department.

War zone was right. She should sue that bitch D'Vyne, she really should. The damage she had done was incalculable. Not least because, without a doubt, it was a blow from that huge-chested freak that had set the camera the wrong way in her cleavage. She should prosecute, really. Even if Champagne would no doubt assume that a charge of GBH referred to her breast size and was a compliment. 'A true journalist,' Belinda raised her head with as much dignity as was possible given the restrictions of the brace, 'never lets *anything* come between her and her duty. In my new capacity as . . . ah . . .'

'Roving Showbiz Party Reporter In Chief?' supplied Laura, now openly tittering.

'I shall be tirelessly working for the good of the paper,' Belinda continued menacingly. 'My new responsibilities are, after all, wide-ranging and, um, very responsible.'

Because whatever Kevin Grayson had said – and he'd said a lot, including that she was lucky still to have a job at all – Belinda was determined to turn this into a triumph. She'd *show* the bastard. All the bastards. She'd get even, no matter what it took. Her first assignment as Roving Showbiz Party Reporter In Chief would be the best thing ever published in a newspaper. It would stand out for future generations as a paradigm of pithy reporting; each word perfectly judged, each phrase brilliantly polished, each sentence carefully weighed, the very syllables balancing each other. Yes, Belinda vowed. No one would cover the *Literary Review* Bad Sex Awards quite like she would.

On the way home Belinda felt she would explode with rage. The effort of keeping her cool, of trying to convince the likes of Laura her change of job was actually a promotion, had been enormous. Now, her feet slamming against the pavement as she approached her flat, her fury at such a professional slap in the face was such that she could barely focus. Belinda ripped leaves off bushes as she passed, but this was no substitute for what she really wanted to do, which was to rip Kevin Grayson's head off. Someone's head off, certainly.

Her hands shaking with anger, it took several attempts to get the key in the lock. The door, in the end, turned out to be on the latch. This could, Belinda realised, mean only one thing. Murderous relief suffused her. The bloody cleaner was still here. The punchbag she wanted, at last. Silent as a panther, lip curling maliciously upwards, Belinda slunk down the corridor in search of her prey.

The cleaner was in the sitting room. Bloody sitting, as well. On one of the bloody dining chairs, Belinda saw with fury. As if she owned the place, not just bloody cleaned it. Only she hadn't cleaned it; Belinda's near-blind rage did not prevent her noticing that this morning's coffee mug, plus the toast plate with the fag butts, remained where she had left them on the floor. Damn it, the woman didn't look as if she had so much as picked up a duster yet. Had she been sitting there all afternoon? Bloody asylum-seeking layabout. Bloody gassing away as well. Into what looked like the very latest in mobile phone technology. How the hell could *Maria* afford *that*?

Snatches of conversation drifted over. 'She ees much better,' Maria was assuring the person on the other end. 'Especially now I got 'er muzzer over as well.' Belinda's eyes narrowed. *Her mother over*? Over from where? Was the bloody woman smuggling refugees now? Amazed, her suspicions mounting, she now heard through the thundering in her ears: 'Ze money? No.' There was a chuckle in Maria's voice. 'Ve haf not discussed zat yet. Eees *soooo* much.' The cleaner sighed happily.

It was too much, too, for the listening Belinda. She sprang. 'So *that's* what you're up to,' she spat, grabbing the cleaner by both shoulders and shaking her fiercely. Maria screamed; the mobile fell from her grasp. As it clattered loudly on to the floor, Belinda noticed, outraged, that it was even more expensive than she had first thought.

'Beleenda . . .' gasped the terrified woman in her grip.

'*Madam* Belinda to you.'

'Ow. Eet hurts,' Maria squealed as Belinda dug her fingers hard into the tender flesh between her shoulderbones.

'It'll hurt a lot more once the police have finished with you,' Belinda snarled into Maria's fear-whitened face. The breath was pouring hot and fast from her nostrils. '*Sooo* much money, is it?' she demanded in furious, mocking imitation. 'So how many other of your bloody asylum-seeking mates are you bringing over in lorries? Or is it rafts across the Channel?'

Maria shook off Belinda's clawing hand. Grasping the top of the dining chair, she raised her head and her chest proudly and met Belinda's incandescent gaze. 'You are wrong,' she said calmly. 'Everything you say ees wrong. You haf, how you say, got ze wrong hend of ze branch.'

'Stick!' screamed Belinda. 'Stick. Stick. *Stick*.'

Maria nodded. 'Oh yes. That's right.'

'So who the hell,' spat Belinda, 'were you talking to?'

'One of my clients.'

Her cool, her ease of manner was the final straw. 'Don't lie to me!' Belinda yelled. In the boiling soup of her mind, she groped for the *coup de grâce*; the one thing that so far she had held back on. The thing that would hurt Maria most.

'You're bloody fired!' she shouted, with a viciousness that almost tore her throat lining. Her head throbbed with triumph. There. Now the real fun could begin. Now she could sit back and watch the pathetic bitch fall on her knees and beg and grovel to be taken back.

To her astonishment, Maria shook her head and smiled. 'No, Belinda,' she said. 'That ees what I came to tell you. I no longer need to work for you. Eet ees you who ees fired.'

CHAPTER TWENTY-THREE

In Grace's confused dream, a terrifying force, a will stronger than her own, was looming at her bedside. She opened her eyes slowly, fearfully, relieved to be back in real life. Safe, if ill, in bed. Except that she *wasn't* safe. It *was* true. A terrifying force, a will stronger than her own, *was* looming at her bedside.

'Mother!' Grace gasped. Her mother. Here, in Archway? It was the first indication to Grace that her mother knew Archway existed; still less where it was.

Lady Armiger was now fully in focus. Grace watched the precisely lipsticked mouth purse and begin to speak. 'Darling. Extraordinary, I know, but it was your cleaner who told me. She rang and said you weren't awfully well.'

Thanks Maria, Grace thought, sinking back into the pillows.

'And she's right. You're in the most *awful* state. Not eaten, dehydrated, exhausted . . . complete bed rest, the doctor says. Poor darling.' Lady Armiger clamped her daughter's hand in the vice-like grip Grace recognised from diplomatic receptions.

Oh God. Her mother would think the flat disgusting. Tomintoul Road was probably as far as it was possible to be from the splendours of the Venice Consulate.

'But at least the flat was spotless,' her mother added. 'Your Maria really is a marvel. One in a million.'

Somewhere in the hallway, Grace heard the familiar smash of Hoover into skirting board and spotted, as it passed the doorway, a flash of purple neon blazing through cropped blonde hair. 'Isn't she just,' she murmured.

A few days later, for the first time in more than a week, Grace left her flat for the Tube. She still felt terrible, but had by now realised that feeling terrible was relative. Literally, a throbbing head, dry mouth and heavy, burning eyeballs were nothing compared to having her mother at her bedside all day. It had, Grace now thought, been very sweet of Maria to contact Lady Armiger at the Consulate with the message that her daughter was ill. But whether the ensuing bustling arrival, much less the lengthy bedside advertisements for the eligible sons of friends, had done much to improve her condition was debatable.

Yet as she descended, already exhausted, into the farty fug of the Underground, Grace wondered whether she might have been too hasty. While getting out of bed meant getting away from her mother, it also meant returning to Hatto & Hatto. Which meant, inevitably, returning to The Book. Red's Book.

The fluey fever that had overcome her during the last week, plus the arrival of her mother, had allowed merciful waves of sickness to obscure recent events concerning Red Campion. Now the fact that, despite making an idiot of herself with the author, it still remained to her to make a triumph of his book, came depressingly back to her. But then, Grace thought glumly, it was hardly the first time this had happened. However, at least Henry Moon's book had been *good*. His behaviour, moreover, seemed positively saintly compared with Red's.

There was Ellie to face, too. Her mother, she knew, had told Hatto & Hatto of her illness, but this still left lots of perfectly healthy pre-flu time in Paris to explain away. A tough call, if Duke's embargo on Campion's identity still stood, as she supposed it did. She was not allowed to say a word. And there was another thing. What if Bill Duke called her, eager for news on how she had fared with Red Campion? Rushing out the way she had hardly constituted the most professional of farewells.

What would she tell him? There was no way of disguising her abject failure. Her utter humiliation. Once again she'd cocked up, both personally and professionally. No doubt Duke really would sack her now. Given The Book situation, that might even be a relief.

Standing on the Tube, stomach twisting, face pushed firmly into a tourist's armpit, Grace felt spent in every sense. Of the professional zeal that had seized her on returning from Venice not a trace remained. She had nothing left to give.

Grace was fond of London, but it seemed particularly drab this morning. The air outside Holborn Tube station was as muggy and polluted as that within. The workers swarming out of it were jostling and bad-tempered; as she walked over the cracked, chewing-gum-spotted pavements, Grace breathed in the hot, appley-fishy-meaty gusts from the sandwich bars. Well, this was her world now. She may have been up in the clouds for a few days, but now she was back beneath the penthouse suites well and truly, down among the drones. And here she would stay.

Arriving at the office, Grace pushed a hand against the peeling front door before noticing, in surprise, that it was no longer peeling. What was more, it had actually been repainted. The windows were positively sparkling, stripped of their usual inch-thick layer of grime. One of them was even open slightly; probably, as it had been nailed shut before, for the first time in a generation. Possibly in several. Was she, Grace wondered, at the right place? Yes – the plaque on the door – which had taken some time to spot, being both uncharacteristically brilliantly polished and highly visible – still claimed the building to house Hatto & Hatto, Publishers.

At the top of the stairs – freshly Hoovered, she noticed – Grace pushed open the press office door. Affixed, she saw, with a shiny new brass sign saying 'Press Corps'.

Ellie glanced up. She looked, Grace thought, extremely smart and businesslike. She also looked uneasy. 'Grace! We, um, weren't expecting you for another day or so. Are you sure you should have come in?'

'I thought I ought.'

'But you look awful.'

'Thanks.'

'No – really awful. Less death warmed up, than death microwaved from frozen, only the microwave broke down halfway through.'

'Like I said,' Grace muttered. 'Thanks.'

Despite her depleted condition, she sensed a purposeful breeze blowing through the press office, and not only from the open window. Other things had changed. There were pot plants, complex-looking new telephones, trendy filing cabinets in bold primary colours. New desks even, or perhaps just the old ones, cleaned. Sitting at one of them was a brisk blonde in pointy glasses and a close-fitting, short-sleeved dress. She looked, Grace thought, very calm and capable. She was, obviously, her replacement.

So it had happened, just as she had been expecting, only rather sooner. No wonder Ellie was uncomfortable. No doubt she'd planned to break the news to her at home, once Grace was up from the sickbed.

'This is Hannah,' Ellie offered. 'She's your, um . . .'

'Yes?' Grace fixed her with a challenging stare. Why should she make this easy?

'. . . new assistant.'

'Assistant?' Grace rubbed her eyes. 'But no one . . .'

'Asked you, I know. But it was an emergency.'

An emergency? Had something, then, actually *happened* in the Hatto press office? 'What emergency?'

'Well, you being away and me having to do all this editorial work . . .'

Ah. That made sense. Ellie had simply seized the opportunity of her absence to complete her move from the PR department. To get someone else in to replace her, to make irreversible her elevation to editorial. No longer, it seemed, did she intend to have a kitten heel in both camps.

'And then, of course,' Ellie added, 'Bill announcing it was all stations go on *The Frogs*.'

'*The Frogs*?' Grace echoed. Was that a new book? Had Hatto branched out into nature publications? And why, when uttering the name 'Bill', had Ellie had gone pink?

'Some freaky book without a title or an author.'

Grace's calm face revealed nothing of the sudden electric convulsion within her. Could *The Frogs* be a reference to non-specific amphibians?

'What is *The Frogs*?' Her voice shook.

'It's about frogs taking over the world.'

Oh God. No doubt about it. 'They're not frogs,' Grace corrected automatically. 'They're non-specific amphibians.' Even as she spoke, she wondered why she was bothering. More to the point; whether the razor-sharp Ellie would wonder the same. The Book, after all, was supposed to be a secret.

But Ellie did not react. Did she, Grace wondered uncomfortably, know what had happened in Paris? Contrary to expectation, she had not yet asked a single question about Grace's stay there.

'Whatever,' Ellie shrugged. 'Anyway, *Bill* . . .'

Was that slight change of tone when Duke was mentioned?

'*Bill* said it was all systems go to send *The Frogs* out to reviewers. Previous campaign strategy had collapsed, or something.' Ellie looked down, the crimson throbbing in her cheeks.

'Collapsed?' A cold shudder slid down Grace's spine. The previous campaign strategy presumably meant her. Ellie *knew*. 'Who told you?' she asked before completing the sentence herself. '*Bill*.' Of course. Just what was going on between the two of them?

Hannah cleared her throat and muttered something about going to the coffee machine. Another innovation. Unless that was Hannahspeak for Gladys's kettle and jar of Maxwell House.

Ellie raised her head. 'He told me a few things.'

'*What* few things?'

'Well,' Ellie cleared her throat and looked more uncomfortable than ever. 'That you and Red spent time together in Paris.'

'Yes,' Grace said flatly. 'We spent time together.'

'And that it all went a bit wrong.'

'A bit wrong, yes.' The image of the two snarling, scratching women, rolling over and over on the shellfish, replayed itself for the millionth time. Hopefully Ellie had been spared those particular details.

'And about the fight with Champagne and that woman . . .'

'Oh,' Grace pulled a face. 'He told you more than a few things. He told you everything.'

Ellie shrugged. 'And for what it's worth I think Red Campion is an utter arse.' She looked up and met Grace's gaze unblinkingly. 'Especially after he called Bill and demanded you be taken off the job.'

'He did what?' Grace gasped. Could it be true? That, far from being concerned about her, far from being embarrassed even, Red Campion had called Bill Duke and dispensed with her services as coolly as he might have cancelled a credit card?

'Bill could hardly believe it. He says he underestimated Campion.'

'*Underestimated?*' Angry now, Grace felt her teeth grinding against each other, her breath shortening and quickening with rage. Was the suggestion that Red had done something admirable in treating her the way he had?

Ellie nodded. 'Underestimated, yes. He's even more of a bastard than Bill thought.'

Grace felt her shoulders heave. 'So *why*,' she snapped, 'didn't *Bill* tell me in the first place? That Red was a bastard, I mean?'

Ellie folded her arms. 'Oh, come on, Grace. How could he? Campion's one of his hottest properties. And like I said, he hadn't appreciated quite what a bastard he could be. Sure, there are all those rumours about sex addiction and dumping the wife by email but Bill's too busy with his business to bother with any of that.'

Grace nodded miserably. If only she'd concentrated on business as well. If only, too, she'd recognised Champagne D'Vyne in the corridor that first time. Everything would have been clear right from the start. She would have known what she was dealing with. But then, Grace thought miserably, I've never been able to see trouble coming. Look at Sion. Look at Henry Moon.

'And anyway, after you'd met him, you wouldn't have taken any notice of anything Bill said. Not if Red was hell-bent on charming you. You'd have been completely dazzled.'

Ellie looked at her speculatively. 'Not that anyone could blame you. *Red Campion!*' She whistled. 'I mean, he may be a bastard. But he's one hell of a sexy bastard.' Her eyes gleamed. 'What was it like . . . no, don't tell me,' she added hastily as Grace's eyes filled with angry tears. 'He's a bastard, that's obvious.'

'But if it was so obvious, why didn't I realise?' Grace wailed. 'I'm just stupid, that's all. Beyond stupid.'

Ellie squeezed her arm. 'Of course you're not. You fell in lust, that was all. Any woman would have done the same. No doubt some woman is doing it now.'

Grace blanched at this.

'He's a famous film star, and he's gorgeous,' Ellie finished. 'Even if he is horrible inside.'

'But now I've lost my job,' Grace groaned. Along with my self-respect, she added silently. But no. That went ages ago. Around the time of the cocktails with Henry Moon, probably.

Ellie released her arm in a reflex of amazement. 'Lost it? Don't be stupid. Of course you haven't. Bill thinks you're great.'

'So why is there someone else in the office?'

Ellie's sigh held a tinge of exasperation. 'Look. You obviously weren't going to do *The Frogs*, and Bill's got to go through the motions to keep Red happy. We all know the book is shite, don't worry,' she added, grinning. 'But it needs to make some sort of impact. Although frankly it would be better for all of us if it flopped and Red stopped writing.'

'I see,' Grace said, although she didn't, entirely.

'So Bill needed to get things moving, even though you weren't on board any more,' Ellie continued. 'And of course I was busy. With editorial . . .'

'Of course,' Grace said, stonily.

'So I called in Hannah. She used to work in a record company and knows all about the counter-intuitive.'

'Oh.' Grace was not sure what this meant. It sounded very impressive, however. The kind of thing Red would love. '*Right.*'

'She got a mailing together in record time. Every literary

editor in London within twenty-four hours. It was a magnificent achievement.'

'Except,' Hannah chimed in briskly, returning with what looked like a really quite respectable cappuccino, 'that none of the literary editors would touch *The Frogs* with a bargepole. The editor of the *Daily Mail* book section said it was the worst thing she had ever read.'

'Did she now,' Grace said, aware, beneath the misery and sense of betrayal, of a faint glow in the bottom of her heart. That the rest of the literary universe did not consider *The Frogs* – quite a good name, actually, despite ripping off poor old Aristophanes – to be the masterpiece that its author did was interesting. Very interesting.

'Which was a bit of a problem,' Ellie was saying. 'And then Hannah had a publicity brainwave. She got *The Frogs* nominated for the *Literary Review* Bad Sex Awards.'

'*The Bad Sex Awards?*' repeated Grace in amazement. 'You mean that party where about four hundred people turn up and hear the worst sex scenes published that year read out by women in silly voices and black rubber gloves?'

'Yes!' shouted Ellie and Hannah.

'And everyone laughs like drains and the writers have the piss thoroughly taken out of them and the whole thing is the most ghastly humiliation?'

'Yes!'

Grace said nothing.

'But great publicity if you handle it right,' Hannah added, shooting a questioning look at Ellie.

'And in the end,' Grace said in a voice which, even to her ears sounded very unlike her own, 'you get splashed all over the papers and your bad sex passage quoted everywhere?'

'Yes,' Ellie confirmed, looking slightly apprehensive. 'Oh no. Don't tell me you disapprove.'

There was a silence. Then Grace's face split in a broad smile. 'Disapprove? *Hell*, no. I think it's the best bloody idea ever.'

Ellie and Hannah clapped their hands in delight. They exchanged glances, 'So,' Ellie said, 'then you won't mind too much when you hear Red might actually be coming to the Bad Sex party?'

The shock of it shuddered down Grace's spine. Her heart banged. 'He's in London?' she croaked.

Ellie nodded. 'Here to do some post-production, apparently. For his latest film – that World War Two one which, between you and me, is apparently not all that great and certainly nowhere near *Legionnaire*—'

'What did you say?' Grace interrupted, her eyes flashing.

'Well, I'm only saying what everyone else is,' faltered Ellie. 'Apparently his days as number one leading man may be numbered . . .'

'Not that. Did you say *post-production*? Voice-overs, you mean?'

'Think so. Only he calls it—'

'*Dialogue*,' thundered Grace. 'And don't I bloody know it. The *bastard*.'

'So I take it you'll be there?' grinned Ellie.

* * *

'The best thing,' Ellie whispered to Grace as, a few evenings later, they entered the party clutching their large, engraved, gold-bordered invitations, 'is that Red apparently thinks he's being given the Booker Prize or something. His assistant tried to warn him it was all a bit more, well, *humorous*, but all that seemed to register were "one of the most fashionable parties in London", "literary prize" and "lots of publicity". He's in for quite a shock.'

Grace nodded nervously. Attractive though the idea of witnessing Red's public humiliation had been in theory, the rapidly approaching reality was making her horribly uneasy. Her cheeks were flushed and her bowels fluttered with embarrassment. She didn't really hate Red, she realised. She just wanted the whole episode concerning him to be over, to be forgotten, for the curtains of oblivion to close on it. Revenge may be a dish best eaten cold, but frankly, Grace decided, as plate after plate of tepid sausages drifted by, she really didn't feel hungry.

'Don't be ridiculous,' Ellie had snapped when Grace had, woollen-tongued, tried to communicate some of this. 'He may be a god, but he played fast and loose with your affections. Which, in my book, means he should be publicly flogged. Not given a prize at a party. You know what you need, don't you?'

Grace had shrugged, aware of her shrunken body inside her thin black dress. 'A good dinner?' It was what her mother – who, irritatingly, had still not left London – kept telling her. And she probably had a point. Grace calculated that she had lost almost a stone in the past few weeks. Something which at one time would have filled her with joy but now just struck her as dull.

'No. A drink. You're nowhere near plastered enough. Just stay here while I get one. And don't,' Ellie warned, 'even *think* about sneaking away while my back is turned.' Grace looked guiltily downwards; Ellie, as always, had guessed her intention. 'You're here to enjoy yourself,' Ellie instructed, 'as well as get closure on Red Campion. And I'm going to make sure you do both. Stay there.' So saying, she plunged into the crowd.

Obediently Grace stayed there, on the wide, red-carpeted stairs, pushed occasionally against the wall as people thrust past holding glasses of champagne in one hand and cigarettes in the other. Everyone was chattering and laughing; after a while, lost in watching them, Grace felt the tension in her shoulder blades ease.

The chandeliers glittered, the gilt glowed, people giggled and grinned, dressed brightly in fuchsias and feathers – and that was just the men. From time to time Grace started at the glimpse of a shiny fair head, but realised it was unlikely, even in a crowd as insouciant as this one, that a Hollywood film star would be wandering around unnoticed. Surely even here, in the midst of not-easily-impressed-highbrow-literary-London, his presence would engender some stir of excitement.

So far, however, the most famous person Grace had

spotted was Tim Rice. He had paused near her on the staircase, unable to make further progress because, higher up, Melvyn Bragg and Beryl Bainbridge had stopped to talk, accompanied by their respective swarms of acolytes.

Tim Rice's politeness deepened to interest as she told him what publisher she worked for. 'Hatto & Hatto, eh?' he said. 'Quite a buzz around them now, what with all this *Neds of Twinky Bay* stuff.'

Grace smiled and nodded. She was now up to speed on what she had missed through Paris and illness. Ellie had filled her in on the mounting excitement in the book trade – not just London, but international – as *The Neds of Twinky Bay* publication date approached. A rash of excited pieces anticipating a 'J.K. Rowling effect' at Hatto had already appeared in the trade press. Adam Knight had even been the subject of an admiring *Observer* profile which had scattered words like 'doyen' and 'legendary' liberally about (Ellie had, to Grace's admiration, been enormously stoical about this). It was, Grace thought, unbelievable, particularly as the whole *Neds* enterprise had begun as a charity project involving her cleaner. That the book had come so far and fast was staggering.

'So who *did* write it?' Tim Rice asked now.

Grace shook her head and smiled in a manner she hoped was enigmatic rather than clueless. She had, after all, asked Ellie the same thing that morning, feeling slightly ridiculous. That she should not know the author seemed impossible – Maria *must* have mentioned the name – why could she not remember it? She would have asked Maria to remind her, but hadn't seen her for several days.

'What do you mean you can't reveal the identity of the author?' Grace had asked Ellie indignantly. 'I brought you the bloody manuscript in the first place. Via Maria, obviously.'

Ellie had flashed her a teasing look. 'You can talk. You managed not to tell me you were working on Red Campion.'

'Hardly the same thing,' snapped Grace. 'If it hadn't been for me, you wouldn't have had that book at all.'

'I can't tell you now, but you'll find out soon enough,' Ellie had trilled in reply. 'The author is coming to the Bad Sex Awards. He says it's been ages since he's been to a party.'

Grace repeated this now to Tim Rice, who looked thrilled. Suddenly, the dam burst, the Bainbridge/Bragg posses eased finally past each other and he was able to continue on his way. Although not, unfortunately, without a minor incident involving someone else coming down the stairs.

'Ouch!' said Louis de Bernières, glaring at his foot.

The minutes passed. Grace glanced at her watch. Buckled at its usual notch, the strap was now positively hanging off her thin wrist. Ellie had been absent now for almost quarter of an hour. But that, Grace supposed, was Ellie, these days. As their editor, her fortunes were rising higher with *The Neds* than they already had with *Spells And The Single Girl*. Which was already poised, if advance bookshop orders were anything to go by, to be a bestseller. 'The hottest young editor in town,' *The Bookseller* had called her. Grace had even started to get inquiring calls in the office about her, from newspapers wanting interviews. The most dramatic illustration yet, Grace thought, of how far Hatto & Hatto's fortunes had changed. Newspapers interested in its editorial staff! They hadn't even been interested in the authors before.

Grace perused the ever-moving crowd, wondering who among them was the author of *The Neds*. None of the men present bore much resemblance to how she always imagined Maria's client; hairy-backed, string-vest-clad, thickly bespectacled and proud possessor of a sink full of soup-stained saucepans. Tattoos as well, possibly, and definitely forearms like tree trunks. But had she been barking up the wrong tree trunks all this time? Could the mysterious author be of completely different appearance – that rather sneery man with the close-cropped hair and aquiline features, for example? That wild-eyed gentleman with the beard and the Spinal Tap T-shirt?

Her eye was suddenly caught by a swiftly moving mass of dark hair. Grace gasped as, flitting like a shadow behind Spinal Tap T-shirt, came someone she recognised all too well. A woman, and one last seen in split-crotch knickers, covered in caviar and trying to scratch Champagne D'Vyne's eyes out.

There was no doubt in Grace's mind that it was the brunette from the penthouse suite cat-fight. For a start, she had the bruises to prove it. A neck brace as well. Although it was too crowded for Grace to see the woman's feet, she seemed to be walking unevenly, with a hopping sort of roll, hinting at a plaster cast.

'Who is it? Who is that woman?' she yelped as Ellie, her strapless black dress almost left behind with the effort, finally extricated herself from the crowd. She was carrying two glasses of champagne.

Ellie glanced, too late, in the direction indicated. The penthouse suite pugilist had disappeared; in her place was a confused-looking woman with a blond beehive and a following film crew. 'That thick Welsh bird from *Big Brother*, isn't it?' Ellie said scornfully. 'Now come on, let's go into the main room. The show's about to begin.'

They joined the throng stuffing itself through the gilded entrance of a room in the centre of the landing. Shoving, shoulder-to-shoulder with Ellie, Grace could hear interested murmurs around her. 'Smaller than he looks on film, but then these superstars always are.'

She turned to Ellie in panic. 'Has he arrived? Is he . . . *here*?'

Ellie nodded excitedly. 'Great, isn't it?'

Great? 'Since when have you been such a fan?' snapped Grace. Or was this Ellie being ironic? She had an odd sense of humour, sometimes.

'Since I was about six,' Ellie replied, giving her a funny look.

'But he wasn't around then. You couldn't have,' Grace challenged.

'Mick Jagger? He's been around since the Sermon on the

Mount. He was old when I was young.'

'*Mick Jagger?*'

'Yes. He's presenting the Bad Sex prize. Who on earth else did you think I meant . . . *oh, I see,*' said Ellie, grimacing. '*Red.*'

Grace nodded, eyes strained and flicking about nervously. Now the moment had almost arrived, she felt sick.

'He's not here yet, as far as I know.'

Fashionably late, obviously. Grace took deep breaths, forcing herself to calm down. Through the crowd pressing against her, she pushed her hands down by her side. The ends of her fingers fizzed; she flexed them, then, quite suddenly, felt someone grasp them from behind.

Grace gasped and tried to tug away, but not before something small, round and warm had been pushed into her palm and her fingers pressed back around it. She struggled to turn in the crush; she could see no one she recognised.

Grace dragged her arm back up with difficulty. Doing so meant almost goosing Jonathan Coe, who stood directly in front with his wife. The press of bodies was almost overwhelming; the voices washed over her in a roar. At last, Grace could see her hand again. Turning her palm over, she opened her fingers and stared down, puzzled. Someone had given her a pound coin. Why?

She nudged Ellie, but Ellie's attention was elsewhere. Along with everyone else, she was straining for a better view of the front of the room, where clearly something of great moment was going on. Grace, whose view was now impeded by Sebastian Faulks's curly hair, tried in vain to see what it was. She nudged Ellie again. 'What's happening?' She could see part of the podium, a bit of microphone, but little else.

'Red's arrived,' Ellie hissed back.

CHAPTER TWENTY-FOUR

Now that Sebastian Faulks had moved slightly, Grace could see, above the mass of heads, the spotlit podium where the readings would take place. Arranged there were a microphone, a lectern and three people. None, as far as she could see, was Red.

Hopefully, reports of his arrival had been exaggerated. A lot of people around her were wearing glasses; the crowd's collective eyesight was evidently not everything it might be.

Two of the people were actresses, friends of the *Literary Review* magazine, inventor of the Bad Sex Award. Their job was to give humorously exaggerated renderings of the five or so shortlisted novel passages which had been deemed to represent the worst examples of sex in fiction that year.

Their performances were relished as one of the most enjoyable aspects of the evening. As usual, they were resplendent in full evening dress, hair in trademark beehives, cleavages a man could get lost down and mouths blazing with bright red lipstick. As a final touch, their arms were sheathed to the elbow in the black rubber gloves they wore to underline the sizzling nature of the material they handled.

The other person was Mick Jagger.

Seeing the legendary rocker there in the flesh – albeit walnuty, wrinkled flesh – would normally have struck Grace as exciting. She wasn't the biggest Stones fan in the world (Tom the banker's hand-twisting, strutting approximation of their lead singer had mortified Grace at the few social occasions involving dancing they had attended together), but there was no doubt the man was an institution.

As Jagger began to speak in his familiar Mockney drawl, he commanded the attention of the entire room. Apart, that was, from Grace. She heard little of what was being said; noticed only faintly the tittering of the crowd as Jagger remarked that, as far as a musician was concerned, there was no such thing as *bad* sex. That *all* sex was good sex. Her entire being was focused – now that Sebastian Faulks had moved further aside – on a spot she had not been able to see before. A spot just to the right of the podium where, beneath the huge portrait of Queen Victoria that hung against the soft red walls, was the top of a familiar blond head. Not his face; just his hair and a bit of his forehead. But that was enough.

She moved immediately to reclaim the sanctuary of the luxurious Faulks curls, and almost as immediately wondered why she was bothering. Red, after all, would hardly care if he saw her. Probably he had not given her a thought for days. She was history now: it was possible he would not recognise her, even if she looked him right in his lying blue eyes. Grace squeezed and unsqueezed her hand round the warm pound coin. It was oddly comforting to have it there, even if its manner of reaching her had been odd. Not least because, writers being famous for their meanness, a literary gathering was the last place she would have expected to come away in credit.

Try as she might, Grace could not quite obscure Red's head. In fact, she could see an increasing amount of it. His face seemed now to shine out like a beacon; that thick, glossy skin she had pressed her cheek to, those sensual lips that had devoured hers, those eyes she had looked into so often but which had turned out to be not quite so deep after all. It seemed impossible, and ridiculously improbable, that over there, over the heads of the crowd, oblivious to her presence and possibly her whole existence, stood the man with whom mere days ago she had sailed on the Seine, shared champagne sunset soirées, made love to so many times. As a riptide of debilitating misery broke, she gripped the coin again. Ellie, sensing her thoughts, squeezed her arm comfortingly.

'Red looks a bit pissed off,' she hissed. 'Probably thought he'd be made more of a fuss of. He should have known better than to pick a literary party. Most writers are so bloody arrogant they think they're more famous than he is anyway. And they do say his career's about to take a dive . . .'

Appreciating this show of loyalty, Grace nodded and tried to look pleased.

'Ooh,' exclaimed Ellie as a round of applause greeted the end of Jagger's speech. 'Here come the readings.'

The first actress stepped forward, clutching her sheet of paper in her rubber gloves. 'The following,' she announced in bright, Joyce Grenfell tones, 'is an excerpt from *Airhead*, by Jenny Bristols.' Whoops of approval followed. The crowd, Grace among them, jerked around as best they could in the crush, trying to spot the author.

'There she is,' directed Ellie. 'Next to Joanna Trollope.' Grace spotted Jenny Bristols, her face white with suppressed rage as she stared murderously at the reader. Next to her, rather surprisingly, was Sassy Jenks, forced there by the pressure of the crowd, Grace imagined. That she might be there as sisterly supporter seemed unlikely, judging by the expression of delighted anticipation on her face as the *Airhead* reading began.

> 'You're huge,' Camilla moaned as Rock's maleness sprang like a cobra from silken boxer shorts. Standing above him, she prepared to climb astride when, in a low, gravel voice, he groaned, 'Not yet. Lick the chocolate off first.'

The crowd whooped. The reader grinned and continued.

> Camilla paused, staring doubtfully at the glistening layer of brown matting his thick chest hairs.
>
> 'What are you waiting for?' Rock demanded, his voice urgent. His member was huge. Glistening. 'Lick the sodding chocolate off, will you?'
>
> 'I can't,' gasped Camilla. 'I just can't.'
>
> 'Why not?' rasped Rock. 'Hell, this is no time to start feeling guilty about your husband. Let alone your children.'
>
> 'It's not that. I've got a cocoa-bean intolerance.'

The audience hooted, Sassy Jenks loudest of all. Jenny shot her a poisonous look. When the laughter had died down, the second actress stepped forward. 'For this next extract,' she announced, 'we have Sassy Jenks and her novel *Shooting Up* to thank.'

It was Sassy's turn to look furious. Beside her, Jenny Bristols's angry face relaxed into a satisfied smile. Grace could hardly hear this reading, so loud were the guffaws. Some sex scene involving a cricket bat as far as she could make out; Mick Jagger, a famed cricket fan, certainly seemed to be enjoying it. Her attention, in any case, was entirely focused on Red. As his blue eyes roamed the room apprehensively, she even felt a twinge of sympathy. He looked alone and rather vulnerable, pressed to the wall beneath Queen Victoria like that. Odd that he had not come with an escort. The giddy, impossible thought struck her that he might be hoping to see . . . her? To apologise for his behaviour? Make amends?

As Grace watched, Red's head suddenly snapped to the side. There was a commotion on the podium. Someone seemed to have arrived. The actress paused in her reading and stared too. Grace strained to see who at, but was once more thwarted by the Faulks bouffant. Being tall was all very well, but not if some people's hair was taller.

'Talk about cantilevered tits,' sneered Ellie. 'She can practically lick her own cleavage.'

'Who?'

'Champagne D'Vyne, of course.'

Obvious now, Grace realised sourly, who Red had been looking about for. Through a gap in the crowd, with a physical jolt of shock, she saw that the golden head of the artist formerly known as Miss Stars In Her Thighs had indeed appeared next to Red Campion's.

'Yah, I love novels,' she could be heard honking to the *Literary Review* editor. 'Matter of fact, I had a diamond stud put in mine the other day.' She nudged the editor hard before cawing with laughter. '*Haw haw haw*. God, I'm funny.'

Neither Jenny Bristols nor Sassy Jenks seemed to think so, however. As the actress resumed reading Sassy's passage, Champagne opened her mouth and hooted with derisory laughter. United in their loathing, Sassy and Jenny glared at the new arrival, then looked back at each other with expressions of mutual, dawning comprehension.

'My God,' Ellie breathed. 'I think they're actually bonding. They've both realised there's one person on earth they hate more than each other. Rather a lovely moment really.'

Grace did not hear. She was far too busy miserably registering Champagne's incredible beauty. The woman she had last seen snarling and smeared with shellfish now radiated a serene and shimmering loveliness. The attention of at least half the audience – the male half, and quite a few of the women as well – was now glued to the plunging dress of transparent black lace that clung to Champagne's curves like Michael Schumacher negotiating a bend. Through the sheer material, almost every inch of her body was visible, her lean thighs tubing floorwards from the slimmest and tightest of hips, her vast breasts pointing chandelierwards like a pair of space probes ready for blast-off.

'That dress deserves an entire Bad Sex Award of its own,' Ellie muttered.

Grace nodded heavily. Who, after all, could possibly have resisted Champagne? But that Red hadn't was not the point. He had lied by omittance. He had not made it clear – given the slightest hint, even – that he and Champagne had a relationship. Looking at the shining, triumphant woman, Grace felt the overwhelming urge to run away. But the crowds pressing behind were too numerous, too dense. She could not move. Instead, she clutched the pound coin for comfort. Strange how it seemed to make her feel better.

Ellie nudged her suddenly. 'Check out Belinda Black. Looks as if she's gone ten rounds with Prince Naz.'

With a shock of recognition followed by a rush of disgust, Grace saw the dark-haired woman she had spotted earlier on the staircase. She was shoving her way determinedly towards Mick Jagger and Red Campion.

'*That's* Belinda Black? With the bruises and the neck brace?' Grace stared, completely unable to reconcile the battered creature before her with the temptress who had snatched Sion, or the journalist who had rudely and consistently – and consistently rudely – turned down every Hatto author for Tea Break. Grace gazed at the figure struggling purposefully towards the podium, trying to summon feelings of outraged loathing. Belinda Black. A few feet in front of her. Not near enough to spill champagne on, but certainly close enough to lob a sausage at.

The outraged loathing, however, was taking its time. Sion, in particular, had not been so very great a loss. Moreover, the hand that had withheld Tea Breaks had also done a hatchet job of epic proportions on Champagne D'Vyne. And finally, while Belinda's presence in Red's suite had been a shock, she had at least been physically assaulting his girlfriend.

Grace gave up on the outraged loathing. All things

considered, Belinda Black had done her a number of favours. In addition, there was something almost admirable about the way her manifold injuries seemed not in the least to have dimmed her determination to mingle with the famous.

'She's obviously headed for Red,' Ellie chuckled. 'Maybe she's hoping to get her job back if she gets an interview with him here. Wonder if she's seen Champagne yet? Stand by for Round Two. Seconds out.'

Grace held her breath as Belinda continued towards Red Campion, realising with reluctant admiration that the reason the crowds before her were parting with such avidity, positively jumping to it, in fact, was because Belinda's hand – the one not in the bandage – concealed a cocktail stick whose point she was employing to painful effect.

Yet as Grace watched, within mere feet of her goal, Belinda suddenly stopped dead and stepped back heavily. Her plaster-casted foot landed squarely on the person behind her.

'Ow!' shrieked Louis de Bernières.

Belinda took no notice. Her entire being seemed frozen with shock and fear as she stared at someone who evidently filled her with terror.

Champagne recognised Belinda at the same moment. Her eyes narrowed, her lip curled, her entire body tensed. Belinda's apprehension, really, was understandable. Champagne looked, Grace thought, as if her Jimmy Choos had knives on the side.

She was unsure about the outcome of the fight at the

Meurice, although it had obviously not been to Belinda's advantage. And Belinda seemed at pains – severe pains, from the look of all that bandaging – not to involve herself in a second round. Already, she was frantically shoving backwards through the crowd, clubbing her way through with her plastercasted foot and talking rapidly into a mobile as she went.

'Mr Grayson, I just don't care,' Grace heard her snap as, white-faced beneath her bruises, Belinda elbowed past her. 'Sack me if you like. Spending the rest of my life on the Somerfield magazine is fine by me. But I'm not going anywhere near Red Campion while that bloody psychopath's there. Unless you want to pay me danger money, that is. No? Thought not . . .'

'Don't know why Champagne's laughing so much,' Ellie remarked. As the Jenks extract reached its climax – in every sense of the word from what Grace could hear of it – Champagne was honking contemptuously once again. 'I mean, how stupid is the woman? Obviously hasn't made the connection between the readings so far and Red Campion. Whereas I *think* Red – oh yes, actually, I'm *sure* – is starting to get the idea . . .'

'Do you think he'll win it?' Grace muttered, digging her nails into her palms.

'I sincerely hope so. Time wounds all heels, they say, although I've never seen much evidence of it myself. But if ever there was a solid gold opportunity for Time to prove it, it's now.'

The first reader stepped forward again. 'And now,' she grinned, eyes twinkling mischievously, 'we come to our final reading. A sex scene which, as I'm sure you'll agree, gives a whole new meaning to Space Oddity.' Grace swallowed and clutched the pound coin. Fortunately, the Faulks bouffant was once more in the way and Red could not see her. Or, more to the point, she him.

The trilling, Joyce Grenfell voice began:

> 'Jed suddenly felt his whole being being sucked upwards towards the dazzling light; not just his body but his soul too. Semi-circular sliding doors opened and shut with a whoosh. He was hovering, surrounded by electrostatic pulses . . .'

Grace clutched Ellie's shoulder. The realisation was dawning on her that, much as Red deserved his comeuppance, the last thing, the *very* last thing she wanted to hear at the moment was anything concerning Red and sex. Even if it *was* fictional. Even if it *did* concern non-specific amphibians. Especially if it concerned non-specific amphibians.

> A profound thrumming resonated through his corpus. He was now flat on his back in what looked like a lecture theatre. There were no seats, but a series of hovering pods disappearing from view as far as the eye could see. He himself was splayed out, suspended in midair. He felt tubes being inserted

> across his whole body, and became aware of fluids and secretions oozing over him. A cold breath was suspended around his body. He realised something near him was aroused . . .'

As the audience roared with laughter, Grace fought to escape from the jam-packed crowd around her. No other obvious way having suggested itself, she took a leaf from the Belinda Black Crowd Management Manual and rammed both pointed elbows backwards into the chest of the person behind her.

'Ow!' protested a familiar voice. But not, Grace realised, with an upright rush of hairs across the back of the neck, the voice of the author of *Captain Corelli's Mandolin*. Rather, the voice of the author of *Sucking Stones*.

'Bloody hell,' said Henry Moon, staggering out after her on to the landing, eyes watering and hand rubbing urgently at his solar plexus. 'I thought you looked thinner. You've got elbows like razors.'

'Sorry.' She wanted to say more, but couldn't. Her tongue lay leaden and useless in her mouth. Something was happening in her stomach too, a queasy surging that might have been connected to the Red Campion reading but equally well might not. The nerves at the sides of her knees were flickering. 'I had to get out,' she muttered.

He nodded. 'Don't blame you. It was pretty terrible. Even by Bad Sex standards.'

There was a small space left to wonder why he looked so apprehensive before waves of self-consciousness overwhelmed her. Despite her best efforts with the make-up bag, Grace could remember few days in the whole of her life when she looked paler or more tired. Or more grey, lank and lustreless, more drained by flu and failure.

Henry, by contrast, seemed to glow with life and health. His greyish pallor had gone, as had the drumskin effect of flesh stretched too tightly over cheekbones. His eyes shone; the bags under them even seemed to have been unpacked to some extent.

'You look well,' she said, trying to sound bright. 'How's the writing going?'

His eyes flickered with surprise. Damn, Grace thought. I should know this. Oh God. A clanger already; a record, even for her. They had only been talking for two seconds.

Henry smiled, the generous mouth stretching to reveal defiantly uncapped teeth. How much more real, she found herself thinking, than Red's Tinseltown tombstones. 'It's going well,' he nodded. 'Really well, actually.' His eyebrows shot up and down like yoyos. He seemed, she thought, oddly agitated.

She nodded, embarrassed at her ignorance, but curious. 'What's the new book called? Is it something different, like you said?'

His smile widened. 'I'll give you a copy. It's about to come out.'

'Thanks,' Grace was surprised publication was so imminent. She had heard nothing about a new Moon. She really hadn't been listening to Ellie. But then, the *Neds of Twinky Bay* excitement seemed to have eclipsed everything else.

'Oh Henry, I'm *so* glad you're writing again.' She spoke sincerely, but sounded, she suspected, over-excited. As her words tumbled out, her hands twisted anxiously round each other.

There was a silence. No doubt he wanted to leave. He must have other people to talk to. Yet he lingered. But why? There was no need to be polite to her.

'You look terrible,' Henry said, not being polite, after all.

She laughed ruefully. 'Thanks. I've been ill.'

'So I hear,' Henry said. She stared in surprise. *How* had he heard? And *why*?

'It's great to see you again,' he said. There was a pause. His face, she saw, looked suddenly drawn. Tense, as if he wanted to unburden himself of something.

'Grace,' Henry said, urgently.

Her heart was banging in her chest. 'Yes?'

'Grace, I've been meaning to ask you . . .'

'Yes?' She spoke almost in a whisper.

'Grace, have you got a pound coin on you, by any chance? For some fags?'

What? Amid the obscure disappointment – what had she been expecting, anyway? – there rose from the floor of Grace's brain the question of *why* Henry wanted to buy fags when the event's sponsors, a tobacco company, had left free cigarettes lying everywhere. The question, however, was forced back down by a larger consideration.

'Pound coins!' she exclaimed with a laugh that came out higher and more hysterical-sounding than was intended. 'Everyone suddenly seems obsessed with them!'

'What do you mean?' Henry's voice was urgent.'Who else . . . I mean, *who's* obsessed with them?'

'Well, the other day I had trouble you wouldn't believe trying to get my cleaner to take back a pound coin that she had obviously left lying around. And just now, someone shoved one into my hand during the readings.' Grace faltered, aware that possibly wasn't all that interesting.

But Henry looked fascinated. 'Really?'

'Yes, so you can have that one if you like.' Grace opened her palm to reveal the coin. Henry peered at it and shrank back dramatically.

'Oh no. I couldn't borrow that.'

'Why not?' Grace looked at the disc in her palm. It looked blameless enough. Rather grimy, hot and sweaty, but that was all. 'What's wrong with it?'

Henry shook his head. 'What's right with it, you mean. *That*, my dear Grace . . .'

A shudder of unexpected pleasure passed over her at this. *His dear Grace.*

'. . . is an extremely rare piece of coinage you've got there. You should hang on to it and never let it out of your sight. *Never*,' Henry added, with emphasis.

'But it's a bog standard coin isn't it? There are millions of them around. Billions.'

Henry shook his head. 'Absolutely not.' He paused. 'That coin is one of the, ah, very rare, ah, *double-chin* stamp of nineteen ninety-eight that the Queen ordered to be, um, completely withdrawn from circulation.'

'*Double-chin stamp?*' Grace inspected the coin. The monarch's profile was, admittedly, bulky. But wasn't it always?

He nodded, hard. 'Yep.' He was speaking faster now, with more conviction. 'She thought the double chin was just too unflattering, got the whole lot melted down and had a new lot done that made her look better. As a consequence, that coin you've got there is extremely rare. The one that got away. Possibly unique. You should never let it go. Ever.'

Grace was staring at him, dumbfounded. 'The Queen ordered a whole load of coins to be melted down?'

'You can see her problem,' Henry grinned. 'Starting off in nineteen fifty-two all taut jawline and youthful beauty, and watching, as the years go by, her face on the coin get saggier and saggier. Like Dorian Gray, but worse. No wonder the poor old love never carries any money . . . and oh, look!' He swooped on a packet of free cigarettes that were lying on a sidetable. 'I don't need your coin now anyway.'

'That's great.' As Grace folded her fingers around the metal disc once more, she was aware of him watching her carefully. Surely he would go now. He'd got his fags. Yet *still* he lingered, the cigarette drawn from the packet dangling unlit in his hand.

She searched for something else to say, but could only find the obvious.

'What are you doing at the Bad Sex Awards anyway?' she asked him.

His grin had a hint of daring. 'Thought it was appropriate, given my performance at the St Merrion.'

Grace's heart rattled against the back of her throat. 'That wasn't bad sex,' she mumbled, before she could stop herself.

'Glad to hear it.' He sounded relieved, pleased. 'But I can do better.' His smile faded; he paused. 'Actually, I was rather hoping I'd bump into you tonight.'

The soles of her feet trembled. '*Were* you?'

A roaring cheer suddenly broke from the room behind them. Grace turned to see a commotion in the doorway, people struggling, then Red Campion, white with rage, emerging on to the landing. Behind him came Champagne D'Vyne.

'Bastards,' Red was snarling, the spittle flying from his mouth. 'They told me it was a *literary* award.' He looked contemptuously at the object in his hand. Mounted on an engraved plinth was a pair of large, naked breasts in glass, which in size, roundness and general upward mobility were remarkably reminiscent of Champagne's own.

'Yah, you told me it was the Booker Prize,' Champagne was honking. 'Should have put an F there instead of the B. *Haw haw haw*. God, I'm funny.'

'Hilarious,' snapped Red.

As Henry stared at the pair in utter amazement, Grace's hand clenched tighter round the hot little disk in her palm. She, Henry, Champagne and Red were the only ones on the landing. If Red looked her way he was bound to recognise her. Even he couldn't fail to, not this close.

The ensuing embarrassment would be excruciating, but it was not just being seen by her former lover that Grace wished to avoid. Depending on what Red had told Champagne about the girl who stormed off in tears from his suite – and he would surely have had to tell her *something* – Grace was, judging by what had happened to Belinda Black, looking at anything between a broken leg and annihilation. Those glass breasts, Grace calculated, almost certainly weighed several pounds; even more certainly they would be the first thing Champagne would hurl in anger.

And there was also the response of Henry Moon to consider. Red recognising her and Champagne attacking her would undoubtedly raise certain questions. Questions she would rather not face just now. She would explain when she had the emotional, not to mention the intellectual, resources. And not until then.

Which meant, now, she must conceal her face. Prevent Red seeing her. Grace looked, panic-stricken, about her. There was nowhere obvious to run, still less anywhere terribly obvious to hide. Apart from one place. There was nothing else for it. Suddenly lunging forward and clutching both lapels of Henry's creased jacket, Grace dragged his face towards her and buried hers in it, kissing him with violent passion.

Her mouth pressed to Henry's, Grace shrank inwardly. What a nymphomaniac he must think her. Or perhaps plain maniac, no nymph about it. Yet what was the alternative? Snogging Henry Moon with not so much as a by-your-leave was forward, but better by far than being battered to death with a pair of glass breasts. The kiss of life, no doubt about it.

And it was working. Out of the corner of her eye, Grace saw Red's irritated gaze and Champagne's bored one sweep round the landing and over herself and Henry before returning to each other.

'Let's split,' Red snapped. 'Let's hit Home House or somewhere.' Clutching his trophy, he stomped down the wide, red-carpeted staircase.

'Yah. Let's go where people *know* a superstar when they see one,' added Champagne, exiting with all the freezing dignity a transparent, skin-tight dress permitted. Freezing, Grace thought, was probably about the size of it.

She pulled her mouth immediately from Henry's. Or tried to. But he had her tight and was drawing her closer, kissing her hungrily, his tongue probing urgently. His need was as overwhelming as it was unexpected; it was also, she realised, pressing up against her thigh. Confused, she pushed away.

'I'm sorry,' she muttered, stepping back, the coin-holding

hand raised protectively. The crowd was now spilling on to the landing, some looking at the pair of them with amusement.

'Sorry for what?' Henry grinned. 'I was enjoying that. Had been wanting to do it for ages, in fact.'

'It was just that there was someone I didn't want to see me . . . *what did you just say*?'

'You heard,' Henry said, taking her face in his hands and pulling her towards him. His mouth had barely covered hers before a splattering noise, which Grace gradually realised was someone clapping, sounded right in her ear.

'Thank God,' said Ellie's voice. 'Now we can get the review copies out.'

Grace yanked her mouth from Henry's.

'Uh?'

'You mean, he hasn't told you?' Ellie's eyes were completely circular with surprise.

'Told me what?'

Ellie folded her arms and looked sternly at Henry. 'The game's up, pal,' she said firmly.

'Not here it isn't,' he replied equally firmly, his eyes flicking guardedly about. 'Too many people.' He gestured a hand into the drink-shrill crowd and caught someone squarely in the face.

'Ow!' shrieked Louis de Bernières, glaring at Henry.

'Let's go outside,' Henry muttered. 'Things are about to get ugly with Louis.'

'Where is it?' Ellie demanded as they hurried down the stairs. Grace followed, trying to decode what was being said.

'In the cloakroom. Hang on, I'll get it.'

'Should be in a bloody safe,' Ellie grumbled, as Henry disappeared round a corner.

'What should?' asked Grace plaintively, fed up with the talking in code.

'You'll find out soon enough.'

Outside, in the orange lamplight, Ellie loitered a polite distance while Henry passed Grace a plastic bag. 'You had to see it first,' he said. 'Before the critics, before the studios, before anybody. I wouldn't let them release it before I'd shown you the first copy. That's why I came tonight.'

'Shown me what?' It was like a language everyone understood except her. Had she left half her brain behind in Paris? Along with everything else? Rummaging in the bag, she pulled something thin, wide and hard into her hands.

A book. With a colourful cover. A children's book. Why did he think she wanted a children's book? She glanced at him uncertainly. He smiled widely, obviously expecting a reaction. Uncomprehending, she looked back at the book.

The picture on the jacket was of a fire-lit beach, where a smiling group of headscarfed fairy types were dancing round a small boy in pyjamas. Above, across a velvet night sky hung with huge stars, looping red letters spelt out by a fat little aeroplane read *The Neds of Twinky Bay*.

'Oh!' Grace gasped. 'The famous book. The book everyone's talking about.' She felt more confused than ever. 'But how did you get hold of this? I thought there was an embargo on it.'

'She still doesn't get it,' murmured Ellie from a few yards down. She crashed her heel against the wall in apparent exasperation.

Henry grinned. 'Ways and means. The fact that Big Bill Duke has a soft spot – or should I say a very *hard* spot – for my clever and beautiful editor.'

'Oi!' said Ellie, sharply, but smiling. Grace looked at her. *Bill Duke*. So clever old Ellie had landed her millionaire after all. Hundreds of times over, probably. But . . . she looked back at Henry. 'Your editor? Ellie?'

'. . . which has given me a certain influence when it comes to getting early copies of my book.'

His book? Grace squinted back at it. In the orange lamplight, she strained to read the author name at the bottom of the cover. 'By Henry Moon', the fat red plane-trail declared proudly in red.

Realisation hit her like lightning. Her head jerked up with the shock. '*You* wrote this? *You're* the mystery author of *The Neds of Twinky Bay*?' Oh God. It was so obvious now. How could she, yet again, have been so stupid? Was that phrase, Grace wondered miserably, to be written on her gravestone?

'Not just me.' Henry's voice seemed to her suddenly slow and distant, like an answering machine whose battery was running down.

She looked down again. Under his name, in smaller letters, were the words: 'With Maria Strupar.' Grace frowned. Strupar. Surely she knew that name. Yes. She wrote it on a cheque every week.

'Maria Strupar? Maria the cleaner? How do you know her?' Grace's voice trailed away. Her head resounded suddenly to a great thundering, as of huge slabs of stone sliding into place. The lightning struck twice. 'I don't believe it. If you're the mystery author, you must be the mystery client as well. Maria's mystery client.'

He nodded. 'Yes. She's my Domestos goddess. And yours as well. And the only way to reach you, after everything else went wrong.'

'Wrong?' Through the clouds in Grace's mind pushed the unpleasant possibility she might be about to receive some professional criticism.

'Every time we met there seemed to be a disaster . . .'

Grace sighed. Yes, here it came. Well, she deserved it.

'. . . and it always seemed to be my fault.' Henry groaned.

'*Your* fault?' She looked at him blearily.

'Absolutely. Me cocking up at the St Merrion Festival . . .' He paused, flicking her a wicked look. 'Although perhaps that's not quite the phrase . . .'

Grace winced. Henry cleared his throat.

'Me messing up on the radio, me making an arse of

myself on the telly, me making a bollocks of it in the bookshop, me coming out with all that stuff about your ex-boyfriend who I didn't realise was your ex-boyfriend.' He ran a hand agitatedly through his hair. '*That* was the end. After that scene in the cocktail bar, I thought you'd never want to see me again.'

Grace was feeling distinctly peculiar now. Her eyes were fixed on his mouth, trying to follow the words. He was speaking rapidly, excitedly. 'I couldn't think how to get back in touch. So one day I was moaning to Maria about it. When she said you were one of her clients as well, I couldn't believe it. That's when I thought of the book idea. Writing something I hoped you would like seemed the best way to reach you. And Maria had lots of ideas for it. She used to live somewhere like Twinky Bay when she was small.'

Grace felt her hands slide down the concrete of the street lamp. Lights flashed against a black sky; she hit something cold and hard. Something small and metallic rolled from her hand. The lights went out.

'Honestly, darling. I *told* you you shouldn't have gone back to work. It was much too soon. You weren't at all well. And going to *parties*, too . . .'

The voice was booming round Grace's head as she woke. In her own flat, in her own bed, with her own mother beside it. Déjà-vu? Or ill again?

She struggled to sit up. 'How long have I been here?'

'A day or so, darling. *Dreadful* flu. You should never have got up.'

A day or so. Grace sank back, fragments of the last thing she could remember piecing themselves together. Henry, smiling at her. Henry, kissing her. A dream, obviously. The hallucinations of a diseased mind.

'Still,' continued Lady Armiger unexpectedly. '*Henry's* been keeping me company.'

'Henry!' Grace felt her spine stiffen with alarm. *Every time we met there seemed to be a disaster*, she vaguely recalled him saying. And now, somehow, he had met her mother. Would she ever see him again?

Lady Armiger nodded briskly. 'We had a lovely chat yesterday while you were sleeping.' Her eyelids fluttered; she sighed slightly. '*Such* a charming boy. And – besides being utterly and devotedly in love with you of course, darling – it turns out he's one of the Hartington Moons. *Terribly* smart family. Wealthy too.'

Grace groaned and closed her eyes.

'Oh darling, *really*, must you be like that? *Still?*' Lady Armiger let out an exasperated breath, but, with an effort, changed the subject. 'But isn't it *too* amazing how you met – well, met *again*, shall we say – through having the same cleaner? Such a shame she's leaving, by the way.'

Grace's eyes snapped open. 'Leaving? Maria's leaving?'

'To set up her own business, yes. Now she's getting a cut of the book profits, she'll be a rich woman. Advance orders like you've never seen, apparently, for this Teds thing.'

'Neds,' corrected Grace. '*The Neds of Twinky Bay*.'

'Whatever, darling. Anyway, it's a dreadful shame, as I was hoping to pinch her for the Consulate.'

'*Were* you now?' Grace frowned, then felt her face relax into a smile. What was the point? You couldn't beat Lady Armiger, so you might as well join her.

'On the other hand,' her mother was saying airily, 'I suppose she *might* have been a bit much in Venice. Terribly fanciful, by the sound of it, always full of amazing stories about magic, apparently. The FO might have found all that rather tiresome.'

'Probably.'

'Still, it's Maria you have to thank for finally getting you two together at last.' Lady Armiger looked almost despondent. 'Really, I feel rather affronted. To succeed where I failed. After all my matchmaking efforts. A *cleaner*.'

Grace hid her giggle in a fit of coughing. Lady Armiger's face, meanwhile, snapped back into brisk and bright-eyed action.

'Ooh, almost forgot, darling, Henry asked me to give you something when you woke up.'

'Did he?' Grace watched excitedly as her mother rummaged in her vast and shiny handbag.

'I'm sure it's in here somewhere. He was *very* adamant you got it, said it was terribly special and valuable . . . ah, here we are.' She produced a small box and handed it over with a beaming smile.

Under her mother's indulgent eye, Grace snapped open the case and emptied its contents into her hand. Not a ring, as her mother so obviously hoped. Instead, a jowly, majestic face lay in profile on her palm.

The chair creaked as Lady Armiger leant to see.

'A *pound coin*?' There was distinct alarm in her voice. '*Filthy*, as well. *Really!* What's so special about *that*?'

Grace gazed at the metal disk. She wasn't entirely certain either, but was now sure its value had nothing to do with double chins. 'It just is, that's all.'

Lady Armiger sniffed disdainfully. 'If you say so.' She glanced at the coin in her daughter's palm. 'Still. Just as long as there's plenty more where *that* came from.'

Pastures Nouveaux

Wendy Holden

From SW7 to rural heaven . . .

Cash-strapped Rosie and her boyfriend Mark are city folk longing for a tiny country cottage. Rampantly nouveaux-riches Samantha and Guy are also searching for rustic bliss – a mansion complete with mile-long drive and hot and cold running gardeners.

The village of Eight Mile Bottom seems quiet enough, despite a nosy postman, a reclusive rock star, a glamorous Bond Girl and a ghost with a knife in its back. But there are unexpected thrills in the hills. The local siren seduces Guy while a farmer fatale rocks Rosie's relationship. Then a mysterious millionaire makes an offer she can't refuse. But should she?

Praise for *Pastures Nouveaux*

'Delicious mayhem. With this updated version of *Cold Comfort Farm*, Holden has pulled it off yet again. Simply divine' *The Times*

'Pacy pastiche of city dwellers gone country . . . an entertaining novel which will no doubt delight' *Daily Mail*

'Clever, naughty, affectionate and good-natured . . . a comic romp engineered with aplomb and dash' *The Sunday Times*

'People will adore this book' *Independent*

'Hilarious look at townies who move to the country' *Mirror*

'Holden at her funniest and most perceptive . . . spot on' *Mail on Sunday*

0 7472 6616 6

headline

madaboutbooks.com